LOVE'S NEW BEGINNING

LOVE'S NEW BEGINNING

Wilderness Hearts
Book One

DOROTHY WILEY

LOVE'S NEW BEGINNING
Dorothy Wiley

ISBN-13: 978-1535020770
ISBN-10: 1535020776

Cover design by April Martinez

Love's New Beginning is a work of fiction inspired by history, rather than a precise account of history. Except for historically prominent personages, the characters are fictional and names, places, and incidents either are the product of the author's imagination or are used fictitiously. Any resemblance to actual persons, living or dead, businesses, companies, events, or locales is entirely coincidental. Each book in the series can be read independently. For the sake of understanding, the author used language for her characters for the modern reader rather than strictly reflecting the far more formal speech and writing patterns of the 18th-century.

DEDICATION

To my new grandson.
You're not even born yet,
and I don't know your name,
but I know I love you.
And always will.

Other titles by Dorothy Wiley

WILDERNESS TRAIL OF LOVE

NEW FRONTIER OF LOVE

WHISPERING HILLS OF LOVE

FRONTIER HIGHLANDER VOW OF LOVE

FRONTIER GIFT OF LOVE

THE BEAUTY OF LOVE

Praise for Dorothy Wiley's books

"A captivating and entertaining tale that uplifts the spirit and warms the heart."

—*InD'Tale Magazine*, Crowned Heart Review

"Skillful, entertaining and sparkly."

—*Historical Novel Society*, Indie Review

"An exciting historical romance that captivates and amazes. Heart-pounding conflict from the start…"

—*Readers' Favorite Five-Star Review*

"This is an amazing frontier tale!"

—*InD'Tale Magazine*, Crowned Heart Review

"A stunning novel with beautiful descriptions and captivating characters. Wiley's novel is, as all of her others, a story to savor."

—Award-winning author Deborah Gafford

"This is a wonderful book, not only for its historical value, but also for its lessons regarding life, love, and honor."

—Melinda Hills, *Readers' Favorite*

"Wiley's books have all received a 5-star rating from me! All I could do was sigh at the end."

—Joanne for *Romancing the Book*

"Give it ten stars! Great read. Hope there are more books!!!!"

—Amazon reader review

"Ms. Wiley's writing skills are powerful and compelling and her books are not to be missed."

—*Timeless Romantic*

"Dorothy Wiley's series just gets better with each book. I was born and raised in Kentucky. To read about my home and the brave women and men who started this great state makes me hold my head a little higher. Thank you Ms. Wiley for representing Kentucky and our history with such passion and love!"

—Donnet Cornett, Amazon reviewer

"A must read. One of the best books I've ever read. A must read!"

—Goodreads reviewer

"This is the best book I have read in a long time…just beautiful."

—Goodreads reviewer

"This romantic adventure takes the reader on a thrilling journey...the light and easy style of writing complements an engaging storyline."

—*Historical Novel Society*, Editor's Choice

"Epic! This first book has convinced me that this story will someday be a movie and winner. It has been a very long time since I have read of men, women and family like this. It has romance, adventure, tradition and history woven into a tale that will capture your heart. And more than that, it gives full credit to God for our lives, our world and our need to be more!"

—Amazon reader review

"Dorothy Wiley takes you on an action-packed adventure on the Kentucky frontier in this enthralling tale of self-discovery, finding true love, and the meaning of family."

—Peggy L. Henderson, Bestselling Historical Romance Author

Character List

Daniel Alexander Armitage – son of Margaret Armitage

Margaret MacGregor Armitage – Daniel Armitage's mother

Daniel 'Bear' Alexander MacKay – adopted brother of the Wyllie brothers

Artis MacKay – Bear's wife

Ann Byrd – daughter of Colonel Byrd

Colonel John Byrd – head of the militia at Fort Boonesborough

Helen Byrd – wife of Colonel Byrd and Ann Byrd's stepmother

Conall Byrd – son of Colonel John Byrd and brother of Ann Byrd

William and **Kelly Wyllie** and their daughter **Nicole**, age 2

Dr. Rory 'Doc' McGuffin – Kelly Wyllie's father

Mrs. 'Wrigley' McGuffin – Kelly's stepmother

Sam and **Catherine Wyllie** and their adopted son **Little John**, age 10, and their baby **Rory**, age 7-months

Stephen and **Jane Wyllie** and their children **Martha**, age 12, **Polly**, age 8, and **Samuel**, age 3

Edward and **Dora Wyllie**

Lucky McGintey – old-timer hunter and friend of Bear and Wyllie brothers

Judge Webb – circuit judge

Bill Wallace – Sheriff William Wyllie's deputy

Daniel Breedhead – general store owner

Charles Snyder Sr. – father of Charles Snyder Jr.

Charles Snyder Jr. – suitor spurned by Ann Byrd

Tommy Dooley – friend of Charles Snyder Jr.

Ed Sanderson – friend of Charles Snyder Jr.

Lem – one of five mercenaries

ANIMAL CAST:

Samson – Daniel's stallion

Camel – Bear's gelding

Glasgow – Artis' stallion

George – Stephen's stallion

Smoke – William's gelding

Whitefoot – Ann's mare

Stirling – Artis' dog

Happy – Little John's dog

Riley – Kelly's dog

Prologue

Onboard the Lovely Nelly ship, Atlantic Ocean
Spring 1775

Daniel Alexander MacKay pushed back from his mother's upper steerage bunk and sank to his knees on the floor. He covered his face with his hands and wept.

"She's dead, isn't she?" his father asked from the bunk beneath her. "I felt her soul leave my heart."

"Aye, Da. She's gone." As was his mother's tender kindheartedness, her strong heart, and her great faith. A woman who loved her only son. A reverent tender love Daniel already missed.

"My son. My son!" his father's hoarse voice whispered. "'Tis also time we part."

"Nay!" He reached for his sire's outstretched hand.

His father's eyes glistened in the dim light of the oil lamp hanging nearby. "Ye kneel beside my dyin' bed," he said, his words tremulous.

He spoke the truth. His father's body, too weak to further bear the throes of the disease that ravaged both his parents over the past few weeks, would not last the day. Maybe not even the hour.

Daniel drew nearer and placed a hand upon his father's head, moist and hot with fever. He closed his eyes, and turned inward in prayer, then said, "I will miss ye Da."

"Do na weep for me. The end of my story is already written in God's own hand. But He is still writin' yer story. Ye have the bold heart of youth and the body of a man, even though ye are but ten and three years. And ye've fought beside me bravely defending our clan."

"Very soon I'll be ten and four."

"Aye, ye will be a man, na just look like one."

"I swear I will be a man ye will be proud of Da."

"Na need to swear it. I *know* ye will make yer Mum and me proud. Now listen carefully, Son. There's a pouch of coin hidden beneath yer Mum's sewin' kit." His father paused to catch his labored breath. "'Tis yours. When ye land in Canada, use the coin to get a decent room at an inn. This grueling, hellishly long voyage threatened to bury us all in the deep. Stay a week to recover your strength, then go south to the colony of New Hampshire. I've heard tell 'tis a beautiful place. Use yer skills as a hunter to keep yerself fed and make a livin'. They pay bounties there to wolf and bear hunters."

It had been a dreadfully long voyage—a seeming eternity in the dark, damp, confined, and foul-smelling quarters below deck. They'd left Scotland at Dumfries, Galloway, six weeks ago for Prince Edward Island, Nova Scotia. And Shipmaster William Sheridan said they still had about two weeks to go.

"Promise me ye'll do as I say."

"Aye Da, I promise."

His father's eyes closed and a single tear slid down his weathered cheek. "I love ye Daniel."

"I love ye too Da." He sat on his bunk, across from his father and waited. Waited because no matter how much he wanted it to be otherwise, he could not stop death from coming.

His father slept quietly for the next hour until his eyelids flew open and his eyes grew large. His Da turned his head and gazed lovingly at him.

Daniel knelt beside the cot, knowing it would be the last time his father's kind face would look upon him.

Slowly, his father raised a quivering fingertip and pointed above. The angels had come to claim him.

Right before Daniel's eyes, the most important man in his life left him.

His father's eyes still shined with tears of love.

Daniel stared at his beloved parents—their bodies resting on planks balanced on the ship's railing—moments away from being severed from his side forever. Their countenances, so pale, so cold, so still, made him shiver. They didn't look themselves.

He struggled to keep his tears in his eyes. He didn't succeed. Great sobs of anguish gushed forth. Their deaths left a gaping wound inside him that made his heart bleed. His father had said that Daniel possessed a bold heart, but now it shriveled and quivered within him.

"Oh, Da and Mum," he whispered to himself, "will anyone ever love me again?"

Shipmaster William Sheridan's strong voice called out to those gathered to see his parents buried in the deep. "I commend you, Mr. and Mrs. MacKay, to God and to the sea to rest peacefully at last!" Sheridan bowed his head and murmured a prayer.

When Sheridan finished, Daniel whispered, "Amen," as did many others.

Two crewman, whose jaded faces reflected that they'd grown too used to their gruesome duty, took a firmer grip on the boards that his parents rested upon. They tilted the planks upwards.

A moment later, Daniel squeezed his eyes closed in pain as he heard the horrifying sound of their bodies slipping into the Atlantic.

As the onlookers dispersed, a young woman of perhaps fifteen or sixteen years, named Margaret, came over and stood beside him. He'd noticed her smiling at him several times during their voyage. Over the past few weeks, when the two of them happened to be on deck at the same time, they had exchanged a few secret words. Each time he felt a pleasurable shiver and something inside his body started to stir.

Close beside him now, she let her shawl slip off her shoulders. It fell between them and covered their hands. For just a brief moment, Daniel felt her slip her hand around his and then squeeze it. Then she left and followed her parents below deck. Her brief touch soothed his crying soul like a burst of summer rain on parched earth.

Daniel was spending his fourteenth birthday alone. No one but Margaret MacGregor knew it was his birthday today.

She smiled at him from across the inn's eatery. Like most of the ship's passengers, she and her parents were staying at the same inn he was although he knew they were leaving tomorrow.

Five lonely days ago, the Lovely Nelly eased up to the dock at Prince Edward Island, Nova Scotia and at long last dropped her anchor.

The island lived up to its reputation for magnificent beauty. Rolling hills, verdant woods, white sand beaches, and misty ocean coves, begged for a young man's exploration. Surrendering to its call, he spent five lonesome days mostly walking and exploring the coastline's beaches, dunes, reddish sandstone cliffs, and saltwater marshes. His legs desperately needed jaunts after being confined to the ship during the long journey across the sea. Each day, he rose at dawn and stayed out until he grew hungry and exhausted. The solitary walks amid the lush, tranquil landscape seemed to gradually ease his grief.

But the beauty that captivated him this morning was Margaret MacGregor. He couldn't stop staring at her. Her warm smile made his face heat as though he'd stayed in the sun for too long.

Then he saw Margaret's father, Mathew MacGregor, scowl first at her and then at him. Daniel quickly glanced away and took a bite of his biscuit. The MacGregor Clan, like his, also came from the Highlands and were too proud for their own good. Perhaps they were so full of pride because one of Scotland's heroes, Rob Roy MacGregor, was one of their clan.

Her father, living up to his clan's boastful motto 'royal is our blood,' had repeatedly spurned him over the last few days and refused to let him court Margaret so he could do the honorable thing and propose to her. Even though she was a bit older—sixteen—it didn't matter to him. He was already man size, taller than her father and most other men for that matter.

But no matter how hard Daniel argued, the obstinate man kept telling him to leave his daughter alone. The family was preparing to move on, but MacGregor wouldn't tell him where. Her father cut him from their fellowship as if he were a rotten branch.

Daniel couldn't blame the man for not wanting to let him anywhere near his daughter. He had nothing but a few coins to his name and those would soon run out. Margaret deserved more.

He smiled, remembering how she came to him deep in the night after his parents died. She'd slipped silently into his bunk, wiggled beneath his covers, and woke him from the cruel dream he was having. She'd tenderly wiped away the tears left by the nightmare and seemed to sense that he needed to feel loved again. To know that not all the life and love in the world had died with his parents. And so she took him to another dreamy world entirely. One he'd never been to before.

Knowing it would be wrong, he'd tried once to stop, and so did she. But his need to feel that he wasn't alone was stronger than his need for respectability.

So, on that life-changing night, Margaret snuggled her lithe little body up next to his. With the sound of waves lapping up against the ship's wooden hull, the two of them had quietly learned the essentials of making love, to the motion of a ship at sea.

Chapter 1

Bristol Township, Philadelphia, Pennsylvania
Summer 1800

Daniel Alexander Armitage stared at his mother's weeping face, unable to believe what she just confessed. If what she said was true, then…he stood and angrily swiped at the air. "My father lies dead less than a week and you disgrace his memory by telling me this!"

Immediately, he regretted his outburst. But how could she say something like that? Since she was lying on her deathbed, succumbing like so many others to the scourge of Yellow Fever, it couldn't possibly be a lie. Could it?

"My son, telling you the truth does not disgrace your father. John knew he was not your real father. When we married I was already carrying you for three months. We told everyone that you were born early. John swore he loved me and would love you as his own son."

At the mention of his father's name, his anger evaporated as fast as it exploded. "Father did love me. Of that, I'm certain."

"I know. He loved you just as much as your brother. And I loved him all the more for it. He didn't care that you were another man's child. His generous spirit loved us both unconditionally," she said as more tears streamed down her still lovely face. "Forgive me. I was so young and in love with your father, or at least what I thought was love at the time."

Daniel wiped her damp forehead with a wet cloth. Fever was only one of her discomforts. As the disease matured so did the horror of the symptoms. He swallowed the bile in his mouth as he remembered what Yellow Fever did to his poor brother Mathew and his father. *His father named John. The only father he'd ever known. Apparently he now had another father. A total stranger to him.*

"Mother, why did you keep this from me all these years?" he asked.

"I was afraid you'd leave us to find your real father. But now, that is exactly what I want you to do." She paused and swallowed. "I want you to find him—he is your only family now."

Daniel's brother, just two years younger at twenty and two years, his only sibling, was the first to die in their family.

Despite being so full of promise and one of the great trading cities of the Atlantic world, Philadelphia now cowered before a merciless disease that claimed one in every ten people.

In the week following his brother's death, he'd found solace in trying to help others suffering with the disease. He would search out those who needed help or food by going door to door in his neighborhood. As a volunteer member of the Overseers of the Poor he helped to guide others trying to help. They would take the poor who were sick to the public dispensary and alert charities to their other needs.

When fear of the disease caused people to race from the city and consequently depleted the ranks of the overseers, he organized a public meeting to raise more volunteers. But in a matter of days, his own parents grew ill and lately he had spent all of his time seeing to their needs. Despite his best efforts, death struck down his father a week ago. Only the need to care for his mother kept his crushing grief at bay.

But he would soon be truly alone in this world. He and his mother both knew it. Once the disease settled in a body, there was nothing anyone could do to stop it.

He offered his mother some water, but she shook her head.

Daniel wanted to honor his mother's wishes, especially now. But he had no desire to go off in search of a man he knew nothing about. "This man—whoever he is—may be my true father, but I don't even know him. He's not family."

She gazed at him with gentle, understanding eyes. "His name is Daniel Alexander MacKay. You were obviously named after him. He's a good man, Son. His mother and father grew ill and died on our voyage from Scotland. He was all alone so I stood next to him when they buried his parents at sea. I felt compassion towards him and, I confess, found him quite attractive too. I could tell his heart was breaking, so in the wee hours of that night, I went to him wanting to console him. 'Twas my fault not his that my comforting led to more."

He shook his head, stood, and started to pace. "I don't want to hear any more of this."

"You must know the truth. Let me finish. He wanted to court me and I'm sure would have married me, but my father forbid him to come anywhere near our family."

"Why?"

His mother took a deep breath and continued. "Daniel was young and appeared to be penniless. My father wanted more for me."

"I can understand that."

"I didn't at the time. All I wanted was Daniel. He was so tall and handsome. But father took us away and we moved from Canada all the way to Philadelphia. Here, at church, I met your stepfather John and we married soon afterwards. There were rumors of impending war with Britain and your stepfather and I wanted to be married before he would be called off to fight so we hurried into marriage."

It was the first time she'd used the term stepfather and he hated the sound of it. "Don't call him that! He'll always be my father." Daniel missed him terribly. His loss had hit him so hard he wanted to drown himself in a bottle of whiskey. But he didn't. Only because his mother needed him.

She started crying in earnest.

Oh, bloody hell.

"I'm sorry," he said, "it's just a lot to learn all at once." He knelt down on one knee and took her hand. "Forgive me, Mother."

"I'm the one who should beg forgiveness," she said between sobs.

"There's nothing to forgive," he told her. He stood and paced back and forth in front of her bed wondering why his mother hadn't taken her secret with her to the grave. "Why is it so important to you that I find this man?"

Her crying abated somewhat and she wiped her nose. "Because he's your blood relative. You come from a proud Scots clan and you can only learn of it through him. You deserve to know your Highland heritage. You are a Scot and no people have a greater right to be proud of their blood. You may live in the colonies, but you have the heart of a Scot. I believe that is why you have not yet found your place in life."

Perhaps she was right. All his life he'd felt as though he were waiting for something. Perhaps this news was it. After graduating from The Academy and College of Philadelphia, he'd studied medicine for a year, but his heart wasn't in it. Most of his professors seemed to know little about what caused diseases. Even worse, their competing claims for cures disheartened most students, including Daniel. He didn't know who to believe.

Then he'd studied law at The University of Pennsylvania Law School. Some of his professors, like James Wilson, one of the signers of the Declaration of Independence and a framer of the Constitution, were profoundly inspiring teachers. But he found many of his professors tedious and boring. They nitpicked at the law like it was some sort of enigma, not the enlightened principles of justice he envisioned the law to be.

In between his studies, he'd wooed numerous women, but none found his heart.

"Mother, you should just rest. Your symptoms are much worse today." He wiped drops of blood away from the corners of her mouth and eyes. The sight didn't frighten him but the prospect of her dying did. He'd refused to let the doctor bleed her after he heard rumors that many of the man's patients simply bled to death. Had he made the right decision? He squeezed his eyes shut—wishing, praying, hoping for some way to help her.

His mother nodded slightly. "Aye. I know I'm worse. That's why I decided to tell you the truth today." She swallowed again with difficulty. "Go to him. Find your father. He's a good man and I know he will love you. He'll help you find a new beginning."

"Where do I find him?"

"He told me he'd promised his father, the one that died on the ship, that he would go to New Hampshire. It's a small state, you'll find him. Just search for a man about thirty and nine years of age that looks very much like you. When you were fourteen, his age when I knew him, I couldn't look at you without being reminded of him. He will be tall. He was already taller than my father when he was just fourteen. He said he would make his living as a hunter. It was enough for me, but not for my father."

"A hunter?"

"Yes. Twenty-five years ago colonial settlements would pay to protect their children and livestock from predators." Her voice sounded weaker.

"Mother, please, rest."

"No, I have too much to say and too little time to say it. We both know I won't survive this much longer."

"Please don't say that, Mother. Perhaps God will provide us with a miracle."

"Thank you for taking such good care of me."

He took ahold of her hand with both of his. "You took care of me when I was young and helpless. I'm happy to do the same for you."

"We've come full circle haven't we? The circle of life." Her hand grew limp in his, her weakness worsening.

He noticed her eyes becoming even glassier. He touched her forehead and found it hotter. He rung the rag out, folded it, and laid it across her forehead. "What else do you need to say? Do you have any other wishes?" He gently stroked damp hair away from her forehead and then pressed the cloth against her temples.

She smiled up at him. "Just two. First, when you find him, and I know you will, I want you to tell Daniel that I'm sorry my father denied us a chance to be together and that I would have married him."

"And your second wish, Mother?" he prompted when she stopped.

"You haven't married yet…so there's no one keeping you here. More than anything, I want you to be happy, to find a woman who loves you and will give you fine children like I had. I want you to be as happy as I have been these past twenty-four years."

"I'm glad you've led a happy life, Mother," he told her, wiping his tears.

"The good Lord blessed your father's shipping business and allowed us to prosper. You will be a wealthy man, Daniel." She smiled weakly. "You've read your father's will?"

Clearly his mother's body was failing, but her mind remained as practical and perceptive as ever. "Yes, Mother. But don't worry yourself about such things." The thought of wealth and the money he was to inherit was not on his mind. Only his mother's dying wishes and her looming death.

She closed her eyes and rested a moment, but he could tell she was still trying to be certain she said everything she wanted to. Even dying, she could not stop being concerned about him.

Through a pained and watery gaze, she said, "Don't be afraid to sell the shipping business and this house and leave here. Our home is one of Philadelphia's finest. With its view of the Delaware, it should bring a tidy sum. I always loved that view."

No, he wouldn't regret selling this place. His childhood home would now only remind him of sickness and his grievous loss—his entire family.

"You've always cared for others. Now it's time to care for yourself, Daniel. Promise me you'll find your father and seek out your own happiness," she said, her voice barely above a whisper as her strength waned.

He gently squeezed her hand. "I promise."

"She's waiting for you, Son. Open your heart and you'll find her. Somewhere out there in the world. A new beginning for your life is upon you. A chance to start again."

Chapter 2

Durham, New Hampshire
Late Summer 1800

His search for his father was senseless from the start. But now it bordered on the ridiculous, Daniel decided as he ate his breakfast of eggs and ham with little enthusiasm at Harry's Tavern and Inn in Durham. Countless people had told him the same thing—they didn't know a tall man named MacKay who looked like him and might be a hunter. He wanted to give up this pointless search that had already taken him five long weeks on horseback. Most of that time, sick with grief, he rode with a heaviness in his chest and an ache in his heart.

For three days after his mother's funeral, he'd lingered around their house. That was all it was. He could no longer call it a home. It wasn't even the same world. The sun still rose and set in colorful splendor; stars still filled the night sky; the Delaware River still sparkled under the sun and lapped waves against the shoreline. But his world, his family, was gone.

Now, he was caught up in this futile search to find a man he didn't know. He couldn't stomach the idea of continuing this useless pursuit even one more day. To do so would be irrational, not the actions of a logical sensible man. No good could come from continuing.

Yet every time he resolved to abandon his search, he would see his mother's face and hear his promise to her. So he kept on, day after day.

Besides, he had nothing to go back to and he was unable to see where his future in Philadelphia might go. His close friends were the only thing he missed about the city. Before leaving, he'd told them only that he wanted to explore the country for a while. A partial truth—but a truth nonetheless.

After he had arrived in Durham late last night during an especially robust thunderstorm, he'd stabled his horse and checked into the inn. Too tired and wet to eat, he went straight to his room and then to bed.

He took a sip of his coffee and decided that for now he would keep on trying. At least he was getting to know New Hampshire well. It truly was a beautiful place. The most scenic he'd ever seen. Most of it was still untouched by man and astoundingly peaceful with quaint towns and even smaller villages dotting the state.

He found the contrast with Philadelphia remarkable. There, it wasn't unusual to see Jefferson, Hamilton, and other prominent people walking down busy Market Street beside laborers, slaves, and other common folk. And before they died, he often saw Benjamin Franklin and sometimes even George Washington. And Philadelphia's port, the busiest in the new world, was a constant hub of activity with ships and their crews coming and going.

After being surrounded by the city's constant noise, and death and dying for so many months, he found New Hampshire's peaceful countryside comforting, even energizing. He could understand now why people who could afford it often owned second homes in the country.

Harry's Tavern must be one of Durham's most popular, because every table was full. Amid the hum of people enjoying conversation and breakfast the scents of fresh-baked goods, pancakes, syrup, coffee, and other breakfast dishes permeated the room. The tavern's staff bustled about ensuring the diners received everything they needed.

A man wearing a stained apron approached him. "Sir, you look like a man who could use some more coffee."

"Indeed," Daniel said. "I didn't check in until late last night. The storm slowed me down. Thankfully, when I arrived here, the light was still on and a man at the desk promptly showed me to a room and gave me a stack of towels."

"Glad to hear it. That was some storm you were caught in. I'm Harry, the inn's owner. I haven't seen you in here before."

Daniel heard just a note of suspicion in Harry's voice, as though the man took it upon himself to question strangers coming to their town.

"I've never been here before. I'm Daniel Armitage of Pennsylvania." He avoided telling people he was from Philadelphia. The papers were full of news of the epidemic there and many people would shun those from larger cities affected by the dreaded disease.

Harry's eyes narrowed and he eyed Daniel from the top of his head to his toes. "You look remarkably like a man who used to live near here."

His heart sped up. It was the first hopeful sign. "Who was that?"

"I don't remember his real name, but his nickname was Bear."

"Bear?"

Harry poured some of the coffee they'd both forgotten about.

"Yes. He was an adopted brother of Stephen Wyllie. Stephen was a regular here every time he made the trip from Barrington to Durham for supplies. But I only saw Bear a time or two. He stood out though, what with his head and face covered in that remarkable color of red hair and his enormous height and breadth. Never saw a bigger man. And he wore a necklace made of bear claws."

Daniel had never heard anything as strange. "Why would a man wear a necklace made of bear claws?"

"He said it was out of respect for the bears he'd killed that strayed too close to the settlements. He called them kings of the forest. He kept a claw to remember each one. But the folks around here were glad to be rid of the wolves and bears he killed. Before Bear, they were as thick as fleas on a dog. After he thinned them out, the area's children and livestock were far safer. He earned quite a reputation around here." Harry chuckled a bit. "I swear that man looked powerful enough to kill a bear with his bare hands."

Daniel's brow furrowed as he took another sip of coffee. Could this be the man his mother described? Surely not. What sane man would wear a bear claw necklace and make his living hunting for predators as dangerous as wolves and bears? Perhaps his father wasn't sane.

"Oh, one other thing. He had a Scots accent. He grew up in the Highlands, I believe. That's where he learned to be such a good hunter. I can't believe how much you look like him. If you grew a beard and dressed like a mountain man, you could be his twin. And even sitting down I can tell you look nearly as tall as he was."

His mouth fell open as he realized this had to be the man his mother described. "Where does he live?"

"He lived near Barrington."

Lived. Was his father dead? Had he come all this way for nothing?

"Bear and his Wyllie brothers—all but one named Edward—left for Kentucky about three years ago. I remember because it was just after a vicious killer and slave trader named Bomazeen showed up around here."

"Where is Edward?" Daniel asked, hopeful that Edward could help him find MacKay.

"Edward Wyllie was a prominent store owner around here but he left earlier this summer to join his brothers. He owned three stores. One here in Durham, another in Barrington where he lived, and I'm not sure where the third one was. He sold all three before he left for Kentucky. I was sorry to see him go. He was a regular here too."

"Where in Kentucky?"

"Hum. Can't say. But my guess would be Boonesborough. I've read it's where most settlers go before they settle elsewhere in the state."

"Can you tell me anything else about this man named Bear? Was his last name MacKay by any chance?"

"No I can't, except that he appeared to be an honorable man and Stephen Wyllie seemed fond of him. Don't know his first or his last name. But if you find the Wyllie brothers, you'll find him. That is if you want to."

"Indeed, Sir. That's why I'm here. I'm in search of my father, Daniel MacKay."

"Didn't you say your name was Armitage?"

"It's complicated," Daniel answered and stood. "How do I get to Barrington?"

THE TRIP TO BARRINGTON PROVED to be pretty much fruitless. He didn't learn much more than what he'd already learned in Durham. The entire Wyllie family, except for Edward, left here some three years ago. Everyone in Barrington knew Daniel MacKay only by his nickname 'Bear' and he was considered a member of the Wyllie family and went with the others to Kentucky. Just a few weeks ago, Edward had followed his brothers to Kentucky with his new wife Dora, described as a sophisticated lady from Boston.

Daniel stepped out into the sunshine from the large general store that once belonged to Edward Wyllie. He found a quiet spot under a shade tree to think. Arms crossed, he leaned up against the large trunk. With his father living on the edge of the wilderness, he needed to make a decision. He could decide to return to Philadelphia society and civilization and reclaim the comforts and lifestyle he was accustomed to. Or he could travel alone nearly a thousand miles to the edge of the frontier and find a man he knew naught about. The decision appeared to be an easy one.

Nevertheless, he hesitated. If he didn't go now, would he always regret it? Would he be breaking his promise to his mother? The decision was not as clear-cut as he thought. He understood one thing for sure. He needed to listen to his heart. Sometimes life's answers lay in unclear choices that only the heart can decide between.

He would go to Kentucky.

Unexpectedly, the idea excited him. It would be his first real journey. It would give him a chance to live boldly and bravely. And, perhaps it would even satisfy his longstanding thirst for adventure.

He marched back inside the general store and shopped for suitable traveling clothes, weapons, and other gear he would need. While he selected the necessary items, he tried to recall everything he had read or heard about Kentucky. It became the fifteenth state in the Union eight years ago in 1792; it was the first state west of the Appalachian Mountains; and land there was plentiful and lush, although land disputes were frequent and often violent. He'd also read that the natives were no longer a serious threat, however, there were sometimes raids by outlaws or renegades who didn't belong to any tribe. And the quickest route there was by keelboat down the Ohio River.

"Did you know Edward Wyllie well?" he asked the store owner while he paid for his purchases.

"Indeed. He was my boss for five years. Together we expanded this store and opened two others. I was this store's manager until he allowed me credit terms and let me buy the place for my own."

"Why did Edward leave for Kentucky?"

"Well, we didn't talk much about that. But I suspect he missed his brothers. They were a close family and after his own wife and children died of Yellow Fever, I guess he had no reason to stay here."

Daniel nodded somberly. "The great killer. My own parents and brother succumbed to it as well." He empathized with how Edward must have felt.

"I'm sorry for your loss, Sir," the store owner said.

Daniel swallowed trying to hide the grief gripping him. "So am I."

He loaded his packages on Samson, his chestnut stallion, whose dark brownish-red coat shined in the sun. He'd owned Samson for several years and the two knew the streets of Philadelphia well. But since they'd left Philadelphia, it took some time for Samson to become accustomed to the many distractions presented by nature. The horse's ears stayed pointed for much of the first week as the stallion took in sights he wasn't accustomed to—a swarm of bird's suddenly fliting before him, a large dragonfly buzzing his nose, a rabbit or deer bounding off into the woods, and a dozen other strange sights for the city horse.

In truth, Daniel wasn't used to them either. He and Samson finally relaxed a bit after the first week of traveling. But riding through the colonies and scenic New Hampshire would be far different than the journey he was about to undertake. With every mile that he traveled, the dangers would grow. But he would face the unknown unafraid. He would find his father and hopefully, someday, a woman he could love.

The journey to Kentucky would take weeks, depending on the weather. The route would take him back to Pennsylvania, heading south and west, to a city called Redstone. The trip there would be about six-hundred miles as near as he could calculate. Once he reached Redstone, he would book passage on a keelboat headed to Maysville on the south bank of the Ohio River, just north of Louisville. From Louisville, he would head to Boonesborough. At least that leg of the journey would be short—a mere hundred miles or so.

Early the next morning, Daniel changed into his new clothing—his wilderness attire as he called them—dark gray leather breeches, a long brown hunting shirt, a thick leather belt, tall sturdy boots, and a leather tricorne. The store owner in Barrington had also suggested a pouch for his lead and a powder horn. He'd bought both and a long-rifle and a large well-honed knife as well. After he attached the sheathed knife to his belt, he stuck the two pistols he'd brought from home into the open-ended leather holsters and attached those as well. Next he donned the powder horn and lead pouch and held the rifle in both hands.

He surveyed himself in the long mirror next to the dresser and let out a chuckle. His brother would be laughing himself silly now if he saw him dressed like this. They had both always enjoyed dressing in the latest Philadelphia fashions, each claiming to be more dashing than the other. And the only weapons they ever carried were a single pistol and their swords. Indeed, a true gentleman could not be considered polite and well-bred without a knowledge of fencing and he and his brother mastered the skill after years of lessons from their highly regarded teacher, Jean Baptiste Lemaire, at Philadelphia's *Academie Pour Les Armes.*

He glanced over at the bag that held his carefully wrapped prized sword—a fine blade that could put a dent in a lesser sword and far worse in a man. Was it too a part of his past? Remembering the competitive and spirited swordfights with his brother during their training, a flash of loneliness ripped through him. Stunned by the emotions that gripped him so abruptly, he let out a deep breath trying to calm the grief that tore at his heart.

He missed his brother. And his mother. And the man who had raised him as his own. Each death wounded his heart in a different way, just as each one held a special place in his life. Now, his heart could only hold a dear memory of each. But that memory would be forever etched—like the letters of their names on their granite tombstones.

With the sun's first rays streaming into the room, he gazed at the strange looking man in the mirror and wondered what the future held in store for him. The sun had set on his old life and today's sunrise signaled a new beginning—not just for the day—for him as well. In Kentucky he would find out who he was.

He thought about that for long hours in the saddle that day until his troubled spirit finally quieted.

Chapter 3

Boonesborough, Kentucky
Six-weeks later

Daniel hesitated for a moment before stepping into the Governor's Ball at the fort in Boonesborough. A sense of accomplishment filled him. He'd finally completed the arduous trip here, fortunately with only the expected obstacles—bad weather, biting insects, constant hunger, and one despicable road bandit that sought to rob him. The formidable thief bragged that he preyed on soft men like Daniel from the big cities of the east. He wouldn't be robbing anyone ever again. Or bragging.

He glanced down at his trail-worn attire and rubbed the rough stubble on his face. After a month on the trail and his nearly two-week trip down the Ohio River, he wasn't as presentable as he would like to be despite getting a bath and purchasing a fresh shirt in Louisville yesterday morning.

But there was nothing to be done about it. As soon as he rode into town, he'd stopped at the local tavern and eatery. When he inquired as to why the establishment was so empty, he'd learned that most of the townspeople and local settlers were at the fort enjoying the annual ball. The gathering would be the perfect time to see if anyone around here knew this man who was apparently his father. So he didn't have the luxury of time to clean up.

Besides he had no place to change into his nicer attire. All the rooms at the town's one inn were full because of the ball.

Letting out a deep breath, he stepped into the large room brilliantly lit with candles and oil lamps hanging from the timbers. For a frontier fort, it was remarkably festive. Ribbons and garlands decorated the walls and the room was packed with people enjoying abundant amounts of food piled high on several tables. Four violin players in the corner provided romantic music. Relief filled him when he saw quite a few other men dressed as he was.

The next thing he noticed was the profile of one of the most astoundingly beautiful women he'd ever seen. Several men were gathered around her and she smiled politely as she listened to them. Her thick ebony hair framed her neck and hung halfway to her waist, its slimness accentuated by a sash. She wore a simple blue gown with white cambric frills at the neck and sleeves. He couldn't see what color her eyes were, but he knew they would be lovely whatever their color.

As if she sensed him observing her, she glanced toward him and their gaze locked for a moment. Something hidden in the depths of her green eyes drew him to her with astonishing force. Something he'd never felt before. He stepped toward her, her lure undeniable, his attraction compelling. Yet without a formal introduction he needed a reason to walk up to her. Although he didn't see a ring on her finger, one of the men she conversed with could be a husband.

Despite the ample attentions of the three men, Daniel noticed that her punch cup was empty and hung from her hand at her side. Never one to ignore an opportunity, he glanced around searching for the beverage table. He quickly spotted it in a corner, hurried over to it, and snatched up a cup of punch. As he strode over to her, he noticed several people simply stopped speaking and stared at him. One man's mouth even hung open. Had no one ever taught these people that it is impolite to stare? Perhaps it was just because he was a stranger in town.

He pulled back his shoulders as he approached the woman and gave her a warm smile. He'd been told by other women that his smile was one of his strongest assets and in this case, he hoped it would prove true.

"I believe your cup has grown empty, dear lady," he told her.

She turned and glanced up at him. Her eyes widened as she took him in. "Thank you, Sir."

Daniel relieved her of the empty cup and handed her the fresh one. He bowed his head slightly and smiled again.

Before he could introduce himself to the four, one of the three young men said, "Miss Byrd does not need you bothering her."

So she wasn't married! The degree of his relief at that news surprised him. "I believe I was refreshing her drink, not bothering her," Daniel replied. "Apparently you three were too self-absorbed to notice her empty glass. A gentleman is required to attend to a lady's wishes."

"We don't need lessons in being gentlemanly from you, stranger. You don't look like much of a gentleman to me. I suggest you *refresh* yourself before you make another appearance here," another man snarled with an upturned nose.

Daniel glowered at the man. He fought to keep his fist from turning that nose up even further.

"Gentlemen, please, you are being most unwelcoming to our guest," Miss Byrd said, with a smile on her sensuous lips. "Welcome to Boonesborough, Sir. Where are you from?"

Before he could answer her, the third man, the largest of the three, stepped closer to Daniel and roughly grabbed his elbow. "I advise you to leave. You are not welcome. Miss Byrd and I have an understanding." The man tried to shove him toward the door.

Daniel held his ground, moved his face mere inches from the brute's dark, insolent eyes, and glared at the man eyeball to eyeball.

WILLIAM WALKED UP TO HIS older brother Sam. "Here, hold my drink. I'd better go put a stop to that," William said and pointed. "That bully Snyder is causing trouble again."

"I know you're the sheriff, but why don't you wait a minute," Sam said. "Snyder may have picked on the wrong man this time. That young fellow looks like he can take care of himself and this might prove amusing."

William took a closer look at the fellow challenging Snyder. "There's something about that young man. He must be a newly arrived stranger in town, but I'd swear I've seen him before."

Thoughtfully, Sam said, "I think maybe we have."

William nodded and they both glanced toward their adopted brother Bear.

DANIEL COULD NOT IMAGINE THAT a woman this beautiful would have any kind of understanding with this coarse man. Drops of moisture clung to his upper lip and low forehead. The man's lips seemed permanently stuck in a contemptuous twist and the lines about his mouth and dark circles under his eyes made him appear as though he were in the habit of drinking too much and sleeping too little. But his body looked powerful. His massive shoulders strained against his ill-fitting coat and he clenched meaty fists against long stout legs.

"Charles Snyder!" she said, placing a restraining hand on the man's arm. "Stop this at once. And whatever understanding we have is all in your imagination."

That was all Daniel needed to hear.

"You have no idea what I am imagining," Snyder told her, still firmly gripping Daniel's elbow.

Daniel handed the empty cup to one of the other two men. "Excuse me," he said to Miss Byrd before turning to the man who held his elbow. "Outside, Sir. We have a matter to settle between us." Daniel slammed the restrained elbow in Snyder's side, then reached up to the man's thick neck and stuck his fingers inside the fellow's plain cravat, and yanked him toward the door.

Snyder coughed and struggled for air, unable to stop Daniel.

Snyder's companions tried to impede Daniel, but they were nowhere near his size and their feeble attempts to pull him back only slowed him down a bit.

Once outside, he threw Snyder into the dirt just beyond the porch step. "You had no right to touch me or interfere in my conversation with that young woman. You need to be taught some manners, Sir. You may apologize now or later, but I will have your apology."

"Like hell," Snyder shouted up at him and scrambled to his feet.

Daniel thrust his right fist into the man's mouth. Not hard enough to break teeth or nose, but a thump solid enough to split the man's lower lip.

Blood rushed down Snyder's chin and onto his white cravat. "You son-of-a…" the man started to say and drew his fist back.

He had no intention of letting this boorish man finish that particular cussword. His left fist came up and under the man's jaw.

Snyder's head snapped backwards but he remained on his feet.

"Stop!" Charles' companions both yelled and wrenched Daniel's arms back before he could hit their friend again.

Daniel jerked his arms free, straightened, and stepped back. "Now, if you three will excuse me, I believe I have a ball to attend." He tidied up his clothes and turned away from the three glaring men.

As he marched back through the middle of the small crowd of onlookers toward the door to the ballroom, he heard murmurings as he went. A few were pointing fingers. So far, this was proving to be a most unwelcoming and impolite town.

"He deserved it," Daniel told them as he passed by.

He stepped into the room hoping to spot the woman named Miss Byrd again. She remained in the same spot, but this time an older couple stood with her. Her parents? Perhaps they would know his father. As he approached, the three of them, and a few others nearby, stared at him. At least most everyone else in the room hadn't noticed the fight or ignored it. Daniel suspected that fights in a frontier town were commonplace.

He strode toward Miss Byrd, trusting that her parents would be more hospitable than those men were when he introduced himself. And hopefully, after he apologized for his scruffy appearance, her father would introduce him to his stunning daughter.

It was the one year anniversary of their engagement and Artis couldn't think of a better anniversary gift for her husband. A year ago, at the first Governor's ball held in Boonesborough, Bear had asked her to marry him. Never had she said yes to anything more enthusiastically. He'd given her a luckenbooth—a Scots symbol of everlasting love. And that love had given them a child.

She couldn't wait to tell him here during the ball. Somehow, she had to get him alone and over to the spot on the far side of the room where Bear had proposed to her a year ago. As usual, though, townspeople and family members surrounded him as they listened to one of his many lively tales.

"Have you told him yet?" Kelly whispered. Artis' sister-in-law, married to Bear's middle brother William, the sheriff of Boonesborough, smiled conspiratorially. Like a sister to her, Kelly was the only person who knew her good news.

"Will ye stop askin' me that?" Artis told her. "I'm just waitin' for the right moment. We have to be alone."

"Why? This couldn't be a better time. The whole family is here to share in your joy. You know we all think of Bear as a blood relative, not an adopted brother."

"I know," Artis said. In fact, she was thrilled that Bear's family were attending the ball with them and would be here to share her good news. The only brother missing was Edward and his new bride Dora. Along with Dora's father, the three just moved to Kentucky from the east coast and visited Boonesborough recently on their way to Lexington, where the three planned to live.

Artis chatted with Kelly as she continued to wait to catch Bear by himself. She finally decided she was just going to have to interrupt Bear's story and pull her husband aside. But to her dismay, Bear's old friend Lucky McGintey approached her husband. If the two of them started exchanging hunting stories, she might never get Bear alone at the ball.

BEAR FELT A TAP ON his shoulder and turned around.

"My friend," Lucky said. "I think you need to see this."

"See what?" Bear asked.

"Well, you'd best just come with me." The aging hunter nodded his head in the direction of the other side of the room.

"Aye, I'll come. Excuse me gentlemen and ladies," Bear said as he turned to follow Lucky.

People seemed to be smiling at him more than normal. Perhaps they were all in a festive mood.

Bear looked back for Artis hoping she was enjoying herself too. She stood next to Kelly. He motioned for her to follow him. He'd already spent too much time away from his beloved wife's side tonight. When she reached him, he took her hand and hurried to catch up to Lucky who stopped unexpectedly. Bear nearly ran into the man's back. Considering the fact that he was probably twice Lucky's size, he was glad he was able to stop in time. "Och man. Do na stop so. I nearly caused ye to tumble over," Bear said laughing.

Lucky turned, peered up at Bear, and stepped aside. "This may make even *you* fall down," Lucky cackled.

Wide-eyed, Bear gaped at the profile of a man across the room who stood talking to Colonel Byrd and his wife and daughter. Astonished, he swallowed hard and heard Artis take a sharp intake of breath. Lucky had been right, he did feel like falling down. Before him stood a younger version of himself. The young man's face was a bit more slender, as was his waistline, but the similarity of his features and build was unmistakable.

How was this possible?

And who the hell was he?

DANIEL GIRDED HIMSELF WITH RESOLVE and introduced himself, learning that the older man was in fact Miss Byrd's father and the colonel in charge of the fort.

"May I present my daughter, Ann Byrd, and her stepmother, my wife Helen Byrd," the colonel said.

Daniel bowed slightly to each woman. "Colonel, ladies, I apologize for my trail-worn appearance, I've just now arrived in town. I've traveled here from Pennsylvania in search of my real father."

"I see," Byrd said. "That is a long journey, indeed."

Colonel Byrd appeared to be in his early fifties and was smartly dressed in a military uniform. His neatly combed light red hair and his fair freckled skin hinted at a Scots heritage. Except for his fine features, he looked nothing like his daughter whose hair was a glossy black. Her flawless soft pearl complexion glowed with a pink rose blush on her cheeks. Unlike the carefully coiffed hairdos of most of the other ladies in the room, Miss Byrd's hair tumbled freely down her back. Earlier, he'd been so preoccupied with her ill-mannered admirers, he hadn't been able to take a close look at her. He risked a few quick glances now and then while he spoke to her father. She looked as though her years of life numbered somewhere around twenty. When her lovely curved lips parted, they revealed straight white teeth beneath. And perhaps most appealing of all, her face held strength and her eyes gleamed with intelligence. He'd never found weak-willed or dimwitted women attractive no matter how beautiful they were.

"Colonel, at my mother's request, I've come from our home in Philadelphia in search of my father. It was her dying wish that I locate him. His name is Daniel Alexander MacKay, however most people know him as Bear."

"I believe you may have found your father, Mr. Armitage," Colonel Byrd told him.

The image of his mother's face entered Daniel's mind. "Do you know a man by that name, Sir?" He held his breath, waiting for the answer.

Before the colonel could answer, Miss Byrd pointed behind him. For a moment he could only gaze at her engaging grin. Then he turned.

At the sight of the man standing a dozen feet away, a jolt surged through Daniel's entire body. His breath bottled up in his chest and his heart raced within him. There was no doubt that this was Daniel Alexander MacKay. At long last, after endless miles and countless sleepless nights, his father stood before him.

MacKay's features quickly displayed shock and apparent confusion.

The man was a bit taller and brawnier than he was, but there was no mistaking the resemblance. In another ten or fifteen years, Daniel would likely look much the same as the man who stood before him.

MacKay strode toward him a foot or two and stopped. He reached a long arm back and took ahold of the hand of an attractive, woman with reddish-gold hair who stood behind him. She seemed reluctant at first, but then allowed herself to be urged forward.

Daniel quickly stepped closer and said, "Sir, is your name Daniel Alexander MacKay?"

"Aye, lad." His bushy red brows furrowed, the man regarded Daniel. "And who might ye be? Ye have no accent so ye're na from Scotland. Perhaps the son of a relative from Scotland?"

Daniel hesitated for just a moment and then raised his chin. "Daniel Alexander Armitage of Philadelphia, Pennsylvania."

"Daniel…Alexander…" MacKay stammered.

"Yes, Sir. My mother sent me in search of you." Daniel glanced at the faces of those gathered around them. Three men, who looked like they might all be brothers, stood next to MacKay. Their faces registered nearly as much shock as MacKay's did. Several others also stood around them listening. "Might we have a few words in private, Sir?"

"Aye." MacKay took off at once in the direction of the door. The crowd parted before him and the same three men and four women followed on MacKay's footsteps. *So much for privacy.*

Daniel turned back toward Miss Byrd and her parents. "It was a great pleasure to make your acquaintance Miss Byrd and yours as well Colonel and Mrs. Byrd. If you will excuse me, I have family business to attend to."

"Of course," Colonel Byrd said and nodded. "We understand."

Miss Byrd smiled at him and he bowed slightly before he left.

As he raced out the door, Daniel saw MacKay, followed by the others, marching across the enclosure with long deliberate steps toward what appeared to be the blockhouse on the fort's northwest corner. The three men must be MacKay's adopted brothers. The ladies, with their skirts hiked up a few inches, struggled to keep up. He suspected the four women were the wives of the four brothers.

Daniel followed behind them all, wondering what he would say to a father he didn't know. A complete stranger in every way but his appearance. Perhaps that was enough of a start.

A warm east wind caressed his face as his search for his father came to an end.

Chapter 4

Bear's mind raced backwards in time as his body marched forward across the fort's enclosure. With each stride he remembered the few women he had lain with in his thirty-eight years. But this young man appeared to be at least twenty. That meant…it couldn't possibly be her, could it?

His brow furrowed as he tried to remember that night long ago on board a ship plowing through the rolling waves of the Atlantic. They'd only been together the one time and he barely knew what he was doing. At the time, he didn't even know if he'd done it right. He only knew she had soothed his aching heart. He'd begged God to forgive them for what they'd done. But sometimes our mistakes shadow us for a lifetime despite the Lord's mercy. And sometimes they follow us, *because* of God's grace. Was this one of those times?

In spite of his tangled emotions, thinking of her again made him smile.

Margaret MacGregor.

His first love. She'd come to him during a dark night filled with terrors and offered him the only thing she had to give. Profoundly sad and lonely, he'd accepted. In the days afterwards, the gentle blossoming of an adolescent heart slowly eased his grief. With every intention of marrying her, he sought permission to court her, even though she was two years older than he was. But her father soundly rejected him.

Now, two decades later, a part of her had come back into his life.

The enormity of the truth hit him.

He had a son. A fully-grown man.

His couldn't think straight and he was having a hard time catching his breath. How should he feel about this? A sense of wonder and amazement began to fill him.

He stopped, realizing he needed Artis beside him. They would face this together. He turned around, and found her walking just behind him.

Artis' eyes sparkled in the dim light of the stars as she gazed up at him.

"Artis," he said, "come my love."

She did not speak, but shook her head slightly and continued on toward William's office. How could she be upset about this? It happened more than two decades ago, long before they met.

He glanced past the other members of his family and saw Daniel hurrying toward them. The clear-cut lines of the young man's profile, strong and rigid against the moonlight, reflected determination and inner strength.

Aye, this was his son, if ever he'd sired one.

Bear told the other members of his family to catch up to Artis and wait for him in William's office. Then he stayed behind, arms crossed, as Daniel marched up to him.

When they stood face to face, Daniel gave him a searching glance.

A lifetime of things unsaid hung in the air between them.

Artis raced inside William's office and stopped in front of the small hearth, her head bent as she stared down at a few still glowing coals.

"I'll put some coffee on," William volunteered. "This might be a long night."

Artis heard Stephen and Sam, Bear's youngest and oldest brothers, amble in, sit down on the wooden floor, and lean back against the rough pine wall opposite the hearth.

Sam's wife Catherine stood next to her and whispered, "Artis, what's wrong?"

Kelly came to Artis' other side, leaned in, and said, "We can tell something is bothering you. Is it the young man who appears to be Bear's son? Whoever his mother is, that happened a long time ago, long before Bear knew you."

Artis shook her head, not trusting herself to speak. She so wanted to tell Bear her good news tonight, but now it would have to wait. He couldn't find out that he was going to be a father twice in the same evening. That would be too much for any man, even Bear.

"I think I know what it is," Catherine said quietly. "I saw how you grimaced at the smell of that fish covered in garlic sauce."

Kelly said. "I can completely understand how this would have upset you."

Artis turned her face toward Kelly. "Ye understand?"

"Of course we do," Catherine whispered. "I would be upset too."

"Upset about what?" Jane asked, just joining them. "Is something wrong?"

"Shush!" Catherine said and held a finger over her mouth before she whispered, "Artis was going to tell Bear tonight that she is with child."

Kelly, who already knew, clapped her hands together and Jane squealed with delight.

So much for waiting until she told Bear to let the others know. The whole room would know in a minute.

"It is wonderful news," Catherine said, "but she hasn't told Bear yet."

"Told Bear what?" William asked as he brought the coffee pot and knelt down between the skirts of their ball gowns.

Artis rolled her eyes and let out an exasperated breath. "Go ahead, ye might as well tell him."

William hung the pot on a rack over the coals and added some more kindling and wood before he stood up.

"Artis is going to have a babe!" Kelly told her husband.

William bounced up and grabbed ahold of Artis to give her a big hug. The handsome sheriff had always been affectionate toward his sister-in-laws. "That's wonderful news."

"But I wanted to tell him tonight!" Artis cried. "It's the anniversary of our engagement. Now I can't"

At that, Sam and Stephen both rose. Sam, nearly as tall as Bear, towered over everyone in the room and looked like the fierce warrior he was. In a surprisingly gentle voice, he asked, "What's wrong, Artis?"

Catherine answered for her. "She was going to tell Bear tonight that he is going to be a father. And then that young man showed up."

"Good Lord," Stephen said. "Talk about unfortunate timing."

Artis started to wail in earnest. She realized she was being self-pitying, but for some reason she couldn't seem to control her emotions.

Kelly and Jane both tried to comfort her, but that just made her cry all the harder. "He told me he'd never been married," Artis whimpered.

"If he said that, it's the truth," Sam said. "Bear doesn't lie—about anything."

"But that means…" Artis started.

"Daniel must have been born out of wedlock," Sam finished for her. "There's no denying the young man is Bear's son. He has the same first and middle names—Daniel Alexander. And the lad looks nearly exactly as Bear did when we were all young men."

"Plus, he said his mother sent him here looking for Bear," William said.

Stephen stepped toward Artis and placed a hand on her shoulder. "These things happen, particularly when we are young and foolish."

Jane scowled at her husband. "These 'things' shouldn't happen, even when we are young and foolish. Now, Bear appears to have a son that he completely missed seeing grow up."

"But he appears to be a fine son, and we have a new nephew," Stephen said. "Regardless of the circumstances, children are always a blessing."

"I do na want any of ye to say anythin' to Bear about our new babe," Artis said. "I want him to get used to havin' Daniel before he learns about this child," she said, placing her palm against her abdomen.

"I'm not sure that's wise, Artis," Sam said. "It's hard enough for one person to keep a secret, much less seven. The more people who know something, the less secret it will stay."

The others shook their head in agreement.

Artis wiped her tears away and raised her chin a bit. "Nevertheless, please do as I ask. 'Tis a small kindness I ask of ye."

"How is your mother?" Bear asked.

"She's dead," Daniel snapped. The bitter words stuck in his throat.

He watched Bear glance down and swallow hard before he said, "I'm sorry for yer loss."

"So am I," Daniel said. "She was a wonderful mother." He hesitated only a half-second and said, "And wife."

"I take it yer father in Philadelphia is named Armitage?"

"He was. He, along with my mother and only brother died earlier this year of Yellow Fever."

"'Tis a terrible loss for ye to lose yer entire family."

"It was," Daniel replied, unable to keep his grief from his voice. "Now, my *father* is apparently named MacKay."

"Aye. And 'tis a good name that ye can be proud of."

"I was proud of the Armitage name!"

"Daniel, there is much to be said between us. And much to be learned of one another. If ye will allow me, I would like to get to know ye and learn of yer life."

Daniel stood there, beneath the stars of Kentucky, in the center of a frontier fort. A whole new world, so different than the one he left behind him. He wondered if he should just leave. He didn't belong here. He'd fulfilled his mother's wish. He'd found MacKay. That didn't mean he had to stay. But where did he belong?

MacKay seemed to sense his hesitation. "I want ye to come and stay with Artis, my wife, and me. She's from Scotland too—from the same clan—but she lived in Achadh an Eas on the south side of Loch Naver. My family lived in Grumbeg, on the north side of Loch Naver. Both our families were forced to leave because of the Highland Clearances. But we never met until we both came here to Boonesborough. She moved here from Virginia after she served her seven-year indenture. I asked her to marry me one year ago tonight, here at the first Governor's ball."

"Congratulations on your anniversary and I thank you, Sir, for your offer of hospitality. But you should feel no obligation to invite me to your home. In fact, I'm not certain I'm even staying in Boonesborough. I only came to honor my mother's dying wish. Now that I've met you, as she requested, it is time for me to leave."

Where would he go? Perhaps one of Kentucky's larger cities like Lexington or Louisville. Then he remembered the woman named Ann, he had just met, the colonel's daughter. Perhaps he could stay for a few days anyway.

"Och, ye did not come all this way just to turn yer tired mount around and go back to Philadelphia. Ye've found yer family, Son, and I want ye to stay with us."

Daniel's heart skipped when MacKay called him son. That was the name Armitage had always used for him. "I'll thank you not to call me that."

"All right. Daniel it is. People around here call me Bear. I realize ye grew up callin' another man father so why don't ye just call me Bear too?"

Bear reached out a hand and Daniel shook it studying MacKay's strong grip and his eyes. Eyes much like his. He detected nothing but genuine warmth in the handshake and what appeared to be kind-heartedness in the man's eyes.

"Pleased, very pleased, to meet ye, Daniel," MacKay said.

Chapter 5

Bear threw open the door to the sheriff's office so hard it banged against the wall. "Sorry, William," he said.

Bear turned and gestured for Daniel to enter. "Come in. Come in and meet yer new family. I warn ye they're an unruly bunch."

Daniel had tried to prepare himself for meeting his new father but he'd never anticipated meeting an entire family. He couldn't remember ever feeling more uncomfortable. His stomach tightened into ball of knots.

All eight people stared at him for a moment. But then, one by one, they started smiling and moved closer to him. The first to extend a hand was a dark-haired man with a scar on his chin who appeared to be in his early forties. Based on his weathered and tanned skin, his buckskin attire, and the exceptionally long knife in his belt, he looked as if he were a seasoned fighter. So much so, Daniel suspected the man would not quake if he came face to face with the devil himself.

Daniel stepped forward and grasped the man's hand with a firm grip. Virtually the same height he was, Daniel looked him eye to eye.

"Welcome to our family. I'm Sam Wyllie and this is my wife Catherine, formerly of Boston."

The dark-haired woman, exquisitely beautiful and dressed in a fine golden gown, extended her hand.

Daniel took it and bowed formally. "A pleasure, Mrs. Wyllie."

"And this is my brother William, the sheriff of Boonesborough. This is his office and jail," Bear said. "And this is his wife Kelly. She's like a sister to all of us. 'Tis a lovely pink gown ye are wearin' Kelly."

"Thank you, Bear," Kelly said.

William and Kelly, both striking blue-eyed blondes, came forward. William shook his hand and Kelly gave him a quick hug. "Welcome," she said.

"Thank you," Daniel told her. He turned to another dark-haired man. Although not as tall as the other men, this brother appeared exceptionally muscular and hale. Daniel noted the man's strong jaw and intelligent eyes.

"And I'm the youngest brother, Stephen Wyllie," the man said, "and this is my wife Jane. We all moved here from New Hampshire."

His wife Jane was another beauty. Wild red curls adorned her head. She wore a green gown nearly the same color as her curiosity-filled eyes.

"Stephen may be the youngest, but he's the one who inspired us all to move here," William said. "In three years, he's built a substantial cattle operation and he supplies beef to all the forts around here."

"Aye," Bear agreed. "Stephen recognized the opportunities in Kentucky earlier than any of us." MacKay proudly wrapped his big arm around the shoulders of the lovely woman Daniel saw standing with Bear earlier. "And lastly, but foremost in my heart, is my precious wife Artis."

Although dressed in a simpler gown than the other women, Artis was every bit as attractive. Soft red-gold hair hung on her shoulders.

Artis extended her hand and Daniel bent to kiss it. When he released her fingers, he looked up expecting to see her smiling like the other women, but she merely stared at him. It had to be a shock for her to find out that her husband now had a grown son.

Other than formal greetings, Daniel hadn't said a word since he entered the room and he didn't know what to say now.

"We have a large family, Daniel. There's quite a few of us," Bear said. "Kelly's father Dr. McGuffin and his brand new wife are watchin' the wee children, all six lads and lasses."

"Mrs. McGuffin used to be our cook—Mrs. Wrigley. Now she's moved here," Catherine explained. "I'm afraid William and Kelly have stolen the best cook in Kentucky away from us."

"I'm still miffed about that," Sam said. "Fortunately she taught our housekeeper Miss Henk how to cook for us before she left."

Bear continued listing their family members. "And we have another brother—Edward—who is married to Dora. They just moved to Lexington, which is about an hour north of here. Dora's father, Mr. Tudor, a respected Boston lawyer, came with them. He and Edward are opening a law school in Lexington."

"Would you like some coffee?" William asked. "I just made a fresh pot."

"Indeed, I would. Thank you," Daniel answered.

After William handed him a cup, MacKay spoke up.

"If ye could all listen for a moment, I have somethin' to say," Bear said. "I've just learned that Daniel's mother, father, and brother recently all passed from Yellow Fever."

Everyone is the room expressed their condolences, nearly simultaneously.

"There's more ye should know. 'Twas his mother's dyin' wish that he find his actual…true…," Bear said, struggling for the right word, "the man who was his sire. That would be me. The night my parents were buried at sea, Margaret MacGregor came to console me. She sought only to show me compassion, but one thing led to another. After our ship arrived in Canada, I wanted to court and marry her, but her father, a stubborn man if ever there was one, refused to let me near her or even tell me where they were movin' to." Bear turned to face his wife Artis. "Margaret was my first love. I cared deeply for her and pined for her for an exceedingly long time after they left. But that was a lad's love. When I met you and married you Artis, I learned the meanin' of a man's love."

Artis smiled at her husband, grateful for his honesty. Then she turned her smile on Daniel. She felt her heart reach out to this young man. He had suffered the worst kind of loss, just as she had, the death of his entire family.

Then he'd set out to find a new life—just as she had.

Her lip quivered a bit at the realization that she was now related to him—his stepmother. "Daniel," she said, trying to keep her voice steady. "Just as ye did, I lost my entire family too, in Scotland during the Highland Clearances. My mother in a most horrible way. I understand what it feels like to be left all alone in this world."

Artis could sense their shared grief as Daniel lowered his head and clasped his hands tighter around his coffee mug.

Artis continued, "But here in Boonesborough, I found a new life and more importantly a new family. And you can do the same. Life has taught me na to be led by heartbreaks and misfortune, but instead by dreams and love. I hope you will come live with Bear and me at our home—Highland—named for our beloved Highlands in Scotland. At least come and stay with us until you decide what you want to do now. Ye are most welcome."

"Aye," Bear said. "Highland will be your home too for as long as ye like."

Artis added, "Oh, I'm na too terrible a cook."

Bear laughed. "Ye can tell the truth of that by lookin' at me. If she gets any better at cookin', I'll have to have the tailor make me another one of these fancy coats."

Daniel raised his handsome head and looked at her. "Thank you, Artis. You are extraordinarily gracious. You're all terribly kind and I am honored to make your acquaintances." He turned to Bear. "I'm sorry if I haven't been as charitable toward you as you have been toward me. It's just...just that I..." He stopped and seemed at a loss for the right words.

"Ye need na explain. We all understand," Bear said. "Life just took ye for a hell of a ride. But if ye can manage to stay in the saddle, you just might like where that ride ends up."

Daniel took a few sips of the coffee while he let Bear's words sink in. Would he want to end up here, with these people? This family seemed so close. He would never fit in. Suddenly, he felt extraordinarily homesick and longed for the life he once had. The hole in his heart opened again and he swallowed his sorrow. There was no going back. That life was gone forever.

He glanced around at their smiling faces and eyes. "You all seem to be such a close family. I'm not sure…"

Sam stepped closer. "Our father raised us to be that way. We were well loved and we were only allowed to fight *for* each other—not *with* each other. He's gone now, but his principles are still a part of us. And, as Bear's son, he would want us to welcome you into our family. From here on, in addition to your father, you now have four uncles—myself, Stephen, William, and Edward—who will fight alongside you if needed."

"And besides them, there's me and yer four fierce aunts—Catherine, Jane, Kelly, and now Dora!" Artis said, making everyone laugh.

When he finished chuckling, Daniel asked Bear, "How long have you been a member of this family?"

"Since I was fourteen. I used to hunt around the area where the Wyllies lived. Mr. and Mrs. Wyllie took me in during the winter months when it was too cold to hunt. After our first winter all together, they adopted me."

Daniel took another sip of his coffee. "That's right, you said your own parents were buried at sea. So you were an orphan?"

"Aye. With no brothers or sisters either."

"Until Stephen befriended him," Sam said. "Soon afterwards, Bear had five brothers."

"Five? I only count four," Daniel pointed out. "Sam, William, Stephen, and the Edward you mentioned."

Bear and Sam glanced at each other. "Our family has suffered loss too," Sam said. Everyone grew quiet when Sam failed to elaborate.

"Well, I'm keeping all of you from the ball," Daniel said to break the awkward silence. "Perhaps we should return."

"Nay, I've had enough excitement for one day and enough food for two," Bear said. "I'm ready to head toward home and help Daniel settle in."

The others nodded their agreement.

"I'll go bid the Governor and his wife goodbye from all of us," Sam said and strode toward the door. "I'll be back shortly."

"Sam and I are staying with William and Kelly," Catherine said.

"We'll stay there tonight too," Jane said. "They need our help with some projects tomorrow."

Daniel wondered if Jane was arranging for Daniel to have some private time with Bear and Artis.

"Our new home is quite large," Artis said. "There's several extra bedrooms upstairs."

"Thank you. I've grown used to sleeping outdoors," Daniel said, "but after my long journey, a soft bed and a roof over my head does sound appealing." In addition to his rifle, knife, and axe, he had with him his bedding, his more formal clothes, a kettle and frying pan, a warm coat, and a few books. With these simple things he had succeeded in making himself reasonably comfortable on his long journey.

When they'd all climbed onto their two wagons, Daniel pulled alongside them riding Samson.

"That's a fine looking stallion you have there," Sam said.

"I would have to agree," Daniel said. "His name is Samson."

"He looks like a smart horse," Bear said with a grin. "My guess is Samson did bring ye to a place ye just might like."

Chapter 6

As they left the ball, Ann glanced up at her father and smiled. "I hope that Daniel Armitage asks your permission to court me."

"It's far too early for you to have such notions about that man. Although I must say he did seem like an agreeable, well-educated, and congenial fellow," her father said and draped his long arm protectively around her shoulders. He grinned and tugged her a little closer. "Of course we only visited with him for a few minutes. But I'm a fair judge of character in a man and he seemed the honorable sort."

"He also struck me as being cultured and gallant," she told him.

Because her father was the commander of the area's militia, they enjoyed fine spacious quarters at the fort. They only had to walk across the enclosure to reach their home, built into the northeast corner of the fortress.

"But he must be a bastard," her stepmother protested, frantically fanning her fan. "He had a different last name than Mr. MacKay."

"So are Alexander Hamilton and Thomas Paine," her father pointed out. "They were both born out of wedlock."

"We don't know that he is illegitimate," Ann said. "There could be any number of explanations." She only knew for certain that he was the most spectacular image of a man that she'd ever seen. And the way he put that pesky Charles Snyder in his place made her chuckle.

"And the way he treated poor young Charles," her stepmother said, nearly echoing her words. "That stranger actually hauled Charles out of the ball! Such course behavior."

"Mother Helen, Charles treated Mr. Armitage abominably. That's why he reacted as he did," Ann told her.

"That's no excuse! I just don't like the man," Mother Helen said. "But I do like Charles Snyder. He is such a polite young man and he's from such a good family. Everyone likes him. And you know he adores you, Ann."

"Well, I think he's a pompous, presumptuous fool," Ann declared.

Her father nodded. "He's much like his father. I am still having problems with that banker." Her father frowned suddenly and drew his pistol. "There's an oil lamp lit inside the house."

Her father entered the house cautiously and Ann and Mother Helen followed. Ann quietly withdrew her own pistol from the entryway table's drawer.

To her astonishment, Charles Snyder Jr. sat in their parlor reading one of her books with a glass of her father's good brandy in his hand.

"Ah, there you all are," Charles said and stood. "I hope it's all right, Colonel Byrd, but after what happened, I decided to wait for you here. Mrs. Byrd said I was free to drop by anytime and make myself at home, so I did and poured myself some brandy. I didn't want to create a scene and disrupt the ball even further by going back inside after that ruffian."

Her father scowled, but didn't say anything.

Charles is a coward, Ann thought. *That's why he didn't go back inside after Armitage.*

"He was a ruffian," Mother Helen agreed entering the room. "I see he split your lip."

Charles rubbed his lower lip and winced.

Ann concealed her smile behind her hand.

Providing her with further evidence that Charles was a fool, he dipped his head slightly and said to her, "I hope that stranger didn't upset your feminine sensibilities too much."

Ann ignored him and stepped toward her favorite spot, one of their blue and gold wing-backed chairs in front of the hearth. She saw feminine sensibility as a glossy patina painted on women by society, especially unmarried women of her age, forcing them to act like fragile china dolls that might easily break. Why should emotions be different for men and women? Why should a woman conceal her strengths? She despised the manipulative social code and refused to adhere to its doctrines.

What she believed in was the freedom to be herself. She flopped into the chair and deposited her pistol on the side table.

With a hint of censure in his tone and an accusing glance, Charles told her, "You really should not have spoken to him, Ann. You weren't introduced to him."

She stiffened as though he had struck her. "Who I speak with is none of your concern."

"Well, we will just have to change that." Charles turned to her father. "Colonel Byrd, I ask your permission to court Ann and then marry her by Thanksgiving."

Ann let out a startled gasp, leapt up from her chair, and spun around toward Charles. "Surely you jest!"

"No, I am very serious. After what happened tonight, I realized I better stake my claim on you sooner rather than later," Charles said. "You're the prettiest girl in Boonesborough and my father says you'd be lucky to marry a man like me."

Ann's eyebrows rose in disbelief. "Stake your claim! I'd be lucky? You arrogant ass!"

"Ann!" Mother Helen cried out. "Such language from a lady!"

"Well, he is," she insisted and fell back into her chair. The very idea! And the only good thing he had to say about her was that she was pretty. She threw up her hands in disgust.

Her father calmly ambled over to his pipe and started filling it with tobacco. "Mr. Snyder, I don't believe I will grant you permission to court my daughter. Ann seems disinclined to favor such a decision or a future union."

"Thank you, father," she said, crossing her arms in front of her.

"Any remaining contact with my daughter must be as a friend only, not a suitor," her father said firmly. "And if I were you, I'd think twice about entering a man's home again uninvited."

"But Sir, we're nearly family. My father told you of my keen interest in your daughter," Charles protested. "I thought the two of you had reached an understanding."

Her father retained his civility, but she didn't miss the hardening of his eyes as he told Charles, "We had nothing of the sort."

Charles snorted and tossed back the rest of his brandy. He took a step toward her father. "I expect you and my father will come to an agreement soon. And I know Ann will undoubtedly change her mind. Women are fickle creatures. When she does, I'll be waiting." He spun on his heels and stormed out, leaving their door open after him as though he expected her to come running after him.

Ann pushed herself up, marched over to the door, and slammed it behind the man. "He'll be waiting until the Lord comes again!"

"Ann!" Mother Helen cried out again. "Such sacrilege."

Ann's stepmother quite often seemed to find her actions or language shocking. Tonight was no exception.

Her father just chuckled.

THAT NIGHT, SOMETIME AROUND MIDNIGHT, Daniel gave up trying to sleep. The room was spacious and the bed comfortable, but he must have tossed and turned a hundred times over the last hour. Perhaps if he had that whiskey he'd declined earlier and sat in front of the hearth for a while he would grow sleepy and quit his lonely brooding.

He tugged his breeches on under his nightshirt and quietly padded downstairs in his bare feet.

Bear, leaning on the handsome mantel and gazing into the sweet-smelling oak fire, turned when Daniel entered the room and asked, "Are ye tired of countin' sheep?"

"Yes, I thought I might count the flames in your fire instead."

"'Tis but a wee fire, just enough to light the room a wee bit. 'Tis too bloody hot for a nice fire."

Daniel asked, "Does that offer for a whiskey still stand?"

"Aye. And another after that if ye have a mind to."

"One should suffice."

"'Tis a dauntin' thing, isn't it?" Bear asked as he poured the amber liquid from a decanter into a nice glass.

"If you mean accepting eight strangers as family, yes."

"Nay, I meant findin' a father ye didn't know ye had and then acceptin' him as your Da."

Daniel exhaled and answered the first part of MacKay's question. "Yes, finding you was daunting. It took me more than a month of searching town to town in New Hampshire. I finally found someone in Durham who recognized my resemblance to you. He only knew you by the name Bear. His name was Harry."

"The owner of the inn and tavern! Stephen was a friend of his."

Daniel nodded. "After I found out that you'd moved to Kentucky, I made the six-hundred mile journey to southwestern Pennsylvania and took a keelboat down the Ohio."

"I admire yer perseverance. Lookin' for me week after week with na luck at all must have been distressin'."

"Finding you is even more unsettling."

"Aye? Why is that?"

"You seem so unlike what I was prepared to find. I expected you to be a hulking uncouth hunter and a selfish bastard who took advantage of a young woman and then did nothing to try to repay what you took."

"What I took could never be repaid."

"I meant doing the honorable thing."

"Aye. I wanted to. To be sure lad. But God did na plan that for either one of us."

"She wanted me to tell you that she would have married you if her father had let her."

"Did she?"

"Yes. Although I have no doubt of her deep abiding love for my father, I think she was still fond of you even after twenty-four years."

"The feeling was mutual." Silence fell between them for a few moments. Then with a questioning gaze, Bear leaned forward and asked, "Do ye think *ye* could ever grow fond of me?"

Daniel heard the hope in MacKay's voice. He took a slow sip of the whiskey, while he considered how he would answer him. As always, the truth was the best answer. "Honestly, I don't know."

Bear took a gulp of the rest of his whiskey. "'Tis gettin' late. Tomorrow, if ye're willin', I want to learn more about ye. Will ye take a ride with me up into the hills? Kelly calls them Whisperin' Hills. Perhaps they will tell us both what we need to know about the other."

Daniel nodded. "I would like that."

Bear left Daniel alone to finish his drink before the fire. He sat down on one of the two comfy tartan covered wing chairs on either side of a massive stone hearth. A magnificent mantel made of polished wood adorned the hearth. Above the mantel, hung a large MacKay Clan coat of arms carved into a plank of butter-colored pine wood. The carving also included what must be the MacKay clan slogan—*Manu Forti.* If he remembered his Latin correctly, it meant with a strong hand. In the center of the badge, a fisted hand held a knife that pointed straight up.

He stared at that fist for a long time before he finally looked away. On the other walls, he noticed mounted rifles, bows, axes, and a variety of animal skins. A bear skin lay on the floor in front of another set of chairs and a small round table. The large rustic logs that formed the walls gave the room a snug warmth.

Could he feel at home here? Part of him hoped so. The other part didn't think so. These people were kind and welcoming, but they were still strangers. It would take more than a warm handshake and a comfortable bed to make him feel like he belonged here.

Chapter 7

Early the next morning, Artis prepared a massive breakfast of ham and eggs, hot corncakes, fresh butter, wild berry jam, and honey. The food gave off tantalizing aromas as she spread it all out on an enormous plank table that Daniel thought would accommodate the entire Wyllie brood.

Bear said the blessing, and surprised Daniel by thanking the Lord for bringing a son to them.

He did his best to eat a generous amount despite feeling uncomfortable and out of place. Try as he might, he couldn't figure out what was making him feel so ill at ease.

After one last swallow of coffee to wash down the hearty breakfast he'd eaten, Bear told him, "Gather yer weapons and get yer horse saddled. If ye have a blanket, ye'd best bring it. The weather here can change faster than a woman's mood."

Artis gave Bear a sideways glance, but Daniel saw a smile in her big green eyes.

"Are yer weapons loaded?" Bear asked Artis. When she nodded, Bear told her, "I want ye to keep a sharp eye out while we're away. If we're na back by sundown, then we'll likely return tomorrow mornin' sometime. Keep the doors barred and the windows shuttered overnight."

"Aye," Artis agreed. "Do na worry about me."

Bear's wife looked to be about the same age Daniel was. Yet she seemed so strong-willed and brave. He had to admire her spirit. In fact, the entire family seemed to possess a good deal of pluck.

As they stood, Artis said, "Do na forget, tomorrow night we are all gatherin' here for a dinner to welcome Daniel. I'll be spendin' the day bakin' and cookin'. What's yer favorite pie, Daniel?"

"My mother never baked much. So I don't really have a favorite." He didn't mention that his mother employed a cook and a scullery maid just for the kitchen. And the cook bought the pies she served from a local bakery.

"Then I'll surprise ye!" Artis declared and turned to Bear. "I'll go pack ye some food to take along."

"Thank ye, my darlin' angel," Bear told her.

Daniel hurried upstairs to gather up his things and load his weapons. He tied his hair behind his head and donned his tricorne before rushing downstairs. When he exited out the back door, Bear stood at the railing, saddling a tall gelding with a rather odd-shaped head.

Bear turned toward him and called, "This is Camel, my loyal friend. I tied Samson there for ye."

Daniel stared at MacKay. Last night at the ball, the man appeared to be a refined well-dressed gentleman who would be comfortable in even the finest homes in Philadelphia. But now…now he was staring at a fierce frontiersman. A virtual armory covered his enormous body. A deadly looking dirk protruded from his belt and he noticed a Scottish *sgian dubh* tucked into the top of Bear's tall leather moccasins. Another knife hung from his thick neck enclosed in beautifully beaded doeskin sheath that looked as though it must have been made by a native. A hatchet stuck out from his belt, which appeared as though it might once have been an Indian's prized tomahawk. Also at his waist, two flintlock pistols, pointing in opposite directions, protruded through leather sheaths open at the ends. And a Kentucky longrifle hung from Camel's saddle.

Daniel decided he was seriously lacking in weapons if Bear was any example of what a well-armed man should look like. "Do you normally carry that many armaments on your person?" he asked as he stepped over to Samson.

"Aye, whenever I'm going into the woods. In the West, you survive by your courage, your senses, and your weapons."

In east coast newspapers, which Daniel read avidly, writers often called Kentucky 'the West' since it was the furthest west that settlers typically ventured. And the common description of frontier was a population density of two people or less per square mile. Most of the state easily met that definition.

Bear slid the bit into Camel's mouth and said, "Sam has taught all of us that there's no such thing as too many weapons when ye face the unknown."

"Sam seems to be a seasoned warrior himself."

"Aye, he is. As a young lad, he joined the Continental Army. For his bravery, several years later he was promoted to the rank of captain. As a captain, there may have been other officers more formally trained in battle plans, but there were none that could out prepare or out fight him. And no man showed more courage."

As he saddled Samson, he said, "My father was also a captain in the army. I wonder if they knew each other."

"Perhaps they did. Now and then, some of us still call him Captain. His ferocity as a warrior earned him another name that's followed him even here, 'Bloody Hand'."

"What does he think of the name?" Daniel asked.

"He hates it. Although, if need be, he and all of us would bloody our hands again for the sake of democracy and independence. But Sam saw enough of death to last him a lifetime."

So had Daniel. He hoped to never see another person die of Yellow Fever. To his knowledge, the dreaded killer had yet to strike Kentucky. He hoped it never did.

They set off in a northerly direction with the sun painting the rolling tree-covered hills in a warm morning light. The air seemed particularly crisp, hinting that fall would soon arrive.

For the first hour or so, the two of them rode quietly. Daniel spent the time absorbing the stunning views and luxurious peaceful scenery just north of Bear and William's homes. Bear had told him that William and Kelly, their daughter, and Kelly's father and wife, lived nearby. The area surrounding their homes was some of the most scenic he'd ever seen—still unblemished by man—so beautiful he now understood why it was worth the risk of settling on the wild frontier with the ever-present chance of sudden death. Many of the early settlers here bought their land with their blood. Natives would creep in when least expected and few settlers escaped their wrath.

Daniel understood that Bear and the Wyllies, and other settlers like them, were part of the young state's growth and that their survival here required both gritty courage and dogged tenacity. At the inn in Louisville, he'd read in the Kentucky Gazette that Kentuckians believed in the values of equality, democracy, individualism, self-reliance, and even violence when necessary. Daniel suspected that Bear was a man who possessed all those qualities.

"I fancy wanderin' these peaceful hills," Bear said. "Even when I'm na huntin'. They remind me of the serenity of the Highlands."

Daniel noted Bear's fondness for finding peace, even though the man was unafraid of using violence or living under its threat.

"Are we going to hunt today?" Daniel asked, noticing that MacKay seemed to be studying the ground now and then.

"Aye, but na for animals."

Daniel wasn't sure what Bear meant by that but didn't ask.

As the terrain's incline grew steeper, Daniel kept Samson on a tight rein, following closely behind Camel. His stallion was now more accustomed to the sights and sounds of the countryside, but these hills and woods were the roughest place he and Samson had ever ventured. Most everywhere else they'd ridden was on well used trails.

As they climbed upwards on a steep forested slope, Daniel's mind turned to Ann. He tried to pinpoint what it was about her that he'd found so attractive. Perhaps it was her smile or the way she'd stood up to that fool Charles. But even from the moment he first caught sight of her, she stood out at the ball like a glowing candle in a dark room. Could someone like her bring light back into his life?

Perhaps his mother was right. She always was a perceptive woman who understood him more than anyone else.

He saw Bear tug Camel to a stop just ahead and look down at something. Daniel shook his head to clear it of his visions of Ann. He needed to pay attention to what MacKay was doing.

Daniel pulled alongside, but not too close to what Bear was studying. He peered down too and noticed horse tracks. It looked like two sets of prints, perhaps even three. Had Bear been following these all along?

"Two mounts," Bear said. "One rider, likely a man by his weight, and a pack animal carryin' a considerable load."

Daniel frowned, wondering how MacKay could tell so much from a few indentions in the ground. "Will you show me how you see so much within those prints?"

"Aye. Dismount for a minute, we need to stretch our legs anyway."

MacKay bent down to point at the track. "These mounts left a good track for us in the dust. The indention made by the hoof print of this horse is spread wide because the mount is carryin' the weight of a good-sized man. The second set of prints there," Bear said pointing, "is spread even further because the horse has a heavy load on its back. We can tell he was not in a hurry because the indention at the top of the print is not as deep as it would be from the impact of gallopin' or trottin'. So, we can conclude that he does na think anyone is followin' him."

"That's amazing," Daniel said.

Bear stood up. "It just takes a wee bit of experience."

Daniel suspected it took far more than a wee bit. "And why are we following these tracks?"

They both raised their eyes to peer up at the sky at the mesmerizing call of an eagle circling overhead.

"Did ye know that the eagle became our national emblem in 1787?" Bear asked.

"Yes, I was there. I was almost thirteen when it was adopted. But before that, my Father, who had a keen interest in all things political, took my brother and me to listen to the debates about that. Franklin wanted a turkey for the national symbol, but they told him to go fly a kite."

Bear laughed. "Do ye tell the truth man?"

"Yes, indeed it is. But Secretary Thomson agreed with the Indians who revered the eagle because it was a symbol of power, nobility, and majesty. In school, my art teacher made a contest of drawing the national seal, an eagle holding a bundle of thirteen arrows in one talon and an olive branch in the other. I won that contest."

Bear smiled and Daniel actually saw pride on his father's face. It was the same look he'd seen on his other father's face when he'd won the contest.

Then Bear scanned around them and said, "These hills may look empty but they're not—they're full of life. The more time ye spend in these woods, the more ye'll see it. And each creature has its own ways and its own strengths and weaknesses. Some are more difficult to understand than others. And some are capable of thievery, aggression, or violence—especially man."

Daniel nodded his agreement.

Bear looked down at the tracks again. "A few things have disappeared from my place over the last few days."

"Like what?"

"A saddle, a sack of seed, and a fine bear skin I was dryin' out."

"Do you think these tracks were made by the robber?"

"Aye. Yesterday afternoon, I spotted fresh tracks on the other side of the barn that pointed in this direction. I would have followed the trail then, but I knew Artis would have been sorely disappointed if we did na attend the ball. She was so excited about it this year."

"Weren't you worried that the thief would get away?"

"Nay. William told me at the ball that several settlers around Highland have noticed items missin' over the last couple of weeks. He's followed tracks north a couple of times, but lost their trail in the rocks. We both thought they might be campin' in the woods somewhere north of us. My guess is that only one of them goes thievin' while the other stays and watches what they've already stolen. What say you? Shall we unleash a little hell on these two?"

Daniel's heart raced with excitement. "Let's go get the bloody thieves."

"Are ye weapons loaded and can ye shoot straight?" MacKay asked.

"They are. An unloaded weapon isn't of much use is it? And yes, I can shoot. I won the annual shooting contest at the academy two years running. And I'm called a fearsomely efficient swordsman by my friends."

"Why do ye na carry a sword then?"

"Too cumbersome for travel. It's stored in one of my bags. I'm equally good with my knife."

"Seems like ye take after yer Uncle Sam."

Daniel smiled as he realized Bear just gave him quite a compliment. Even though he didn't share Sam's blood, he would be proud to share his brave uncle's temperament.

For another hour they proceeded at the same pace. As the terrain turned rockier, MacKay spotted the place where the two thieves had apparently been camping. Bear pointed to a pile of ash, discarded bones, and coffee grounds. Several mounds of fly-covered horse dung lay on the ground next to two nearby trees. The sound of the buzzing flies was the only sign of life in the deserted camp.

After Bear dismounted and studied the area for a few minutes, he said, "The two men have four rifles with them."

Daniel's eyes widened. "How can you tell that?"

With a cheeky grin, MacKay pointed to the ground. "By the imprint of these rifle butts. They leaned two here against this tree and two there in front of that pine."

Daniel regarded MacKay with even more respect for his tracking skills. With a few more minutes, Bear could probably tell him what the men ate and drank for dinner.

"They've moved on now, not too long ago. Probably to trade what they've stolen with Indians," Bear explained.

The blindingly bright sun hung high in the cloudless sky by the time they stopped to eat and rest by a little waterfall. But they didn't tarry long. Just time enough to water the horses and let the mounts rest for a while.

Within a half hour, they reached the top of a sandstone cliff. Bear dismounted and tied his mount and Daniel did as well. Carrying their rifles, they hiked to the edge of a rocky outcrop and Bear knelt down to peer into the narrow ravine below. A small stream trickled across the bottom of the rock-covered gulley.

Two men lay on their stomachs watering themselves and their horses.

"We must surprise them," Bear whispered. "We'll follow this ledge to the east about a hundred yards and then make our way down. We can come up behind them."

"All right."

"Daniel?"

"Yes."

"Have ye ever killed a man?"

"Yes, Sir. A thief who tried to rob me on the way here."

"I hope it will na come to that, but it might. If it does, ye shoot the one with the red cap. I'll take the other. Do na be afraid to aim to kill. If ye hesitate, ye'll be dead before yer next breath. I'd hate to lose ye after havin' just found ye."

Daniel nodded. He felt the same. "You be careful too."

"And watch where ye step so we don't alert them by snappin' a twig. Surprise is our best asset."

"Yes, Sir," Daniel said. "Let's hurry, before they set off again."

Moving swiftly, the two of them wove their way silently through the white pine, red maple, and oak trees that lined the ridge. Bear soon found a place to begin their descent and headed down the narrow path likely made by the area's elk, deer, and other wild animals.

For a large man, Bear could move surprisingly stealthily. Hidden by brush, they were able to make their descent undetected. Daniel followed MacKay as he wove his way behind one tree after another until they were a mere twenty feet from the two men whose backs were to them.

"Ready?" Bear mouthed.

Daniel nodded.

They moved out, rifles pointed, and Bear yelled. "If ye take another step, I'll shoot ye."

The bodies of both men grew rigid.

One man peered behind him. "What do you want?"

"I'm curious to see what that pack horse is carryin'," Bear said.

The two men whirled around and faced them. The rough-looking bearded men just stood there, their faces snarling and defiant.

Daniel had never seen men dressed as they were. Despite the warm weather, they wore vests made of animal skins decorated with feathers and beads. One man wore a bright red woolen cap on his balding head and the other an old brown leather tricorne over straggly, shoulder-length hair.

"Lower yer weapons to the ground before we each put a ball in yer soft bellies," Bear told them.

Daniel kept a steady aim on the man who stood directly in front of him, the one wearing the red cap. Out of the corner of his eye he could see MacKay's rifle aimed at the other man.

The two slowly stooped and laid their rifles on the ground.

"Your pistols as well," Daniel yelled. Relief filled him when they did as he ordered.

Bear marched closer. "Now, start unloadin' those two pack horses."

"Why? It's none of your damn business what we carry with us," the one on the left protested.

"Maybe," Bear said, "we'll just have to see."

"You're not the law," the one on the right said.

Daniel removed the two rifles that were tied on the sides of the pack horses.

"Start now!" Bear said. "Or I'll put a ball in yer leg and let ye limp to those animals."

At once, they both moved toward the horses and started unpacking their sizable loads. The first thing that came off one of the mount's back was the bearskin covering the other items.

Daniel glanced at Bear and he nodded without taking his eyes off the two men.

Next came a variety of other items and finally a saddle.

"Yours?" Daniel asked.

Bear stepped nearer. "Turn it over."

One of the men did as he said and Daniel saw D.A.M. carved into the leather. Daniel Alexander MacKay's saddle.

"Sure as hell, 'tis mine," Bear growled as he stared down at the saddle. "Pack these animals up again."

Daniel kept his weapon pointed at the man wearing the red cap who remained frozen where he was.

As Bear glanced down to examine the other items, the other thief wearing the beat-up leather tricorne put a hand on the long knife sheathed at his side.

"Don't do it!" Daniel warned.

Without looking up, Bear told the man, "Ask yerself, Indian trader, if there's anythin' on that horse worth dyin' for?"

Chapter 8

Ann spun her horse around. "Stop following me!"

"Ann, I *will* make you listen to reason!" Charles threatened.

"Make me! You'll do no such thing. Go back to your father's home and leave me the hell alone."

"Such language. Your sweet stepmother would be appalled. You need an escort. A woman as attractive as you shouldn't be unaccompanied on this road," he protested.

"Oh, so only attractive women should be protected?"

"Only the one I'm interested in," he said with a leer.

She loathed the man. She'd tried to make that perfectly clear without coming right out and saying it. But rejecting him kindly several times didn't seem to work. She wanted nothing to do with him. Why couldn't he get that through his thick skull and into his small brain?

"My father is the head of the militia. He's taught me how to defend myself with a pistol, knife, or my hands if necessary. And if you don't leave me alone, I'll be forced to show you just what I've learned." Her knife was hidden in her boot, but she placed a hand on the pistol that hung from her belt. She would never shoot him, of course, but perhaps the coward would scare easily.

Charles harrumphed in his typical pompous way. "Someone needs to teach you how to be a proper lady."

That utterly ridiculous statement revealed how little the man knew her. She would never seek to be a 'proper' lady whose interests were entirely domestic. Proper ladies could have their needlework, looms, and spinning wheels. She wanted no part of that. She'd always been far more comfortable outdoors and on the back of a horse or perched in a tree along the Kentucky River.

"Go away, Charles," she said with as much firmness as she could muster.

"I hope you don't live to regret sending me away," he said staring at her in an unsettling way. He finally turned back toward Boonesborough.

Glad to see him go, she released a deep breath. If Charles were the only choice she had, she would remain unmarried forever.

Her father often said she took after her mother, a strong, self-reliant, and beautiful woman. Her mother's life was cut short when, out riding by herself, Indians brutally murdered her. Ann was seven at the time, old enough to remember her mother and that horrible day well.

She'd grown up at the fort, surrounded by an adoring militia. Perched up on the ramparts, she often watched their drills to improve their fighting skills. Her father made his men, mostly yeoman farmers and planters, regularly perform exercises of arms to teach his militia how to fight in the military fashion. Independent and largely unsupervised, she learned to be self-reliant.

She spun her mare around and continued her ride toward her friend Kelly's home about a twenty-minute ride from Boonesborough. Kelly's handsome husband was the sheriff of Boonesborough and she'd become good friends with both. But today, it was more than friendship that motivated her visit. She wanted to learn more about that young man, Daniel Armitage, who was evidently related to Mr. MacKay.

When she arrived, Kelly and her stepmother Mrs. McGuffin, were hard at work making five pies. The buttery fragrance of fresh-baked pie crusts filled the cabin. Several loaves of bread, waiting to be baked in the hearth, were also rising on the counter.

"Why are you making so many?" Ann asked Kelly.

"Because we are all gathering tomorrow evening at Bear and Artis' place to celebrate Bear's son Daniel becoming a member of the family."

At the startling confirmation that Daniel *was* Bear's son, Ann's mind filled with questions. *Was he an illegitimate son? What did that mean exactly? Why did he have a different last name?* She hoped Kelly would explain.

"Why don't you join us?" Kelly asked.

Disappointment filled her. "I'd love to, but father wants me there at the house to greet a visiting member of the Kentucky legislature."

"That's a shame," Mrs. McGuffin said.

"It certainly is," Kelly agreed. "Daniel is such a handsome fellow. I saw the way he looked at you at the ball."

"What way?" Ann asked, although she already knew.

Kelly thought for a moment, touching her chin with a flour covered fingertip. "Like a starving man would look at one of these pies."

The two of them giggled for a moment.

Smiling at them, Mrs. McGuffin asked, "Does he truly look that much like Bear?"

"He does!" Kelly said. "But he's not quite as tall or filled out as Bear. And he's younger, of course."

"And even more handsome," Ann said. In truth, the man was outlandishly good-looking. His strong jaw and compelling eyes conveyed strength, as did his powerful body. His dark reddish brown hair needed trimming and his short beard could use shaving, but beneath she could see a princely face. *Perhaps he was her prince.*

Kelly added, "There's no doubt he's Bear's son."

"I saw your entire family leave together and head to William's office," Ann told Kelly. "Did Daniel tell all of you much about himself?"

"A little. Bear did most of the talking. Daniel seemed somewhat withdrawn. Almost wary," Kelly said. "You won't believe what Bear had to say!"

"Well, tell me what he said!" Ann declared, unable to control her eagerness to learn more about the handsome stranger. She'd flirted with a number of young men at the ball trying to find one that could make her feel some kind of spark within herself. But none made her feel close to the way she reacted when Daniel spoke to her. Even his voice had caused a tiny but delicious shiver to race though her.

"I don't think Bear would mind if I told you in confidence. But only if you'll help roll out these pie crusts," Kelly bargained.

"I don't know how," Ann said, trying to get out of the task.

Mrs. McGuffin held out a rolling pin. "I'll teach you."

Ann shrugged, pushed her hair back, and donned an apron. Learning more about Daniel would be worth a few baking lessons.

THE DESCENT DOWN THE HILLS took less time than the trip up since Bear did not have to search for tracks. Late that afternoon, Daniel and Bear arrived in Boonesborough with the two thieves, their hands and feet bound to their saddles. Each led one of the Indian traders' mounts, with the pack horses tied behind. The people they passed waved, but none seemed surprised that Bear had captured two men.

As Daniel and Bear tied their own mounts in front of William's office, his uncle and his deputy stepped out and the sheriff said, "I see your first day together was an eventful one."

"Aye," Bear answered. "These two stole some of my things and I followed the tracks they left at my place. Daniel and I caught the Indian trader thieves for ye."

"I'm grateful," William said. "Bill and I have been trying to track them down for two weeks and we would have gone after them again this morning if Judge Webb hadn't needed us in the courtroom. Daniel, this is my deputy, Bill Wallace."

A tall lean man moved down to shake Daniel's hand. "Pleased to meet you, Sir."

"Ye have plenty of evidence. That pack horse is carryin' one of my saddles, a bear hide, and a sack of feed that belong to me," Bear said. "Ye will have to find the owners of the rest."

"It looks like one of them gave you some trouble," William noted as he scowled up at the two thieves.

"Och, a wee lassie could have handled these two feartie-cats. The only real trouble we had was endurin' their stink," Bear said.

The thieves glowered down at Bear.

The man in the red cap snarled, "Someday, we'll get some of our Indian friends to pay you a visit. Then you can see how they stink."

William glared up at the man with narrowed eyes. "I'll be sure to pass that threat along to the judge."

"My guess is you just doubled your sentence," Wallace said.

Their faces scowling, William and Wallace untied the feet of the thieves, wrenched them down from their saddles, and shoved them inside.

As soon as they locked the Indian traders safely inside their cells and gave them water, they unloaded all the stolen goods onto the back of a wagon. The deputy would use the wagon to take the things to the rightful owners.

After they finished stacking the stolen items, they stabled the Indian traders' pack animals and horses. When they finished, William turned to Daniel and Bear. "You two deserve an ale or two in thanks."

Bear nodded. "After that long, hot ride I could use one or two. But na more, Artis will be worried and I want to get home soon."

"Deputy, keep a good eye on those thieves while I take Bear and Daniel to the tavern," William instructed.

"Certainly, Sir," Wallace said. "Take your time. I'll make an inventory of all this stuff and figure out who reported what missing and map out where I need to deliver it all to tomorrow."

Daniel glanced across the fort's enclosure, hoping to catch a glimpse of Miss Byrd but sadly she was nowhere in sight.

As they walked toward the tavern, Daniel followed behind William as Bear told his brother all about capturing the thieves and where they found them.

"And Daniel here," Bear said, and turned back to look at him, "showed he's got a good deal of gumption."

"Thanks for helping Bear out," William said. "If you hadn't been here, I know Bear would have gone after those two thieves single-handedly."

Daniel suspected that going alone would not have been a problem for Bear and that William knew it.

Bear pushed open the tavern door and headed toward a table already occupied by an older man. The well-used longrifle leaning against the table and the man's wilderness attire made Daniel think he might be a local hunter.

"Daniel Armitage, this is Lucky McGintey," Bear said. "A good friend to all of us."

"Greetings," Lucky said as he stood and gave Daniel's hand a firm shake despite his gnarled fingers. Lucky wore a black hunting shirt, buckskin leggings, and moccasins. A coonskin cap covered his long grey hair. He carried a pistol, tomahawk, and long knife in his leather belt and intricate artistic carvings covered his powder horn. His sun-darkened weathered skin bore the seasoned look of someone who must have coped with the elements for some time.

William explained who the man was. "Lucky was one of the first stouthearted men to come to the Kentucky frontier."

"I came with Daniel Boone," Lucky said proudly. "Helped him hack the Wilderness Road out of the forest in '75 so folks could use it. And then I helped him build and defend this settlement."

Awestruck, Daniel's mouth dropped open. Here was a man who was a companion of the legendary Daniel Boone and worked alongside him as they built the famed Wilderness Trail! When he could speak again, he said, "An honor to meet you, Mr. McGintey. Colonel Boone was born in Pennsylvania, only about sixty miles from Philadelphia where I was born and raised."

"Yep," Lucky agreed. "Heard all about his boyhood home across many a campfire." For a few moments, the older man's eyes and face filled with nostalgic remoteness.

"Around here Lucky's called a backcountry long-hunter," Bear said, "because of the far-reachin' distances he covers huntin' fresh meat for the settlement. When I have time, I sometimes join him."

"And Bear can outhunt me on one of his bad days," Lucky said, and chuckled a bit.

Bear shook his head. "Nay. Na man has a truer aim than Lucky."

Gratitude showed in Lucky's eyes and he said, "Sometimes we come across the strangest things while hunting. For instance, around a hundred miles north of here, near Beaverlick, there's a place we named Big Bone Salt Lick. A couple of years ago, Bear and I found the bones of a giant bison. That animal must've been as tall as this ceiling," he said pointing up, "more than twice the size of the buffalo roaming around Kentucky these days."

Bear added, "Local natives think some of the bones at Big Bone Lick belonged to ancient monsters. Indians describe seein' the bones of immense buffalos as tall as trees with horns sticking straight out of their foreheads. They call them Witch Buffalos."

"I'd like to see that place for myself one of these days," Daniel said. "I wonder how they came to be there."

"Some natives say the ancient animals were poisoned by salty water and died off," Lucky answered. "Others say they got stuck in a marsh."

After a woman served ale to all of them, Bear told Lucky the story of capturing the thieves, but this time MacKay embellished the details a bit more. If Daniel had to guess, the facts of the story would get more exaggerated each time Bear told it, especially if he had a few more of the strong ales they were drinking.

"Did those varmints give you any trouble?" Lucky asked.

"Nay," Bear said, "except that one thief tried to bite me when I tied his hands."

Lucky pointed a crooked finger at Bear and said, "A native once tried that nastiness on me during a fight. I looked down and he had a good part of my leg in his Indian mouth. You know what flashed through my mind at that point?"

"What?" Daniel asked intrigued.

"I remembered what my ma used to say—if a snapping turtle bites you before sundown, it won't let go until after sunrise. It's a funny thing what goes through a fellow's mind when he's in harm's way. Since it weren't no damn turtle hanging from my leg, I sent that vicious fellow to meet his Great Spirit."

Daniel chuckled and took another sip of his ale. "Well, Bear certainly made the thief pay for trying to take a bite of him. He knocked the fellow so hard I heard the man's brain rattle inside his muddled head."

"I needed to teach him na to bite," Bear said.

Daniel added, "And after Bear pummeled the jaw of the biter, the other thief decided to run. I took the liberty of kicking his backside."

"Daniel's boot hit so hard the thief's red cap flew off and 'twas a while before the man could stand up," Bear said chuckling. "'Tis my opinion that bitin' is a filthy habit and na a gentlemanly way to fight, as I explained to both men afterwards."

"Quite thoroughly," Daniel said.

"I'm glad the encounter didn't get any more serious," William said. He eyed Daniel for a moment and turned to Bear. "Are you ready to tell your old friend Lucky where this fine young man came from?"

Daniel saw a gleam of interest and a faint twinkle in the depths of Lucky's eyes. He suspected that Lucky had already concluded where Daniel came from.

They all listened as MacKay related the same story he'd told his family the night before, although this time Bear smiled more and his eyes brimmed with compassion.

"You picked a fine family to join," Lucky told Daniel. "There's not a throwaway in the entire bunch. And as far as a father, you'd be hard pressed to find a better man anywhere."

Bear's chest seemed to expand a little and he flashed a warm smile at Lucky and then at Daniel. "My son is stayin' with Artis and me. 'Twill give the three of us some time to get to know one another."

Daniel took a sip of his ale and let out a long slow breath, thinking he'd already learned a lot about Bear in that one day.

Chapter 9

The next evening, a storm of doubts grew within Daniel as he dressed for the family gathering in his honor. His elegant ruffled shirt, embroidered waistcoat, and his perfectly tailored dark blue coat ornamented with shiny brass buttons down the wide lapels, did little to improve his confidence or mood.

He didn't want to do this. He didn't feel like celebrating with this large boisterous family. His head swirled with doubts as he slipped on his low-cut shoes with decorative buckles and then tied his shoulder length hair in a long queue with a black ribbon. He checked himself in the mirror. The man who stared back at him was the same man he'd been in Pennsylvania. Somehow, though, this conventional dress of a Philadelphia gentleman no longer seemed quite right.

But why? These were just garments. He was the same person.

Or was he?

A realization hit him, so strong it shook his soul.

Here, he was a bastard!

His entire life he'd believed himself to be the son of one of Philadelphia's finest and most prominent businessmen. He'd been proud of his family and his family's renowned name. They were descendants of distinguished men from Yorkshire, England. But his mother took all of that away from him with her admission. He understood why she revealed what she did. But the impact on his life was difficult to accept.

Now, he was nothing more than an illegitimate son of a Scottish orphan who was little more than a stranger to him. In Philadelphia society, families went to great lengths to keep such a guilty secret under wraps. And his mother had done just that for twenty-four years because the humiliation of illegitimacy would have made him subject to social and legal discrimination.

The realization hung over him like a low, dark cloud. Anger swelled within him and threatened to grow and rupture into a fearful storm. His chest felt as though it held a fiery thunderbolt that needed a place to strike.

He had wanted to get away from Philadelphia, but at least no one there knew he was a bastard. *No one but him.*

Here, everyone knew or soon would.

He could hear Bear's family members arriving, laughing, and speaking loudly to one another downstairs. The joyful sounds only angered him more. The world seemed to spin. Grinding his teeth, he pounded his fist on the small table beside the bed, making the pewter candle holder shake. Why was he doing this? He took deep gulps of air trying to calm himself. He was too angry to go downstairs. He wished there was another way out of the house—a way to get away from these people. He opened the window and glanced down. He could climb down, take a long walk until it grew late and they all left.

Then he remembered how hard Artis had worked all day to ready the food and the house for the party. And Bear had been roasting a wild boar since early morning, basting it often with a honey mustard sauce that smelled suspiciously like whiskey. He hated the thought of disappointing them. And Sam and Catherine, and Stephen and Jane, had postponed returning to their homes near Cumberland Falls just to stay for the gathering tonight.

Still, he couldn't seem to move his legs and make himself go down there. As much as Artis and Bear tried to make him feel otherwise, he didn't feel welcome here. This was not where he belonged. He was an intruder here. A stranger. An interloper into a family that wasn't his.

But where did he belong?

"Daniel?" Bear's deep voice called from behind his door. "Everyone's here. Are ye coming down soon?"

He didn't answer Bear. He didn't know what to say.

MacKay knocked and when Daniel didn't respond, his father opened the door a bit. Bear eyed Daniel sitting on the bed and entered. "Ye look like a fine gentleman. Such a handsome fellow," Bear said with a hearty chuckle.

Carefully controlling his voice, Daniel told him, "I don't think I can do this. I don't want this celebration."

"Why?"

"I don't know exactly."

Bear studied him for a moment. "Ye do na know exactly? Well, what do ye suspect?"

Daniel stood and glared at Bear. He pointed downstairs. "Why should they welcome your bastard into their midst?"

"Because ye're my son and they're family."

His mind refused to accept the significance of Bear's words. "I have no family."

"Daniel, ye're soul sick," Bear said. "We both lost our parents at a young age. And ye lost yer brother too. Ye've got a poison in yer veins. A poison brewed from grief, confusion, and shock. I know because the same venom once poisoned me for a time."

Was there an antidote for this poison? Daniel wondered.

"But a family's love cured me. A great man and good woman welcomed me into their home and hearts, as Artis and I are doing now for ye."

Every muscle in his body spoke denial. "I thank you for that, Sir. But you can't love me. You barely know me."

A sense of conviction settled on Bear's face. "Daniel, ye *are* loved for who ye are inside—a good and honorable man. And as my son and a member of my family, ye're loved by me and by all of them. And ye always will be. Ye're na my bastard. Ye *are* my son born of love."

"Love? You two didn't know what love was."

"Perhaps, perhaps not. I only know that her good kind heart reached out to mine and she gave me hope and compassion in a world filled with fear and darkness. If that's na love, I do na know what love is."

Daniel squeezed his eyes shut. "She did have a good, kind heart."

"Yer mum knew well what she was askin' of ye when she told ye to find me."

"It was a lot to ask. As I searched, I questioned the wisdom of it many times."

"She did it out of kindness for both of us. Because that kindness gave ye back to me. And now I can give ye my love and friendship and my family's as well. Ye will *always* be a member of this family because they're my family."

"They're not your family. They're Wyllies."

"Aye, they *are* my family, just as surely as we are all children of God. Family is na just those born of the same parents. 'Tis those who share yer heart and those who nurture yer soul. And it is those who will defend ye with their life. Every one of those men and women down there would do that for me. And I would gladly give my life to save each and every one of them. I've fought many a battle doin' just that. In fact, the ancient middle name we share—Alexander—means defender."

"I've never had to defend a family member from anything except disease. And I lost all three battles," Daniel admitted, remembering the horror of their deaths.

Bear sat down next to him. "Death of loved ones is hard to accept. We can only grasp 'tis the way things must be. There are just some events this side of heaven that we are na meant to ever understand."

Or this side of hell. Helplessly watching his much-loved family die one at a time was the worst kind of hell.

He stood and turned his back to Bear until he could regain control. "I think I should just leave, return to Philadelphia. Your family may accept me, but they won't be the only ones who learn I'm a bastard. Soon everyone will know, including Miss Byrd's parents. I'm not prepared to fight that battle."

"A man does na run from a fight. In fact, a man does na run from anything."

Daniel spun around and hands fisted faced MacKay—his father. Bear was right, of course. He needed to be a man about this. He released his clenched fists and started pacing the room.

"We saw an eagle yesterday, remember?" Bear asked.

Daniel nodded.

"Ye're a bit old for fables, but here's an ancient one that might help ye, an Aesop's fable, *'The Eagle and the Arrow.'* An eagle was soarin' through the air. Suddenly it heard the whizz of an arrow, and felt the dart pierce its proud breast. Slowly it fluttered down to the earth, its lifeblood pouring out. Lookin' down at the arrow with which it had been shot, the eagle realized that the deadly shaft was feathered with one of its own plumes."

Daniel remembered the fable from his studies. "And the moral is we often give our enemies the means for our own destruction," he said.

"Aye, but there's another moral to the wee fable. Sometimes we let ourselves become our own worst enemies. When we do, the means of our destruction comes from within us."

"What do you want from me? There's no denying that I'm a bastard. I don't know how to be a son to you, much less a member of your sizable family. I lived with my family for twenty-four years and I haven't even known you four days!"

"I'm just askin' ye to stay. To be my friend first," Bear told him. "Do na yield to your fears or let yer doubts about yerself become your enemy. Be the man I know ye are. Here in the West, that's what counts. Here a man is valued for his honor and courage, not his lineage."

Head bent, Daniel considered Bear's words. *Was there a chance for him to grow whole again here? To be the man he once was? And was there a chance for something more to grow between him and Ann?*

Daniel peered up at Bear. "What kind of pie did Artis make?"

Chapter 10

As Daniel slowly descended the stairs, his father came down behind him.

All eyes in the room searched Daniel's face first and then glanced up at Bear as if seeking an explanation for the delay.

Daniel had none to offer, but his father came to his rescue.

"Daniel just needed a bit of time to get spruced up for all of ye. Have ye ever seen a more handsome lad?"

Everyone laughed or chuckled and greeted Daniel when he reached the bottom of the stairs. Afterwards, his father told the children to stand in front of their parents and Bear introduced Daniel to the youngsters—first ten-year-old Little John and seven-month old Rory, the sons of Catherine and Sam; then Martha, Polly, and Samuel, ages twelve, eight, and three, the pretty daughters and son of Stephen and Jane; and finally Nicole, nearly three, the adorable blonde-headed daughter of Kelly and William. With her arms wrapped around one of William's long legs, Nicole peered up at Daniel and gave him a toothy heartwarming grin.

Daniel smiled at her and then all of the other children. It suddenly dawned on him that all these youngsters were his cousins.

Bear also introduced Kelly's father, Dr. Rory McGuffin, and his wife, a plump woman with graying hair and laughing eyes.

"She's always been dear to us," Catherine said, smiling. "But we're so glad she's part of the family now." Catherine explained that the former Mrs. Wrigley and Dr. McGuffin married recently while Catherine and Sam were on a trip to Boston.

Although middle-aged, Dr. McGuffin was still a vigorous and strong man with a ruggedly attractive face and only a sprinkle of gray sparkling in his dark hair. With the exception of Kelly's violet-blue eyes and her bright blonde hair color, it was clear that she inherited some of her good looks from her father.

"We couldn't wait until they got back from Boston to get wed," Mrs. McGuffin said, giving the doctor a lively smile. "Or at least I couldn't."

After everyone finished laughing or snickering, Little John proudly introduced Daniel to the three large dogs in the room. The black one named Happy belonged to the boy and the other black dog, Stirling, belonged to Artis. The third one, Riley, a handsome golden color, belonged to Kelly. Each dog had at least one child hanging on him.

Artis pointed to Stirling. "I let Little John borrow Stirlin' while he was visitin' his Uncle William and Aunt Kelly. Most days, Stirlin' is my shadow followin' me everywhere I go at Highland."

"I wanted to race the dogs!" Little John blurted out. The boy seemed tall for his age and on his forehead his straight blond hair hung nearly into his big blue eyes.

"Oh, and who won?" Daniel asked, petting the dogs. He loved dogs himself and fondly recalled his own childhood dog. One day he would have one again.

"Stirling," Little John said, sounding a bit disappointed.

"Happy would have beat him if he hadn't caught the scent of a rabbit," Polly explained. The girl's dark hair and crystal blue eyes looked just like her father Stephen's.

Little Samuel perked up at the mention of a rabbit. "Wabbits run fast!"

Daniel chuckled. "Yes, rabbits can run pretty fast. Did Happy catch it?"

"No, he just chased it away," Polly said.

"He brought us a stinky, dried-up animal skin once," Martha said. This girl looked more like Jane, with wild red curls and green eyes.

Daniel told them, "When dogs do that, it means they are bringing you a present."

"I told you we should have kept it!" Little John told his cousin.

Everyone laughed again and Jane encouraged the children to play some checkers on the floor so the adults would have a chance to talk.

The rest of the evening consisted of lively conversations and a bountiful banquet of roasted hog, several vegetables, freshly baked cornbread and butter. For dessert, Artis served a superb apple pie and Kelly and Mrs. McGuffin's melt in your mouth custard and wild berry pies. Afterwards several of them enjoyed a glass of wine or a 'wee droppy of whiskey' as Bear called it.

"My compliments ladies. I had to sample each of those pies and all three kinds were sublime," Daniel told them. "A little piece of heaven."

"Ann Byrd helped us make them," Kelly told him.

"Did she?" Daniel asked. At the mere mention of Ann's name, his pulse sped up.

Kelly grinned mischievously. "Ann would always prefer to be outdoors but she can do anything she sets her mind to."

Daniel believed her. Ann seemed to possess an air of self-reliance which he liked.

Around eight, the children were all sent to bed under Martha's supervision and it surprised him that he was almost sorry to see them go. The men took seats in the large front room to sip brandy while the women and Dr. McGuffin, who apparently did not consume strong drink, put up the dishes and food. Daniel offered to help, but Artis shooed him away.

As Bear poured the brandy, Little John, dressed in a night shirt, snuck down the stairs, placed a small hand on Daniel's knee, and quietly asked if he would race the dogs and horses with him tomorrow. "Aunt Artis said I could race her stallion Glasgow against your stallion," Little John told him.

"She did?" Daniel asked.

"Yup! My horse is named Dan, after Daniel Boone. He's a good one, but he's not as big or as fast as Glasgow. I rode Glasgow a lot while my Pa and Ma were in Boston."

Daniel glanced over at Sam whose eyes widened with astonishment.

"Of course I will race the dogs with you, but we can only race the stallions if it's all right with your father," Daniel answered. "What say you, Captain Sam?"

Sam winked at Little John and gave the answer all parents use when they're stalling. "We'll see."

"Captain Sam is not my real father," Little John explained. "He's dead and in heaven with my first mother."

It seemed Daniel and this boy had much in common.

"But my new Pa is just as good a father. Maybe even better." The boy smiled affectionately at Sam before he turned and raced back up the stairs.

Sam cleared his throat and took a sip of his brandy.

"Ye should see how he can ride now," Bear told Sam. "While ye were away in Boston Artis taught the lad to ride with the wind."

"Glad to hear it," Sam said. "He's always been a good rider and I'm glad to hear Artis taught him to race. But are you sure he's ready to race Glasgow?"

"He's been ridin' him for weeks, but only with either Artis or me ridin' with him," Bear said. "He even beat me."

"I'm not too surprised by that," William said, laughing. "Carrying a portly man like you always slows a mount down."

"I'm na blubbery. I'm big boned," Bear protested, "and ye well know it, William Wyllie!"

William shook his head. "Let's just say Artis' good cooking is beginning to show on those bones."

Bear glanced down at the beginnings of a belly and laughed. "Well, perhaps just a wee bit. I need to get more exercise."

"Daniel, do you have any plans yet?" Stephen asked. "Will you be buying land and building a home?"

"This is his home!" Bear declared. "There is na need to build another one."

"Bear is quite the builder," Sam said. "He helped me construct our home and then he built Stephen and Jane's home."

"He also built this beautiful place," William said, gesturing around them. "It's large enough for the biggest family."

Bear eyed Daniel and said, "Aye. Artis and I want a big family. And I'm drawin' up plans for a new inn and lumber mill I want to build in town. Catherine, Sam, and I are goin' to be partners. And if ye'd like, Daniel, ye can be too."

It was way too soon to think about where he wanted to live or investing in a business. The future still only looked vague and shadowy to him. "I have no firm plans as yet. I'm just taking life a day at a time, at least for a few more days." Daniel fidgeted in his chair, wanting to move the conversation away from him.

McGuffin joined them and provided a perfect diversion.

"Dr. McGuffin, have you had any interesting cases lately?" Daniel asked. "I studied medicine for a year before switching to law for the last couple of years."

Daniel saw the brows raise on all the men's faces.

Bear's face brightened. "I thought as much. Ye're an educated man!"

"I graduated from The Academy and College of Philadelphia and attended the University of Pennsylvania Law School."

"Are you a lawyer?" Sam asked. "We could use one around here."

Daniel frowned into his glass. "Not yet. I didn't quite finish. I found myself restless and unable to tolerate some of the professors I had. Then the epidemic broke out and I quit for a while to take care of my family. Perhaps I'll finish someday. Hopefully, they will have more interesting professors by then." *Why did he just say that? Did he intend to return to Philadelphia?*

"Daniel, please just call me Doc or Rory. We're family now. I did have an interesting case just today," McGuffin said, rubbing his chin. "A poor child was brought into the apothecary by her parents. She was quite ill."

"And your diagnosis, Doctor?" Daniel probed.

"Milk sickness due to the family's cow grazing upon the numerous poison ivy plants growing in the same vicinity as their home," McGuffin said.

"Poor thing," Stephen said. "Were you able to help her?"

McGuffin nodded. "Indeed. I gave her parents a tonic to give her that should have her feeling better by tomorrow. I also told her father to feed their cow only grain for a while until he hoed up the poison ivy as far as the cow grazes."

"Doc saved Artis' life," Bear said.

"And Catherine's," Sam added. "That's why we named our son Rory, after him."

No wonder this family seemed so fond of the good doctor. Dr. McGuffin seemed to be a man of keen intelligence and a calm nature, though Daniel suspected he would not let anyone take advantage of him or his family.

"Doc is also the physician for Colonel Byrd's militia," William said. "The militia is a great deal of help keeping us all pretty safe around Boonesborough. Unfortunately, we occasionally have renegades and outlaws who prey upon folks, like the two thieves you and Bear captured."

"Colonel Byrd seems like a fine gentleman," Daniel said. "Do any of you happen to know much about his daughter?" Ann's smile filled his mind. The night of the ball, her glowing smile felt like a light shining upon his dark soul. "Is she promised to anyone?"

"No, she's not," Kelly said, joining them. William stood and she took his seat. "And Artis and I are her closest friends," she said.

Daniel's heart filled with glorious hope.

Perhaps there was an antidote for his sick soul after all.

Chapter 11

The next morning, Daniel waved goodbye to all the others as they left to return to Whispering Hills after spending the night at Highland. "I'll see you all again in a little while," he yelled to them.

Before William left, he told Daniel that today they would be putting meat up in the smokehouse and William invited him to join them. The women, except for Artis who was very tired after entertaining everyone, were going to harvest the season's first apples and prepare them for storage. Winter was coming in a few months and now was the time to prepare for the great, howling storms to come.

Daniel grabbed his tricorne and as he stuck it on his head he turned to Bear and Artis. "I'm going into town later today. Do either of you need me to pick up anything while I'm there?"

"Nay," Artis said, wearily taking a seat. "But could ye do me another wee favor?"

"Anything, just name it," Daniel told her. "I owe you a favor or two after that wonderful dinner party you put together. I hope we didn't wear you out too badly."

"Nay. 'Twas my pleasure," Artis said. "I enjoy havin' parties. In fact, I have been meanin' to invite Colonel Byrd and his wife here for dinner.

Would ye mind stoppin' by the fort and findin' the colonel's home? Ask them if they would be available to come this Saturday night about 6:30."

"All right," he agreed, hoping he would see Miss Byrd while he was there. Perhaps her parents would even bring Ann along with them. At least he hoped they would. He turned to leave.

"And Daniel?"

He turned back to face Artis. "Yes?"

"Tell the Colonel to bring his daughter along as well."

From the wide grin on Bear's face, Daniel could tell that Artis was engaged in that pastime many females are inclined toward—matchmaking.

Well, she didn't have to ask him twice. "I'll be happy to suggest that," Daniel told her.

"Enjoy yer day," Bear said. "Are ye goin' to stop by William's on yer way back?"

"No, I'm going there now. I made that promise to Little John to race and I don't want to keep him waiting. Sam said they were returning to Cumberland Falls tomorrow didn't he?"

"Aye. William talked Stephen into stayin' one more day to help him butcher the hogs and prepare the meat for the smokehouse. And Sam volunteered to cut firewood and get it stacked up and dryin' for winter. I'll be doing the same here today. Then I'm goin' to start on diggin' a cellar."

"I'll try to be back in time to help. I saw that Little John took Glasgow. Is it all right for the boy to race your stallion?" Daniel asked.

Artis nodded. "Aye, I told the lad that he could. William and Kelly's place is only a few miles up the road. I can get my horse anytime. But when Little John races ye, Daniel, do na let him run Glasgow more than a quarter mile."

"Why?" Daniel asked.

"I do na want Little John ridin' at Glasgow's full speed just yet. I've trained Glasgow to hold back on the first quarter mile and then let himself go on the last quarter mile of any race."

"Then I'll hold Samson back a bit too."

"Ye do na have to let Little John win," she said. "Competition is good for them both. I've trained Little John to ride well and Glasgow is a winnin' stallion."

"She proved that," Bear said proudly. "But we'll tell that story another time."

"Where did you learn so much about horses and racing?" Daniel asked Artis.

"During my indenture, I worked on a large prosperous plantation in Virginia. I was assigned to work in the stables and care for the horses. Soon I started trainin' them as well. I did well enough that the owner asked me to train his stallion for racin'."

"I'm impressed," Daniel said. "Few women I've known could even ride a stallion, much less race one."

"What a woman must learn as a servant on a plantation, or even as a settler on the frontier, is far different than what a woman in a big civilized city needs to know."

"Turn Samson to the right when ye leave," Bear said. "Whisperin' Hills sits a few miles up on the right."

WHEN DANIEL ARRIVED AT WHISPERING Hills, he decided William and Kelly's home was nestled in a perfect spot. For a moment, he just sat there on Samson admiring the spectacular view. Rolling hills covered in trees beginning to don their fall colors rose on either side of a little valley. Limestone boulders and outcrops speckled both sides of the slopes to the east and west and a small stream trickled over rocks through the bottom of the ravine.

As he dismounted Samson, William strode up.

"Beautiful place," Daniel said.

"The stream normally has much more water flowing through it," William explained rolling up his sleeves. The day had already grown warm. "But for a couple of months now it hasn't rained enough to fill a thimble. It's really hurt our apple crop this year and the vegetables."

Daniel heard the crack of an axe splitting a log in two and saw Sam hard at work creating a sizeable stack of firewood between the two cabins. Nearby a lean-to shed held several animal skins that Daniel assumed were being stretched and dried, although he'd never seen it done.

William pointed to the larger cabin of the two. "Kelly, Nicole, and I live in the main cabin. Catherine, Sam, Little John, and baby Rory are staying in the upstairs loft. And the doctor and his good wife live in that second cabin. Mrs. McGuffin helps out with the housekeeping and cooking for all of us."

"What about Stephen and his family?" Daniel asked.

"They've been bunking at Bear and Artis' place. But they started staying with Doc and his wife on the night you arrived. They wanted to give you and Bear some private time together. We all decided that there must be a lot for you both to learn about the other and having a bunch of noisy relatives and children about could make that a bit difficult."

"I must admit, having such a large family around takes some getting used to," Daniel confessed.

"Kelly had to make the same adjustment as well. She was an only child and her mother died when she was young, so for several years she lived by herself for months at a time in a remote mountain cabin in the woods of Virginia while her father was away working," William explained.

They hiked a short way up an incline toward the smokehouse. A large flat board sitting on sawhorses served as a work table beside the smokehouse. Stephen, hard at work butchering a hog, wiped his brow against his shirt sleeve. A plucked turkey also lay nearby apparently awaiting its turn in the smokehouse.

"He does this every time I come to visit," Stephen complained halfheartedly. "Somehow he wrangles me into doing the worst jobs."

"As the youngest, it's your duty," William said, grabbing the turkey.

Stephen gave his brother a scowl worthy of an ogre. "Next time you come to visit, William, I'm putting you to work digging up the biggest stump I have."

Daniel laughed at the two. "Well, I'm the youngest now. Show me what I can do to help."

Stephen handed him an apron and explained how Daniel could help finish butchering the dead hog while he slaughtered another one. When the butchering was finished, they would salt and smoke the meat.

When the children spotted Daniel working with William and Stephen, they raced up excitedly, escorted by the three dogs. Based on their soiled clothing and messy hair, Daniel suspected the three oldest had been playing outdoors for some time.

Daniel told them that he would join them for the dog race as soon as they finished preparing and salting the meat.

"With the three of us working on getting the meat ready for the smokehouse, we'll soon be finished," William assured the youngsters.

Every ten minutes or so for the next hour, Little John ran up and asked, "Are you finished yet?"

Finally, after completing some of the most revolting and foul-smelling work he'd ever done, Daniel was able to say yes. It would be a long time before he would have a taste for ham again.

After Daniel discarded the heavily stained apron and washed up thoroughly, Little John grabbed him by the hand and dragged him toward where Martha, Polly, and little Nicole were waiting with the dogs near the apple orchard. William followed behind them but Stephen stayed behind to finish cleaning up the mess.

Little John bent down and looked his big dog in the eyes. "All right Happy, this time win. Okay?"

As Daniel watched, the boy reminded him so much of his brother Mathew that his heart clenched for a moment. He could vividly remember, when they were young boys, his brother doing the same thing as they'd played with their dog. The dog was long gone and now, so was his brother.

After Martha and Polly let the dogs go, Happy did win the race being the first dog to snatch up the large bone William held in the air. But then William had to toss Stirling and Riley a hog bone too to keep the three dogs from fighting over the first bone. They fought anyway for a minute until each dog ran off with his bone gripped tightly in his drooling jaw.

Daniel chuckled to himself. The whole boisterous scene reminded him of politics.

Soon afterwards, the children and the men gathered to see Little John and Daniel race the thoroughbreds. The women, too engrossed in their apple harvesting and preparing the fruit for storage, could not stop.

When they were ready, Daniel told Little John, "I warn you, my Samson is a strong runner."

"Not as strong as Glasgow!" the boy retorted. "Wait and see." Little John hoisted himself onto the back of the stallion smoothly and righted himself.

They cantered around in a circle for a few minutes to warm up the two stallions.

"Just stay on the road to Boonesborough," William said. "It's well used and pretty smooth. I'll be waiting a quarter mile down the road. When you pass me, it's over. Understood Little John?"

The boy nodded and William took off on his mount named Smoke.

Sam lined them up and said, "After you've taken off, I'll follow behind you on my horse."

Daniel glanced over at Little John. The boy appeared settled in the saddle, his feet were well placed, and he had the animal well under control. "Remember, pull up when you pass William," Daniel told him. "Okay?"

"Okay, cousin Daniel."

Taken aback, Daniel glanced at Little John. It was the first time anyone called him cousin.

Sam called the start of the race and the two were off. Glasgow accelerated from a standing position to a full run in a blink. Although Samson was an even longer-legged stallion than Glasgow, Daniel was already lagging behind. He urged his big horse to catch Glasgow, but it was obvious from the beginning that they couldn't win. The boy was an excellent rider and weighed far less than Daniel. Samson didn't stand a chance.

In about twenty seconds, it was over. Little John tugged Glasgow to a stop and Daniel did the same with Samson.

"And the winner of the first annual cousins' race is Little John!" William declared loudly.

Sam came racing up behind them on his mount.

"I did it Pa! I won!" Little John declared.

"Congratulations, Son," Sam said and leaned over to tousle the boy's hair. "I'm proud of you. You've become a real fine horseman while Catherine and I were in Boston."

The two seemed extremely fond of each other. Daniel suspected though that it was a lot easier for a child to grow close to a new father than it would be for an adult.

"I want a rematch buddy," Daniel said.

"Okay," Little John readily agreed. "Now?"

"No, one race a day on a prized stallion is enough for a boy," Sam told his son.

"Yes Pa."

"Now what did we bet on this race?" Daniel asked rubbing his chin. "I remember now—it was a sack of candy from the general store."

Little John beamed. "Candy?"

Actually, there had been no bet, but Daniel was more than glad to pay up and it would help to entertain the children during their long ride home tomorrow. "I'll bring a sack back from town later today."

"Thanks!" Little John told him. "I'll share it with our cousins."

"I'll say my goodbyes when I deliver the candy on my way back," Daniel told Sam. "I understand you're leaving for home tomorrow."

"Yes, we'll be leaving early so we'll say our goodbyes today," Sam said. "Daniel, I want you to know that you're invited to Cumberland Falls Horse Farm for a visit anytime." Sam regarded Daniel with an air of calm self-assurance.

Daniel knew it was battle-hardened patriots like Captain Sam who were responsible for winning the Revolutionary War. Someday, Daniel wanted to hear some of the tales this uncle could undoubtedly tell.

"Yup, you just gotta come for a visit soon," Little John said. "We have lots of fine horses we can race and I have a rabbit that I thought was a boy until he had babies. And my Pa has three men who work for him. Maybe you could work for him too."

Daniel smiled at that and told him, "I guess I'll be staying here a while, but I promise I'll come see you one of these days. I'd like to race that fine stallion Stephen rides. He looks magnificent."

"His name is George," Little John said.

"George is a fine horse," Sam agreed. "His sire, who was also named George, saved my life once."

"Truly?" Daniel asked.

"Indeed," Sam said, but did not elaborate.

Daniel sensed that the story should wait for another time.

"Perhaps you can come with us at Christmas," William suggested. "We all gather at Sam's big house for the holidays."

"Yes!" Little John said. "You can sleep in my room!"

"We have plenty of rooms, Little John," Sam said.

"I know. But Daniel is my friend. Aren't you Daniel?"

Daniel's smile widened and he nodded, even as he realized it would be his first Christmas without his family. But being with his father's family last night and today gave him an undeniable feeling of rightness. "I'll try to come," he said.

It wasn't much of a commitment, but it was a start.

Chapter 12

Daniel dismounted and dusted himself off to clean up from the ride into Boonesborough. He removed his tricorne and then knocked on the door of the Colonel's quarters.

The flutter in his stomach surprised him. This was just a simple invitation to dinner he was delivering.

The moment the door flew open, the air fairly shimmered with Miss Byrd's presence. Her compelling eyes captivated him again, even more strongly this time.

She extended her hand. "Mr. Armitage. Welcome to our home."

His senses leapt to life and her closeness caused a quiver to surge through him. He shook her hand and her touch upset his balance even more. He swallowed, cleared his throat, and said "Miss Byrd. A very great pleasure to see you again." It wasn't just a polite greeting, it was the honest truth.

"Please come in," she said, holding the door open and waving him inside.

As he passed her, a lovely soft fragrance filled the air between them. The room was neat and well-furnished but rustic compared to Philadelphia standards.

"I've come to see your father. Is he available?"

"No, he's out scouting with some of his men. But my stepmother is here. Could she be of some help to you?"

As if on cue, Mrs. Byrd stepped into the room, wiping her hands on an apron. "Mr. Armitage. Why are you here?"

The incivility of her tone surprised Daniel.

"I have come at Artis MacKay's request. She asked me to invite you and your husband to dinner at their home this Saturday night at 6:30. She also requested your daughter's presence," he said and smiled at Miss Byrd.

"I believe we have other plans," Mrs. Byrd said. "Please thank Mrs. MacKay for her invitation."

"I don't have other plans," Miss Byrd said. "And I would be delighted to attend."

Mrs. Byrd's face grew taut and scornful. "Ann!"

Ann ignored the woman. "I can ride there by myself, but would it be possible for you to escort me home, Mr. Armitage, since it will be after dark by the time I return? Father prefers that I not ride alone that far from the fort at night."

"Of course. It would be my pleasure. I'll pick you up and escort you both ways." He couldn't believe his good fortune. He would have Miss Byrd all to himself for the nearly half-hour ride to the MacKay's place and then back to Boonesborough.

"Well, you must get your father's permission first," Mrs. Byrd insisted. "After all, this man is a stranger to us, and therefore not a suitable escort." Her judgmental eyes glowered at him.

Daniel was stunned by her curt remarks and surly appraisal. Never had a mother of a young lady he'd called upon been anything other than welcoming and cordial. In fact, several of them fawned over him, knowing he was among Philadelphia's most sought after bachelors.

"He's suitable enough for me," Miss Byrd said.

Mrs. Byrd's scowling face flushed with something between irritation and shock.

"Perhaps I should speak with Mr. Byrd when he returns," Daniel suggested quickly, trying to ease the tension between the two women.

He glanced at Miss Byrd for an answer.

Shockingly, her answer was a wink. Then she said, "I'll speak to my father when he returns. Please thank Artis for her kind invitation and tell her I am earnestly looking forward to it."

"Unless I hear otherwise from your father, I will plan on picking you up a little before 6:00 Saturday evening. Do you have a mount to ride or should I bring one?" he asked. "Or if you prefer, I'm certain I could borrow a wagon."

Miss Byrd giggled. "Of course I have a horse. I love to ride. I'll have my mare saddled by the time you arrive."

That surprised Daniel. It was uncommon for women in Philadelphia to ride horses. Perhaps it was more commonplace here.

"Well then, I wish you both a good day." He bowed slightly and then left, closing the door softly behind him.

As he settled himself onto Samson's saddle, Daniel tried to figure out what that was all about. Why would Mrs. Byrd be so hostile toward him? *Because she must know I'm a bastard*, he suddenly realized. He'd told Colonel Byrd right in front of her that he was looking for his father—a man with another last name. Mrs. Byrd considered him an unfit suitor for her stepdaughter because he was a bastard. He guessed Mr. Byrd felt the same way.

Anger welled up inside of him again. At least Miss Byrd didn't seem to care. Or maybe she just hadn't put two and two together yet. He let out his anger and frustration on a long sigh. Somehow, he would prove himself to her and her parents.

If he had to, he would prove himself to all of Boonesborough. But for now, he just had to buy a little boy some candy.

Sam, Catherine, Stephen, Jane, and their children all left early the next morning for their homes about a day and a half ride to the south. It surprised Daniel that he was truly sorry to see them leave for home, particularly Little John. He'd grown quite fond of the rambunctious little boy. If he was still in Kentucky, perhaps he would visit them at Christmas after all.

He planned to spend the rest of the coming week helping Bear and Artis and William and Kelly with one project or another. After just a few days, he recognized how trivial his old life in Philadelphia had been. There, when he wasn't in school, he spent his days attending teas or parties with young pampered ladies, or shopping with his brother for clothes and other things neither one of them really needed. In between, he learned swordsmanship, horsemanship, marksmanship, the fine art of dancing, and other skills considered necessary for young men of Philadelphia's upper sort, as his class was referred to there. And his evenings were often spent in taverns playing cards, drinking, or listening to music. Common pursuits for young men of his age, but it shocked him to realize just how humdrum and unimportant they all seemed now.

Here, everyone was required to learn and use skills that could mean the difference between life and death. Or between going hungry or being well fed. If you wanted food, you had to slaughter and skin it or spend a growing season prying it from the soil. They spent their days being productive—raising and harvesting crops to sell, hunting, working livestock, felling trees and turning them into logs or lumber, and making other useful items. It astounded him how little he knew about such things. In Philadelphia, his family or their servants bought everything they needed. Someone else always did the hard work. Not so here. The wilderness was no place for the lazy or amateurs.

But he was learning more and more every day. And he was realizing the value of a hard day's work and helping family. At breakfast, Bear had asked for his help in trying to save what was left of the growing season. The drought had severally lessened the yield they would normally have gotten from the garden. The dry withered plants needed to be taken up and new seed planted along with prayers for rain.

He chuckled to himself. Already this morning he'd learned just how hard dry packed earth can become under the blazing summer sun. And how painful blisters can be. He'd earned himself several on each hand hoeing the garden for Artis and helping Bear plant a fall garden of carrots, peas, squash, pumpkin, and other vegetables. His hands were embarrassingly soft and his father had rightfully teased him about having the silky hands of a Philadelphia gentleman. Bear's hands, however, were the hands of a man well used to hard work.

He glanced down at the red blisters realizing how much he was changing. Someday he would have strong hands—*Manu Forti*—and be able to live up to that clan motto hanging above Bear's hearth.

His clan's motto.

ARTIS HAD JUST GONE INSIDE to prepare the noon meal, but Daniel and Bear both glanced up at the clatter of approaching horses.

At the sight of the riders, Daniel's heart sank. It was Miss Byrd approaching and a man accompanied her, but he wasn't one of the three fools from the ball. This man was about Daniel's size and handsome. And he sat his mount well, his back straight and his body relaxed.

As they rode closer, the fellow seemed to eye Daniel warily.

He squinted his own eyes as he assessed the well-dressed man. Daniel quickly glanced down and realized his own clothes were covered in garden dirt and his body glistened with sweat. And clumps of damp hair clung to his forehead and neck. Worse, as he worked this morning he'd ripped one shirt sleeve and stained the other. It was a far cry from how he planned to look the next time he saw Miss Byrd.

Why were they out riding the countryside together? His hackles rose quickly in suspicion. Of course, he had no claim on this young woman, and no right to be jealous, but he couldn't help himself—for some reason he was.

He finally pulled his gaze away from the man and smiled at Miss Byrd as she brought her mount to a stop in front of him. She wore a tailored brown and green riding habit, with a drawstring vest over an ivory blouse with flowing sleeves. He waited for her to greet him, but she didn't. Appearing nervous for some reason, she removed her riding gloves and ran her hands across her hair trying to tidy it.

The man with her brought his horse up close to Ann. The fellow dismounted and stepped next to Ann's mount. His big hands circled her waist and he easily lifted her down and then gave her a quick hug.

Daniel's mind reeled as he tried to comprehend what he was seeing. Within his chest, his heart felt like it was shrinking and beat chaotically. His chest tightened and his breath hitched.

The man strode toward Bear, hand extended. "Mr. MacKay."

"Welcome," Bear said.

The man then turned to Daniel. "I'm Conall Byrd. Ann's brother."

The relief that surged through Daniel surprised him. How could he have misunderstood so spectacularly and reacted so strongly? He found the ferocity of his feelings both frightening and exalting. And they could not be denied. He smiled awkwardly and said, "I'm Daniel Armitage."

After Daniel shook Conall's hand, Ann said, "Hello, gentleman. My brother has just returned from school in Virginia," she explained, still not looking Daniel in the eye. "I wanted to ride out and ask if it would be all right for him to come to your dinner Saturday night, Mr. MacKay."

"Aye," Bear said quickly. "Conall is always welcome here. I'll let Artis know."

"I'll tell her," Ann said. She handed her reins to Daniel, and hurried inside.

"I'm pleased to make your acquaintance, Sir," Daniel told Conall. "What school in Virginia are you returning from?"

"William and Mary," Conall said.

"Ah, Thomas Jefferson's alma mater," Daniel said. "I've heard it's an excellent school. What year student are you?"

"Praise the saints in heaven, I just graduated."

"Congratulations!" Bear and Daniel both said at once.

"This calls for a wee droppy of whiskey to celebrate. Let's get these horses watered and in the shade so they can rest," Bear said, putting a hand on both Daniel and Conall's shoulders and directing them to lead the two mounts to the water trough. "I've had enough of gardenin' for this day anyway. The sun grows too hot for a man as furred as me."

While they watered the horses, Bear pulled off the sweat-soaked shirt he wore and threw it over one of his massive shoulders. Bear was right—he was a rather hairy man, much more so than Daniel. But then his father was more of everything than most men. Taller, bigger, fiercer, stronger. But also thoughtful and caring. His father was an interesting paradox—the fiercest warrior type he'd ever met and yet he was also the most kindhearted man he'd ever known.

Bear washed his face and hands with a bucket of water he drew up from the cistern and Daniel did the same. "There's hardly any water in there," he told Bear when the bucket came up half full.

"Aye, and it has been so long since it rained 'tis gettin' stale. Only good for washin' the dirt off ye before goin' inside. And haulin' water up from the creek for cookin' and bathin' is gettin' tiresome. If it does na rain soon, I plan to dig a well. The creek is spring fed so there's always water in it, but gettin' it here is na an easy task. I have to take the wagon down there with a dozen buckets in the back. It takes three trips to get enough water for a few days."

After rinsing off himself, Daniel followed Bear and Conall to the house. As he walked behind them toward the back door, he pondered his intense reaction to seeing another man with Ann. The mere thought of a potential rival had gripped his very soul and shaken it to its core.

Chapter 13

Daniel raced up the stairs to change into a fresh shirt and comb his damp hair. He snatched a couple of shirts from the tall dresser. The blue or the ivory? The blue, he decided, it was less wrinkled. He badly needed a haircut and a shave, but for now all he could do was run a comb through his hair. When he finished, he fairly flew down the stairs wanting to make the most of Miss Byrd's unexpected visit.

They were all gathered in the kitchen drinking the cool tea Artis had just served everyone. She handed him a cup as he entered.

"Let's go sit in the big room," Artis said, pointing to the large room with the hearth. "The windows are open and there's a wee bit of a breeze in there today."

"I'm goin' to go change my shirt too," Bear told them. "Then I'll join ye for that wee droppy I promised."

Daniel sat across from Miss Byrd and her brother wanting a good view of her lovely face.

"So, what are your plans now, Sir?" Daniel asked Conall, even though he was sick of people asking him the same question.

"I'm going to stay here in Boonesborough until Christmas and in January I'll be moving to Lexington to attend the new law school there.

Hopefully, I can earn enough money between now and then to pay for at least my first term there. Father says he will try to pay for the rest."

Daniel doubted that the wages of a military man would pay for a legal education.

Ann smiled at her brother. "My father met Edward Wyllie and Mr. Tudor when they stopped to visit William and Bear on their way to Lexington and he learned of their plans to build a new law school. Father was impressed with both men and encouraged Conall to consider attending law school closer to home. Since I will get to see him more, I couldn't agree more."

"I've studied law myself," Daniel told them, "although I didn't finish."

"Well then, perhaps we might be attending together."

"I don't know yet what my own plans are," Daniel said.

"So, Mr. Armitage…" Miss Byrd began.

"Please call me Daniel," he interjected.

"And we'd be pleased if you would call us Ann and Conall. Wouldn't we Conall?"

"Indeed," her brother confirmed.

"Tell us how you are related to Mr. MacKay," Ann said. "The resemblance is unmistakable."

"Aye, Daniel's a fine-lookin' lad, just like my husband," Artis said and beamed at Bear.

Daniel swallowed. There was no easy way to say it, but he wanted Ann to know the truth. "I'm his son. His illegitimate son, actually."

"Indeed?" Ann said. "So Mother Helen was right."

That explained the woman's rude behavior toward him, Daniel thought.

"Did you know that Alexander Hamilton was also born out of wedlock?" Conall asked.

"That's what father told Mother Helen," Ann said to her brother. "And he said Thomas Paine was too."

"What of your mother?" Conall asked.

Thankfully, Artis answered for him. "Daniel's entire family—stepfather, mother, and brother—recently died of Yellow Fever."

Ann looked dismayed. "Oh my, how dreadful for you."

Conall turned back to Daniel. "We're sorry for your loss, Daniel."

He nodded and glanced away, grateful when Conall changed the subject and asked him another question.

"Ann tells me you just arrived last week from Philadelphia. How on earth did you find Bear here in the wilds of Kentucky?"

"He persevered. He did na give up," Bear's voice boomed as he came out of his bedroom downstairs. His father made his way into the big room, wearing a fresh shirt, and added, "He spent weeks horseback travelin' all over New Hampshire lookin' for me. I'll be forever grateful that he never gave up." Bear poured a small measure of brandy for Artis and Ann and then a generous portion for the men.

Bear held his cup high. "Here's to Conall. Congratulations on becoming a man of learning. Remember, even for an educated man, life is hard work and some of the choices ye will have to make will na be easy ones. Rely on God to guide ye, yer integrity to strengthen ye, and yer heart to find the courage to love." With a hopeful glint in his eyes, Bear glanced over at Daniel.

After everyone saluted, Daniel drank deeply, savoring the brandy's rich flavor. The strong drink along with Bear's wise words, clearly directed at him as well as Conall, settled Daniel's rattled nerves. Perhaps he *could* find the courage to love a new family and start a new life. He'd admitted to them that he didn't have any firm plans for the future but if the truth be known, the plans he was just beginning to mull over now revolved around Ann. Lost in thought, he gazed at her, wondering if it might be possible that they could have a future together.

Now that Ann knew he was illegitimate would she be agreeable to courting? Even if she was, would her father be amenable? The odds were not in his favor. With regards to their daughters, most fathers treated bastards like lepers.

"I'm looking forward to our dinner here," Ann said. "Can I bring anything Artis?"

Artis laughed. "Nay, ye know ye're a terrible cook."

Ann chuckled. "Unfortunately, yes. I've never learned that particular skill. But I've decided to start. Mrs. McGuffin gave me a lesson in making pie crusts."

"It'll take more than a wee lesson or two to get ye ready to serve up a meal fit to eat," Artis said in a playful voice.

"How about a bottle of wine then?" Conall suggested.

"How about two?" Ann countered.

FROM THE MOMENT SHE'D ARRIVED at Highland, Ann could not keep her eyes off of Daniel. When they rode up, his sweat drenched shirt clung to his broad chest and his rolled up sleeves revealed glistening, rippling arm muscles. He'd looked exceedingly powerful and strikingly handsome. At once, the sight of him quickened her pulse and forced her to look away before she became completely overcome.

Determined not to too quickly reveal her joy at seeing Daniel, she'd volunteered to run into the house and speak to Artis about Conall coming to dinner.

To make matters worse, Artis seemed to be playing matchmaker. "And whose idea do ye think it was to invite ye to dinner so ye could get to know Daniel?" she'd quipped before the men came inside.

She and Artis must have giggled and chatted on for a full five minutes.

After the men had washed up and come inside, Daniel had excused himself and went upstairs.

She had thought he was withdrawing to his room to rest and her heart plummeted. But when she heard his boots stomping hurriedly down the wooden stairs, she decided he was as eager as she was to visit. And when he took a seat across from her and smiled, a warm glow flowed through her.

Throughout the conversation, despite Daniel's closed expression and carefully controlled voice, she sensed his vulnerability. The deaths of his family members clearly left an open wound upon his soul. But something else, seated deep within Daniel, made him appear guarded.

Unfortunately, after only a few minutes of conversation, her brother cut their visit short. "Thank you for the drinks Mr. and Mrs. MacKay, but Ann and I should be on our way. It was good to see you both again and I appreciate your letting me join your upcoming dinner party."

What was her brother thinking? They just got here!

"We will see you again day after tomorrow," Artis said. "And do na be late."

"I will have Ann here by 6:30 sharp," Conall said.

Conall addressed Daniel. "Thank you for volunteering to escort my sister, but now that I am here, that honor falls to me."

Conall's tone surprised her. Did she detect protectiveness in her brother's voice?

Ann saw Daniel struggle not to reveal what looked like disappointment "Yes, of course," he said. "I'll look forward to seeing you both again at our dinner party then." Daniel bowed slightly to Conall before turning to her.

For a moment, he stared wordlessly at her and then he bent to kiss the back of her hand. When he glanced up, his gaze caught her eyes and a peculiar excitement surged through her. She stared at him, mesmerized by the shared touch and the feel of his lips brushing lightly against her skin.

"I SAW HOW YOU LOOKED AT Daniel. I hope you're not developing feelings for him," her brother said as they started their ride toward Boonesborough.

"Why on earth would you say something like that?" Ann asked. "First of all, it's none of your business. And second, he's a fine gentleman and, to be honest, I do find him quite appealing. I sincerely hope he finds me appealing as well."

"I assure you he does."

"How can you tell? Tell me!"

"Because he looks at you as though you were Venus herself."

The possibility that Daniel found her attractive sent a shiver through her chest. "Why are you so opposed to him?"

"Ann, he's a bastard." He spoke with resolute firmness. "It's unfortunate, but it's the truth. You heard it from the man's own mouth."

Stunned by his bluntness, her lips tightened before she said, "So what if he is? That wasn't his fault."

"You're the daughter of a colonel from a respected Virginia family. It would ruin our family name if you were to marry him."

"Marriage? Who said anything about marriage?"

"For proper young ladies, that is the only goal of a relationship. And proper young ladies don't marry bastards. Legally bastards have no standing in society."

She rejected such ideas as absurd. "I have never had an interest in being *proper* or what society thinks. You know that."

"Well, perhaps you should start."

"Never!"

"You're not a child running around the fort playing soldier anymore. You are of marriageable age now and must conduct yourself accordingly."

"Bah!"

"Ann, I think Mother Helen may be right about this man. We know nothing about him. He's a rough-looking stranger."

"You sound like Mother Helen. And that is *not* a compliment."

"No, it's not," Conall agreed. "Think about this then. The man is not very forthcoming and today we learned little about him. He studied law but quit or got asked to leave. We just don't know. He has no plans for the future or at least none he would reveal. He doesn't appear to have a visible means of supporting himself or a family. He's probably penniless. And he's living with a father he didn't know until last week. The man is unstable and unpredictable."

Disappointment filled her. "I thought you liked him."

"I have to admit, I do. He might make a friend for me—but not you."

"Well, father likes him. And so do I!"

"You hardly know him. Even if we learn more about him during the dinner Artis has planned, he'll still be a bastard. There's no changing that. Surely there are other suitors here you might be interested in."

"There are other suitors, but none that I'm interested in. Particularly that pesky Charles Snyder."

"I never liked him either. When his family moved here two years ago, I told father they would cause us grief sooner or later."

"Father says Mr. Snyder Sr. is causing him problems."

"What kind of problems?" Conall asked.

"I don't know. Father wouldn't say and I didn't press him. I'm having enough trouble dealing with Charles Junior."

Conall peered over at her, his face concerned. "What kind of trouble?"

Ann choked on a bit on road dust and then said, “He refuses to accept that I have no interest in him. And he’s taken to following me, although I sent him away in no uncertain terms.”

“I’ll beat the bastard silly if he tries that again or touches you.”

“Daniel already did. At the Governor’s Ball. It was a delightful thing to see.” She told him all about the incident and then how Charles showed up afterwards at their house uninvited.

“Hmm. Perhaps I need to give Daniel some further thought,” Conall said.

Ann smiled as she took Whitefoot to a full gallop, knowing her brother would race her back to the fort. And lose.

Chapter 14

The next morning Daniel saddled Samson to go into town to pick up a few things Artis needed for the dinner the following evening, including more flour. With two men as sizeable as Bear and himself to feed, it was no wonder she rapidly used up her supplies. He refused her coin saying he would pay for the supplies this time.

As he rode, he admired the splendors of nature on display despite the dry conditions. Blossoming vines and wildflowers lined both sides of the road and a lush canopy of tree limbs hung overhead. Perhaps because of the drought, brilliant fall foliage already flashed through the forest. Later, as the trees dropped their leaves for winter, it would open the view into the woods. He wondered if people were like that. Did they need to drop the things of the past to be able to see into the future—things like grief, regret, and heartache.

His thoughts of the future soon made him turn away from the stunning scenery to someone he considered even more beautiful. Ann. She carried herself confidently and appeared to possess an inner strength. But her self-assurance didn't lessen her femininity or her natural beauty. She seemed anything but prissy, in fact, now that he thought about it, she didn't act like the prim and proper women he'd known in Philadelphia.

She spoke her mind and didn't seem to act according to the customary code of polite behavior for a woman in society. Perhaps that was because her mother had died when she was young. Girls typically learned their gender's roles from the example of their mothers. He didn't know how long ago her father married Mrs. Byrd, but heaven help Ann if she tried to learn anything from that woman.

Since Ann and Artis were good friends, he wondered if Ann might have conspired with Artis on this dinner idea as a means to get to know him better. If she had, it was all right by him. He wanted to get to know her better too.

He decided he would buy her a small gift and get Bear and Artis something for their home too, as a thank you for their hospitality.

When he rode into Boonesborough, the frontier town was humming with activity. Wagons and people—merchants, planters, tradesmen, trappers, and many other frontier types—were everywhere going in every direction. Most appeared to be good, honest, hard-working types who would help the new state of Kentucky grow to fulfill its potential.

He drew his stallion up before the big general store and tied him securely. As he stepped inside, he was shocked by the enormous assortment of goods available for sale. You name it, it looked as though the store offered it. The air inside held that unique fragrance common to all such places—a mixture of new leather, cloth dyes, spices, beeswax candles, and a dozen other scents that combined to make even the most miserly shopper want to part with their money.

Today he would spend some of his own coin. He could afford it after all. He was rich. But far more importantly, he was rich in youth, education, and valor. And the desire to make something of himself. Someday he wanted use his assets to help him accomplish something significant. But for now, his wealth and his plans would remain his secrets.

He and the store manager gathered the things Artis had on her list and then he focused on finding the perfect gift for Artis and Bear. After some minutes of searching, he finally spotted it—a crystal cut-glass decanter. "I'll take that too," he told the store manager and pointed.

"Well, Sir, that one is quite expensive. One of a kind. Imported all the way from Ireland. Perhaps you would be interested in one of these other glass decanters?"

The manager was clearly judging Daniel on his appearance. He'd worn his work clothes to town knowing they would be covered in dust by the time he got back. And he hadn't yet gotten that haircut and shave.

"I am interested in the crystal one, Sir."

The manager told him the price and Daniel nodded. "Just add it to my total bill. And wrap it well, please, I have a good ride to deliver it."

He saved finding Ann something for last. He wanted to take his time and find the perfect gift. Nothing too significant yet, just a little something to let her know he was thinking of her. The manager showed him a case containing things that might interest a lady. He shook his head at most of the items. Some were too domestic, like scissors or pin cushions. Others too lacey or frilly. Then he spotted the perfect gift—a pair of fine brown leather riding gloves with decorative stitching. He'd noticed that the gloves she'd worn yesterday, when she rode with her brother, were quite worn. "I'll take those," he said, pointing at them.

"They're meant for horseback riding or handling a wagon team—not for dressing up," the manager pointed out.

"That's exactly what I want. How much do I owe you?"

Daniel counted out enough gold and silver to pay for his purchases. "I'll be back later to pick them up. I'm badly in need of a visit to the barber."

"Go see Poppy. He's a freed black man and has a shop right next to the tavern. Just look for the red and white stripped sign."

Daniel grimaced, knowing the red in barber signs meant they also bled people. Opening up a vein and draining out blood was a popular medical treatment, but Daniel considered it barbaric and antiquated.

"Before you go, Sir, has anyone ever told you that you look remarkably like…"

"Yes, they have. I'm his son."

"Well, welcome to Boonesborough, Mr. MacKay! I'm Daniel Breedhead. It is an honor to meet you. I owe your father a great deal. Very probably my life. Get Bear to tell you all about it someday."

"My name is Daniel too. But it's Daniel *Armitage*."

Breedhead gave him a curious look.

This was getting tedious. He had no interest in explaining to this man why his last name was different than Bear's—that yes, he was a bastard. "If you will excuse me, Sir, I have several other errands."

"Certainly. I will see you later then, Mr. *Armitage*," he said with raised brows.

Daniel left and stepped out into the bright sunlight. Looking left and then right, he saw Charles Snyder and his two companions coming straight toward him. He had spotted them earlier, as he rode through town, and was able to avoid them. He wasn't that lucky now.

"Mr. Armitage," Snyder called to him. "I just want to apologize for the other night at the ball. We all had a bit too much strong beverage to drink—not used to the stuff."

Daniel eyed the man wondering if his apology was as sincere as it sounded. "I hope your jaw and lip have recovered," he told him.

"Yes, I'm fine." Snyder introduced him to his friends. "This is Tommy Dooley and this fellow is Ed Sanderson."

Daniel nodded and waited for Snyder to continue.

"We were just going for a cup of coffee. Want to tag along?" Snyder asked.

Daniel decided it was better to have friends than enemies in Boonesborough. Or any town for that matter. He might as well go. Coffee sounded good. Thinking about Ann, it took him several hours to fall asleep last night.

They walked down the street together to an eatery and entered. Snyder selected a table by the door and they took their seats. They all ordered coffee and then Daniel spotted Lucky McGintey across the room. "Excuse me, gentlemen." He strode over to Lucky and shook his outstretched hand.

"I'm surprised to see you sitting with those three," Lucky said. His tone left no question as to his meaning.

"I'm surprised myself. They apologized and invited me for coffee. Decided I should give them another chance."

"I'd be wary of them if I was you. Giving some men a second chance is like giving a wolf another chance to bite you."

"Why is that, Sir?"

"Snyder would enjoy playing cards with the devil. And that Dooley is nuttier than a squirrel's turd."

"What about Sanderson?"

"Oh, he seems harmless enough. He just follows Snyder around like a puppy dog."

"Thanks for the word of warning, Lucky. I'll see you later." Daniel turned and strode back to the table.

"What were you doing talkin' to that useless old man?" Snyder asked. "He's nothing but a ragged frontiersman, not much beyond a stinkin' native."

Daniel regarded Snyder with a critical squint. "He's not a useless old man. Perhaps you didn't know, Sir, that he was one of the founders of Boonesborough along with Daniel Boone. His appearance may be that of an older, rumpled man, but he has the heart of a lion. We wouldn't be sitting here if it weren't for the bravery of men like him."

Snyder gave Daniel a tight-lipped smile. "Maybe, maybe not."

Daniel took a swallow of his coffee. It was bitter but maybe that was because it was now lukewarm. He took another sip before it cooled any more. "Furthermore, what I was doing talking to him is my business. But since you asked, he's my father's friend and I hope someday Lucky will call me friend as well."

"Which father? MacKay or the other one?" Dooley asked, making the other two snicker.

So gossipers wasted no time spreading the word that he was a bastard. Daniel ignored Dooley's question, narrowed his eyes, and said, "I thought this was a friendly invitation."

"It was," Snyder said. "We just wanted you to get to know us a little better. Since you're new to town, we thought you could use some friends."

So far, he didn't like these men any better than he did the night of the ball but he would give them another chance. Just one. "All right, then. Tell me about yourselves."

Snyder spoke first and told Daniel that he'd come to Boonesborough two years ago with his father who had opened a local bank. He had a decent education, but never attended a university. His mother was deceased and he was an only child.

An overindulged, willful child, Daniel suspected. "What kind of job do you have?" he asked.

"I do things for my father."

"What kinds of things?"

"Take notices out to people who have failed to make their loan payments. Evict them from their land. That type of thing."

A despicable occupation, but at least he worked, Daniel decided.

Then Dooley and Sanderson told him they'd all been friends for life. They'd moved here from North Carolina when Snyder did. Both their fathers perished in the Revolutionary War when they were young.

Daniel could tell the two suffered from the lack of a father's discipline and training. They'd never learned what it meant to be a man from the example of a strong, principled father. Neither one had much of an education or held a steady job. They preferred doing odd jobs around town and they liked helping Snyder when he evicted people from their homes. They said their work gave them more freedom.

Daniel yawned, suddenly tired. Clearly, he didn't get enough sleep. Perhaps he should get going and get done with his tasks in town. He was anxious to get that shave and haircut so that he would look more presentable tomorrow evening at the dinner party.

"Hey let's show Daniel the horse I'm thinking about buying," Snyder suggested and turned to Daniel. "We saw you earlier, riding a fine stallion. I'd like your judgment of a gelding before I buy him."

Horses were something Daniel knew something about. "All right, but I'll have to make it quick. I have some errands to get done." He took another sip of the coffee and stood.

They let Daniel pay, which didn't surprise him.

They took him to the livery down the street, quickly marched through the stable to the far side, and exited out the back.

"He's tied behind the barn," Dooley told him.

Daniel was beginning to grow suspicious until Dooley said, "There he is," and pointed to a tall gray gelding.

Daniel wondered why the horse was tied back here. He ran a hand along the gelding's hips and then bent to examine a back hoof. At once, his head spun and his eyelids grew heavy. He blinked, trying to clear the blurry hoof he held in his hand. But his eyes closed instead and he crumpled to the ground.

"The bastard's already passed out. He won't know who beat him." It was Snyder's voice, but Daniel couldn't respond.

One of them roughly rolled him onto his back. Disoriented, his head swam and his stomach lurched in a black, rolling sea. No matter how hard he tried, he could not open his eyes.

Dooley and Sanderson both flanked his face and repeatedly yelled, "Bastard!"

The barbed insults were hurtful but Daniel knew they were just the beginning as soon as the kicks started. The booted blows came one after the other—each more painful than the last.

The last thing he heard was Snyder's fading voice saying, "I'll teach you to stay away from Ann, you bloody bastard."

BEAR WIPED THE SWEAT FROM his brow with his sleeve. Digging this food cellar into the hard earth behind the house was getting tiresome. But they needed a cool place to store the vegetables for the winter. At least he hoped they'd have vegetables. If they didn't get some good rains soon, they'd have little more than wild garlic and mealy apples to store.

As Artis hiked toward him with a pitcher of cooled tea and a pewter cup, he admired the sway of her well-formed hips.

"Ah, there ye are my beautiful angel," he said. He accepted the tea and tossed it back at once.

"I wonder what's keepin' Daniel," Artis told him. "I was plannin' to bake bread and make a pie this afternoon with the flour I ordered, but 'tis growin' late. He's been gone for hours and he said he'd be home in time for the noon meal." Artis poured him another cup.

Bear gulped the liquid down again. "Aye, I've been wonderin' the same thing myself. He promised to help me dig this cellar today."

Artis glanced uneasily over her shoulder toward the road. "I do na think he's the type to avoid hard work and 'tis already 4:00. Something is amiss."

"We're probably just being worrywarts. We're both new to this parentin' business."

Artis shook her head. "New or not, 'tis worrisome just the same."

"I'll saddle Camel and go see what might be keepin' the lad." He stuck his shovel well into the pile of dirt and wiped his hands on his dirty breeches. "I'm sure the lad's fine. He looks like he can take care of himself. But accidents do happen. He could have been thrown from that big stallion."

She flinched at his words. "Do na suggest such a thing! Just get goin' and find him!"

"Aye, my angel. I'll find him."

ARTIS SIGHED AS BEAR RODE away. She placed a hand on her belly. "Aye, I need to tell him about ye. I will tonight, Lord willin'."

Chapter 15

Bear stormed into William's office just as his brother was putting on his hat to leave for the day. "I need ye to help me find Daniel!"

"Find him? Is he missing?" William asked.

"Aye. He came into town to buy a few things for Artis, and he was supposed to return in time for the noon meal. But he never came home. I came here first but when I didn't see his horse tied outside your office, I started searchin' all over town. I've been lookin' for the last half hour at least and I have na spotted him."

"Did you check the Colonel's house? Daniel seemed quite taken with Ann."

"Aye, I just spoke to Mrs. Byrd before I came here. She said they have na seen him today and then she shut the door in my face before I could ask anythin' else."

"That woman. She's a strange bird, pardon the jest."

He was in no mood for quips, but he had to agree. "Aye, she is at that."

"Perhaps Daniel decided to return to Philadelphia," William suggested.

"Nay, he did na take any of his things when he left for town." Impatient, he waved an arm toward the door. "Let's go!"

William followed him out and mounted his already saddled horse. "Where do you want to look?"

"I've searched down the main street of town. Let's make a circle of the town and look around."

For some time they searched and found nothing. As they rode back through town, Bear said, "Look, there's Samson tied in front of Breedhead's store. Do na tell me Daniel is just shoppin'."

"How did you miss seeing Samson earlier?" William asked.

"The street was busy. There must have been a covered wagon blockin' the stallion from my sight."

He and William stepped inside and questioned Breedhead.

"He was here earlier today, bought some things, and said he would pick them up later. But he never came back. I've been waiting for him, but I need to close. It's been a long day."

"Can you deliver the things he bought to my office?" William asked.

"Certainly. I go by there on my way home anyway," the store owner said.

"Just put them inside behind the door. We'll pick them up later," William told him.

"What direction did Daniel go?" Bear asked Breedhead.

"To the left, I think. He was on his way to the barber's shop."

He and William hurried outside. Samson's head hung low and his eyes looked sunken. "This poor animal needs water," Bear said. "Let's take him down to the stable to get him watered and fed. Perhaps the stable owner will have seen Daniel."

They left their own horses tied next to where Samson had been. In case Daniel came back, he would know they were there and would figure they took Samson to get him watered.

As they passed the local eatery, they peered inside. Although customers filled their tables eating their dinners, Daniel was not one of them. Nor was he at the tavern or at Poppy's barber shop. Next they checked with the gunsmith, but he wasn't there either.

"This is beginning to worry me," William said. "A man just doesn't disappear like this unless something is wrong."

Bear quickened his pace and marched down the street toward the stable. "Nor does he leave his prized stallion tied for hours."

They quickly turned Samson over to the stable owner to get him watered, fed, and put in the shade. "Take care of him until one of us or Daniel Armitage comes for him," William said, handing the man a coin.

"Did you happen to see a young man today that looks much like me?" Bear asked him.

"Nope, but I saw four men who looked to be in their twenties walk through the stable and go out back earlier this morning. I didn't get a good look at any of them. I was busy at the time and they seemed to be in a hurry."

"Did they come back through here?" William asked.

"Come to think of it, I don't think they did."

Bear took off running toward the back of the stable with William close on his heels. When they exited the back and came outside they looked around and found nothing. Crestfallen, Bear asked, "What has the lad gotten tangled up in?"

William frowned. "No good, I'm afraid."

Then Bear heard something. It sounded like a growl or maybe a moan. "Did ye hear that?"

"Yes, behind that shed, I think."

They both raced toward the back of the shed and when they reached it, Bear's heart clenched. "Bloody hell!"

Daniel lolled in a heap face down on the ground. Bear rolled him over and his son moaned loudly, but did not awake.

Bear knelt to his side. "Daniel, what happened to ye lad?"

William told Bear, "He won't answer, he'll still completely out. I'll go get Doc."

"Nay, go be sure Doc does na leave for home. On yer way ask the stable owner to help me carry Daniel to Doc's office. Doc will have all he needs to help Daniel there."

William took off running and Bear scooped Daniel's head and shoulders into his arms. He ran a hand lightly across his son's bloodied forehead and cheek. *Someone would pay for this.*

He examined Daniel's hands, noting that the knuckles were not red or swollen. Why hadn't his son defended himself?

The stable owner ran up and said, "Dear Lord. Who did this?"

"I do na know. But I'll surely find out. Ye can bet yer horses on that."

Bear grabbed his son from behind under his arms and the stable owner put his forearms and hands under Daniel's legs. The two gingerly carried Daniel through the stable and down the street to Dr. McGuffin's office.

William held the door open for them as they brought Daniel inside and said, "I helped Doc get set up. He's all ready for him."

"Lay him here on this table," Doc said. "And help me get this filthy shirt off him."

After they got Daniel's shirt off, Bear thanked the stable owner for his help. The man said he would pray that Daniel would come around and then he left to take care of Samson.

Bear stared down at his son. Scrapes covered Daniel's chest, and arms and ugly bruises were already visible around his ribs. Bear said his own prayer. Someone must have punched or kicked Daniel's ribs and stomach repeatedly. At least his face only suffered a few abrasions and welts.

Daniel moaned again and tossed his head from side to side.

"He's beat up pretty good," Doc said. He bent down to examine a cut just below Daniel's right shoulder. When he did, he bent closer to Daniel's mouth, pried it open and sniffed. "Drugged."

"Drugged!" Bear nearly shouted.

"Indeed," Doc confirmed. "That explains why he hasn't woke up. How long ago did this happen?"

"We think it happened this morning," William said. "That's when the stable owner saw four men walk through his stable and go out behind it."

"Then he should be coming around soon," Doc told them, "if he didn't suffer a heat stroke lying in the sun all day."

Worry gripped Bear's heart. "Will he be all right, Doc?"

"I think so," Doc replied as he continued to examine Daniel. "He's young so he should have been able to bear today's heat fairly well. I don't see any evidence of major damage or broken bones. They were trying to give him a strong message, not kill him. Let me get all this blood and dirt washed off and then I can give you a better assessment of his condition."

Bear and William watched Doc work on Daniel for some time as McGuffin carefully cleaned all the scrapes and scratches and then applied an ointment.

While McGuffin worked, Bear and William determined that Daniel's knife, pistols, and coin pouch were missing.

"Maybe this was a robbery. Or maybe they took his things just to make it look like a robbery," William pointed out.

Bear shook his head. "I do na think it was robbery. Daniel would have fought back. Look at his knuckles. There's na a mark on them. I think he knew his attackers and the cowards somehow drugged him. Then they took him behind the stable. Caught unawares or passed out, the three pounced on him. I bet it was the same three scamps he tangled with at the ball."

"I saw that fight myself," Doc said. "Thought I might have to patch Snyder up, but Daniel went easy on him."

"Daniel will wish he hadn't when he wakes," William said.

Bear placed a hand on his son's shoulder, nearly as broad as his own, and leaned in close. "Ye're strong Daniel. Ye must wake so we can go get the bastards that did this to ye."

Daniel moaned again and coughed. Then, praise the saints, his eyelids flew open. Immediately, Daniel tried to sit up, but he groaned and sank back down.

"Pour him some of that water, William," Doc said, pointing to a pitcher on his counter. "His mouth will be desert dry."

"Daniel, boy, I know ye must feel rotten," Bear said. "Doc is gettin' ye fixed up. Ye'll feel better soon."

Daniel nodded slightly and rubbed his eyes.

Bear lifted Daniel's head so he could sip from the water cup William offered up to his mouth.

"My head hurts," he said and rubbed his forehead.

"It's from the drug they gave you," Doc said, "and the beating."

"Drug?" Daniel croaked.

"Aye, Doc smelled it on your breath," Bear told him.

"A laudanum tincture," Doc said, "made from opium and whiskey."

Daniel blinked a few times and squeezed his eyelids. "The coffee! The son-of-a-bitches must have put it in the coffee."

"Who?" William asked.

Daniel's expression grew tense and he took a deep breath. "Snyder, Dooley, and Sanderson."

"Why were ye havin' coffee with that bunch?" Bear asked.

"They apologized for their behavior at the ball—or pretended to. Then they invited me to have coffee with them. I thought it was the gentlemanly thing to do." Daniel paused a moment to catch his breath. "We drank some coffee at the eatery before we went to the livery stable. Dooley said he had a horse he wanted me to look at."

"Do na worry Daniel, William and I will see to their punishment. Take care of him Doc," Bear said. "We're goin' to go find those three blackhearts."

"No," Daniel said and winced when he raised his head. "I'll take care of them myself. This is my fight. Not yours. Help me up."

"Why did they beat you up?" William asked.

Daniel grimaced again when Doc took a bottle of something and applied it to another open cut. "The last thing I heard was Snyder saying he would teach me to stay away from Ann."

Bear balled his fists. "I'm goin' to teach those buggers a thing or two! Or three! First, to stay away from my son!"

William shook his head. "Bear, I know you're anxious to make them pay for doing this, but we have no real proof yet that it was them. The stable owner didn't get a good look at the four, remember? And it will be the word of the three of them against Daniel's word. They'll just deny everything and blame it on robbers."

Bear scowled at William and crossed his arms. "I am na goin' to stand by and let those bloody arses get away with this. Daniel and I will take care of it."

Daniel held up a hand. "I'll be the one who goes after them. Not you two. I want you both to stay away from them."

"Ye just try to stop me," Bear growled. "No one does this to my family!"

William put a hand on Bear's arm and told him, "I will see to it that the men who did this are punished. But you have to give me time and you must follow the law or you'll wind up in jail instead of them."

"Sometimes havin' the sheriff for a brother is a real pain in the arse," Bear grumbled.

"No one, I repeat, no one is going to do a damn thing about this but me," Daniel hissed.

Bear had to admire his son's spunk.

Doc finished up wrapping Daniel's ribs. "That should give you enough support to allow you to ride home," he told Daniel. "You can take it off tomorrow. Your ribs aren't broken, just bruised. You'll be feeling much better by this time tomorrow."

Bear opened the door and shook most of the dirt off Daniel's shirt. Then he helped Daniel to put it back on, gave him some more water, and helped him to stand. When Daniel wobbled a bit, Bear took a firm grip on his son's arm. "Ye're just a little unsteady right now. Hold on to me. I won't let ye go."

Ever.

Startled by the depth of his feelings, Bear realized that Daniel became his son the moment he'd laid eyes on him. His heart swelled with feelings of protectiveness and a father's love.

Chapter 16

While Bear retrieved Samson from the livery and William loaded Daniel's purchases on Camel, he remained at Doc's office until all four of them were ready to go.

Daniel decided the ride home was the longest thirty minutes he'd ever spent in his life. Every muscle in his pain-racked body ached worse with each step Samson took. Bear and William rode close on either side of him and Doc rode off to the side. Despite his reassurances that he felt well enough to ride, they remained worried that after taking the pain medicine Doc gave him, he would pass out again. He tried his best to stay alert. The last thing he wanted to do was fall off before they reached home.

He realized he'd just called it home. Was he beginning to think of it as his home?

"Thank you for coming into town to find me," he told Bear.

"That's what families do for each other," Bear told him.

Daniel swallowed, realizing how good it felt to have someone who cared about him again. He'd missed his Philadelphia family's love, particularly his mother's. There is something special about a mother's love and he recognized that it could never be replaced. He cleared his throat, refusing his emotions when they tried to rise to the surface. After a few moments, he glanced over at Bear again. "Thank you for taking care of Samson too." He turned toward William and Doc. "And I appreciate your loading my purchases, William. But Doc, I am truly grateful for your help. It almost made me regret giving up medical school. It's a real gift to be able to help someone desperately in need of care."

"It is," Doc agreed. "I forgot that for a while. But then the good Lord sent some folks to remind me."

"We were all glad to help ye," Bear said. "I'm sure ye've noticed that they took yer pistol, knife, and coin pouch. I'll replace them for ye when we get home."

"I only took a modest portion of my money to town. I have enough to last me quite a while," Daniel said. "When I need more I can go to the bank."

"Snyder's father owns the bank," William said. "I wouldn't trust him with your banking affairs."

"Aye. I wouldn't trust him with one of yer hogs," Bear told William and then turned to Daniel. "Wait till ye're feelin' better and we can make a trip to Lexington. They have a bigger bank there that does na charge outrageous fees to handle your banking business. 'Twill give ye a chance to meet Edward and Dora. Her father, Mr. Tudor, was a well-respected lawyer in Boston until he decided to found a law school here in Kentucky."

Daniel nodded, "I heard about that from Ann and Conall." But his mind was elsewhere. The loss of some of his money and being beaten near to death didn't bother him nearly as much as the loss of his precious pistols and being made a dupe of. "I can't believe I was naïve enough to think they actually wanted to be friends."

"It just shows how good yer heart is and how black theirs are," Bear said.

They soon reached the turnoff for Bear and Artis' home. William and Doc said goodnight and continued on toward Whispering Hills, a few miles further down the road.

Bear and Daniel proceeded up the lane at a slow pace.

"Artis will be worried sick," Bear said.

"Will she?"

"Oh aye. When she finds out what happened, she'll likely tend to ye like a mother would her babe."

Daniel chuckled. "But she's about the same age I am."

"Artis' difficult life before she came to Kentucky made her wise beyond her years. Besides, age does na matter to a woman. By nature, they are carin'. Mark my words, she'll worry ye to death tryin' to nurse ye back to health."

"My own mother was the same way. Whenever we even sniffled, she'd make a pot of chicken soup and made us drink the broth."

Bear smiled. "That does na surprise me. She seemed to be an especially carin' person."

"She was. And I loved her dearly."

"I'm sorry she had to carry the burden of her secret for all those years. And I'm so sorry ye lost her Daniel. And yer da and brother."

Daniel didn't reply for a few moments as he remembered the three.

"But now ye have a chance for another life and another family. Maybe even yer own wife and family if Artis has anything to say about it."

Daniel chuckled. "What do you mean?"

"Who do ye think came up with the idea to have the dinner tomorrow night just so ye could get to know Ann?"

"Let me guess—Artis."

"Aye. But she'll probably want to cancel it now and give ye a chance to heal up."

"I'll be fine by tomorrow night. I just need a good night's sleep and a day to rest."

"Aye, your body needs to have a little rest. All right then. We'll na cancel it. But I predict ye'll likely have two women fussin' over ye then."

Bear was right. When Artis got over her outrage at what happened, she fussed over him that evening like a protective mother goose. And his father was nearly as attentive. But he couldn't complain. He actually welcomed the help. He'd never felt so bad, but he already felt better than he did at Doc's office.

Bear helped him up the stairs and out of his boots and clothes. After he settled into bed with extra feather pillows propped behind him by Bear, Artis brought him a tray of food and tea.

"I think we should cancel the dinner," Artis told him.

"No, by tomorrow night, I'll be perfectly capable of eating a meal and carrying on a conversation," Daniel insisted.

With her hands on her hips, she said, "Well then, just eat this food and get to sleep. We'll let ye sleep late in the morn."

After eating, he did feel somewhat better and quickly dozed off. But his dreams were not peaceful. He kept feeling the punches and kicks into his stomach. Again and again they came and he couldn't stop them. And he couldn't stop the pain. Barely able to breathe, the dreams woke him from sleep gasping for air and clutching his stomach. He finally took another dose of the pain killer the doc sent home with him and drifted into a sound sleep.

When the warm rays of the sun streamed in through his bedroom window, he woke and opened his eyes feeling much better. He snuggled back under the covers and was nearly asleep again when he heard a soft knock on the door. "Come in."

"Daniel, are ye awake yet?" Bear asked. "Artis sent me up to be sure ye are decent and covered before she brings up a tray of food for ye."

"Yes, I'm awake. But I was just drifting off to sleep again."

"Would ye rather sleep or are ye hungry?"

"In truth, I'm suddenly ravenous."

"Do ye want to come down or eat up here?"

"I'll come down. Moving around a bit will probably help ease the soreness. Hand me my shirt and breeches."

Bear helped him dress but he didn't bother putting on shoes or boots. He'd be heading back up to bed again soon.

"Ye need to rest today and enjoy the dinner tonight as much as yer able, but tomorrow mornin', if ye're up to it, I think we should go after those three," Bear told him as they left the room.

"I'll go after them. I don't need your help." Fortunately his legs suffered only a few bruises from the kicks that landed on them, so he was able to start down the stairs on his own.

"I know that. But ye have it anyway."

Daniel turned around and eyed his father. "Bear…"

Bear motioned toward the stairs. "Let's hurry now. Artis will na be pleased if the big breakfast she made ye grows cold."

DANIEL WINCED NOW AND THEN as he dressed in nice but comfortable, cool attire for the dinner. After sleeping most of the day, Bear brought him several buckets of water and a wood tub so he could take a warm bath. Without his clothes, he looked nearly as bad as one of William's butchered hogs, but he felt remarkably well considering his beating. Earlier, after breakfast, he'd removed the bandaging from around his ribs and that allowed him to move more freely. The swelling and redness had gone down considerably, but the cuts and bruising made him look blotchy and sickly.

Again, this was not how he wanted to appear when he saw Ann again. But it couldn't be helped. Counting tonight, he would have seen her four times and each time he had not looked his best. It wasn't vanity that made him regret it, it was that he very much wanted her to find him appealing. He couldn't remember ever wanting to make a favorable impression on a woman more than he did now. Tonight, he would just have to rely on his smile and charm.

He came down the stairs, carrying the cloth wrapped gift for Artis and Bear under one arm and the gift for Ann under the other arm. He sat both on a side table.

Ann and Conall were just arriving. They were a little early, which surprised him. In his experience, most women typically arrived late.

Ann saw him and her face went from joy to shock in an instant. "Daniel! What happened?"

"Were you thrown from your horse?" Conall asked.

"No," Daniel replied simply. "It's a long story, let's save it for another time."

Conall handed Bear the two bottles of wine he brought.

Artis took Ann' elbow and said, "I'm so sorry yer parents could not join us this evenin'."

"Mother Helen wasn't feeling well," Ann told her.

Daniel remembered the woman saying they had other engagements.

"Are you sure you're feeling up to having dinner?" Ann asked Daniel. "We could come back another time."

"Yes, I'm quite recovered. Thank you," he told her with a slight smile. *Well, he was almost recovered.*

She grinned back and with concern in her eyes reached up to draw a lock of his hair away from one of the scrapes on his forehead.

The simple gesture caused his heart to gallop and his skin to prickle pleasurably. "You look exquisite this evening," he told her, as Conall spoke with Bear and Artis.

She blushed at the compliment and thanked him.

He spoke the absolute truth. Her seductive body and wind-swept good looks made his senses spin. The half-hour trip here on horseback had done nothing but make her look even more appealing. She'd pinned her hair up for the ride, but loose tendrils hung on both sides of her face and down her neck. He desperately wanted to reach up and curl one of those wispy strands around one of his fingers.

Drawn to her again, he moved closer and took her elbow. "Shall we have a seat by the hearth?"

Even to him, his invitation sounded like it was more than simple courtesy. And touching her for the first time made his body extremely aware of her sensual appeal. He already wished they could be alone together, even to just hold her hand, but of course propriety made that impossible. At least until he formally made his intentions known to her father.

Did he have intentions?

After a drink before dinner, Daniel stood and picked up the gifts he'd set on the table and presented the larger package to Artis. "A gift to thank you both for your warm hospitality," he said to Artis. He turned to Bear and added, "And for accepting me so readily into your family."

To his surprise Bear stood, enfolded Daniel in his long arms, and hauled him against his broad chest. Then Bear leaned his head back a bit and looked Daniel in the eye. "*Our* family."

Bear released him, but rested his long arm across Daniel's shoulders.

Artis untied the twine and unwrapped the cloth protecting the fragile crystal. When she caught her first glimpse, she squealed with delight.

"'Tis magnificent, Daniel. It must have cost ye a fortune." She held it up to the oil lamp's light to see it better. "'Twas so thoughtful of ye. We'll treasure it always."

Seeing the joy on Artis' face made Daniel realize why he had always, even as a boy, enjoyed giving gifts to people. "It's a token of my appreciation," he said. "And this is for you, Ann" He handed her the small package.

Ann's eyes widened with surprise. "You got me a gift?"

"Just a little one. To thank you for being the first person who welcomed me here in Kentucky. I will never forget your kindness that evening when I first arrived."

Ann opened the gift and her hand flew to her mouth as she gazed at the gloves. "They're lovely," she said and tried them on. The fit appeared to be perfect. "My riding gloves were so worn, my fingertips were coming through. Thank you, Daniel. This was so thoughtful if you."

They moved to the dining table, already set by Artis with shining plates and sparkling crystal wine glasses. A bouquet of wild flowers sat in the middle with lit beeswax candles on either side.

"Your table looks magnificent, Artis," Conall said and took a seat between Daniel and Bear.

"Thank ye. I hope the food is as well," she replied.

Bear took the new decanter to the kitchen to rinse it out and fill it with the wine Conall had brought. He returned and placed it on the dining table next to Ann, who sat next to Artis, directly across from Daniel. "Would ye do the honor of bein' the first to pour from Daniel's gift?" he asked Ann.

Ann stood and took hold of the crystal, glistening in the candlelight. "It would be my great pleasure."

Bear returned to his seat at the head of the table as Ann filled Artis' glass first and then the men's. When she leaned next to Daniel, the sweet scent of her caused a tingling in the pit of his stomach.

Fortunately, neither Conall nor Ann pressed him any further on what caused his injuries. Perhaps, like him, they did not want to spoil their evening with unpleasantries.

"It must have been hard for you to leave your childhood home behind and set off for the wilderness of Kentucky," Ann said.

"No, actually, it wasn't. With my family—first my younger brother, then my father, and finally my mother—all dying there in our home, I couldn't wait to sell it. And the prospect of a trek all the way to Kentucky seemed exciting. I'd always wanted to take an adventurous journey."

"I think we share adventuresome spirits, Daniel," Ann said.

"Sometimes on life's adventures, at the end of them, we find ourselves," Bear said. He smiled at Artis. "And if we are very lucky, we find our futures too."

"Aye, 'twas exactly what happened to me," Artis said.

During their delightful dinner, he could barely pull his attention away from Ann to make polite conversation with the others. Every time his gaze met hers, his emotional link to her grew stronger. Yet, the physical distance between them seemed to lengthen. She sat just across the table, but the space between them seemed so great it might as while be a mile wide canyon. He wanted to touch her so badly his fingers ached with the need.

Yes, he decided, *he did have intentions toward her.*

After he dealt with his attackers, he would visit with her father and ask permission to court Ann.

It was time to truly start his new life.

Chapter 17

Well before first light, Daniel rose anxious to find Snyder and his two cohorts. He quickly donned fresh clothing and weapons, including his sword and the pistol and knife Bear loaned him. He'd loaded the flintlock the night before with powder and ball. Then, carrying his boots, he cat-footed down the stairs trying not to wake Bear and Artis. In the kitchen, he tugged on his boots, drank some water, and hurried outside to saddle Samson. Daniel halted abruptly and sighed.

Bear stood there, decked out in all his armaments, his muscular arms folded across his chest, waiting.

"Well, let's get goin'," Bear said, "we've got men to punish."

"Bear, I told you this was my fight."

"Aye, ye did."

"And you're going to ignore what I said?"

"Aye, I am."

Now Daniel understood where he got his stubborn streak. "All right then. But promise me you'll let me do the talking."

"When I go to a fight, I do na go to talk."

"And promise me you won't kill them. I don't want either one of us to wind up getting hung because of a senseless fight. I just want to give them a taste of what they gave me."

"There are many ways to punish a man without killin' him."

"Let's get the horses saddled," Daniel told him.

"They're both already saddled."

"Why doesn't that surprise me?"

"I'll lock the back door to the house while ye bring the horses out from their stalls," Bear told him. "I left them stalled to give them time to eat their grain. Grab their bridles. They're hangin' in front of each stall door."

Daniel found Samson chewing the last of his grain, a few pieces escaping to the ground, that the birds would find later. He slipped the headstall over Samson's big head, buckled the jaw strap, and led him out. Then he went back for Camel.

After Daniel handed Camel over, Bear asked, "How are ye feelin' this mornin'? Are ye sure yer up to this?"

"I've never wanted to do something more."

"Ye did na answer my question."

"No, I did not," Daniel told him. "Let's go."

The two nudged their mounts to a slow gallop and rode into town without speaking further. When they reached the edge of Boonesborough, they slowed and Daniel turned to Bear. "I don't know where they live exactly. They said it was east of the fort."

Bear eyed him. "I do."

They proceeded through town headed east and about a mile down the road Bear turned south. They soon came upon a large well-built home with a rock fence leading up to it. A smaller log cabin stood to the right, well behind the main house. Both the house and the cabin appeared quiet and still dark inside.

"That's the banker's place," Bear said, tugging Camel to a gentle stop about a hundred yards from the dwellings. "Snyder will likely be inside his father's house. I suspect the other two are living in that cabin to the right."

"What if his housekeeper or cook lives in the cabin?" Daniel asked.

"Nay, she'll be in the banker's bed. She's also his mistress."

Daniel gaped at Bear. "How do you know all this?"

"'Tis na that difficult. A man can na spit in Boonesborough without everyone knowin' about it. And Lucky makes it his habit to know just about everythin' about everybody. Yesterday, while ye were recoverin', I rode into town and asked Lucky to tell me what he knew about the three weasels and about Snyder's father, the banker."

"That was smart."

"If ye know yer enemy, and yerself, ye need not fear any battle. What's yer plan?"

Daniel's brow furrowed. "I don't have one yet."

"Well, would ye like my suggestions lad?"

"Yes, of course."

"Make a noise against that cabin's door and then hide. When one or both comes out to investigate, we'll grab them and haul them into the woods. Then ye can do to them exactly what they did to you."

Anger smoldered on Bear's face and boiled in Daniel's chest at the mention of the terrible beating.

"What about Snyder?" Daniel asked.

"When he wakes and comes lookin' for his friends in a bit, ye can surprise him too." Bear turned Camel into the forest away from the house and Daniel followed. They kept far enough away that the sound of their mounts could not be heard from the house. Well behind the cabin, they tied the horses and then made their way closer on foot.

With his heart beating rapidly, Daniel rattled the front door to the cabin and quickly slid behind the side wall. Bear was already hiding on the other side of the cabin.

Just as Bear anticipated, Tommy Dooley came out and looked around. Not seeing anything, the man went toward the side of the house where Daniel was hiding. As soon as Dooley turned the corner, Daniel's fist struck the man solidly. Dooley wilted and slumped to the ground.

Bear was there in the next instant and his father dragged Dooley away by his boots.

Daniel waited a few moments longer and when no one else came out, he rattled the door again, a bit louder this time. Quickly, he hid again. After a minute, Ed Sanderson stepped out scratching his belly and said, "What the hell? Where'd you go Tommy? Are you taking a piss?"

Daniel sprang out from behind the wall and lurched toward Sanderson, but the man hurled himself away and landed in a crouch, knife drawn. Daniel jumped him and, with his left hand, grabbed the wrist that held the knife. With his other hand he planted his fist under Sanderson's jaw, hard enough that the man went limp and flopped over. Daniel tossed the knife, grabbed Sanderson underneath his arms, and hauled him toward where Bear and Dooley were.

Within a few minutes, they had the two men leaning up against trees, hidden from view, a good distance from the house.

"Honor requires us to wait 'til they wake," Bear said.

"Agreed."

"It will na be long."

As Bear predicted, Dooley soon shook his head and came awake. The man's eyes went round at the sight of Daniel standing before him fists clenched, but when he noticed Bear standing a few feet away, Dooley actually recoiled.

Daniel moved closer to Dooley and demanded, "Are you willing to come with us and tell Sheriff Wyllie what you three did?"

"We didn't do a damn thing," Dooley sneered.

"You deny beating me?"

Dooley shrugged. "I don't know what the heck you're talking about."

Daniel had heard enough lies. "Stand up!"

Dooley pushed off the ground and sprang up swinging.

Daniel put up an arm in time to block Dooley's punch and delivered one of his own into the man's stomach.

Dooley gasped for air but rotated his body and kicked, landing a blow to Daniel's right knee.

Daniel's leg nearly buckled but he managed to stay on his feet.

Dooley charged, fists flying.

Using the footwork he'd learned in swordsmanship, Daniel easily evaded Dooley's blows.

When punching didn't work, Dooley resorted to head-butting, but again Daniel side-stepped away smoothly and delivered a kick to Dooley's backside. Daniel continued to get the best of the man no matter what Dooley tried. Incensed, Dooley charged again, arms extended and hands out, intending to choke him.

Using both his hands, Daniel grabbed Dooley's wrist and forearm, twisted in opposite directions, then pushed down, forcing Dooley painfully to his knees.

Dooley yelped and glared angrily up at him.

Using his knee, Daniel delivered a solid blow to the man's chin that knocked the man out again.

"That was entertainin'," Bear quipped and let out a belly laugh.

At the sound of Bear guffawing, Sanderson woke, coughed, sat up, and glanced around him. "What the hell?"

Daniel squinted his narrowed his eyes and hissed at the man, "That's just what I'm here to give you—a little taste of hell. Just as you did me."

Panic filled Sanderson's face. "Daniel, I'm sorry. I was just doing what Snyder told me to. It was supposed to be just a punch or two to scare you off of seeing Miss Ann. But Snyder kept kicking you. I told him to stop, but he wouldn't. He was talking wild and filled with hatred."

"I seem to remember more than a little hatred coming out of your mouth too," Daniel told him. "What was that you called me as I lay there drugged up? Say it again to my face. I dare you!"

Sanderson paled and fear crossed his face. He glanced at Dooley who was coming awake.

Bear hauled Dooley to his feet and then, twisting the man's nose and arm at the same time, pushed Dooley up against a tree.

Glowering, Daniel stared down at Sanderson. "Will you be willing to testify to Sheriff Wyllie—tell him what you just told me about Snyder?"

Sanderson ground his jaw. "Well…I couldn't…Charles…he would kill me."

The poor answer fueled Daniel's already heated anger turning it to rage. He picked Sanderson up with one hand and threw a punch into his stomach. When the man doubled over, Daniel grabbed a fistful of the top of his hair, lifted his face, and pummeled his whisker-covered jaw.

Sanderson tried to fight back, wildly swinging his fists, but he was a poor fighter, not nearly as good as Dooley, and he never landed a solid blow.

With a final punch to Sanderson's nose that knocked him out again too, Daniel let the man drop to the ground.

He straightened and stood there, breathing hard, as Bear marched up to him.

"I've got Dooley tied up over there. I'll tie this one up too," Bear said removing a small coil of rawhide from his sporran. After Bear tied Sanderson's wrists securely behind his back, his father hauled the man closer to Dooley and Daniel followed.

The corner of Daniel's mouth lifted when he caught sight of Dooley. He bent down to get a better look. Bear had cut all the hair off Dooley's head leaving just a wisp sticking straight up on the top of the man's scalp. He'd also been gagged with a foul-smelling piece of what looked like some kind of animal skin.

Bear bent and shoved a similar piece of skin into Sanderson's mouth and secured it with a strip of cloth. His father stood and said, "That should keep the pigs from squealing while ye find Snyder."

Daniel stared down at the two. "What are those gags? They smell dreadful."

"A wee bit of hog skin," Bear answered. "Before we left this morning, I stuck them under Camel's saddle so they're seasoned with a bit of horse sweat too."

Daniel turned his gaze on Bear. "I'm ready to find Snyder."

Bear yanked out his long hunting knife. "Just as soon as I give this one a quick haircut too."

Daniel grinned and said, "Leave a little more on top."

DANIEL AND BEAR WOVE THEIR way through the trees on foot as they hurried back toward the main house, staying out of sight as much as possible.

As they neared the banker's house, they saw someone open a back window and peer out. It was Charles Snyder Jr. "Dooley, Sanderson," Snyder yelled toward the cabin. "Get your lazy asses up and let's get going. Father has some work for us."

They watched as Snyder waited at the window and finally turned back inside. Five minutes later, he came out the back door of the house and headed toward the cabin. "What are you two doing still asleep?" Snyder yelled. "Didn't you hear, we've got work to do. Some delinquent squatter refuses to leave his land down by the river."

Some poor farmer must have used his land as collateral for a loan from the bank. High-interest coupled with little business experience often put farmers and planters at risk for foreclosure.

Snyder threw the door to the cabin open, stepped inside, and then quickly came out again looking around.

With his hand on his pistol, Daniel strode out from behind a tree and marched toward Snyder with a firm challenge in his stride. "I ought to shoot you full of holes."

As Daniel neared the man, Bear stealthily made his way around and came up behind Snyder, but kept his distance.

"Why are you here?" Snyder asked pretending to not understand.

"You know why."

"I don't know what you're talking about."

"You don't know anything about a beating?"

"You do look a bit roughed up. Rotten luck," Snyder said coolly.

Daniel eyed Snyder with deadly menace. He truly wanted to kill the rat.

Snyder's fingers slipped closer to his pistol and he cocked his head to one side. "I warned you at the ball to stay away from Ann. Have you learned your lesson, *bastard*?"

"He's my son and no one's bastard!" Bear swore.

Snyder whirled around and then glanced back and forth between Bear and Daniel. For the first time alarm glittered in the man's eyes and Daniel caught the tensing of Snyder's face and body. "Father!" he screamed toward the house. "Help!"

"Ye scream like a woman ye damn coward," Bear said, his vexation building. "Fight Daniel like a man if ye have the ballocks. I'll na interfere."

For the third time, Daniel asked the same question. "Will you come with us and admit to Sheriff Wyllie what you three did? And will you return my things?"

Snyder's lips pursed and he scowled at Daniel for a moment before he said, "There ain't nothing to admit. And I know zilch about your things."

A middle-aged man with a soft-looking white belly came rushing out of the back of the house wearing only his breeches. A disheveled woman wearing a nightdress stood in the doorway. The banker pointed his pistol first at Daniel and then at Bear. "What's the meaning of this, Mr. MacKay?" Snyder Sr. demanded of Bear.

Bear faced the banker. "Mr. Snyder, this fight is between the lads. If ye try to interfere, ye'll be fightin' me, Sir."

"They're threatening to kill me Father. And they've done something with Dooley and Sanderson. They're gone!"

Bear pointed in the direction of where they'd left Dooley and Sanderson. "Ye will find your friends chewin' the fat in yonder woods."

Daniel's eyes bored into Charles. "If you won't admit your guilt to Sheriff Wyllie, it's time for you to fight me."

"Why are they doing this?" the banker asked his son.

"I have no idea, Father," Charles answered.

"Ye know why," Bear challenged with furrowed brows. "Because you and your two weasels beat and robbed my son."

"You stole my pistols, knife, and coin pouch," Daniel added. The pistols had belonged to his father in Philadelphia and they were precious to him. "I intend to get them back."

"How much coin?" Snyder Sr. asked.

"A lot," Daniel answered. "He's a coward and a thief!"

"Lies!" Charles screeched at Daniel. "We didn't steal anything! Someone must have found you and beat you up after we left."

"Fight me, you damn liar," Daniel swore, his voice hardened ruthlessly. "Or can you only fight when it's three against one and your opponent is passed out because you drugged him?"

Charles took a long hard look at Daniel's clenched fists and then took a step back. "This is all because you're jealous that Ann and I have an understanding."

"According to Miss Byrd, you have no understanding," Daniel told him.

Charles snorted. "Understand this. Her father will never allow her to marry a bastard."

Snyder Sr. regarded Daniel with icy contempt. "Anne's father and I are working out the details. I expect the Colonel and I will reach an agreement for a marriage contract soon. You would be wise to stay out of this arrangement. Little good can come from your interference."

Daniel studied the man's eyes and the meaning behind his words. Snyder Sr. was just as unscrupulous as his son. Daniel ignored the banker, and his threats, and turned to Charles. "Saddle your horse," he ordered.

"I'm charging you with assault and theft. Your two lackeys already got their punishment so we'll leave them here. But you're going to see Sheriff Wyllie."

"Father, stop them!" Charles cried. He sounded pathetic and panicky.

The banker sighed heavily and then stepped closer to his son. "I've warned you time and again that if you kept up your foolish ways, something like this was going to happen. But don't worry, I'll take care of this mess soon, just like I always have. Give me your pistol and get your horse saddled. I'll take care of your friends."

Chapter 18

Bear told Daniel, "There's moral justice and there's legal justice. If ye want to stop along the way and deliver a little morality to this one too, I'm agreeable." Bear nodded toward Snyder who rode just ahead of them, his hands tied.

Snyder turned and peered back at them, more fear than anger in his beady brown rat eyes.

Daniel shook his head. "Nothing would give me greater pleasure. But I've always tried to live my life on the side of right and that wouldn't be right."

"Aye, but I'd surely enjoy it. And I think a good haircut would improve his sorry looks."

"This man needs to learn a hard lesson. One that will last longer than recovering from a beating or a bad haircut," Daniel said.

"Aye, Judge Webb will likely order him whipped."

They soon pulled up to William's office at the fort and Daniel dismounted stiffly, his soreness returning.

Bear noticed his discomfort and quickly moved over to yank Snyder down from his mount. Then his father shoved Charles onto the porch, threw open the door, and hauled him in by his shirt collar.

"William," Bear said, "since 'tis Sunday, I did na think ye'd be here. I was going to hand our prisoner here over to yer deputy." Bear turned to Daniel. "William's deputy lives upstairs in the blockhouse."

William stood up quickly from his desk. "I'm preparing a brief for Judge Webb on the two thieves you caught. The judge is coming into town tomorrow. What's going on? Why is Charles tied up?"

Daniel stepped forward. "This morning Bear and I paid a visit to Snyder's home and the cabin of his two friends."

William scowled, clearly annoyed. "I asked you not to do that!"

"The three needed some disciplinin'," Bear told his brother.

"The other two are still alive?" William asked.

Bear nodded his big head. "Oh, aye. But they're likely wishin' they weren't."

William frowned. "I can just imagine."

"They tried to kill me," Snyder blurted out. "If my father hadn't come out with his pistol drawn, they would have." He faced Daniel. "This man said he was going to shoot me full of holes."

Daniel turned to Snyder and met the man's accusing eyes without flinching. "That's two lies. Anymore and Bear and I may take you back and give you what your companions got."

"Aye," Bear snarled. "Only worse, you poor excuse for a man."

Snyder stiffened and raised his chin defiantly. "My father will take care of all this. You'll see. I'll be the one to court Ann." He put his sneering face right up next to Daniel's. "Not you—you bastard!"

With one of his meaty hands, Bear grabbed Snyder by the throat and raised him off the ground. "I told ye, he's my son!"

"Let him go Bear and take him to one of the cells," William said, "until we can sort this all out."

Bear released Snyder and gruffly ushered him down the narrow hall to a cell. Daniel untied the man's hands and shoved him in.

William locked the cell and followed them toward his office.

"He may be your son, Mr. MacKay," Snyder shouted, "but he's still a bastard."

Daniel and Bear both halted in their tracks, but William pushed a hand firmly against both their backs. "Ignore him!"

William closed the door to the cells behind him. "Coffee?" he asked, bending down to the pot hanging above some coals in the tiny office hearth.

Daniel nodded as did Bear.

Still snarling and grumbling, Bear plopped down onto a ladderback wooden chair. One of the legs snapped and Bear nearly tumbled. His father growled, snatched up the broken leg and hurled it into the hearth. He crossed his arms and leaned against the wall.

William poured them each a cup. "Sit down, Daniel, a bit easier than Bear did, and tell me everything that happened this morning. And I mean everything."

Daniel reported exactly what happened and concluded with, "I want you to charge Snyder with assault and theft."

"Did you tell Charles you were going to fill him full of holes?" William asked.

Daniel sighed. "I said I ought to, not that I was going to. I never laid a hand on the contemptuous man."

"But you beat up Dooley and Sanderson," William said. "You'll be lucky if the judge doesn't charge you with assault too. I know they deserved it. And probably more. But you can't go around punishing people for their crimes. That's the job of the court."

"But Snyder started this," Bear protested.

William leaned forward and said, "The fact that those guys started it doesn't matter. What does is whether or not there was an immediate threat to you just before you took action. You set out to go there this morning, with no immediate threat present. In actuality, you brought a threat to *them*."

Irritated with William's legalistic assessment of the situation, Daniel gave an impatient shrug. "Sir, a gentleman is required by the code of honor to defend himself from the violence and insults of abusive persons."

"This is not polite Philadelphia society, Daniel. You're on the frontier now and the law here is strict for a reason. If we tolerated men fighting with each other, we would soon have bedlam and anarchy."

Daniel frowned and said, "I will agree that your laws appear to be necessary, because there seems to be a distinct lack of honor among some frontier men."

"Unfortunately, yes. Did you learn or solve anything this morning?" William asked him.

"Before I ever laid a hand on them, I tried to get each one to agree to tell you the truth of what happened, but they all flatly refused. Only then did I fight Dooley and Sanderson. And I would have fought Snyder too if he'd been man enough."

"Nay, he wasn't," Bear said, uncrossing his arms and leaning forward.

"So you learned nothing?" William asked.

"Sanderson told me it was Snyder who delivered most of the kicks to my stomach and ribs. That he tried to stop him, but Snyder was acting wild and wouldn't stop."

William's voice held a note of impatience as he said, "It's my job to investigate crimes, arrest prisoners, and secure appropriate punishment. That's the way the law works. You should know that Daniel since you've studied the law."

"Agreed," Daniel said. "But as Bear said earlier, there is moral justice and legal justice and sometimes the law is a barrier to the former."

"Daniel, I understand why you did what you did. But Charles Snyder Sr. is a powerful man and getting more powerful all the time. The banker is filing claims on the land of long-time squatters. His son and his two minions push farmers, who can't make the payments on their high-interest loans, off their properties and threaten them with violence if they protest. So most just move further west. I've been trying to build a case against him and his son. That's why I wanted to be sure we had proof before you did anything."

Bear stood over William his hands on his hips. "They did it. What more proof do ye need?"

"All we have is Daniel's word against theirs. They made sure there were no witnesses. You can bet that the top-notch lawyer from Louisville that banker will hire to defend his son will point that out to Judge Webb."

"How do we get proof?" Daniel asked.

William heaved a sigh. "I had planned to go to Snyder's home this morning and search his son's room."

"Can't you still do that?" Daniel asked.

"Don't you think that the banker is smart enough to search his son's room himself and hide or destroy anything he knows doesn't belong to Charles? Your pistol and knife are likely already at the bottom of his well. And your money will be hidden in his bank before it opens tomorrow."

Daniel exhaled. William was right.

William continued with more discouraging news. "They can claim that you were drunk and someone else must have come along and robbed you after you passed out. They may even say that you tried to attack them and that they were just defending themselves. Your obvious size and strength would make that possible."

"What about the fact that they drugged me?" Daniel asked.

"Did you see them put something in your coffee?"

Daniel shook his head. "No."

William tapped his finger impatiently on his desk. "So again, we have no proof."

"'Tis a sad state of affairs when the truth is not proof enough," Bear growled.

William stood and faced Daniel. "Let me take care of this from here on," William said, his voice firm. "I'll talk to the judge when he gets here tomorrow."

Daniel and Bear decided to go to the eatery for breakfast before heading back home. Shoulder to shoulder, they strode out of the fort and down the street, drawing numerous glances their way. Daniel guessed it was because it was rare to see a man of their size, much less two together, and both well-armed and scowling. They must have presented a formidable appearance.

In equally black moods, they ate their eggs and ham in silence. Daniel traded his ham for one of Bear's biscuits, his memory of butchering the hogs still too fresh.

After a minute of brooding, Bear said, "I'm sorry I did na try to stop ye from goin' after them. I should have known better. I'm doin' a poor job of bein' a father to ye."

"You couldn't have stopped me even if you had tried."

"But I should have listened to William. I know better than ye what a wise man he is. I'm sorry I did na listen to him."

"The only thing to be sorry about is that we didn't stop to teach that pompous ass some of that moral justice you suggested."

"Aye," Bear said, thumping one fist against the other palm and scowling.

"But I'm the one that should apologize to you. I've studied the law and I know better. I let my need for honor squash my reason." Disgusted, Daniel shook his head. "If I'm ever going to be a lawyer, I'll need to do a better job of clamping down my anger."

He'd made a real mess of things. Now, if Ann's father heard about this, the man would likely think of him as a brute as well as a bastard.

"Do na worry over much. I know we'll find a way to make this all right," Bear told him. "Whatever happens, I'll be by yer side."

Chapter 19

Standing in the kitchen at Highland, Daniel told Artis what had happened that morning. "You should have seen the haircuts Bear gave those two." He couldn't help a whole-hearted chuckle and Bear's deep belly laugh joined his. It felt good to laugh. It had been a long time since he had.

Artis, however, failed to see the humor in the situation and shrugged impatiently. He could tell she disapproved of what they'd done.

"I wanted to scalp them," Bear said, "but I held my hand."

Daniel turned serious. "I'm afraid our encounter got us sideways with William."

Artis frowned and said, "'Tis na good if ye've caused William concern."

"Do na worry, my angel. William will figure somethin' out. He always does," Bear told her.

Daniel decided he wanted to be there when William met with the judge. "I'm going to go into town tomorrow morning and, if William will allow me, I'm going to speak with the judge myself. Perhaps if I can talk to him, I can convince him of their guilt."

"I know Judge Webb well," Bear said. "He's a plain-speakin' judge who is known for his impatience. Perhaps ye should just leave it to William as he requested."

"Do you truly think that's for the best?" Daniel asked him.

"Aye, I do. William will let ye know when the judge is ready to speak with ye. Now let's quit worryin' about it and get to work on finishin' up that cellar."

They spent the rest of the day continuing to dig the soil away from a spot behind the house where the ground sloped downward. Bear explained that the slope would keep rainwater from draining into the cellar. He wanted the cellar to measure sixteen by sixteen feet with eight feet extending beneath the home's kitchen where the cellar could be entered without going outside through a trap door on the kitchen floor. The other eight feet would be covered by a slanting roof that would also carry rainwater away from the cellar. The cellar floor would be six feet below ground surface. Into that floor, they would construct rock-lined storage pits for root vegetables. Once they removed all the soil, they would start lining the walls and floor with mortar-laid fieldstone.

As they worked, Bear described the kinds of food that would be stored in the cellar for winter, including apples. "We gather the apples from William's orchard about noon on the day of the full of the moon each month between July and September. Then we put them on shavings of pine in casks or boxes and store them in the cellar where they will be safe from frosts. They'll keep until the last of May."

"Do you lose many?" Daniel asked.

"Nay. Only one in fifty will rot."

"How did William come to have such a mature orchard when he just moved here three years ago?"

"Whispering Hills was given to him by Daniel Boone when he left Kentucky for good. Boone was there when William was sworn in as the new sheriff and Boone knew that William needed a place to live. Boone said it was a symbol of the faith and trust he was placing in William to protect the town Boone founded and loved so much."

"That was quite an honor!"

"Aye. We were all proud of William."

It amazed Daniel that William and many of the other settlers here actually knew a legend like Boone. The famous trailblazing hero lost both his son and brother to brutal native attacks. Many of the older pioneers also suffered great losses as their loved ones died defending the fort and settling the town. After many long years of struggle, these settlers had successfully planted a sturdy stake in the vast western wilderness. And that stake would undeniably become the cornerstone for westward expansion.

But Daniel knew living here would still not be easy. There was much to learn about living in this strange wild place. Without the right skills, a man put his very survival at risk. One of the first things he needed to learn was how to hunt. "Will you teach me to hunt Bear?"

"Aye, it would be my honor just as soon as we finish the cellar. My grandfather in Scotland taught me in the hills of the Highlands. Now I can teach ye in the hills of Kentucky."

After filling a large bucket with dirt ready to be emptied outside by Bear, Daniel stuck his shovel into the ground and leaned on it. "Thank you for helping me teach those men a lesson this morning. I'm glad you were there."

Bear grinned. "I'm prepared to provide ye help whenever it's needed—whether 'tis wanted or not."

Daniel smiled at his father, admitting to himself that he was now very fond of Bear. "Can I ask your opinion about something?"

"Aye."

"I'm planning to speak to Colonel Byrd soon about getting permission to court Miss Byrd."

"I thought ye might have feelings for her and I'm glad to hear it. She a fine young woman with a spirit worthy of ye." Bear picked up the filled bucket.

They were now about five-feet below ground level and Daniel took a deep breath of the earthy scented air. "I'm worried that because I am considered a bastard he will not grant his permission."

With a thud, Bear set the heavy bucket down again. "Aye, 'tis possible."

"What can I do about it?"

Bear's bushy brows furrowed in thought for a moment and his father studied the ground between them. Then Bear looked up and with glistening eyes said, "I can adopt ye."

Daniel's heart filled with a curious deep longing. The compelling sentiment brought a lump and tightness to his throat. Did his heart recognize that this was his father? Could his mind embrace the thought of it? As he stared at Bear, a single tear slid down his father's dirt-covered face. It left behind a track that revealed far more than his father's ruddy complexion.

Ann sat in front of her father's large desk, covered in papers and maps. "But father, Daniel told Artis that he was from a fine Philadelphia family. That his stepfather was one of the most prominent businessmen in that city."

"I'm sorry darling girl, but legally and socially he's a bastard. He faces legal repression and social discrimination. The stigma will follow him the rest of his life."

She stood and stamped her foot. "I don't care."

"Truthfully, neither do I," he said. "But it's my duty to watch over your interests. Your future is at stake. I must insist that you give up the notion of getting to know him better. In fact, I want you to stay away from him entirely."

She straightened in her chair. "I don't think I can do that, Father."

Losing his patience, her father's expression darkened. "Perhaps I will send you to a school for young ladies on the east coast."

Panic gripped her chest. "You wouldn't! Would you?"

"I don't want to. I'd miss you terribly. But if you persist in this, I certainly will."

"Father, I would be miserable. You know I love it here with you, living on the frontier. This is my home."

"Then you must learn to become the *proper* young lady that Mother Helen wants you to be."

Ann threw her arms in the air and marched off. "You condemn me, Sir, to a life of utter misery!"

"Ann!"

She spun around and faced him again, every fiber of her body filled with defiance. In a rush of words, she said, "I love you father. But I will not let you ruin my chance to find the same kind of love you had with my mother."

Triumph flooded through her when she saw the truth of her words reach her father's eyes.

BEAR'S UNEXPECTED OFFER UNLEASHED SOMETHING within Daniel. Something rekindled somewhere in his heart.

Daniel swallowed hard and boldly met his father's gaze, shocked to see this warrior of a man's eyes suddenly filled with tender sparkling.

Struggling to control his own emotions, Daniel could only stare, unable to find his voice.

As if Bear understood, his father cleared his throat and said in a strong voice, "Yer honorable heart beats with the pulse of my own heart. Yer blood flows with the same courage as my blood. And the fire of Scotland's spirit burns brightly within us both. Whether we make it legal or not, I swear here and now that ye are and forever will be, my son. But if ye will consent to this, na man can ever again call ye bastard."

Wave after wave of emotions rolled through Daniel. He could tell that everything Bear said was both true and heartfelt. But could he give up his Armitage name? Could he forever become a part of a family he knew nothing about before his mother's shocking confession? His jaw clenched tighter as he tried to control the overwhelming feelings exploding within him. He lowered his gaze and tried to force his tumultuous emotions into some kind of order.

Bear turned a couple of the larger buckets over and sat on one. "Sit," he said, pointing to the other bucket.

Daniel sat down with relief, taking a moment to catch his breath and slow down his racing heart. But his mind still reeled with confusion.

"Ye're tormented by conflicting emotions," Bear said.

"Yes," Daniel admitted.

"To become a MacKay does na mean ye must forget yer Armitage heritage. That will always be a part of ye too. I would na respect ye if ye felt otherwise. But if ye chose to become a MacKay, there will be no turnin' back. I will expect ye to become my son in all ways."

Daniel looked up, his decision made. "And I will likewise expect you to be my father in all ways."

Bear put a hand in the air between them, palm facing Daniel. "Take it."

Daniel grasped his father's big hand tightly, palm to palm, knowing what was coming.

"*Manu Forti*," they both said. "With a strong hand."

Chapter 20

On his way home that evening, William stopped by. Daniel and Bear were just emerging from the cellar, ready to quit for the day and celebrate their decision. Tired and covered in dirt and sweat, but in high spirits, the two gazed up at William, who remained horseback.

"Ye're just in time to join us for a swim in the creek," Bear told his brother. "We've got a fair amount of grime to wash off."

"No one who saw you would argue that," William said with a grin. "But I must decline. I have a beautiful wife who has a fine dinner waiting for me. Another time perhaps?"

"Aye," Bear said. "We can all go to the Kentucky River for a swim. I'd like to see if Daniel here can beat ye at river wrestlin'. I *know* I can." He turned to Daniel. "We wrestle in the water so no one gets hurt."

"No, just nearly drowned," William said, with a chuckle. Then he asked Daniel and Bear to appear in court the next morning to hear Judge Webb's decision about charging Snyder.

Daniel pressed William hoping to learn what the outcome would be, but William offered no hint saying they needed to wait to hear from the judge.

Delighted to hear about Bear adopting Daniel, William told them that first thing in the morning, he would add it to the judge's court agenda for the matter to be addressed tomorrow as well.

The sooner the better, Daniel thought. He'd grown to despise the word bastard and vowed to never again use it in anger or to describe someone. The origin of a person's paternity was something between a man or woman and God—and no one else's.

HUMILIATED AND DEFLATED, DANIEL WATCHED in disgust the next morning as Charles Snyder Jr., a satisfied smirk on his face, strode out of Webb's courtroom. Located at the back of the fort on the opposite end of the big room used for meetings as well as a ballroom, the courtroom held the fifteen-star flag of the Union, a sizable desk where Judge Webb sat, two smaller tables, and a dozen chairs. A pistol rested on the top of the judge's desk.

The mocking sneer must be a family trait because Snyder's father, who followed his son out the door, wore the exact same expression. Their lawyer sauntered confidently behind them both.

Standing beside Daniel, Bear also watched with silent distaste. But Daniel sensed the frustration and tension smoldering within his father.

And William, who stood nearby, was clearly making an effort to quell his anger. He turned toward Daniel and said in a low voice, taut with anger, "I was afraid this would happen."

Frustrated that the truth had not been enough, Daniel stood there struggling to keep his embarrassment from turning into raw fury. He should have known better. He *did* know better. When the judge reprimanded him and Bear for doling out their own forms of punishment, Daniel's face grew hot with humiliation and he was sure he must have flushed to a deep crimson.

William had been right. Judge Webb reluctantly released Charles because William failed to provide proof of guilt. Daniel could tell that the judge knew Charles was guilty of drugging and beating him, but they hadn't proven it with evidence or witnesses.

Judge Webb squirmed in his chair and looked uncomfortable. "I'm sorry, Mr. Armitage. But the law is clear on this. I must have firm proof of a crime being committed. And, in the future, please allow Sheriff Wyllie to handle these matters. However, I must say that if I were in your boots, I might have done the same thing."

Daniel nodded at the judge, appreciating the man's candor at least.

"Now, in the matter of the formal adoption by Daniel 'Bear' MacKay of his illegitimate son, Daniel Alexander Armitage. Mr. MacKay, is this your wish?

Bear stood. "Aye, 'tis my fervent hope your Honor. I have great affection for my son and I am deeply concerned for his welfare. I wish to legally give him my clan name—MacKay—for he is in fact a MacKay."

I have great affection for my son. Daniel repeated the words in his mind with a sizable lump in his throat. *I wish to legally give him my clan name—MacKay.*

"Mr. Armitage, do you agree to this?"

Daniel stood, realizing he would never again be called Mr. Armitage. But he answered in a firm sure voice, "I do, your Honor. I would be proud to carry the MacKay name and even prouder to have this man be legally named as my father." He glanced to his right where Bear stood and saw his father's chest expand a little.

Daniel was sorry Artis could not have been there. She'd planned to be, but this morning she wasn't feeling well. While she made breakfast Artis had run outside and retched, blaming it on the heat in the kitchen. Bear didn't want to leave her, but she insisted she would feel better after she cooled off. She adamantly wanted Bear to keep his scheduled time with the judge to make Daniel's adoption official.

The judge hit his gavel on the pine table. "Adoption granted! You are now officially and legally Daniel Alexander MacKay Jr."

Junior! Daniel had never thought of that.

Apparently neither had Bear because his father let out a bellow of laughter and then hugged him fiercely. Afterwards, Bear invited William, Judge Webb, and Lucky McGintey, who'd been quietly watching the proceedings, to go to the tavern to celebrate his adoption. "Let's put this whole nasty business with the Snyder's aside for the day," Bear said. "Although he's na a wee babe by any means, I feel like celebratin' becomin' a father."

"Yes, congratulations are in order," Judge Webb agreed.

"I'll join ye at the tavern in a just wee bit," Bear said. "I have a quick errand to run first."

"All right," Daniel told him. "But hurry. I want to see if my father can hold his ale as well as me."

"That's one competition I know I can win," Bear said, laughing. "Go on now, all of ye," he said shoving them all out the door.

Despite losing to Snyder, Daniel was in a mood to celebrate. No longer was he Daniel, the bastard, the recipient of slights and the butt of gossips. He was a MacKay now. Now there would be no questions about his paternity. At last, he had a legitimate name again.

As SOON AS THE OTHERS LEFT through the fort's gate and turned toward town, Bear spun around and headed to the Colonel's home. He knocked vigorously, still excited about adopting Daniel.

The Colonel opened the door. "Mr. MacKay, what a delightful surprise."

"Ye know, Colonel Byrd, I've asked ye before to call me Bear," he answered.

"Yes, I'd forgotten. Please come in. Helen and Ann are outside in the garden collecting herbs they have been struggling to keep alive. We pour every drop of our used bathing water on them. They should be coming inside in a few minutes and can serve us some refreshments."

"I thank ye, but that will na be necessary. I have only a minute." Bear entered and came to the point right away. "Colonel, I just legally adopted Daniel Armitage as my son."

"That's wonderful news! Congratulations, Bear."

"That means he is no longer illegitimate."

"Again, that's great news."

"It is!" Conall said, joining them. "I overhead you tell father."

"So, I've come to ask ye to join us now over at the tavern to celebrate Daniel's adoption. Would ye both do me the honor of bein' part of our merrymakin'?"

"It is us who would be honored, Sir."

"Thank ye, Colonel."

"Let me just get my hat," father and son said at once.

After they stepped outside, Colonel Byrd yelled over to his wife and Ann to let them know he and Conall were leaving with Bear.

The three of them made their way across the enclosure and headed toward the tavern while Bear told them about the beating Daniel took, along with the early morning visit he and Daniel had paid to the three, and the decision just made by the judge to release Snyder.

The Colonel shook his head. "That no-good Charles has had an eye on my Ann for some time. But she despises the man. And so do I. Although somehow Snyder has managed to favorably impress my wife Helen."

"And ye know, I'm sure, that Daniel has also had an eye on Ann. But he has been reluctant to ask yer permission to court her, Colonel, believing ye would have denied it because of his legally being a bastard."

"He's right. Father would have," Conall said. "And I would have supported my father's decision."

Bear stopped, took hold of the colonel's elbow, and peered into the man's eyes. "Can ye reconsider now?"

"I already have," Byrd answered with a smile.

DANIEL GLANCED UP FROM HIS nearly finished first ale and saw his father walk in with Colonel Byrd and Conall. The three seemed to be in an especially jovial mood. When they approached their table in the busy tavern, Daniel stood and shook the Colonel's outstretched hand and then Conall's.

"Congratulations, Daniel. You have joined a first-rate family," Byrd told him. "I've never known men with more integrity, principles, and honor than your father and his brothers."

"Exactly my sentiments, Colonel," Daniel said. "Thank you both for joining us."

The Colonel, Conall, and Bear took their seats and ordered ale.

The moment his drink arrived, Bear held it up and said, "To my first-born son Daniel. Here in Kentucky you are part of a new family and a new world. May you experience life and adventures, peace and love, greater than you have ever known. I'm proud to call myself your father and welcome you to clan MacKay."

"Here, here," everyone said.

"Another toast," the Colonel said. "To Daniel and his good fortune in joining a fine family." A thoughtful smile curved the man's mouth as he regarded Daniel.

Daniel could have sworn that the Colonel's eyes conveyed more meaning in his statement. Was that a hint? Should he speak to him now? Yes, he decided. He couldn't wait even a minute longer. He opened his mouth to address Byrd, but William spoke up first.

"And another toast," William said, raising his glass. "To Daniel's proud father and my brother, our family wouldn't be the same without you, Bear."

Everyone took a swallow and Bear said, "I'd hate to see the muddled messes you Wyllie boys would have gotten into all these years had I na been there to keep ye in line."

"That sounds like God's truth to me," Lucky agreed.

"I think it's William who will have his hands full," Judge Webb said, "with *two* Daniel Alexander MacKays in town!"

Daniel glanced over at Bear who gave him a knowing grin. Daniel smiled back, already proud to have a man like Bear as his father.

Then Bear inclined his head a bit toward the Colonel. His father clearly wanted him to speak up about Ann. He was more than ready. As casually as he could manage, Daniel said, "Colonel, Sir. May I have a word with you?"

"Certainly, Daniel. Speak your mind."

"Privately, Sir." Daniel stood and motioned the Colonel over to an area away from their table and other people. When he reached the spot, he turned back to Byrd and said, "I would like to ask for the honor of calling on Miss Ann, Sir."

"You don't know how relieved I am," Byrd said, "that the issue of your paternity has been resolved. But what of your means of supporting my daughter? Do you have an occupation or trade?"

"I assure you, Colonel, on my honor, that you should have no concerns whatsoever in that regard. Ann will not only be supported, she will have the means to live in as much luxury as she would like—servants included. So the fact that she spurns domestic duties is of no concern to me. But I would prefer, Sir, if you would keep my wealth between the two of us for now."

Byrd cocked his head and eyed him, but asked no further questions. "Then you have my permission."

Daniel shook the colonel's hand vigorously, as he said, "Thank you, Sir." Then they returned to the table.

"I've just given Daniel permission to court my daughter Ann," Byrd told the others and took his seat.

The table erupted in cheers and applause.

"But," Byrd said, stopping them with a hand in the air. "Ann will have to be the one to agree to let you court her, Daniel. She has a mind of her own."

Conall nodded and said, "That's for sure. Although something tells me you won't have too much convincing to do."

"Colonel, you don't know how happy this makes me," Daniel told him. He sat down again even though he was so wound up he didn't know if he could sit still for long. His heart and pulse beat so fast he became a bit breathless. And, for a change, his chest felt light. He could hardly keep from laughing out loud.

Bear slapped the colonel on the back. "Perhaps we'll be Grandpas by this time next year!"

Startled, Daniel's elation curbed and his eyes widened at the mere mention of babes. He had never considered that.

"Grandpa Bear," William said, "I never thought that day would come this soon."

"Whoa now," Daniel protested. "I haven't even courted her yet."

"Aye," Bear said, "but ye will soon. And we can all tell ye and Miss Ann are a perfect match. What handsome and beautiful bairns ye two will have."

Judge Webb turned to Lucky. "When are you going to find another wife Mr. McGintey?"

"My flint wore out a long time ago," Lucky answered, causing everyone to laugh so hard they shook the table.

"Lucky, I think you could make a stuffed turkey laugh," Conall said.

"And if he did, he was probably the one who shot it too," Webb agreed. Still chuckling, the judge rocked back on the hind legs of his chair.

Lucky continued to laugh in a deep jovial way and the old hunter seemed ten years younger.

Although Daniel was enjoying the friendly bantering, he grew anxious to speak to Ann. If she said yes, his joy would be complete. "Colonel, if it is all right with you, I'd like to go see Ann now."

"He's certainly not a procrastinator," William said.

Byrd nodded. "Yes, Daniel, go see her. Her mother's there so you will have a chaperone."

Daniel leapt up so quickly, his sore ribs protested and he knocked his glass over. Fortunately, the pain passed quickly and he'd already emptied his mug. "Thank you all for your good wishes," he said, straightening the glass. "If Ann says yes, would it be all right if I brought her back here for a few minutes, Colonel?"

"Yes, indeed. I can hardly wait to see her smile," Byrd answered.

Daniel asked the others, "Would you all wait here until we come back?"

Every one of them nodded and smiled up at him. He turned and strode away, ready to ask the most important question of his life.

Chapter 21

Daniel dashed to the home of the Byrds and skidded to a stop at their door. He bit down on the wide smile on his face and tried to calm his breathing as he smoothed his clothing and knocked.

Ann answered the door and met him with sparkling eyes and a warm smile. "Mr. Armitage," she said. Her voice sent ripples of pleasure through his chest.

"It's Daniel," he replied.

"Who is it?" he heard Mrs. Byrd call out.

"Come in, Daniel," Ann said and then whispered, "rescue me from this fool."

He quirked his eyebrows questioningly, surprised she would speak of her stepmother so disparagingly.

She motioned him inside. "It's Mr. Armitage, Mother Helen."

As he removed his tricorne and stepped inside, Mrs. Byrd stared blankly at him, her mouth open. Then Ann's stepmother pressed her lips together firmly as he greeted her.

"Good morning, Mrs. Byrd."

The woman's austere face and manner could only be described as haughty. "Mr. Armitage, Ann already has a caller," Mrs. Byrd said and pointed across the room.

Snyder Jr., his mouth twisted dryly, stood up from his chair and said, "You're an obstinate fellow."

Daniel narrowed his eyes and glared at Snyder with contempt. "And you're a coward."

"Mr. Armitage!" Mrs. Byrd declared. "Do not insult the guests in my home. Mr. Snyder is a friend of ours."

"With respect, Mrs. Byrd, this man's honor is not what you think," Daniel tried.

Her eyebrows shot up. "Ann, please escort Mr. Armitage to the door at once."

He ignored the woman and turned to Ann. "Ann, you are invited to join our fathers, your brother, and our friends at the tavern for a celebration. You're invited as well, Mrs. Byrd."

Mrs. Byrd's eyebrows shot up nearly to her hairline. "Tavern! Never!"

"What are you celebrating?" Ann asked.

It was difficult to ignore Snyder's irksome presence, but he decided to go ahead and answer her. He wanted Charles to know.

"Your father has just given his permission for me to court you," he answered.

Ann's face broke into a broad smile while Snyder and Mrs. Byrd both gasped.

Mrs. Byrd scrunched up her face. "But that's impossible. Don't believe him, Ann."

A muscle in Snyder's jaw twitched. "Yes, he's lying."

"If you call me a liar just one more time," Daniel warned, "I will yank that lying tongue of yours out of your rude mouth and nail it to a wall."

Mrs. Byrd's face paled, but Ann smiled.

Snyder took a threatening step toward him and snarled, "Colonel Byrd would never give a *bastard* permission to court his daughter."

Daniel struggled to keep from thrashing the man. If he weren't inside the Byrd home, he would have. "I'm not a bastard anymore."

Ann's mouth fell open, but she evidently took his word for it because she glanced up at him with a look of relief.

Snyder's nostrils flared and his eyes widened oddly. "Ann, I refuse to let you go with him."

Ann grimaced as if she'd been struck. "You will never, ever have any say over what I do." Then she put a hand on Daniel's arm and told him, "Please escort me to my father."

He placed his palm on top of her hand and eyed Snyder. "In the future, you will stay away from Miss Byrd. If you ever come near her again, I'll make sure it's the last time."

ANN GAZED UP AT DANIEL a little breathlessly as they made their way to the tavern. She couldn't believe her father had given Daniel his permission to court her. And what did Daniel mean when he said he was no longer a bastard?

As if he read her thoughts, he abruptly stopped under the magnificent and massive sycamore tree that held a place of honor in the center of the town. The tree's far-reaching branches shielded them both from the already blazing sun.

His face grew serious and holding her hand he told her, "You should know that Bear MacKay officially adopted me this morning in Judge Webb's court. So I am now his legal son, Daniel Alexander MacKay." He said the name with pride and held his head a bit higher now.

"Pleased to make your acquaintance, Mr. Daniel Alexander MacKay."

He gave her a heart-melting smile. "And, although it was an honor to receive your father's consent to court you, I would also ask your permission."

"Yes, Daniel, you have it." She winked at him and added, "As long as I may also woo you."

At first she saw shock register on his tanned face and then his lips parted in a dazzling smile. She'd never seen teeth that white and that straight on any of the men at the fort. She'd also never seen one as handsome and well-built as this man.

But good looks and a great build weren't enough for her. Daniel had to accept her for what she was now and what she intended to be in the future. She wasn't going to change for any man. She told him, "You might as well know now that I tend to speak my mind. I am brutally honest, impetuous, and I am prone to say things that are not considered proper for a young lady."

Daniel crisscrossed his arms over his chest and stood there regarding her. "And what of your conduct? Are you prone to improper behavior for a young lady?" he asked, with humor touching his eyes and mouth.

"Most definitely."

His look of enthrallment mirrored her own feelings about him.

They stood there for a moment gazing into each other's eyes and perhaps into their future as well.

DANIEL'S CHEEKS GREW WARM AS Ann peered up at him with a steady gaze. He knew she was trying to gauge his reaction to her forthrightness. He drew his hand across his moist brow and tried to quash the desire growing within him. He'd never known a woman as frank as Ann and he had to admit that he found her directness beguiling. Even exciting.

She gazed at the ground for a moment. "Do not misunderstand me, Sir. Of course I am speaking of my insistence on maintaining my freedom and independence. I ride where and when I want to. I hate staying inside, especially drinking tea with gossipy women. And I will never learn how to use a spinning wheel or sew or do many of the things expected of a woman."

"Or a wife?" he asked, enthralled by her every word.

"Or a wife."

"You sound perfect. Let's go."

He smiled and took her elbow. He was not the least bit concerned about her disdain for domestic duties or by her spirited, outspoken nature. In fact, he admired her for it. He could afford to hire all the cooks, housekeepers, and tailors they would need. He took hold of her hand and they headed across the street to the Bear Trap Tavern.

He'd been told by Bear that taking a woman into the popular tavern was not a concern because the Bear Trap was also an eatery and the owner refused to cater to the rough types in town and no longer allowed prostitutes to work there. The tavern on the other end of town appealed to rougher types and not just because of the ale they served. Ladies were welcomed at the Bear Trap and often met their friends there. The frontier seemed to be whittling away at some of society's outdated norms. And the presence of women in taverns was one of them, although proper decorum required that a lady be escorted.

His father and their friends were all still there and several empty mugs sat before all of them. All the men stood at once and welcomed Ann.

She nodded to each and took a seat beside her father. "Thank you," she told him, placing a hand on her father's sleeve and smiling warmly.

"Yes, Colonel," Daniel said, pulling a chair up beside Ann. "Thank you for your trust in me."

"If you're anything like your father here, my faith in you as a suitable suitor for Ann is well placed," Byrd said. "Some of her admirers definitely did not earn my endorsement."

"One of them is sitting in our living room yet again," she told her father.

"Charles Snyder?" her father asked, incredulous.

Ann nodded. "When he showed up, Mother Helen insisted on entertaining the loathsome man."

"He must have gone there shortly after court," Bear said.

"Court?" Ann asked.

"I brought charges against him for assault and theft," Daniel explained. "But Judge Webb said there wasn't enough evidence to charge him."

Bear nodded. "Aye, the weasel and his two minions beat Daniel near to death."

"They attacked you?" Ann demanded. "That's how you got hurt?"

Daniel realized he'd never told her about the incident. He didn't want to spoil their dinner the other night. "Yes. The three of them put a drug in my coffee and then duped me into looking at a horse out behind the stable. After the drug took effect, they attacked me, stole my possessions, and left me there. Fortunately, Bear and William came looking for me and took me to Dr. McGuffin."

"They must have slipped that drug into your coffee while you were talking to me," Lucky said.

"It's a shame Snyder didn't get what he deserved," Byrd said.

Judge Webb scowled. "I was forced to release him because we had no witnesses or evidence that the three of them assaulted Daniel."

"Why did they attack you?" Ann asked Daniel.

Everyone remained quiet for a moment as Ann glanced from man to man. "Why?" she repeated.

"Because they wanted me to stay away from you," Daniel said.

Ann sprang up, her fists clenched at her sides. "That slimy pompous no-good snake. I ought to shoot him myself!"

"Ann, sit down," her father told her as he stood. "Stay here and enjoy Daniel's celebration. I'll go be sure Snyder knows he's no longer welcome in my home!"

Conall leapt up. "I'm going with you, Father."

"Do ye want company?" Bear asked.

"Now Bear," William said. "I'm certain a couple of *Byrd*s can take care of a *worm* like Snyder." Amused at his own pun, William regarded Bear with laughing eyes.

Of all the Wyllie brothers, William seemed to possess the greatest wit and sense of humor.

They all chuckled, even Daniel, although he considered Snyder more of a snake than a worm.

"Indeed, we Byrd's can handle that worm," the Colonel said. "Give me five minutes to get rid of him and the rest of you are invited to my home to continue our merrymaking so Daniel and Ann can have some time together and get to know one another better."

Bear stood. "I'm sorry, Colonel, but I must decline. Artis was feelin' poorly when we left and I want to get home to her. Perhaps another time?"

"Of course," Byrd said and turned to Daniel. "Do I have your word as a gentleman that you will behave honorably toward my daughter?"

"Indeed, Sir. You have my word."

"Very well then. You may have the rest of the day with Ann. I will expect her home before dinner time."

"Thank you, Sir," Daniel said. His heart leapt at the prospect of an entire afternoon alone with Ann.

Chapter 22

After the others left to join Byrd and Bear departed for home, Daniel turned to Ann and asked, "Where do you want to go? Or do you want to just stay here and talk?"

"Let's ride. I'm still dressed for riding," she said, glancing down at her brown riding habit and white blouse. "There's a place I'd like to show you."

After they retrieved her mare, Whitefoot, from the fort's stable and saddled it, they mounted and soon left the town behind them.

He glanced over and the sight of the beautiful woman riding beside him filled Daniel's wounded heart with new hope. Was this the woman his mother promised he would find someday? It seemed Ann had already found a place in his heart. Did she also have a place in his future?

As they rode, his desire for her seemed to mount by the minute. When she wasn't looking, he allowed his gaze to drop from her face to her breasts to her slim waist and down to her curvy hips. The motion of her body undulating in rhythm with the horse's slow lope made the sight even more beguiling. His attraction to her suddenly escalated and he struggled to control the surge of longing welling within him.

To distract himself, he focused on the beauty of the forest again and the feel of the wind on his face, letting it cool some of the heat of his fervor.

"Daniel, we'll turn into the forest up here. The path's narrow, so follow behind me."

He nodded and let Samson fall in behind Whitefoot. Ann's horse seemed to be an excellent mount. She was a brown-colored mare with black on her legs, mane, and nose and she had one white foot. It reminded Daniel of an old adage he'd once learned:

One white foot – buy him,
Two white feet – try him,
Three white feet – deny him,
Four white feet – do without him.

ANN RODE WHITEFOOT IN GOOD form. Better than any woman he ever saw on the back of a horse and she seemed to know these dense woods remarkably well, never once hesitating or looking around to determine her direction.

But riding this far away from town and the protection of the fort left them vulnerable to attack from both man and beast. He would keep his guard up.

The trail climbed steadily upward until it wove them into a secluded spot where a 60-foot waterfall cascaded over sandstone cliffs. With the drought, the waterfall had to be spring fed. At the bottom of the falls, the water flowed in a peaceful blue-green pool surrounded by boulders and rocks.

As they drew closer, the rhythm of the steady flowing water as it gushed over rocks and outcrops grew louder. The spring that fed the creek above the waterfall must come from deep within the earth. The second thing he noticed was the lung-cleansing scent of the misty air. It smelled fresh, like pine and sunshine and rain all mixed together.

"It's breathtaking," he told her as they dismounted and tied their horses. "What is it called?"

She hesitated for a moment, swallowed, and said, "Bad Branch Falls."

He removed his tricorne to let his head cool and placed the hat on a large boulder. Then he took off his coat and laid it next to it. "Why is it called bad?"

"Because my mother died along the branch that feeds these falls," she said, her voice faltering a little.

"Ann, you don't have to tell me about it."

"I want to." She moved closer to the falls until she stood in its cooling mist. "Around 1788, when I was seven, Shawnee attacks in northern Kentucky, especially around Maysville and Kenton's Station, became quite frequent. A Kentucky Board of War was appointed. But there had been no attacks near Boonesborough. Everyone believed we were safe here because we were south of the Kentucky River. Then one day my mother disappeared. She came up here often to bathe and when she didn't come home, my father and the militia searched for her for hours. He finally found her scalped and..." she stopped herself and squeezed her eyes for a moment. "They normally just steal women away, but father said he could tell she fought them fiercely. So they scalped her for it. When he brought her back, carried in his arms, he wouldn't let me see her. She was wrapped in a blanket. I knew why."

Daniel could envision the horror Ann must have felt. And her father.

"Soon afterwards, father was given command of the second Brigade of the Kentucky militia. He led men from Lincoln, Madison, and Mercer counties to help Mad Anthony Wayne's Legion for the rest of the Northwest Indian War. He was part of their decisive victory at the Battle of Fallen Timbers."

No wonder she was so independent. She'd been forced to grow up too soon. And mostly alone.

She bit her lip and pointed up to the top of the falls. "She was up there, face down in the creek when they found her body. She likely took her last breath there in that stream."

Daniel peered up at the top of the waterfall and then down at Ann. "Is that why you brought me here?" he asked as gently as he could.

"Yes. This is my favorite place and I come here often. This is why I like my freedom. Because when I come here I feel like I'm with her again. I believe that the water that comes down from these falls was once a part of her."

Daniel could tell that even now, after all these years, her heart longed for a mother's love. She still nursed a wound that would not heal.

She choked back a sob. "Sometimes, I can even see her beautiful face here."

He took her into his arms and held her. For a long moment, neither one spoke. He let his heart reach into hers and take some of her pain. "I can understand why you come here. It's a gift to be able to feel her presence here."

With tears dampening her dark lashes, Ann gazed up at him. "Today, I wanted her to meet you."

To the sound of the water falling behind them, he kissed Ann and in that glorious moment his heart fell into hers. As he held her, his kiss fiercely passionate, love rushed through him with a force as powerful as the strongest waterfall. Finally freed, it surged, flowed, and pounded him with astonishing force. It was a kiss with enough power to wash away the stain of grief and carry him into the future.

And then, as he gentled the kiss, love settled within him in a peaceful pool. A pool that beckoned, inviting him to plunge into its healing, soothing waters.

When she opened her eyelids, he saw a difference in her as well. Love shined in her eyes and softened her exquisite face. The pain he'd seen when she'd spoken about her mother was gone.

"Thank you," Daniel told her, "for bringing me here."

"You're the first one I've ever brought here."

This time she kissed him, letting her tongue trace the fullness of his lips as she wove her fingers through his hair. Then she grew more confident and explored his mouth with the hunger of a woman who had never kissed another with passion. A kiss full of possibilities and promises.

A kiss that pledged her love.

He tugged her body up against his and drank in the sweetness of her. His lips seared a path down her mist moistened neck and back up to her opened mouth. The feel of her soft breasts pressing through the fabric of his shirt made his heart thud against hers.

She ran her hands up and down his back and over his shoulders, as if her fingers were memorizing the feel of his muscles.

Her touch made his body shudder and sent a tremor through him that compelled him to grasp her hips and tug her even closer and kiss her even harder.

Then she drew back a bit, correctly sensing that he was losing control. She waited until their breaths slowed and then she placed the softest kiss he'd ever felt on his lips.

For a long moment they were lost, together, in the dreamy intimacy of their perfect kiss. In this perfect spot—this little piece of heaven that was hers.

And now it was theirs.

Too soon, it was time to back away. His honor and hers demanded it. Reluctantly, he slowly pulled his lips from hers and kissed her forehead. When he took a step back, he gazed at her for a moment, awed by her beauty. A fine mist resembling a luminous delicate veil now covered her hair. The tiny droplets looked like diamonds and sparkled in the filtered sunlight that broke through the trees. Her eyes glowed with the beauty of her soul. Her lips parted with a smile that came from her heart.

"Ann, I love you."

"I could feel it in your kiss," she said. "Could you feel my love too?"

"Yes, I felt it in my heart."

Chapter 23

Bear unsaddled and fed Camel as quickly as he could and then rushed inside. "Artis!" he called. The house was strangely silent. "Artis! Where are ye?"

"In here," Artis called to him from their bedroom.

Bear rushed to their room and found her resting on the bed. A slight breeze wafted through the open windows. "Are ye all right love?"

"Aye, I was just takin' a wee nap."

"A nap? Ye never take naps."

"Not often," she said. "How did it go with Judge Webb?"

He grimaced. "The judge was forced to release that weasel of a man because we could not provide proof that it was Snyder and his friends who carried out the attack on Daniel."

"Och, Bear, that's dreadful."

"Aye, but justice has a way of findin' its own path. He'll receive his due in time."

"What about the adoption?"

"We are now his proud parents, Artis. Are ye happy about it?"

"Aye, I am. We have much to be thankful for."

"Aye, my angel. We do. He's a fine son, that one."

"And this one will be too." Artis placed a hand on her belly.

Bear's heart jumped to his throat. "Yer carryin' a bairn?"

"Aye, for nearly three months now."

They both laughed with joy and he sat on the bed next to her, leaned down, and kissed her. "Why did ye not tell me sooner?"

"I was goin' to tell ye the night of the ball, as my anniversary gift to ye. But then ye found out that same night that ye were Daniel's father. I figured ye needed some time to get used to the idea."

"Ye were right. I did."

She giggled a bit. "Ye might have swooned had I told ye then."

He laughed, imagining the possibility. "Why did ye not tell me since then?"

"I was plannin' to, but when poor Daniel got beaten, I wanted to wait until that nastiness was behind us. When I got the mornin' sickness, I knew I needed to tell ye soon. I wanted to wait until just the right moment, and I guess today was it—the day we adopted Daniel."

He clutched both her hands and kissed them. "Any moment is the right moment for such joyous news. But, aye, today is the perfect day. Ye've made me so happy my angel."

"And ye've made me happier than I ever dreamt I would be. When I was young, I used to daydream about the man I would marry someday. Never did I imagine someone as magnificent as ye. Someone who would make me this happy. I'm so glad ye will be my baby's father."

Her words touched him all the way to his soul. "And ye will be a wonderful mother and give our babe yer kindness and strength." He squeezed her hands and asked, "When will our bairn be born?"

"Sometime between Thanksgiving and Christmas."

"Aye? 'Tis a magical time of year."

She smiled suggestively. "Would ye like to…"

He leaned down and kissed the mother of his child.

THE NEXT MORNING DANIEL LEARNED that he would soon have a brother or sister. The welcome news gave him one more reason to feel at home here. Together, they truly would be a family.

For the next week he helped Bear construct the cellar during the day, then cleaned up, ate a quick dinner with Bear and Artis, and rode into town to call on Ann.

Every evening they strolled around the fort's enclosure, partly to avoid the company of Mother Helen and partly to enjoy the cooler evening air. They talked for hours. Occasionally, he would hold her hand or slip an arm around her waist. But he allowed himself to do no more. He found Ann so enticing that if he whisked her away to some private place and started kissing her again, he would want all of her.

Surprisingly, the fort was a quiet, peaceful place when the militia wasn't there going through their drills. Much quieter than the town's streets. And above them, there was nothing but shimmering stars sprinkled across the velvet canopy of heaven.

Most of the militia went back to their own homes at night, Ann told him. Only a few single men lived at the fort, including William's deputy Bill Wallace. He was leaning on the porch railing in front of William's office studying the half-moon as they came by.

"Evenin'," Bill called out.

"Good evening to you, Sir," Daniel replied.

"Nice evenin' for a walk," Bill said.

"Indeed it is, Deputy. Hope all is quiet for you and Sheriff Wyllie," Ann told him.

"It is, at least for now," Bill replied.

"Are you expecting trouble?" Daniel asked.

"Snyder has been seen around town with some of the roughs. The sheriff and I are worried that he's up to something."

"Do you have any idea what it is?" Ann asked.

"No, but where that man is, there's likely to be trouble," Bill said.

Daniel had to agree. "Have you seen him anywhere near Ann's home?"

"Nope. I doubt he will show his face inside this fort again after the way the Colonel escorted him out," Bill said with a grin.

"What happened?" Daniel asked.

"Yes, what?" Ann asked too. "My father wouldn't say anything about it."

"I happened to be standing out here on the porch having a smoke. Your father shoved Snyder's hat so far down on his head that it nearly covered his eyes and then with his sword held to Snyder's back, he escorted the man up to the gate. Each time, Snyder slowed even a bit, the Colonel poked him in the back and I think he pricked him a few times because Snyder yelped now and then."

Daniel and Ann both laughed, picturing the sight.

Bill continued, "By the time they reached the gate, they had quite an audience, laughing and scorning the man."

"Did you see my stepmother in all this?" Ann asked.

"Yes, she was standing on your porch, hands on hips looking like she'd gotten herself all riled up. I heard her yell at your father, 'You're off your head, John!'"

"I hate to say it, but I think she's the one who is daft. She actually thought I should want Charles Snyder to marry me. The very idea is sheer lunacy," Ann said.

Daniel grew serious. "I'm worried that Snyder may want to pay the Colonel back for humiliating him."

"My father can handle Snyder," Ann declared.

"Snyder's not man enough to stand up to the Colonel," Bill said.

Daniel nodded. "I agree. But he's not likely to forget a grudge. And I don't think he'll give up pursuing Ann either. He thinks too much of himself and expects her to do the same."

"You're right on both counts," Bill said.

"Ann, I think it would be wise for you to curtail your rides for now," Daniel told her.

"Now Daniel, I told you…"

"Just for a few days. Just until we figure out what Snyder may be up to," Daniel said. "I need to determine just how much of a threat he may be."

Ann's face registered her displeasure, but she said, "All right. But only a few days. I won't have Snyder limiting my freedom."

Daniel took her hand. "Ann, he's a dangerous man. Not because of his strength, but because of his lack of it. He's a bully. Until he's under control or behind bars, you may be in danger."

"I think you should heed what Daniel is saying," Bill told her. "I'm sure Sheriff Wyllie would agree too if he were here."

Ann threw up her hands. "All right. I give up. I'll stay home for a few days. But I warn you, I may be as daft as Mother Helen at the end of it."

IT WAS FRIDAY NIGHT AND TIME to have some fun, Daniel decided. He'd asked Ann to be dressed and ready to go by 6:00. They were going to the dance held every Friday during the summer under the big sycamore in the center of town. It would be the first time he could show Ann his dancing skills. And tonight he was going to dress befitting a gentleman—sword included.

Because tonight, he would ask Ann to marry him.

He'd already ordered a ring from the general store's catalog. With the discovery of diamonds in Brazil a few decades past, diamond jewelry was now readily available, for a price. He'd ordered a diamond cluster engagement ring of small rose-cut diamonds arranged around a larger center stone. He knew it would be lovely on the hand of a woman as beautiful as Ann.

As he and Ann strolled toward the dance, she carried a pie she'd made and explained that, except for the more formal Governor's Ball, dances this time of year were always held outdoors because of the heat. As they approached, people stood in clusters under the sycamore in the center of town. He was surprised to see how many folks were there, including a number of children. A dozen or so musicians played lively music that added to the festive atmosphere. Chairs formed two half circles and desserts, contributed by the women attending the dance, were spread out on tables. In one spot, several men and women were serving Syllabubs, a blend of wine, cream, sugar and lemon juice.

As soon as they arrived, they greeted William and Kelly, who said they'd left Nicole with Kelly's father and his wife. Then they said hello to Conall and the pretty young woman he was with.

"You're looking particularly dapper and gallant with that fine sword," Conall told Daniel.

"In Philadelphia, a gentleman wears a sword to all important occasions," he answered. "You never know when gallantry will be called for."

"Where are Bear and Artis?" Kelly asked.

"They stayed home. She said she didn't have the energy for a dance," Daniel explained.

"Being with child will do that to you," Kelly said.

"Let me just put my pie on a table," Ann told him.

He nodded and followed her. Remembering what Artis had said about Ann's cooking abilities, he wondered if her cherry pie was any good.

"I baked it myself. Would you like some now," she asked, "before everyone else has at it?"

She seemed so proud of herself, he didn't have the heart to say no. "Of course," he told her.

She cut a piece and he noticed that it took her a while to slice through the crust. It did appear rather crispy. At least it wasn't burnt. But the cherries looked suspiciously lumpy.

Handing him a piece and a fork, she beamed up at him, waiting for him to take a bite.

Daniel smiled back indulgently.

The musicians had started playing *Goin' to Boston*, a popular dance tune.

Ann glanced toward the dance floor. "I adore that tune. I can sing it too!"

"Then let's dance first," he said, setting the plate and fork back down on the table. He took hold of her hand and they quickly joined the line of dancers and then sashayed to the other end of the lined up couples.

Along with most everyone else, Ann exuberantly sang the song's lyrics. *"Goodbye, girls, we're goin' to Boston, goodbye, girls, we're goin' to Boston, goodbye, girls, we're goin' to Boston, early in the mornin'."*

When the song finished, they made their way back to the table. Daniel hoped someone had picked up his piece of the cherry pie, but he wasn't that lucky.

Ann immediately thrust it back into his hands and he cautiously took a bite. It actually didn't taste that bad, but then he realized he had a mouthful of pits. He stood there for a moment wondering what to do.

"Is it good? It's the first one I ever made!"

He nodded and tried to say the word delicious, but it came out more like delirious.

Ann's brow furrowed. "What's wrong? Why haven't you swallowed?"

Daniel's lips puckered as his tongue massaged the pits, trying not to swallow them. He was certain he must look like a fish out of water gasping for air. Then a bit of cherry juice slipped out the corner of his mouth. There was nothing to be done about it. He spit the pits out into his plate. "Pardon me," he said, as he wiped his mouth.

Ann stared down at the pits in disbelief. She looked devastated. "Mother Helen said the cherries were ready for the pie," she nearly wailed.

"I think she must have assumed you would pit them first," Daniel said. "It's an understandable mistake."

"No, it's not!" She slipped a hand under the pie pan and stomped off.

Daniel followed closely behind her, not sure what else to do.

When they reached the edge of the forest, she kept going. "Where are you going?" he asked. But she didn't answer.

Finally, she stopped and threw the remaining pie into the trees with surprising force. It splattered against a pine's trunk and he wanted to laugh but didn't as they watched the cherries and juice slowly ooze down the bark. The dented pie plate clung to the trunk for a few seconds before it fell ignobly to the ground.

"I'll never bake again!" she vowed and spun away from the tree. Her foot caught on a root and she tripped, landing on her hands and knees.

He hurried over to help her up and asked, "Are you all right?"

She sighed heavily. "Yes, I'm just humiliated. First I make you eat a *pitiful* pie! And then I lose my temper, stomp off, attack that poor tree. And for a finale, I take a graceless fall to the ground. I'm sorry." She turned distraught eyes toward him.

"Don't make yourself miserable over a pie," he urged. "You have many other talents."

"Like what?"

He enfolded her in a comforting embrace. "You are an exceptionally good kisser."

"You truly think so?"

"I most certainly do," he said and lowered his lips to hers. His fingers ached to explore her every curve, but his honor stopped him. He locked her safely within his embrace, wanting to protect her from the world.

Chapter 24

Daniel wiped his moist lips with his sleeve as they headed back toward the dance and Ann straightened her yellow gown. The frock was a bit too short and wasn't the latest fashion, but on her it seemed fit for a queen. "That's a lovely gown," he told her. "And you look particularly stunning tonight."

She grinned up at him. "It's old, but I like the color. I need to order some new ones from the east. Perhaps you could help me pick out one or two from the catalog at Mr. Breedhead's store. I'm sure you're more familiar with the latest fashions than I am."

Daniel suspected her father's salary didn't permit many new gowns. Someday he would dress her in the best gowns his money could buy. And he'd buy her shoes and gloves that matched each one. Even though she was an outdoors type, every woman he ever knew loved getting new clothes. He suspected she was no exception.

"I bet the ladies in Philadelphia wear splendid gowns," she said.

They did but he wasn't going to tell her that. "A gown is only as beautiful as the woman who wears it."

She smiled, took his arm, and they started down the path that led back to the dance. When they finally took their eyes off of each other and looked ahead, Daniel's heart sank.

Snyder blocked the path.

With his mean beady eyes and hooked nose, the man reminded Daniel of a buzzard waiting for a meal.

"Have you been off in the woods having your way with Miss Byrd, Daniel?"

"Snyder!" Daniel hissed the man's name with loathing. "Apologize."

"Hey fellows, look who is walking out of the forest together," Snyder called. "My lady friend and that fancy Philadelphian."

A group of rough-looking men emerged from the trees and stood all around them. Dooley and Sanderson weren't among the five. Perhaps the two were too embarrassed to show themselves and their new haircuts in town. Snyder must have a new group of lackeys to do his bidding. They were probably hired with the coin Snyder stole from him. Daniel suspected one of the five men took the job because he needed a meal. The fellow stood there, looking hesitant, clothes hanging on his nearly skeletal frame. But the other four appeared menacing enough that Daniel thought they might be mercenaries—guns for hire—usually men of the worst sort that moved from town to town.

Snyder stepped closer and peered at Ann. "Your lips look awfully red, Miss Byrd. You been sucking on something?"

Ann gasped and stared at Snyder in astonishment as her fingers flew to her mouth and covered her lips. Then she blushed furiously and glared angrily at the man. She could not have looked any guiltier if she tried, although Daniel doubted that she even understood what Snyder implied.

Daniel's fist seized Snyder's cravat and he jerked the man's head in front of his own snarling face. "How dare you? Any insult to a lady under a gentleman's care or protection is considered a greater insult than if the insult is given to a gentleman personally," Daniel formally pronounced as he quoted the required statement for a duel. "Charles Snyder, I challenge you to fight me. As the challenger I am obligated to give you your choice of weapons, time, and place. But fight me you will. I won't let you back out this time." He released Snyder's cravat with a shove.

Snyder burst out laughing. "Did you hear that, fellows?"

The men joined Snyder in laughing uproariously and one said, "He sounds like a bloody aristocat."

"It's *aristocrat*, you ignorant fool," Ann snapped.

"Move aside," Daniel told Snyder. "Ann and I are together now and I dare you to try to take her from me." He almost hoped Snyder would try so he would have a justifiable reason to kill the man.

Snyder remained planted where he was, feet spread apart and arms crossed. "These men and I don't think it's proper for you to treat Miss Byrd with such disrespect."

"I'm sure her father wouldn't either," another man said. "We'll tell him how we found you two. And how her gown got those dirt and grass stains." He pointed to Ann's knees.

They all gawked at Ann's gown. Dirt from her fall had caused two stains on the front of the skirt. Several of the men snickered.

Looking panic stricken, Ann tried to dust off the dirt but the stains clung to the fabric. Then, incensed, she glared up at Snyder. "I fell earlier and my father would send you straight to hell for insulting me, you blithering idiot."

Worry filled Daniel. If these men spread their lies, her reputation would be ruined. And a reputation, once lost, was never fully recovered.

"Ann, go back to the dance," Daniel told her. "Stay with Conall or William until I get there."

She straightened and raised her chin defiantly. "No, I won't leave you to be beat up again by these ruffians."

"Ann, please do as I say," Daniel pleaded.

She pursed her lips and glared at Snyder. Then in a huff she marched off toward the dance.

Snyder moved aside to let her pass but his leering eyes followed her bottom. "Perhaps I should join Miss Byrd," Snyder said. "I'd enjoy a dance with that one clutched in my arms."

"Like hell!" Daniel swore and proceeded to follow Ann.

Two of the men grabbed him by the arms. "We'll watch him," one said.

"Yes, keep him entertained for a while," Snyder ordered and started after Ann.

Daniel shook off the two men, but the rest of Snyder's minions stepped forward and blocked him, preventing him from following Charles.

"You son-of-a-bitch," Daniel shouted after Snyder.

"Ann, you owe me a dance!"

Ann jumped at the sound of Snyder's voice and whirled around.

He grabbed her by the wrist and hauled her into the dance amid all the other couples. His hands, massive and strong, turned her in a circle.

Her body stiffened in shock. "Unhand me!" she told him. "I don't want to dance with you."

But Snyder wouldn't let go. In fact, he put his other hand behind her back and yanked her closer still, smiling the entire time as though they were a happy couple.

The feel of his beefy hands on her body made her want to retch. "Let go of me!"

Several couples around them stopped dancing and stared.

"Isn't she beautiful?" Snyder asked them, as he spun her around. "I don't blame you for staring."

"Conall! William!" she yelled, looking around frantically. "Get the sheriff," she told a nearby man.

Snyder finally released her when he saw Conall running toward them. Snyder shrugged and told her, "I guess we'll have to dance another time. I promise you—we will."

"I will *never* dance with you," she spat.

"Ann, are you all right? Snyder, what are you doing with my sister?" Conall demanded.

"Just giving the lady a good time," Snyder said with a wink at her. "I found her off in the bushes with Mr. Armitage—that's his real name you know—but she said she was tired of his fancy ways. She's ready to dance with a real man."

The eyes of the women around them widened and Ann heard their quick intake of breath. The men with the ladies gasped and huffed in indignation. At the sight of them reacting to Snyder's lies, anger welled inside of her. "Liar!" Ann reached up and slapped Snyder as hard as she could. The impact stung her hand, but it was well worth it.

Conall glared daggers at Snyder. "Where's Daniel? What have you done?"

Daniel stepped back from the five men, unsheathed his sword, and glowered menacingly at each one in turn. "All of you. Go back to the bottle Snyder found you behind."

Each of the men's eyes took in the length of the sword from pommel to point. The blue-tinted metal glistened menacingly with the last rays of the late-summer sunset.

"What if we don't want to? Are you going to stop all five of us with that pointy stick?" one said and the others laughed.

"Leave now or you'll feel this finely honed *stick* slice across your chicken necks."

"He looks like he knows how to use that thing. Let's get," the skinny man said. "I don't relish havin' my neck slit open."

Prudent man, Daniel thought. But the others stood their ground. One fool stepped forward, his long knife drawn and said, "Snyder said we couldn't shoot anyone just *yet*, but he didn't say nothing about a knife."

Incredulous, Daniel gawked at the man holding the blade. "Are you really so foolish to think that you can fence with a knife?" He saw hesitation in the man's eyes. Perhaps he didn't even know the meaning of the word fence. It was, after all, the sport of gentlemen.

Daniel widened his stance and glared menacingly. "Leave now! Or die a fool's death," he warned.

"Come on Lem," one of the hired guns said. "If you kill this dandy, they'll be after you and you'll wind up hangin' from a rope. And Snyder sure as hell ain't worth dying for."

Daniel had to agree.

The man named Lem said, "This ain't over yet. We don't like fancy dandies like you and don't approve of what you've been doin' with the woman Charles was meant to marry." Then, scowling, he turned and followed the others.

Quickly, Daniel sheathed the sword and ran toward the dance.

SNYDER HELD HIS PALM TO his reddened cheek and his mouth took on an unpleasant twist as William hurried toward them.

"What are you up to, Snyder?" William demanded.

"As usual, he's telling lies," Ann answered. "But forget about me. His men have Daniel, there in the woods!" she said pointing.

"Conall, keep Snyder here," William ordered and sprinted toward the timber.

Ann started to follow him but Conall held her back.

"Let the sheriff handle this," her brother told her. "I don't want you anywhere near trouble."

"*Trouble* is standing right next to us," she said with a sideways glare at Snyder.

They watched as Daniel emerged from the trees at about the same time William reached him. The two spoke a few words and then marched purposefully toward her and Conall.

Daniel came to a halt in front of Snyder and glowered at the man with the fierceness of an angry bull. "Mr. Snyder!" he said in a voice loud enough for all to hear. "You have been officially challenged to a duel for disparaging the honor of Miss Byrd while she was under my protection." Clearly livid, he clenched his fists and hardened his face.

Snyder's brows rose. "I don't think Colonel Byrd would call what you were doing protection," he mocked, and gave those around them an insinuating look.

The implication made her want to reach for Conall's pistol.

"You lying fiend," Conall swore. "I'd like to shoot you myself, but I'll leave that privilege to Daniel since he challenged you first."

"A fiend is just what you are—a beastly, wicked man," Ann hissed. Right now, she hated him. But she hated the idea of a duel more. Someone would be killed. It would very likely be Snyder, but she didn't want to be the cause of the man's death, no matter how much she despised him. She turned to Daniel. "Please don't fight a duel over me. I am not worried about my honor."

"It is my honor that requires it," Daniel told her, his voice sharp. "If he had insulted me, I could let it go. But he insulted you and that cannot be overlooked." He turned back to Snyder. "What will be your choice of weapons, Sir? Sword, pistol, or knives? Any of the three will suit me just as long as I get to kill you."

"There will be *no* duels," William said in a voice of authority. "Go home Snyder. You've made enough trouble for one evening."

Ann saw denial in Snyder's eyes, but he said, "All right, Sheriff Wyllie. I don't want any trouble. Sorry for the misunderstanding."

"I didn't misunderstand anything," Daniel swore.

"I'm pleased to hear it, Sir," Snyder said and turned to her. He bowed slightly. "Good night, Miss Byrd. I enjoyed our dance." With a cold spine-prickling grin at Daniel, Snyder left.

William turned to Daniel. "You too. I want you to go home."

"But, William…" Daniel started.

"Don't challenge my authority," William warned. "I didn't ask. I'm telling you to go home, before there's any more trouble. I'm trying to keep you safe. We'll all go back to the fort together. We'll escort Miss Byrd back to the Byrd house and you can go home while I speak to Ann and her father."

Profoundly disappointed, Ann was on the verge of tears. This evening was definitely not turning out the way she'd wanted it to. It had been a disaster from start to finish. "Sheriff, at least let me tell you exactly what happened," she pleaded.

William told her, "You can tell me on the way to your house. You and Conall wait here while I go and get Kelly. You too Daniel."

Daniel glanced over at her. Anger still blazed in his eyes. A vein pulsed on his neck and a muscle jerked on his clenched jaw. She could tell that he was still too furious to speak.

She hoped there would be no duel, or any other fight for that matter. But if there was, she wondered if Snyder realized what a powerful opponent Daniel would be.

Chapter 25

Riding toward home, Daniel wasn't sure what bothered him more—not being able to ask Ann to marry him; being sent home from the dance like a misbehaving schoolboy; or not being able to do the honorable thing. Kill Snyder.

He tried to reassure himself that he wanted the duel for honor's sake—that it wasn't just for retaliation or a settling of scores. In his heart, he knew he wanted it more for the sake of protecting Ann's honor. Snyder deserved to be sent to hell. But William, to his credit, knew it would still legally be killing a man.

Beneath him, Samson's hooves crunched a layer of fallen leaves into the dusty ground. Denied moisture for too long, the trees had picked today to start shedding their leaves.

He also heard wolves howling in the distance. In law school, a professor once told Daniel and his fellow students that they needed to become more like wolves because they had to be so darned ruthless and cunningly smart. But he didn't feel smart right now. He'd failed Ann and himself. He had tried to deal with Snyder within the bounds of the law and the code of being a gentleman. Perhaps here, the frontier called for new rules.

Behind him he heard a flurry of hoofs. He turned Samson sideways to get a better look. Six riders.

Daniel didn't need to see their faces to know it would be Snyder and his five hired guns. He'd underestimated Snyder. He never thought the man would follow him. But he had. Since he'd gotten away with the first beating, perhaps he believed he could do it again.

He had no intention of taking another beating.

His mind raced. He had three choices. None of them good ones.

He could try to outrun them. He was about halfway home and he was certain Samson could outrun any of their mounts. But that would bring this trouble to Bear and Artis. Both would insist on joining the fight with him. He couldn't do that to Artis—especially now that she carried a child.

He could take Samson into the woods and hope that he could evade them among the trees when they gave chase. But these men would know the woods far better than he did and they would likely circle around, trap him, and kill him in some hidden or remote spot where only a bear or a wolf would find his body.

Or, he could stand and fight.

Quickly, he pulled his pistol and clutching it firmly, he rested it on the saddle in front of him. He'd made sure it was loaded before he left town. But if they each had a pistol, that gave them six shots to his one. And one or more of them could also be carrying a rifle on their mounts. He would likely be badly wounded or killed. Even if he managed to survive, again it would be his word against theirs. And they would say he fired first.

There had to be a fourth choice. But what was it?

When Samson snorted and pawed the ground, it hit him.

The six men were now lined up across the road, approaching him.

He stuck the pistol back in its sheath and hauled his sword from its scabbard. The steely sound of the sword's release always strengthened his heart. He raised the tip above him, took a deep breath, and charged, urging Samson to a full run. Like a fired cannon, the powerful horse launched forward.

As Samson raced toward them, they looked confused. They hadn't expected him to come *at* them. They'd expected him to run away.

Samson thundered toward the group and Daniel brought his sword level with the men's heads. At the sight of the gleaming sword, like the rod of Moses, they parted, hastily peeling off to the left and the right.

Samson flew by them and Daniel lowered his sword and his body to help the stallion run faster. It was a good thing he did. He heard the report of two shots and felt them whiz by over his head. He glanced back and saw gunsmoke, gray and threatening. They were trying to kill him!

He urged Samson to run even faster. Behind him, he heard Snyder yelling and soon he could hear the sound of six horses chasing him. Thank God he rode such a strong mount, he would need all the stallion had to give. Samson seemed to sense the danger and Daniel felt him draw on an even greater speed from his valiant heart.

Soon he'd left the group of men well behind and Daniel sheathed his sword. He would find William and demand that he agree to let him have a duel with Snyder. He wanted to put an end to this once and for all. Hopefully William and Kelly would be on their way home by now.

He slowed somewhat, but kept Samson at a gallop and before long spotted William up ahead. His uncle rode next to Kelly and her long blonde hair stood out in the darkness. They were on their way home now. He worried that Kelly would be endangered.

He galloped toward them and then tugged Samson to a stop. The lathered stallion released great puffs of steamy air into the darkness as Samson caught his breath.

"Daniel, what's wrong?" William asked at once.

"Snyder and his five men are coming up behind me! They followed me. I decided to do what they least expected. I turned about, and charged through them to come and get your help. But I don't want Kelly harmed. We have to get her out of here!"

William faced his wife. "Kelly, turn around and go back to the fort. Get my deputy and the Colonel and tell them to come here. You stay with Ann. Hurry!"

Without saying a word, Kelly whirled her mare around and headed back at a gallop.

As soon as she left, Daniel turned Samson around and peered into the darkness. "I can hear them. They're coming. About a quarter-mile away now."

William dismounted and hid his horse behind a copse of trees. "Leave Samson where they can see him and take cover behind that large pine," William said pointing.

Daniel did as he was told. Then William hid too a few feet away from him.

"I don't want them to know I'm here with you," William said. "Let's see what Snyder does. Maybe we can finally get that evidence we need."

Daniel nodded and glanced over at William. His face was grave. Two against six were not great odds either.

"I'm sorry I brought this trouble to you, Uncle," he told him. It was the first time he'd called William uncle and he prayed it would not be the last.

William smiled. "Don't worry. I make my living handling trouble. It's me who should apologize for sending you home by yourself. I didn't think Snyder would take it this far. He normally backs away when it comes to a fight. Keep a watch, but don't let them see you."

The six men were nearly upon them. When they spotted Daniel's stallion, they all cruelly yanked their mounts to a sudden stop. The night air filled with the dust kicked up by their horses. One gelding, not appreciating the harsh treatment, pawed the air with his front hooves.

"The coward's hiding in these woods somewhere," Snyder yelled as he dismounted "He couldn't have gone far. Tie your mounts and find him. You can beat him to a bloody pulp. But don't kill him, I want that pleasure."

Ann finished loading and then strapping on her pistol while ignoring Mother Helen's frantic and repeated protests behind her back. She dashed through their door and ran toward the stables to saddle Whitefoot. With resolute clarity she knew she must to go to Daniel.

Kelly called after her, "Ann, stop!"

As Kelly closed the distance between them, Ann whirled around and faced her. "I will not sit in my parlor drinking tea while Daniel and your husband face six men."

"Your father, Conall, and Deputy Wallace are all on their way, they will reach them well before we can," Kelly said. "The last thing Daniel and William need is to be distracted by us."

"I can shoot as well as my father."

"And I can shoot as well as William, but that doesn't mean they want us in the middle of a fight."

Apprehension caused Ann's heart to thump within her. The moment Kelly came rushing into their home calling for Ann's father, concern for Daniel had gripped her with an astonishing intensity. Ann had wanted to go with her father and Conall then, but her father would have stopped her if she had tried. Although it had only been five minutes or so since they left with the deputy, she couldn't stand to just wait.

Now, she stood in the darkness of the fort's enclosure, frozen with uncertainty. Her fists clenched and unclenched at her sides, as she tried to decide what to do. The pulsing knot formed in her stomach. A moment later, she knew. If there was even the slightest chance she could help Daniel, she had to try. She couldn't risk losing him to Snyder.

Kelly shook her head. "Ann, I know what you're thinking. And I want to go too."

"Then come with me!"

"All right. I will," Kelly said, surprising her. "I don't want you to go by yourself." Kelly spun on her heels and headed to her mare, tied by the Byrd home.

As soon as Ann saddled and mounted Whitefoot, the two rushed through the fort's gates and headed toward where Kelly last saw William and Daniel.

What if Daniel has been killed? She fought hard to control the sob in her throat as she realized just how much she loved him. Her initial attraction to him had led to an infatuation. But the more she learned about him, her feelings had quickly evolved into a deep-seated love. The sound of their horses' galloping hooves matched the pace of her thunderous heartbeat and the reins shook in her trembling hands. She could not let herself be paralyzed by fear. She needed to be ready to help. But the tenseness between her shoulders only grew tighter as she rode. She took a few deep breaths trying to calm her fears.

If Snyder killed Daniel, she would not rest until she saw him hang.

How could she have prevented all of this? Why couldn't the man just leave her alone? Why was he so obsessed with having her? Maybe this wasn't even about her. Maybe Daniel had somehow threatened Snyder's manhood and the fool was trying to prove himself by challenging Daniel. How would this end? One question after another hammered her mind nearly as fast as Whitefoot's hooves pounded the dusty trail.

SNYDER JUST CONFIRMED DANIEL'S WORST fears and William had heard it too. Snyder didn't just want to scare him away from Ann with another good beating, he wanted him dead. Jealousy and envy had caused the man's mind to sink to an evil and twisted place.

All but one man dismounted and tied their huffing horses.

"I've no stomach for this," the skinny man said who was still atop his mount.

"I paid you!" Snyder said.

"You didn't pay us to murder the man, just scare him. And we already done that tonight. I want no part of a killin'," he said. The man turned his horse and took off toward town.

Snyder and the others moved forward.

William stepped out, pistols drawn. "Halt! Stay right there!"

Daniel also showed himself, his flintlock drawn.

"I told you to go home," William told Snyder. "You should have listened."

"That man wants to kill me," Snyder whined and pointed to Daniel. "He's threatened and insulted me more than once. I'm just defending myself."

"Defending yourself with five hired thugs to do your dirty work? Only after they roughed me up were you going to fight me," Daniel said, making his voice as cutting as his blade. "You're a bloody coward."

"You four, get your things from town and leave. I don't want to see any of your faces in Boonesborough ever again," William told them.

Only one of the men spoke up. "I'm leaving, Sheriff." He turned, mounted his horse, and took off in a hurry.

That left Snyder and three others.

"I'm not going anywhere," one of them said. It was Lem, the same one who had threatened Daniel with his knife at the dance. Lem heaved his pistol out and gave William a crazed hostile look, openly daring the sheriff.

The other two hired thugs didn't pull their pistols but their hard faces filled with menace.

"I don't know what Snyder is paying you," William said, "but trust me, it's not worth it. If Daniel or I don't kill you first, you will be punished severely."

Snyder advanced like a stalking cat toward Daniel. "Men, don't let him scare you off like those other two quitters. We can handle these two."

A seething undercurrent rippled the air between the four men and William and Daniel.

"Snyder, I'm warning you," William said. "You've taken this too far. Judge Webb won't go so easy on you this time. Tell your man to put his pistol away."

"Will you do the same?" Snyder asked. He turned to Daniel. "Or are you both too much of a gentleman to fight us with your fists?" He stared tauntingly at them. Snyder was counting on the four being able to whip the living daylights out of the two of them. He was making a big mistake.

"Yeah, he's an aristocrat, through and through," Lem said. "Just look at those fine clothes and that sword. I bet we could sell that sword for several pieces of gold up in Louisville."

"I ought to use this blade to run you through," Daniel told the man. "But I'll remove it and put away my pistol. I don't need either to thrash weasels like you." Daniel slid his flintlock back in its holster and then unstrapped his sword and set it aside.

He nodded at William and his uncle put one of his two pistols away but kept the other trained on Lem.

Snyder told his man, "Put your pistol away, Lem."

"All right," Lem agreed, his sinister smile revealing tobacco stained teeth. He stared threateningly at Daniel and tossed his hat aside. "I'd rather put my fist into his pretty face anyway."

William put his remaining flintlock away and instantly two of the mercenaries sprang forward toward his uncle.

Both snarling, first Snyder and then Lem lunged toward Daniel. As they charged, Snyder's eyes oozed hatred, but Lem's chilling face held a crazed look.

Daniel doubled his leg at the knee and drove his boot as hard as he could into Snyder's middle. He put everything he had into it and Snyder's back slammed against the hard ground. "That's payback for the kicks you gave me."

With Snyder out of his way, Daniel sprang at Lem. Lem hurled a punch toward Daniel's face. He sidestepped smoothly and sent his balled fist cracking against the back of the hired gun's head. Lem stumbled and collapsed face first.

Daniel glanced over at William who seemed to be holding his own against the two men fighting him.

Gulping in air and looking a bit unsteady, Snyder pushed himself up while Daniel waited.

Snyder regained his feet, and took a couple of deep breaths, before he leapt toward Daniel.

Daniel's knuckles rasped against the flesh of the man's face, but Snyder landed a punch on Daniel's jaw that shook his teeth to their roots.

Thrown off balance by the vicious blow at Daniel, Snyder's back was turned and Daniel took the opportunity to whack the blade of his hand against the back of Snyder's neck.

The chop to the neck made Snyder have to lean up against a pine to remain standing. Daniel took hold of Snyder's shoulders, turned him around, and smashed his back against the tree's trunk. As the fellow gasped for air, Daniel delivered a blow to Snyder's jaw that sent him collapsing to the side and he slid down the trunk to the ground.

When Daniel looked over at William, two men were still attacking him. One held his arms while the other repeatedly punched his uncle in the stomach, although William twisted and delivered a good kick into his puncher's leg.

Daniel ran toward them, grabbed the puncher by his hair and jerked the man backwards. He hammered his tightened fist into the side of the man's head. The fellow went down limply and didn't move again.

When Daniel glanced up, William had just finished disposing of the other man that had held him. The fellow was sprawled on the ground in a contorted heap.

Daniel whirled around when he heard Snyder moan and try to sit up, his hand clutching his pistol.

Daniel raced over to Snyder who was several yards away, shoved him back down, and slammed his boot against the hand that held the pistol.

Snyder squealed like the pig he was.

Daniel leaned down, snatched the weapon and tossed it away.

Snyder whimpered as Daniel grabbed a fistful of the man's shirt.

"This is for insulting Ann. Do it again and I'll put a lead ball through your ugly face instead of my fist." Daniel released his pent up anger in a mighty blow to Snyder's face that knocked him out. Daniel wanted to keep thrashing Snyder, but he forced himself to release the pitiful excuse for a man. Snyder flopped back down to the ground.

Daniel turned at the sound of horses approaching.

"You've done all the work for us," Colonel Byrd said as he glanced around and brought his panting mount to a stop in front of William. He almost sounded disappointed.

"My nephew did most of it, Colonel. He fights just like his father." William gave Daniel a knowing grin.

Pulling in a deep breath, Daniel drew his shoulders back a bit and returned William's smile, pleased to hear the pride in William's voice.

"Colonel, will you help me remove all the weapons from these men?" William asked.

"Indeed," Byrd said, and dismounted.

Conall rode over to where Daniel stood and peered down at Snyder. "I was really looking forward to putting my fist into that one's boorish mouth."

"Don't let me stop you!" Daniel told him, panting. "Have at him."

"Look out!" Conall yelled.

Daniel grabbed his weapon as he spun and faced Lem's raised pistol pointed directly at his heart. In that instant, all the love he would never be able to give Ann made his heart ache as though it were already shot.

Then the report of a pistol being fired exploded above Daniel's ears.

Lem's eyes widened in shock as his chest absorbed the searing lead. A moment later, the man toppled like a felled tree.

Daniel swung his head around and peered up at Conall.

With scornful eyes, Conall stared down at Lem, his pistol still aimed at the man. Smoke from the weapon's black powder filled the air between the three men.

A shudder vibrated within Daniel. Taking a deep, unsteady breath, he stepped next to Conall's mount and reached up. "Thank you."

Conall appeared a bit shaken, but leaned down and grasped Daniel's hand. "That was the first time I've ever shot a man."

Daniel shook Conall's hand. "You saved my life."

Colonel Byrd and William hurried over to Lem and William kicked the man's pistol away. The sheriff checked to see if Lem was still alive. He wasn't.

"Well done, Son," Colonel Byrd told Conall, and then he began removing the weapons from the other three men.

Deputy Wallace pulled his winded mount up next to them and said, "Sorry it took me so long. I stopped two men racing toward town. They both urged me to come help you and said that they wanted nothing to do with what Snyder was up to. So I let them go. I hope I did the right thing, Sheriff Wyllie."

William nodded his approval. Looking down at Lem, he said, "They were the smart ones."

Wallace dismounted and withdrew several pieces of rope out of his saddlebag. "I'll tie these three up for you."

Still breathless from the fight, William said, "I'll let you."

"All but Snyder," Daniel said. "I'll tie this worthless prick."

Chapter 26

Within a few minutes Ann and Kelly came upon Daniel, William, her father, and Deputy Wallace riding toward them. The four of them surrounded three men, including Snyder, with their hands tied in front of them. Ann cringed at the sight of another man's limp body hanging across a mount's saddle.

Relief filled her, though, when she saw that Daniel appeared to be unharmed. *Thank God.* "You're all right?"

Daniel's smile reassured her that he was. "Indeed," he answered.

Then she glanced at her father and brother. "And both of you?"

"We're all fine," Conall answered.

"What happened?" she asked with a nod in the direction of the dead man. "Did you have to kill him, Daniel?"

"No, your brother did, saving my life," Daniel answered.

Ann gasped. "Oh, good Lord. Tell me what happened!"

"We'll explain that later. Ann, what on earth are you doing here?" her father demanded.

"I couldn't just wait at home!" she declared. "You were all in danger!"

"Kelly, you shouldn't be here either," William said, a touch of anger in his voice.

"I didn't want her to come alone and Ann was determined to help if needed," Kelly said. "In truth, I understood how she felt."

Ann drew her mount closer to Daniel. She could see reddened spots on his knuckles and his clothes were dirtied and in disarray. She turned to glare at Snyder. "Mr. Snyder, I don't know what to say to you to make you give up this irrational obsession."

"Don't worry, Judge Webb will know exactly what to say to him," William said.

Snyder appeared to have suffered a beating. His swollen eyes conveyed a fury seething deep within him and he glowered at her and then at Daniel.

"It's over," Daniel told him with a hostile glare.

Snyder shook his head and, tightlipped, stared off into the woods.

"Let's get these three locked up and see if we can salvage what's left of this night," William said.

"William, I really want to get home to Nicole. I think I'll go on home," Kelly said.

"Not alone," William said. "Daniel, will you escort Kelly home? Deputy Wallace and I can take care of these fellows."

"Of course," Daniel told him.

"Ann, will you come too?" Kelly asked. "You can sleep in the upstairs loft and then come back tomorrow. I could use your help in the morning planting the root and leaf crops for the fall harvest. I'll lend you some work clothes."

Ann had to wonder if Kelly was just arranging for her and Daniel to have some time together. Both Kelly and Artis were conspiring to foster romance between the two of them. In any case, planting vegetables was one domestic chore that Ann actually enjoyed. She loved being outdoors and liked the feel of soil in her hands. And seeing seed blossom and grow into food always seemed like some sort of extraordinary miracle to her. "I'd be happy to help," she said.

Ann said goodnight to her father and brother and they set off for Whispering Hills with Kelly riding on her left and Daniel on her right.

As they rode, walking the horses at a leisurely pace, the night air felt good against her face. She glanced over at Daniel and found him staring at her. The look in his eyes made her heart race with excitement.

"I'm sorry the dance turned out to be such a miserable evening," he said. "My intentions were quite the opposite."

Ann wondered exactly what he had intended. "It was disappointing. I wish I could convince Snyder to leave us both alone."

"I doubt he'll ever give up," Kelly said. "William said that once a man that crazed sets his mind on a woman, trying to stop him is like trying to stop an avalanche. There's no telling what he'll do."

"The man is an overindulged, self-centered, dim-wit," Daniel said. "A gentleman would never behave in such a manner."

"Agreed," Ann said. "But he's also cunning, deceitful, and malicious. He's capable of doing anything to get what he wants."

DANIEL HAD TO AGREE WITH Ann's characterization of Snyder. And what Kelly said was probably true too—Snyder wouldn't give up. He had to find a way to stop the man from pursuing Ann.

If Daniel married her, perhaps Snyder would finally admit he'd lost. He intended to wait until the ring he'd ordered arrived to arrange a wedding ceremony, but now he was of the opinion that they should marry as quickly as possible.

They soon arrived at Whispering Hills and Kelly and Ann dismounted. "I'll unsaddle and stable your horses before I leave," Daniel told them.

"I'll help," Ann said.

"Thank you," Kelly said. "I'll say goodnight then. Ann, I'll put your work clothes for tomorrow upstairs in the loft and some fresh water too."

"Thank you, Kelly," Ann told her. "I'll be there soon."

Kelly winked at her and said, "Take your time. I'm going to bed early. I feel particularly tired for some reason." She said goodnight again and strode off toward her cabin.

While Daniel watered and then tied Samson outside the barn, Mrs. McGuffin, who had been watching Nicole, emerged. She waved at them and headed back to her own cabin, a few yards away.

Then they led the other two horses into the stable. The air inside smelled of grain, dry hay, and fresh droppings. As they approached, the milk cow scrutinized them warily with big brown eyes. Two other mounts that must belong to Doc and Mrs. McGuffin whinnied.

He gave his own eyes a moment to adjust to the darkness before he removed the saddle and blanket from Kelly's mare. Then he led the horse into a stall and turned it forward before taking off the bridle. Ann did the same with Whitefoot. Next, they filled a couple of buckets with water from a rain barrel just outside the stable and found two pails for their feed.

It felt pleasant and comfortable working beside Ann, as though they'd been doing it for years. If she said yes to his proposal, perhaps they would be. The notion made him grin. And the prospect of lying beside her luscious body for years in the marriage bed brought an intense heat to his male regions. But he told his unruly manhood to back down. He meant to keep his promise to the Colonel.

"Ann, will you take a walk with me down to the creek?" he asked when they'd finished.

"Of course, it's a beautiful night and there's a full moon," she said.

He took her hand and they strolled unhurried down the slight hill toward the stream. When they reached the creek bed, they stood there for a few moments just listening to the sound of the water trickling over the rocks. The peaceful sound was set against the music of the night forest—leaves rustling in the breeze, crickets, an owl's hoots, and a far-off wolf howling.

"William said there is normally a lot more water flowing through this creek," Daniel told her.

"Yes, the drought has lowered a lot of branches and streams, but most of them are spring fed so they never completely dry up," Ann said. "I'm told that is one of the things that makes Kentucky so appealing to settlers."

Daniel was ready to settle here himself. When his mother lay dying, she'd made him promise to find a woman he could love. Someone who would make him happy. She told him that woman was somewhere out there in the world waiting for him to find her. And she was right. At the end of his long journey to Kentucky, he not only found his father, he found Ann.

And he loved her.

His breath quickened as he readied himself to ask her. It only took one glance at her, though, to remove all hesitation. Bathed in the soft light of the moon, her beauty seemed ethereal. She had the face of an angel and the body of a goddess. Her skin glowed like the surface of a fine pearl. And behind her sparkling eyes he saw both intelligence and strength of character.

"Ann, there's something I want to ask. Never in my life have I known a woman who touched my soul as you do. You are all I could have ever asked for in a woman and then some. You're beautiful, honest, and strong. You make me want to love you as a man should."

Even in the moon-lit darkness, he could see the blush that crept onto her cheeks, but with every word he spoke, her smile broadened.

"Ann, I love you and I would be so honored if you would marry me. I still must get permission from your father, but if he consents, will you marry me, my darling?"

"Oh Daniel, I did not expect this so soon. But yes, yes, yes! A thousand times yes!"

His joy was so great, he grabbed her around the waist and lifted her into the air. She squealed with delight as he twirled her around in a circle. Then he put her down and wrapped his arms tightly around her before lowering his lips to hers. He kissed her with wild abandon. She would be his wife soon so he allowed his hand to grip her bottom as he deepened the kiss.

She took his face in her hands and kissed his chin and his neck before she brushed her lips across his cheek. Instinctively, she pressed her body against his.

The sensation sent bolts of desire surging through him and his body instantly responded. His hand found her breast and he cupped it through her gown. The feel of it—full and firm—made his entire arm throb with heat.

She groaned deep in her throat and then whimpered in his ear.

The sound of her ardor made his own need nearly uncontrollable. Oh how he wanted her—all of her. Now.

No, no, no, his mind told his rebellious body. *Not yet.*

"Daniel, what's happening to me?" she asked, revealing her innocence. She'd probably never felt the sensations her young body was now making known to her.

"It's called passion," he whispered in her ear. "What you're feeling is only the beginning."

She leaned back and gazed up into his face with a glint of wonder in her wide, guileless eyes.

"But we can't give in to our passion until we marry. I won't go back on my word to your father. A gentleman's word is everything."

"Then I sincerely wish you weren't a gentleman," she said, her teasing voice full of longing.

Daniel chuckled. He had to agree with her.

Chapter 27

The next morning, as she dressed to work in the garden with Kelly, Ann smiled and thought about Daniel and his proposal. She was engaged and going to marry! She couldn't wait. Last night, after he had left her with a final soul-reaching kiss, she had quietly climbed the stairs up to the loft trying not to wake Kelly and Nicole. William had not yet returned from town.

She had tried to fall asleep, but her excitement had been too great and she was still awake when she heard William finally get home. She hoped Snyder and his men hadn't given him too much trouble at the jail.

Instead of slumbering, she'd spent most of the night imagining what it would be like to be married to Daniel. He'd told her that the new, exhilarating feelings his kisses and caresses caused were only the beginning. She couldn't wait to discover on their wedding night what the rest of those feelings would be like.

After a hearty breakfast cooked by Mrs. McGuffin, William and Dr. McGuffin left for town. Doc had a few patients coming in early and William had to take Snyder and the other prisoners to the judge's courtroom to be tried. He planned to meet Daniel there at 8:00 sharp. Judge Webb always started his court precisely on time.

FROM THE DISPLEASED LOOK ON Judge Webb's beard-covered face, it appeared that Charles Snyder Jr. had exhausted the judge's scant patience. Daniel sincerely hoped that this time Snyder would get the punishment he deserved.

Before the proceedings started, William told Daniel that the judge's leniency was even scarcer than his patience. But, William warned, the judge precisely followed the letter of the law.

After William summarized the facts of the incident for the judge, Webb sentenced two of Snyder's three men to only a week in jail since they never used their pistols. Deputy Wallace led the two off to the jail and then Judge Webb eyed Snyder. "You confronted Mr. MacKay with malice aforethought—the intent to kill or to cause grievous bodily harm. In other words you meet the *mens rea* requirement for attempted murder."

Daniel already understood what the legal term meant, but Judge Webb turned to William and said, "That's Latin for guilty mind."

William nodded and then whispered to Daniel that Judge Webb was mentoring his study of the law.

Snyder's balding attorney popped up and argued, "However, because Sheriff Wyllie and Daniel MacKay stopped Mr. Snyder before he took action, he does not meet the requirement for *actus reus*. Liability requires both a guilty mind and a bad act. In this case there was no bad act. In fact, my client was the one attacked and savagely beaten. Just look at his swollen lips and black eye. I've never seen one blacker."

Daniel hid his slight smile behind his hand, pleased that his whack managed to severely blacken Snyder's eye.

Judge Webb exhaled a deep sigh and gave Snyder's attorney a withering glance. "Luck normally favors the noble. But sometimes luck gets befuddled and she favors the ignoble."

Daniel was representing himself and he rose, realizing what the judge was thinking. "Your honor, I beseech the court to consider this. Snyder specifically told his men, and I quote, 'Don't kill him, I want that pleasure.' He made his despicable intent clear. He ordered his men to beat me and then he planned to kill me himself. And Sheriff Wyllie heard him say that as well. When he and his men approached us, it was with weapons drawn. Clearly Snyder is guilty of intent to commit murder."

Snyder's attorney interrupted, "Merely preparing to kill someone or planning to do so is not sufficient to satisfy the components of attempted murder. The direct act of attempted murder must consist of using a weapon against another, such as a gun or knife, with the intention of inflicting mortal harm. Charles Snyder never fired his weapon at Mr. MacKay or Sheriff Wyllie."

"Because Daniel stopped him!" William barked. "Snyder had every intention of doing so. He had his hand on his weapon right before Daniel had to hit him."

"Did Mr. Snyder ever shoot his pistol or use his knife?" the lawyer asked William.

"No, Sir."

"Did he even *aim* his flintlock at anyone?"

William rolled his eyes. "Well no…but Lem did."

Judge Webb held up a hand stopping William. "Sheriff Wyllie, Lem is not on trial here—he already received what he deserved and a coffin awaits him. I am well aware of the sequence of events. We have previously gone over those." He turned to Snyder. "Tell me why you said, 'I want that pleasure'."

"I didn't want any of my men to kill Daniel and, actually, I would never have killed him either. This is just a trifling and foolish fight over a girl. And I guess I'll have to admit defeat. Mr. MacKay has won Miss Byrd's heart. I just had a hard time accepting that. You know how it is, your honor, a girl can make a man behave a little outlandishly." Snyder turned to Daniel. "Please accept my apology, Sir. I promise I will cause you no further trouble."

Judge Webb narrowed his eyes at Snyder and then, with a sigh, told Daniel, "The law says that attempted murder must go beyond merely preparing to commit the crime. It must cross over into actually perpetrating it."

Unfortunately, Webb was right.

The judge shook his head in apparent dismay. "So, I cannot find this man guilty of attempted murder, as much as I'd like to do so."

Daniel gave a sideways glance at Snyder and saw a sly smile on the man's cunning face. His fists ached to wipe that smirk off Snyder's face with another punch to his lying mouth.

Judge Webb turned a hard gaze on Charles. "But it is clear to me, Mr. Snyder Jr., that you possessed a guilty mind—*mens rea*. For that, I hereby fine you ten gold dollars to be paid to the court."

"Ten dollars! In gold?" Snyder protested.

"You're lucky it's not more!" Webb retorted angrily.

It was a hefty fine, but Daniel suspected Snyder would be paying it with the gold the man had stolen from *him*, and that made his stomach sour. As he remembered that Snyder had also stolen his cherished pistols, an intense loathing for the man filled him.

William said, "May I confer with you for a moment, Judge Webb?"

"Come here," the judge said, motioning William forward.

The two whispered back and forth for a few moments and then Webb addressed Snyder's lawyer. "His full fine must be deposited with Sheriff Wyllie within two months. I will now release your client into your hands, Sir. He is to report to Colonel Byrd immediately for the second half of his punishment—a year's service in the militia. Perhaps Sheriff Wyllie is right and the Colonel will be able to drill some respectability into him."

"A year!" Snyder turned around and peered at his father. "Father do something!"

Charles Snyder Sr. wisely shook his head. The man was smart enough to realize that a protest would likely make the judge lengthen the sentence.

The lawyer rose and motioned for Snyder to do so as well.

Snyder slowly pushed himself off the table and stood. The man's anger was palatable. With hard flinty eyes he glared at Daniel. "This is all your fault."

"Hush up, Charles!" the lawyer scolded.

"I warn you both, if he appears in my courtroom a third time, I will see the man flogged. And then I will hang him."

Astoundingly, Snyder snorted his contempt and stood there sullen and glowering.

The judge furrowed his brow and shook a long finger at Charles as he said, "Do you understand me, Mr. Snyder? This is no idle threat. I will have no more nonsense between you and Mr. MacKay. None!"

Snyder raised his chin and a vein in his neck twitched. "Yes, it is understood very well indeed."

Daniel could almost see bitterness—black, menacing, and vengeful—winding tentacles around Snyder's heart and mind.

Judge Webb pounded his gavel on the wooden table. The ominous sound echoed off the courtroom's wooden walls and ceiling. "Court dismissed."

Charles Snyder Sr. stood up from his chair and clamped a hand on his son's shoulder. "Let's get out of here, Charles."

With a backward sneer at Daniel, Snyder and his father left the room with their lawyer in tow.

"I'm sorry, Daniel," Judge Webb told him as soon as the Snyders were out of earshot. "Sometimes the technicalities of the law make it difficult to see justice done."

Daniel decided right then and there that if he did become a lawyer, he would work to see that laws were changed to ensure right would always triumph over wrong.

"Technicalities aside, that man is guilty as hell," Daniel snapped. "This won't be the last time you see him, Sir. That man's repentance was a sham. As Snyder left, I could see in his eyes that he was already fantasizing violence. The man is wicked to his core."

"I know," the Judge said. "I saw it too. You'd best keep your guard up." Webb turned to William. "Sheriff, let me know at once if he tries anything. He's been warned. I will show him no mercy if this happens again."

Daniel only hoped that someone wouldn't have to die for Snyder to get what he deserved.

"Let's go," William said. "I can still smell that man's stink in here."

William was right. It was the stink of an evil man.

Chapter 28

Under a high sun, Ann and Kelly worked diligently in Kelly's fall garden. They'd already been at it several hours. Sweat from Ann's forehead dripped into her eyes and she could feel the moisture accumulating between her breasts as she hoed and planted alongside Kelly. They were planting root crops of onions, parsnip, carrots, rutabaga, and beets and when they finished those they would plant leaf crops of beans, Brussel sprouts, cabbages, and cauliflower.

"I know you're having a hard time concentrating," Kelly told her, "and it's understandable, but try to keep those rows straight will you."

Ann glanced up and realized the row she'd been hoeing was as crooked as a snake's track. "I'm sorry," she said laughing. "I'll straighten it up."

Mrs. McGuffin came out carrying two glasses of milk. "I supposed you young ladies might be thirsty by now."

"Thank you," Ann said, reaching for the milk. "I truly am."

"Congratulations on your engagement," Mrs. McGuffin said. "I was so busy at breakfast I forgot to say anything about it. Kelly told me that Daniel proposed to you last night in the moonlight. That's so romantic."

"It was," Ann agreed. She smiled as she remembered his passionate kisses and the way he had held her.

"When will the wedding be?" Kelly asked.

"Daniel said he wanted to get married as soon as possible," she answered. "Today would suit me." She was anxious to learn more about what Daniel described as passion.

Kelly shook her head. "You shouldn't rush this. We'll need to have a fine gown made for you by that seamstress in town. You'll have to set a date with the traveling preacher, and hire a few musicians so we can dance. And, of course, we need to send invitations to the rest of the family."

"And I'll need to bake a wedding cake," Mrs. McGuffin said. "And plan a feast that…"

"Wait, both of you. We don't need any of that. If my father gives his consent, Judge Webb can marry us this evening if that's what Daniel wants," she told them. "And I don't need anything fancy to wear. And the rest of the family was just here visiting. There's no point in making them make that long trip again."

"But Ann…" Kelly started.

"I just want to marry him. That's all I want. The sooner the better."

Giving up, at least for now, Kelly took a long sip of her milk. With a white mustache she said, "I hope all goes well in court this morning."

Despite the seriousness of the topic, Ann had to smile and pointed at Kelly's mouth.

Kelly giggled, gulped down the rest of the milk, and wiped her mouth off with her apron. "Thank you," she said handing the empty glass back to Mrs. McGuffin.

Ann said, "I expect the judge will give Snyder what he deserves."

"He deserves to be whipped," Mrs. McGuffin said. "My husband said Snyder and his two friends beat Daniel senseless the first time. And to think Snyder was going to do it again. Maybe worse. It's contemptable."

Ann finished the milk and handed her empty glass to Mrs. McGuffin. "Hopefully, this mess is behind us and Snyder will leave Daniel and me alone."

They all nodded their agreement and the portly woman made her way back to the cabin after telling them that she'd have a nice lunch ready for them when they were ready to eat.

"You know, when I get married, I just might have to hire that cook and steal her away from you," she told Kelly, with a mischievous smile.

"Oh no you won't," Kelly declared. "She's family now. And I'm keeping her. I've really grown to love her."

"I wish my stepmother were that kind."

"She will be," Kelly said as she picked up her spade. "Once she gets to know Daniel better."

Ann shook her head in doubt and set about trying to straighten her crooked row.

In a few more hours, they were done. Ann stood next to Kelly as they both leaned on their hoes and admired all their hard work.

"I'm so grateful for your help, Ann," Kelly told her. "With Mrs. McGuffin watching Nicole, this would have taken me two or three days by myself."

"All you need now is some rain," Ann said, tugging off her work gloves.

"We all need rain. And soon," Kelly said. "It feels like the entire state and everything in it is dusty."

"Including me," Ann said, brushing the dust off her apron and skirt.

"Until it rains, I'll have to haul buckets up from the creek to water this. In fact we should get some now before we go in."

"All right, but let's soak our feet before we bring the water back," Ann suggested. "Race you there!"

After they each grabbed two buckets, the two friends set off at a run. Tired from her labor and lack of sleep, Ann soon gave up and let Kelly win, but not by much. Laughing, they removed their boots and stockings and they each rested their feet upon a rock with water swirling over and around it.

"Ah, that feels good," Ann said, wiggling her toes against the smooth stone.

"Wish we could just take off all our clothes," Kelly said.

"Why not?" Ann told her. "It's just us women here today."

"Ann, that would be scandalous!"

"That's no reason not to do it."

Kelly appeared to consider the idea. "I am awfully hot. And I do need a good bath."

"Me too," Ann said. "Everything under this skirt and shirt is dripping wet."

They both pounced up at the same time and started stripping their clothes off and laying them on rocks to dry.

The air, even though it was warm, felt good on Ann's bare skin but as she eased into the creek, the cool spring water felt even better. "That's heavenly."

"Blissful," Kelly agreed. "I needed this."

Ann cupped water in her hands and poured it into her parched throat. Then she splashed water onto her face. As some of the water ran down her neck and between her breasts she remembered the unbelievable feel of Daniel's lips and his hands as they caressed her body. "Kelly, last night, when Daniel was kissing and hugging me…"

"You didn't let him take your maidenhead did you?"

"No, of course not. Although honestly I would not have stopped him if he had tried. But he's too much of a gentleman. He said he didn't want to break his promise to my father."

"You have to admire that."

"I do. It makes me respect him even more. But what I was going to ask is this. I started feeling the strangest sensations. I've never felt them before."

"I know what you mean, you don't have to describe them. It's normal, Ann."

"Daniel called it passion."

Kelly leaned her head back in the water and let her long blonde hair swirl beneath the water's surface. Then she raised her head and said, "Physical closeness between a man and a woman who truly love each other is one of God's greatest gifts. You know how this water feels so incredible as it caresses your skin?"

"Yes."

"Well the feel of your husband's loving hands on you is ten, no a hundred times, better. Your body will explode with fantastic sensations that send you to a kind of paradise. It's hard to describe, but it's sheer ecstasy."

"Really?"

"Truly. You have nothing to fear and everything to look forward to."

"Thank you, Kelly. I wanted to know what to expect. I've seen animals do it of course, but that hardly compares."

"No, it certainly doesn't. Between a man and a woman in love there is tenderness, affection, and an ardor that makes you crave one another more than you've ever desired anything."

"Ardor?"

Kelly smiled. "Ann, you'll just have to experience it for yourself."

Ann giggled and then with a start glanced up.

Behind Kelly, Snyder came out of the woods.

He held a burning torch in his hand.

Chapter 29

Snyder came closer, the glint of lust in his eyes nearly as hot as the torch's flames. "Well, well, well. Look what I found. And I assumed I would find you two hard at work. I must say, I like this far better."

Kelly covered her breasts with her hands and sank lower into the water, but Ann leapt out, grabbed her chemise, and threw it over her head. Then she tossed Kelly's to her. After Kelly caught it, Ann slipped her boots on and took a step toward Snyder. "Get out of here Snyder. If Daniel or William find you here, this time they will kill you. That is if I don't kill you first."

Snyder sneered at her. "They'll be busy with other things. And I don't think you'd have the nerve to try to kill me. Women are so *delicate*."

The way he said the word made Ann want to prove him wrong.

Kelly stood, keeping her back to Snyder, slipped the chemise over her head, and tugged on her boots. Then she turned and faced Snyder too.

His burning eyes stilled them both.

The burning torch stilled their hearts.

"What do you mean?" Ann asked. "Why will Daniel and William be busy?" She tried to keep all emotion from her voice. She had no intention of letting this man scare her.

"Simply this." Snyder calmly moved over to a patch of tall dry weeds. He lowered the torch.

"Don't!" Kelly screamed.

"Charles, please don't do this," Ann pleaded.

Snyder raised the torch a bit. "So it's Charles now is it? I thought we weren't using familiar names any longer," he said, his curt voice lashing out at her.

Ann swallowed and approached him. "Charles, please stop this. You know I cared for you—as a friend."

"I don't need another friend. I want to marry you. We can go live in New Orleans."

"I can't marry you. I'm going to marry Daniel. I love him," she said.

His lips thinned with anger and his dark eyes grew wild.

She put her hand behind her back and motioned Kelly toward the house.

Kelly took off running.

"Charles, please there's a young child and an older woman in that cabin. Your quarrel is with me, not with them."

"No, my quarrel is with Daniel and William. If I can't have you, nobody will. I guess the only way I'm going to keep him from marrying you is to have you first. You'll be spoiled goods and he won't want you."

Ann could not stop the gasp that escaped her.

"Or maybe I'll just kill you. I'll even use Daniel's pistols. Wouldn't that be ironic? Then I'll go to New Orleans to find a smarter woman who *will* want me."

Two fine pistols, with carved embellishments on the stock, stuck out from Snyder's belt. She remembered seeing them on Daniel when he first arrived at the Governor's ball.

Was this man capable of killing her? His twisted logic and darkened thoughts might justify killing her in his mind.

"If your quarrel is with Daniel, why are you threatening to burn William's farm? You'll also set these dry woods on fire. Surely you don't want to do something this cruel."

"Oh, but I do. It was William's idea to have the judge sentence me to a year in the militia. I'll be damned if I'm going to waste a year of my youth with that foolishness. And I don't give a damn about this forest. I'm leaving anyway."

"Charles, please listen to reason. William was only doing his job and Daniel was only trying to protect me."

"Protect? Hah! He came to my father's house and beat up my two friends. That wasn't protecting you. *I* was protecting you when I beat *him* up." Broodingly, he studied her for a moment. "If Daniel had just left you alone at the ball like I asked him, none of this would have happened."

"Charles, I don't love you."

"He's the one who turned your heart cold toward me. You might have grown to love me. If he'd never come to town, you would have married me and I could have taken over as head of the fort's militia when you father retires in a couple of years. I could have been respected in Boonesborough. And your stepmother was going to give us her inheritance after we wed. We would have been set."

"Why would she do that?"

"Because she has no children of her own," he said, his tone shrill, "and I told her she was like the mother I never had."

"And she believed you?"

"Indeed, especially after I promised her I would name our first daughter Helen, after her."

Ann's gaze darted toward the cabin as Kelly rushed out, armed with her rifle.

Ann watched him warily, afraid he might try to shoot Kelly. "Charles, I'm warning you. Cease this reign of terror. If you don't, you will surely die today."

"No, I'm going to New Orleans later. But my revenge starts now!" He lowered the torch to the tall grass and it exploded into hissing flames.

Right before Ann's horrified eyes, the flames multiplied and leapt, devouring the dry grass feverishly.

"No!" she screamed. "Stop!"

Snyder hurried to another nearby patch of grass, keeping behind the trees where Kelly would not have a clear aim. He set fire to the grass and then threw the torch toward the orchard as hard as he could.

Ann wanted to run but she hesitated, terrified he would shoot her in the back. Best to keep her eyes trained on him.

Suddenly, Kelly dashed toward them, rifle raised.

Ann started backing away from Snyder, moving toward Kelly, but before Kelly could take aim, Snyder darted for her and yanked her in front of him.

Twisting her arm to keep her from resisting, he lugged her toward his tied horse. The animal could smell the smoke now and pranced nervously as they approached.

Kelly would never risk hitting her and wouldn't be able to take the shot. She saw Kelly glance nervously back toward her home.

Dear God, the flames were spreading so fast.

"Go back!" Ann yelled to Kelly. "Save Nicole and Mrs. McGuffin."

Kelly hesitated for a moment, her face stricken. Then, thankfully, she turned and ran toward the cabin.

For an instant, Ann wondered if it would be the last time she would see her dear friend.

Snyder's brawny arms encircled her waist as he prepared to throw her over the saddle.

She struggled against him, beating him with her fists, but she couldn't free herself from his strong grip. She shoved her boot down on his toes and her elbow into his side, but it had little effect.

He yanked out his knife and she froze, biting her lip to stifle an outcry. The malevolent look on his face made her finally give in to terror. Until this moment, she'd allowed herself to feel only disbelief and anger. But now, she realized she was in severe danger and fear spurted through her. She might never see Daniel again and that thought stabbed at her heart more sharply than Snyder's blade ever could.

Confirming her fears, Snyder said, "No more resistance or I'll shoot your legs and dump you where the flames will finish you."

"ARTIS!" BEAR YELLED INTO THE house. "Artis!"

"What's got ye so fashed?" Artis called. "Do not be troubled, I'm right here husband."

"Smoke!" Bear told her. "First I smelled it and then I saw it driftin' up into the higher hills behind William and Kelly's!"

"Good Lord! Is Camel saddled?"

Bear nodded. "Aye. I'll saddle Glasgow for ye."

Outside, Stirling's high-pitched bark signaled looming danger.

"Shall we take Stirling?" she asked.

"Nay, it might be too dangerous. But if we leave him outside, he'll follow us. Bring him inside. Then grab some blankets and wet them in the water barrel."

Bear turned and raced toward the stable his heart aching with worry for Kelly, her daughter, and Mrs. McGuffin.

"Do ye think William is still in town?" Artis asked as she ran out carrying the blankets. She tossed them into the water barrel, drew them out, and tied the dripping blankets onto Camel.

"Aye. Since Daniel's na back, I do," Bear answered. "And Doc will be at his apothecary today. Artis, since ye are with child, I do na want ye to gallop fast. I'll ride ahead. Ye ride slower and catch up to me." He was surprised when she didn't argue with him.

He rode off at a fast gallop, soon covering the few miles between their places, and turned Camel to the right onto the short trail that led downward to Whispering Hills.

Bear's eyes widened at the grim sight before him and he raced to Kelly. The entire pasture in front of the cabins was aflame along with part of the orchard. The fire hadn't reached the cabins or barn yet, but it soon would. Kelly looked frantic as she hitched up the wagon team. Little Nicole stood in the back of the wagon with Mrs. McGuffin. Also in the back, Riley barked continuously at the fire. The milk cow, shuffling nervously behind the wagon, strained at the rope that tied her.

At the sight of Bear, Kelly screamed, "Help!"

Bear heard the desperation in her voice as she struggled to control the nervous horse team.

An immense amount of smoke encircled the two cabins, barn, and smokehouse. Bear leapt off Camel, tied him, and helped Kelly finish harnessing the team. By the time they finished, Artis rode up.

With tears welling in her eyes, Kelly cried, "Snyder took Ann! You've got to help her!"

"Did he do this?" Bear demanded.

"Yes! He brought a torch with him. While I ran to the cabin to get my rifle he set the fire and then stole Ann away on his horse."

"I'll find Ann! But these woods will soon be on fire, Kelly. Ye must leave now with Nicole, Mrs. McGuffin, and Artis."

"Nay, I'll stay and help you," Artis insisted.

"Love, there is na help on earth that will stop this fire. Their house and farm are doomed." Bear turned to Kelly. "Kelly, I know 'tis hard, but ye must stay calm and get your child and stepmother to safety."

Kelly shook her head. "Mrs. McGuffin is going to take Nicole into town. I've got to saddle my mare and Ann's too and help you find her."

Behind them, they heard crackling sounds as the fire began to consume tree limbs and dead wood lying on the ground. They could see long flaming tongues spreading through the orchard, licking the trunks of the apple trees. Between the creek and the house, dry grass shriveled into withered black stubbles, weeds disappeared before their eyes, and pine needles sizzled and popped.

"There's na time to saddle yer mare. Go! Ye must leave now!" Bear shouted, losing his patience. "I'll free the horses and then I need to go after Snyder at once before the fire spreads and blocks the way."

Artis tried to coax Kelly. "The fire is comin' this way. Ye both must hurry. I'll go with ye, Kelly."

Nicole started coughing as smoke reached them.

"All right," Kelly said with a glance at her daughter. "I'll leave. But promise me you'll not give up until you find Ann. You must find her. Snyder might kill her."

"Ye have my word," Bear told her. He tugged the wet blankets off of Camel and tossed them into the wagon. "Cover the child and yerself," he told Mrs. McGuffin. While she drew one over Nicole's head, he ran into the barn to free Kelly and Ann's mares. He slapped each horse's hip and sent them running off, knowing they would take the familiar path into town.

"We must outrun this fire," Artis yelled as he ran back to them. "Bear, I think ye should come with us!"

"Nay, I must find Ann. Kelly, where was Snyder's mount tied when he set the fire?" he asked.

She told him as he mounted Camel. "Go! Now!" he ordered.

As soon as Kelly's wagon team and Glasgow took off, he turned Camel and raced toward the creek. He forced the horse to leap over patches where the grass was already on fire. Once he reached the creek, he dismounted and threw himself in the water. If the fire spread to the north side of the creek, he wanted to be prepared. He tied a wet handkerchief around his nose and then took the bucket he had tied on Camel earlier, filled it, and poured its contents over Camel's mane, tail and head. His trusted stead did not flinch, but Bear could tell the smoke was making him anxious. But Camel was an intrepid horse and would take him through hell's flames if Bear needed him to.

After he mounted, he found the spot where Snyder's mount had stood tied. The pile of horse droppings on the ground made it easy to find. He followed the tracks up an incline and into the woods on the other side of the creek. He felt certain that Snyder would ride away from the fire and stay on the north side of the creek where they would be safer.

But Snyder was far from safe. Ann was very nearly Bear's daughter and no one threatened a member of his family like this. No one!

This time Snyder would not escape justice. He intended to kill the maggot.

Chapter 30

Behind them, Artis heard the sound of a tall pine explode into flame as they reached the road that led to Boonesborough. It sounded like a cannon blast. The drought had already claimed the lives of many water starved pine trees and their dry needles would feed the fire's savage hunger.

She glanced over at Kelly who slapped the team's leathers again and hollered at the horses trying to get them to gallop even faster. Tears flowed down Kelly's face.

Her friend's heart was breaking, both for the loss of her beloved home and for Ann.

Artis was worried about Ann too. But there was nothing either one of them could do for their friend now, except call upon God. Artis turned her burning eyes heavenward and prayed that God would send his angels to protect both Ann and Bear.

As Kelly turned the wagon left, onto the road to Boonesborough, burning trees began to shower fiery missiles around them. Mrs. McGuffin threw another wet blanket over Nicole, who was crying pitifully, and she tugged Riley under the blanket as well. The poor woman was choking on the smoke herself and she stuck her own head beneath the blanket too.

They hadn't even traveled a mile before gusts of ash-laden smoke, which blinded and choked them, soon filled the air. Artis' own treasured home, Highland, lay another two miles down the road toward Boonesborough. Would the fire reach it too? Would Stirling be trapped inside a burning home? The thought of losing her beloved dog horrified her.

"The fire is spreading fast and this bouncing wagon is too slow," Kelly yelled over to Artis. "Take Nicole and race Glasgow into town. If it spreads into town too, take her to the river and keep her there until William or I find you."

"Nay, I can't leave you," Artis shouted.

As the inferno worsened, they heard a sudden roar that sounded like an angry animal. Artis glanced behind them. The sight of the blaze sucking more and more of the beautiful forest into its hungry mouth horrified her.

Kelly turned to her with a sober look. "Artis, I'm begging you. Save my child. Your horse can't carry all of us and the fire might catch up with us."

"I'll let Mrs. McGuffin ride Glasgow and I'll stay with you," Artis yelled to her.

"No!" Mrs. McGuffin bellowed over the noisy bouncy wagon and the roar of the fire. "I've already lived a full life. Kelly, I want you to get on that stallion with Artis. Nicole needs you. She's terrified. Glasgow can easily carry the both of you and the child and still run like the wind."

Artis eyed Kelly. They both knew the kindly woman was right. As if to reinforce the terrible but only option they had, a large branch came crashing down onto the road, nearly blocking the wagon's path. Kelly hastily maneuvered the horses around it.

Riding Glasgow next to the wagon bench where Kelly was seated, Artis could see her friend struggling with the heart-wrenching decision.

The wagon team was becoming more and more unruly. And Riley began whimpering. She could tell he wanted to jump and run but the faithful dog wouldn't leave his family.

Mrs. McGuffin reached over the wagon seat, grabbed the team's leathers, and jerked them to an abrupt stop. The two horses halted, but continued to prance and whinny in fear.

Artis tugged on her stallion's reins, turned, and brought Glasgow alongside the wagon bench.

In a firm voice, Mrs. McGuffin said, "Kelly, get on that stallion right this second. Do it for your daughter. And your father."

Kelly hesitated for only a moment and then tied the leathers and grabbed Nicole. She put a palm up against Mrs. McGuffin's reddened cheek. "Thank you. We'll send help just as soon as we can."

"Tell your father I love him," Mrs. McGuffin said, her voice cracking.

Kelly nodded and said, "We love you too." With her daughter clinging to her neck Kelly jumped off the wagon and handed Nicole up to Artis. Riley jumped out as well.

With tears in all their eyes, Artis nestled Nicole on the saddle in front of her and then reached down and to help Kelly swing herself up onto Glasgow's big hips.

"Mommy," Nicole cried.

Kelly wrapped an arm securely around Artis and reached the other one up to pat Nicole's shoulder. "I'm here honey, right behind Aunt Artis."

"Artis, ride for your lives!" Mrs. McGuffin ordered.

Riley ran behind them. He wouldn't be able to keep up for long, but the dog would follow their scent and find them. Artis peered back before taking Glasgow to a faster gallop. Her heart broke as she saw Mrs. McGuffin cough dreadfully. Then she climbed over the wagon seat, sat down, and took the reins in her hands.

After their time in court, Daniel had spent the rest of the morning, speaking with Colonel Byrd, who happily granted his permission for Daniel to wed Ann. When he'd explained to the colonel that he thought Snyder might finally admit defeat if he and Ann wed, Byrd agreed that they should marry as soon as possible. Then Mrs. Byrd left the room in a huff and the Colonel hurried after her.

He invited Conall to lunch and before they'd even ordered their food, he asked if Conall if he would be his best man. Ann's brother was the only friend he had here but he was certain they would be close friends in the future. And he owed Conall his life.

During lunch, the two of them decided upon 4:00 o'clock tomorrow afternoon for the wedding.

"Conall, you know Ann better than anyone. Do you think she'll mind if I go ahead and make all the arrangements myself?" Daniel asked.

"As long as it means marrying you sooner, I think she won't mind one bit," Conall told him. "If I know my sister, she likes to keep things simple and isn't formal and fussy. She'll just want to marry as soon as possible. Patience is *not* one of her strengths."

After lunch, they set about making preparations for a wedding at Bear and Artis' home. *Now it was his home too.*

He found a lovely gown on display at the dressmaker's shop and they both thought it would fit Ann so he bought it and several pieces of jewelry to match. And he bought new shirts, cravats, and boots for both he and Conall. He also bought a nice waistcoat for Conall since it was too hot for a full dress coat. As the groom, he would need to wear one, but there was no reason for Conall to have to suffer.

Then they spoke to Judge Webb about conducting the ceremony. Afterwards, with Lucky McGintey's help, they located three musicians who were willing to play for them. Lucky volunteered to hunt for fresh meat and said he would bring it to Highland early in the morning for Bear to roast. He said he would also bring a few dozen ears of corn. Of course, Daniel asked Lucky to join them as a guest as well.

Next, they stopped at the bakery and ordered a cake, six pies, and several loaves of bread to be delivered tomorrow afternoon so Artis and Kelly wouldn't have to bake all day. Afterwards, he made a stop at the general store for a case of the best wine that they carried. He asked Mr. Breedhead to deliver it to the baker and have them bring the wine with their delivery. He also bought a new doll and some candy for Nicole. It surprised him how much pleasure it gave him to plan a special wedding for Ann.

Their last task was to go by the town's only inn and arrange for a room for the wedding night. But to his extreme disappointment, the inn's owner said they were completely full and no rooms would be available for at least a week.

Conall helped him load all his wrapped packages on Samson, who was tied in front of William's office. He thanked Conall for his help and put his boot in the stirrup. Then he froze. He took a deeper breath and looked to the sky. Smoke billowed in an ominous gray cloud from the direction of Whispering Hills.

Ann. Bear. Artis. William's family. They would all be in danger.

"Bloody hell, the forest is on fire!" Daniel called to Conall who was walking away. Then he turned toward his uncle's office and shouted, "William! Fire!"

Conall turned around, realized what was happening, and began shouting, "Fire!" toward all the men milling about the fort.

William and the deputy came running as did all the other men who were in the area. With one look to the sky, they all knew the entire town, surrounded by the tinder dry woods of late July could be in grave danger. At least the north side of Boonesborough and the fort were protected by the immense waters of the nearby Kentucky River. And a few days ago, he'd learned from Lucky that deep dirt trenches, dug to stop forest fires and hold sewage, bordered the town on the west and east sides. The area to the south was too rocky to dig trenches, he'd explained, but the townspeople had also wisely cleared the area of trees and thick brush, using the grass to feed livestock and the lumber for buildings.

"Let's go!" William said, tightening Smoke's cinch strap. "Deputy, help the Colonel. The militia can start protecting the town by filling buckets."

"Conall, take all these packages to your home," Daniel told him as he hastily removed the items. "I'll need Samson to fly."

Wallace helped Conall with some of the packages and the two took off running through the enclosure toward the Byrd home.

Daniel and William's mounts tore through the fort's gates and raced to the trail that led to Highland and Whispering Hills. He couldn't believe how much smoke there was. He could feel the breeze blowing it toward them. That also meant it was sending the fire toward the town!

Fear for Ann, Bear and Artis, and William's family filled him. He urged Samson to an even faster run.

They soon rounded a bend in the road and spotted Whitefoot and Kelly's mare running riderless toward them.

Daniel glanced over at William. His uncle's expression was extremely distraught.

"What does that mean?" William asked. "Why would they just turn the horses loose?"

"They must be coming in the wagon," Daniel told him, hoping it was true.

"But they would have tied the horses to the back of the wagon."

"Perhaps there wasn't time." Daniel and William both knew, if that were true, they could be in real trouble.

Unwilling to slow down, they just let the horses run past them. Whitefoot would head for the fort's stable where she was used to getting fed and Kelly's mare would likely follow.

Within a few minutes, they caught sight of Artis on Glasgow, with Nicole in front of her and Kelly riding behind.

"Thank God!" William yelled to him.

"But where is Ann?" he shouted. A shiver of sheer panic raced down his spine, but he forced an iron control on himself.

Artis tugged the stallion to a stop and Kelly, dressed in only a sheer chemise, leapt off as did William. Surprisingly, she immediately rushed to Daniel and gazed up at him with frantic eyes. "Snyder took Ann! He set the pasture on fire." Then she reached for William and told him, "Our home will be in flames by now."

"Bloody hell," William swore.

"Where did Snyder take Ann?" Daniel demanded. "Is she all right?"

"I don't know where he took her. He surprised us down by the creek. We were bathing and he came out of nowhere," Kelly cried.

William removed his waistcoat and put the vest on Kelly as she continued to tell them what happened.

"I ran for my rifle, but I couldn't take a shot without risking hitting Ann," Kelly explained.

Artis told them, "Bear went after them! I'm worried that he'll get caught in the fire but he wanted to save Ann. Who knows what Snyder might do to her."

Daniel swore, "I'll kill that son-of-a…"

William interrupted. "Kelly, take care of Nicole. We're leaving now! We'll find Ann. And Bear."

Kelly shook her head. "Wait. Go save Mrs. McGuffin. She's behind us, in the wagon. The fire was moving fast and she made us go on ahead without her because the fire was catching up to us. We left her a little more than a mile from home. You've got to find her!" Kelly was understandably nearly hysterical and tears began flowing down her cheeks.

Artis also appeared frantic. "And after ye find Ann and Bear, if the fire is nearin' Highland, tell him to let my dog out of the house. But only if he can do so safely," Artis told them.

Not waiting for William, Daniel nudged Samson to a full run and rushed ahead. A moment later, he heard William's horse galloping behind him.

A few minutes later, he spotted Riley hurrying up the road. The poor dog's head was hanging low. He was clearly exhausted.

"Riley," William called and dismounted.

The dog perked up at the sound of William's voice and came running.

"Do you think he'll make it all the way back to town?" Daniel asked.

"Yes. He'll stop along the way to rest. Go on ahead. I'm going to give him some water and then I'll tell him to find Kelly. Riley is devoted to her and he'll find her. I'll catch up to you in a minute."

Daniel soon raced past Highland, which still appeared to be untouched by the fire. About a mile further up the road he spotted the wagon. Leaves scattered around the back wheels were on fire and a burning log lay across the road in front of the wagon blocking the wagon team from moving any further. They'd been tied securely so they couldn't move, but the terrified horses pranced wildly and rocked the wagon violently.

Mrs. McGuffin lay slumped over in the wagon seat. She had a blanket over her head and she wasn't moving. She must have been overcome by the smoke and became too weak to try to run away from the fire.

Around the wagon, on the north side of the road, the closest trees flickered with flames only around their bases. Further into the woods, on the drier pines, he saw fire wind its way up their trunks, like fiery dragons intent on roasting their prey alive. What once was a stunningly beautiful forest full of fall hues was now dotted with brighter, glowing versions of the same colors. At least the fire hadn't crossed the road to the south side.

Daniel leapt off Samson and tied the frightened stallion so he would not bolt. Then he scooped Mrs. McGuffin up.

"Is she breathing?" William asked as he raced up on Smoke.

"I think so. Take her to safety. I'm going after Ann and Bear." He handed Mrs. McGuffin up to William, who was still mounted, and they positioned her across his lap.

William supported her upper body with his left arm and took Smoke's reins in his right hand. "I'm sure Doc has been alerted to the fire and is on his way," William said. "I'll find him."

As Daniel unhitched the wagon team to release them, William hastily told him, "The fire won't cross the Kentucky River so if you get trapped, head for that. If you can't get to it, the creek behind my farm is the same one that runs behind and on both sides of Bear's property. Unless the wind picks up, the creek bed should stop the fire from reaching Highland."

Daniel thought it would take a miracle to keep Highland from being destroyed too.

William continued to speak rapidly, his voice growing hoarse from the thick smoke and heavy waves of heat. "Don't take the road, there's too much burning in that direction and if the fire crosses the road, you could be trapped. Go north through those woods," he said and pointed. "Then angle back. Bear probably crossed the creek to stay on the safe side and Snyder would have done the same."

"William, you need to leave," Daniel urged, as he unfastened another leather.

"I'm not leaving until you are safely in Samson's saddle again."

William shielded Mrs. McGuffin's face against his chest when a sudden shift in the direction of the breeze caused bits of ash to rain down onto them. It also brought choking smoke that burned their lungs and eyes and caused Mrs. McGuffin to cough. At least that meant she was breathing.

Two deer bounded out of the woods in front of the wagon and ran down the road—more terrified of the fire than men and horses.

Daniel removed the last of the wagon team's leathers and with a slap to the rumps of the two horses, he sent the frightened animals racing away. They both leapt over the burning log, and headed for Boonesborough.

Smoke whinnied and pranced, wanting to follow the two, but with some difficulty, his uncle was able to hold the anxious gelding back. "Whoa, Smoke. Whoa," William soothed.

Daniel leapt up onto Samson. "William, go! Take Mrs. McGuffin to Doc. I'll be fine." Also uneasy, the stallion stomped the ground, more than ready to leave.

"I hate leaving you, but it can't be helped. Please be careful," William urged. "And I'm giving you the authority to kill that bastard if he's hurt Ann." His uncle turned Smoke and galloped off.

Holding Samson's reins in his teeth, Daniel quickly tied a handkerchief over his nose and pointed the stallion into the woods. He headed due north. He would find Ann.

Snyder's day of reckoning had come.

Chapter 31

As Daniel passed a burning tree he could not maneuver around, he talked and petted Samson trying to keep the stallion from giving way to fear. The horse's courageous heart kept him steady even as a sudden flaming ember landed on Daniel's arm. Before he could knock it off, the flame burnt a hole in his shirt sleeve and seared a spot on his arm. The sweet, acrid, smell of burning flesh touched his nose and hit the back of his throat. He sincerely hoped that would be the last time he would smell the repulsive scent as he searched for Ann. Even the choking smell of the fire's smoke was preferable.

As he rode, he ignored the burn's sting, too preoccupied to care. He had to find Ann—that was all that mattered. And he sincerely hoped Bear was safe from the fire. He knew his father could track Snyder with little difficulty and once he found the coward Bear would have no trouble dealing with him. At least that was something Daniel didn't have to worry about.

But what if Bear didn't find her in time?

He prayed guardian angels would protect her from harm. He tried to swallow his fear for her, but it seemed to stick in his throat. It wasn't from the heat and smoke. It was the stomach-churning uncertainty of what he would find.

Would Ann be dead? At Snyder's hand or the fire's?

Please, God, no!

He nudged Samson to a faster trot and wove the stallion through the trees. Fortunately, the pine-needle covered forest floor grew a minimal amount of brush and he was able to keep a rapid pace.

They were soon out of the area with the most flames, but there was still a lot of smoke. Then, miraculously, the wind increased and shifted direction, blowing east to west and the air abruptly cleared. If the direction the wind blew kept up, it would take the fire away from town and leave Highland intact.

It would be the miracle he'd hoped for.

He yanked the handkerchief down from his nose and surveyed the area surrounding him. The land sloped downward and Daniel guessed that a flood-carved creek must lie at the bottom of the incline. It had to be the same one that ran behind Whispering Hills. Weaving his way around boulders and large rocks, he hurried toward it.

He knew he'd guessed right when he heard the sound of the spring-fed waters rushing over rocks and against the creek's limestone banks. Finding a spot where elk, deer, and other wildlife had made a trail to the water for him, he rode straight into the creek and paused long enough to let Samson take a much needed drink.

Looking up, he could see smoke still rising into the sky to the west and south of where he was but at least the smoke cloud wasn't growing in size. Even better, he could see the wind chasing the gray cloud away from their home and the town.

But his fear for Ann, a captive of a crazed man, mounted.

Bear wasn't far behind them, no more than a couple hundred yards further up this hill. He wanted to surprise Snyder, so he slowed Camel to a walk…until he heard a woman scream in terror.

It had to be Ann.

He booted Camel's side and tore toward the alarming sound.

Ann screamed again and Bear's insides twisted with anger.

If Snyder harmed Ann he would remove the bastard's head. He yanked his hatchet from his belt and thundered into the clearing where he spotted Snyder.

The man's arms and legs pinned Ann to the ground. The bloody bastard intended to rape her!

Like a flash of violent lightning, he bolted toward Snyder, hatchet poised to strike with lethal force.

At the thunderous sound of his approach, Snyder lifted his head and then raised up on his knees, revealing his engorged manhood.

The sight disgusted Bear so greatly that he bellowed a Scottish war cry, filling the forest with the threatening sound.

DANIEL HEARD A STARTLING ROAR reverberate through the trees. He'd never heard anything like it, but he knew at once that it must be Bear. Probably a Scots war cry, known to make even the bravest of men quiver on the battlefield.

With a sense of foreboding, he rushed Samson toward the dreadful, chilling sound. What did it mean?

Did Bear find Ann dead?

His heart thundered in his chest and a suffocating sensation of intense despair swept over him.

Within moments, he spotted Bear racing Camel toward a clearing.

Hurry, Bear, hurry!

Daniel looked in the direction Bear was headed. He spotted Snyder, pushing himself to his feet, his head turning toward the sound of Bear approaching. When Snyder took a step back, Daniel caught sight of Ann. She was lying motionless on the ground in front of Snyder!

Dear God, what had the man done?

Fear and rage warred within him each competing for control of his mind and heart as he raced toward them, still a few moments away. Helpless to do anything until he reached them, he could only watch the confrontation unfold.

Snyder pulled his pistol and took aim at Bear.

His father continued his charge, hurtling straight toward Snyder.

He heard Ann shriek as she leapt from the ground. *She was alive!* She lunged toward Snyder. He caught the glint of a knife in her outstretched hand.

Snyder turned back to face Ann and then howled as she plunged the knife into the center of the man's chest.

Bear skidded Camel to a halt beside the two and leapt off, ax readied to strike. Bear prepared to take Snyder's head off.

"No!" Ann yelled, stopping Bear in mid-swing.

Even over the sound of Samson's thundering hooves, he heard Bear's angry growl. His father looked like he wanted to behead the man anyway. Bear bellowed from deep within his heaving chest and his formidable expression turned even more fearsome. His father still held the ax above his broad shoulders, poised to strike.

A second later, Daniel galloped Samson right up to Ann. He hurdled off the stallion in a fluid motion, pistol drawn.

Snyder dropped to his knees, but didn't fall over.

Daniel glanced at Ann to be certain she was all right. Her ripped chemise left one breast exposed that she tried to cover with her hand. Red welts stood out on her beautiful face.

Daniel pointed his flintlock at Charles' head. "You filthy son-of-a-bitch."

Still kneeling, Snyder peered up at Daniel and nodded his head as if he'd expected him. Thwarted and defeated, Charles simply waited for Daniel to take the shot.

The forest seemed eerily quiet as Daniel rotated the flintlock's cock from half to full and took aim at the center of Snyder's forehead. He heard blood drip down Snyder's waistcoat and onto the dry leaves. The man was clearly dying.

Daniel uncocked and lowered his pistol and Bear brought his deadly weapon down to his side.

Struggling to breathe, Snyder glared at Daniel. Blood dripped from the side of Charles' mouth as he sputtered, "You'll always be a bastard."

Bear snarled and raised his ax again, but Daniel held up a hand stopping him.

Daniel tried to speak but he couldn't find the right words to say to a dying man. He searched Snyder's face, hoping to see some sign of repentance or contrition. Or at least shame. He saw only the same willful, malicious man that he met his first night in Boonesborough. Even as he faced imminent death, Snyder could not embrace goodness.

Snyder turned back to Ann and his eyes glowed strangely for a moment before they grew flat and unfathomable. Then he finally collapsed to the ground.

Daniel grabbed Ann, wrapped his arms tightly around her, and hugged her against his still galloping heart. "Thank God, you're all right." He kissed the top of her head several times, needing to feel her against his lips.

"Daniel, I fought back. But I couldn't stop him. He was going to…he put it…he was nearly inside."

"We know. Bear and I saw him," Daniel said, soothingly.

She started crying. "He touched me…he almost…that's why I had to kill him. I had to!"

She stared down at Snyder's body. Her mouth fell open in dismay as her mind confronted the hard realities of both being violated and killing another human being.

Daniel knew she was in shock. He felt her shudder and draw in a sharp breath as she continued to sob. As he'd seen William do for Kelly, Daniel gave Ann his waistcoat and buttoned the vest for her. It was so long on her it hung down below her thighs.

"Ye had to kill him," Bear agreed, still breathing hard. "And if ye hadn't, then I would have a second later. Or Daniel would have put a lead ball in his head. But ye were strong lass. Ye defended yerself as every woman has a right to do."

"And I would have killed him too," Daniel assured her. "He tried to dishonor you in the worst way. A man deserves to die for that."

Daniel and Ann both watched, almost transfixed, as Bear stood over Snyder's body, retrieved her knife, and wiped it clean on several large leaves before handing it back to her.

"It was hidden in my boot," she said, taking it with trembling hands. Her voice was a tear-smothered whimper.

"Put it back now," Daniel told her. "I want you to carry it with you always."

While she put the knife back, Daniel reached down and removed his treasured pistols from Snyder's belt. He stared at them for a moment and his father Armitage's smiling face came into his mind as clear as if he were standing right before him. His father appeared pleased. "Father," Daniel said out aloud.

"Aye, son?" Bear said.

Daniel glanced up and Bear gazed at him.

"Let's go home," Daniel said.

"I'll ride Snyder's mount," Daniel told Ann. He didn't want her to have to ride the same horse used to abduct her. "You can ride Samson. In this heat, it will be easier on Samson if he doesn't have to carry two people." Daniel peered over at Snyder's tied gelding. "I wonder why his mount has a traveling bag and bedroll on him."

"He was going to take me to New Orleans, with his two friends. When I told him I loved you, he threatened to kill me and take my virginity first, so you wouldn't want me anymore if you came after us."

Daniel's anger returned. "Even if he'd succeeded, nothing could ever stop me from loving you and wanting to marry you."

Bear threw Snyder's body over Camel's big hips, and said, "I'd like to leave this whoreson for the wolves, but for his father's sake, we'll take him back."

"What of the fire?" he asked Bear. "Did it take William and Kelly's home?"

"Aye, from what I saw, I think it must have. And the McGuffin's cabin as well. Everything at Whisperin' Hills will likely be gone."

"Do you think it will take our home too?" he asked.

As Bear securely tied Snyder's body onto Camel, he said, "Nay, 'tis surrounded on three sides by the creek. I doubt the fire will cross all those rocks and the steep bank. And when I built our home, I used all but a few of the largest hardwood trees, clearin' the land to make grazin' pastures for the horses. With the drought, our horses have kept the pasture grasses grazed down to nothin'. And a while ago, I felt the wind shift toward the west. I'm hopeful our home is untouched."

"That's good, because we're going to have a wedding at Highland tomorrow."

Ann turned her still glistening eyes toward him. "Truly? Tomorrow? After all that's happened?"

Especially after all that's happened, he thought. Ann needed something positive to think about.

Daniel wiped the tears from her face with a gentle finger as he said, "Yes, tomorrow, if that's all right with you, and Bear and Artis. I think we could all use a joyful event after this."

"Even William and Kelly?" she asked.

"Especially William and Kelly," Bear answered. "”Twill be a needed distraction."

Ann nodded and squeezed his hands. "Yes! Let's have a wedding!" She started crying again, but this time they were tears of happiness.

"Life goes on," Bear said, "if the fire stopped at the creek and burned itself out as I suspect, ye can make all the arrangements tomorrow."

Daniel smiled at Ann. "I already have. Before the fire started, I decided the best way to stop Snyder was for us to be married as soon as possible. So I bought you a gown and a few gifts, and some wine, and I arranged for Judge Webb to marry us and for musicians to play. Of course, now that Snyder's dead there's not as much urgency. We can wait as long as you want to if you'd rather plan a big wedding."

She sniffled and shook her head. "I just want you, Daniel. The sooner the better."

Bear cleared his throat and mounted Camel. "We'd best be gettin' back to check on Artis and the others."

Daniel nodded. "Yes, I found Mrs. McGuffin overcome by smoke in the wagon on the road between Whispering Hills and Highland. Kelly and Artis had to leave her with the wagon because she insisted that they take Nicole and hurry to safety on Glasgow. William took Mrs. McGuffin to Doc."

"We must pray she'll be recovered by now," Bear said.

Daniel led the way back with Ann riding beside him on Samson. Bear stayed well behind them so Ann wouldn't have to see Snyder's body.

The good news about holding the wedding tomorrow seemed to shake Ann out of her shock. She no longer seemed fragile and she wasn't shaking now. As they rode toward town, she even managed a few smiles and he saw a hopeful glint in her lovely eyes.

His own heart felt lighter too. Now, nothing and no one would stand in the way of their wedding or their happiness.

Chapter 32

When Daniel arrived at the edge of Boonesborough with Ann and Bear, it seemed as though the entire population scurried around the sycamore at the center of town. The townspeople must have banded together to stand against the fire. Hundreds of buckets and small barrels filled with water stood lined up to one side. Women filled buckets from the town's well while men loaded them onto wagons. Hoes, axes, shovels, and whatever other hand tools they could find to fight the blaze, leaned against the big tree.

Even though the wind sent the fire away from town, the townspeople were wisely getting prepared in case the wind's direction shifted again before the fire burned itself out. They all knew a sudden strong wind could fan the flames into one gigantic blaze that could last for days and burn thousands of acres of woodland and destroy homesteads. At its worst, it could claim many lives as well. The town itself was particularly vulnerable to fire because nearly every structure was a timber-framed building. The town would literally explode into flames if a forest fire reached Boonesborough.

Still mounted on Samson, and a good distance away, Daniel peered over all the activity trying to spot Glasgow. He finally caught sight of Artis' stallion tied to a tree. Artis and Kelly sat nearby in the shade. Both appeared to be okay, although Kelly looked distraught. Nicole sat in Kelly's lap and Riley was asleep next to them. Colonel Byrd and Conall looked busy directing the activities of the townspeople.

Bear shifted Camel so that Daniel and Ann's mounts stood between him and the townspeople and then said, "Artis looks to be fine. And so do Kelly and her wee lassie. Go, join them and find out how Mrs. McGuffin fares. I'll take Snyder's body and his horse to his father. That way the whole town does na have to learn what happened. Perhaps we can keep this quiet. Tell Artis I'll find her a wee bit later."

"I should go with you," Daniel said.

"Nay, I think the man will take it better if it's just me who tells him."

Daniel nodded and he and Ann dismounted. He handed the reins for Snyder's mount over to Bear and then took hold of Samson's reins.

Ann peered up at Bear with imploring eyes. "Please don't tell Mr. Snyder what Charles almost did to me. Just tell him that it was self-defense—and I'm sorry that it came to this."

Bear nodded and his father kept the body hidden by Snyder's horse as he left the edge of town and rode east toward the banker's home.

Leading Samson, he and Ann hurried over to Artis and Kelly.

Both women leapt up as soon as they drew near. "Ann!" Kelly and Artis cried out and rushed up to them. Both hugged Ann.

Daniel's head turned when he heard Ann's name shouted by two men—Colonel Byrd and Conall. Both men hastened toward them.

"We were so worried," Kelly said. Tracks of tears streaked her reddened and ash-blackened face. "When Snyder carried you off, it tore my heart apart."

The hair and clothes of both Kelly and Artis were covered in a fine gray ash and they looked exhausted.

Colonel Byrd rushed up and enveloped his daughter in his strong arms and when he released her Conall did the same.

"I'm so relieved to see you unharmed," her father said. Then his expression hardened in dismay as he took in her ripped chemise and the fact that she was wearing Daniel's waistcoat.

"You are unharmed aren't you?" Conall demanded.

Daniel saw a flash of still raw recollections rip through her, but she bravely held her tears in check as she nodded.

"What happened?" Artis demanded. "That monster hit you, didn't he?"

Ann touched the reddened spot on her cheek.

Daniel answered for her. "He's dead."

Colonel Byrd turned to Daniel "Did you kill Charles?"

"Or did Bear?" Artis asked.

"I killed him!" Ann blurted. Her reply rang with finality.

The eyes of her father and brother grew wide and Artis and Kelly paled.

"Are you all right?" Kelly asked. "He didn't…"

"No," Daniel answered for her. "But he was about to. My brave Ann defended herself and probably saved Bear's life too. She had a knife hidden in her boot and when Snyder took aim at Bear, she charged."

"That's my daughter!" Byrd said, and hugged Ann again. "Kelly told us what happened and that Bear had gone after you. And William told me that Daniel went to find you too. Conall and I were just about to leave to go after you as well, but first I had to quickly get the townspeople organized in case the fire came this way. If it did and we weren't prepared, we could have a disaster. A great many lives could have been lost."

"Where's Bear?" Artis wanted to know.

"He's taking the body to Mr. Snyder," Daniel said. "He didn't want the whole town to see it and start asking a lot of questions. He'll be back soon."

"Good," Artis said. "We need to check on Highland. And Stirling is still inside the house."

"Highland should be fine," Daniel said. "When we rode by there the fire was still more than a mile away and then the wind changed and shifted the fire's direction away from our home." It felt good to say our home, though soon he would build a house for Ann and him.

"Thank the good Lord," Artis said.

"Amen to that," Byrd said. "That means the town should be spared too. Come on Conall, let's finish getting these people ready in case the wind shifts again. Then you and some others can go with Sheriff Wyllie to check on his place. Perhaps some of it can be saved."

"Mommy, I'm thirsty," Nicole said, pulling on Kelly's hand.

Kelly gave Ann a quick hug. "I'll get you both some water too," she volunteered and walked away holding Nicole by the hand.

"Artis, how is Mrs. McGuffin?" Daniel asked. "Is she…"

"She'll be fine. She's at the Doc's office. He shooed us all away and said she needed to rest for a wee bit. The smoke made it difficult for her to breathe. Doc said his wife should be fine in a couple of hours," Artis explained.

"Thank God," Ann said. "When Daniel told us what happened, we feared the worst."

"I thought Kelly might be crying because Mrs. McGuffin didn't make it," Daniel said.

"She's cryin' because she was so worried about Ann. And because she's lost her beloved home, Whisperin' Hills," Artis said.

"That will be terribly difficult for her and for William. But we can rebuild it," he said. "I'll gladly pay for its construction. I feel responsible."

Ann and Artis both looked at him skeptically, undoubtedly wondering how he could afford it. Aside from his fine sword and his father's pistols, he'd deliberately kept evidence of his wealth secret.

"I can and will take care of it," he repeated without explaining. "But please don't tell anyone just yet."

Lucky McGintey ambled up to them, carrying his well-worn longrifle. "You folks all right?"

"Yes, Sir," Daniel said. "Everyone made it out all right. Kelly and Nicole just went for some water. But the fire undoubtedly scorched William and Kelly's place. Snyder deliberately set their place on fire and then he abducted Ann and took her off into the woods. Bear and I found them, but Ann was forced to kill Snyder just before we arrived."

"I'm glad you're all right, Miss Byrd," Lucky said. "Killin' a man is never easy, but you bravely defended yourself. I'm not a bit surprised it came to that. Sooner or later someone would have had to kill that no good."

Daniel, Ann, and Artis all somberly nodded their agreement.

"Did you run into any fire while you were searching for Ann?" Lucky asked Daniel.

"Indeed, but the creek banks that run alongside and behind Highland slowed the flames and kept the fire on the north side of the road into Boonesborough. It might have jumped the creek, but thankfully, the wind shifted it away."

"If it crossed the creek, the Kentucky River would have stopped it," Lucky said. He glanced up at the cloudless sky. "I wish that sky would grow black as the Earl of Hell's waistcoat and rain ten inches and then drizzle until it all dries up."

Kelly returned with the water and Daniel gulped it down his parched throat. Never had water tasted so good. "Thank you," he told her. "Where is William?"

"He's borrowing a fresh mount from the fort's stable. After racing to the fire, then carrying both William and Mrs. McGuffin back into town, and breathing all that smoky air, Smoke needed a rest," Kelly explained.

A few minutes later, William rode up to them on the borrowed horse. His uncle dismounted and Daniel quickly told him everything that had happened.

William turned to Ann and put a hand on her arm. "I'm sorry you had to experience that. I should have realized just how demented that man was. Daniel tried to tell us."

"The important thing is that Ann is safe now," Daniel said.

Tears of joy found their way to her eyes. "And we're going to be married."

Colonel Byrd gave her another hug and then issued orders to several members of the militia to ride out and assess the damage with William and Conall.

"Come with us, Daniel," William said. "I'd appreciate a family member being with me when I have to face what's waiting for me."

"Of course," Daniel answered quickly, pleased at William's reference to family. "Why don't you ladies all wait at Ann's house and rest there until we get back? Bear will figure out where you went."

"I'll tell him," Lucky volunteered. "I'll keep a lookout for him."

"First I need to find Whitefoot," Ann said. "She's probably waiting for me at the stable."

"If you have any trouble finding her, let me know," Lucky said, leaning on his longrifle. "I'll hunt her down for you."

"Thanks Lucky," Daniel told him. "Ann, when you get home, don't open any of my packages."

"Packages? At my house?" Ann asked.

"Before I left to search for you, I asked Conall to take them there so they wouldn't be loaded on Samson while I looked for you. They're some of the things we need for the wedding." He grinned and winked at her and then mounted Samson and took the horse to the water trough. As Samson drank he smiled to himself despite all the chaos and commotion caused by the fire. *Ann was safe now and they would soon be married!*

When Samson finished drinking, Daniel joined William and Conall, waiting with the others on their mounts. He turned Samson toward the road and scanned the sky. The grey cloud that had hung over Whispering Hills was now just a wisp of smoke.

ANN, ARTIS, KELLY, AND LITTLE Nicole walked together across the fort's enclosure toward the stable. Riley scampered just ahead of them, wagging his furry tail, and Artis led Glasgow behind her.

As Ann suspected, Whitefoot was waiting for her in front of the stable. Kelly's mare, her wagon team, and the milk cow were all clustered together nearby.

At the sight of the cow waiting with the horses, Kelly managed a small chuckle and Nicole pointed her tiny finger and excitedly squealed, "Cow."

"Since they're stable mates, I guess they must all be chums," Kelly told Ann and Artis.

"Friends stick together in a crisis," Ann said.

Kelly set Nicole down on a pile of fresh hay and then they got all four horses and the cow stalled, fed, and watered. Artis watered and fed Glasgow too, but only loosened the girth strap, leaving him saddled for the return trip home.

As the three exhausted women, Nicole, and Riley, strolled across the enclosure toward Ann's home, the fort's tall walls and buildings cast long late-afternoon shadows. The closer she drew to home, the more anxious Ann became about how Mother Helen would react when her stepmother learned that she had killed Snyder. The woman would likely become hysterical or at the very least distraught. She might even faint.

By the time she reached their front door, Ann decided it didn't matter what Mother Helen thought. She had done what she had to and Snyder got what he deserved.

All three women brushed most of the ash from their clothes and then Ann entered first, holding the door open for the others. Riley slipped in on Kelly's heels.

Daniel's packages stood piled in the corner of the parlor. She wondered what they contained but she was too tired to examine them.

"Nicole, would you like to play with my old dolly? Her name is Susie," Ann told her. "She's in my bedroom, right over there, sitting in the chair. Suzie would like a visitor as sweet as you."

Smiling, Nicole toddled off toward the bedroom and Riley followed her.

"Don't touch anything else, Nicole," Kelly called after her.

"Ann!" she heard Mother Helen call from the kitchen. The woman came running into the parlor, holding her dish towel.

Ann had to wonder why she wasn't helping all the other women fill buckets. Perhaps because she considered herself too good for anything that resembled strenuous labor. The woman believed women's work was restricted to the inside of a home.

Mother Helen froze when she noticed Ann's disheveled appearance and state of dress. "Good grief? What happened? Did you have an accident at Kelly's? And why are you dressed so indecently? That's a man's vest!"

Ann sighed. "Mother Helen, we are all exhausted and filthy from the fire. Can you please get some wet towels so we can clean up a bit while we talk? And some water to drink. And Nicole's in my bedroom, can you take her a cup of water too?"

"Of course," her stepmother said, and went to the kitchen. She brought back three small dampened towels, handed one to each of them and took a cup of water to Nicole. While she poured the water into three glasses, she asked, "Kelly, Conall said that the fire was over in the direction of your home. Is your place all right?"

"No," Kelly answered without elaborating. She collapsed into a nearby chair, hung her head, and rubbed her red eyes with the cool towel.

Artis took a seat as well and explained further. "William, Conall, Daniel, and some of the militia have just left to go check the fire and the extent of the damage to Kelly's home. We fear it will be extensive."

"And your home?" her stepmother asked Artis.

"We think 'tis safe," Artis answered.

Her stepmother turned to Ann. "You never said what happened to you."

"I was abducted by Snyder."

"Oh, surely you exaggerate. Men can be…"

Kelly rose, her hands clenched at her sides. "She is not exaggerating! I saw it happen myself. After she labored in my garden all day without a single grumble, we were bathing in the creek by my home to cool off. Snyder surprised us, carrying a torch, and the demon set fire to my farm for revenge. Revenge against my husband and against Daniel!"

Ann stopped her pacing and took over. "Then Charles grabbed me, forced me onto his horse, and took me off into the forest, high in the hills."

Mother Helen gasped and her eyes flew open. "Did he…"

The rest of it rushed out of Ann. "He threw me on the ground and tried to have his way with me."

"His way?" Mother Helen asked, startled.

"He tried to rape me!"

"Rape?" her stepmother asked in a suffocated whisper.

"Yes!"

Mother Helen's brow furrowed. "Did he?"

"No, I killed him just as he was about to."

Her stepmother's fingers flew to her mouth and she just stared at Ann for a few moments before she asked, "You killed Charles?"

"Yes, Mother Helen, I put the knife I carry in my boot in the center of his chest." The bitterness she heard in her own voice soured her stomach. "The man was obsessed with having me. He wouldn't give up, no matter what I said to him. He was determined to keep me away from Daniel by whatever means necessary—even raping me. Bear and Daniel came to my aid. Just as they got there, Snyder took aim at Bear and I leapt up with my knife…now Charles is dead."

Her stepmother shook her head, squeezed her eyes shut and said, "Lord have mercy on his soul."

"He was a wolf in sheep's clothin' and he does na deserve mercy," Artis swore. "Only those who turn from their wicked ways deserve the Lord's mercy."

Mother Helen stared at Artis for a long moment before she turned back to Ann. "I'm stunned by all this. He was always so nice to me."

"Because he wanted your money," Ann said. Mother Helen often made it clear that she considered her inheritance her money. She'd never volunteered to use any of it for Conall's education. She believed the responsibility for paying for Conall's legal studies rested solely with her husband. "Snyder told me you were planning to give him your inheritance once we married."

"I was..." she said, her voice dying away as she left the room.

Chapter 33

The three of them went to Ann's bedroom and cleaned up. After Kelly scrubbed Nicole's face and hands and wiped her little dress with a dampened towel, the little girl continued to play with the doll and Riley on the green and brown braided rug that covered most of the wooden floor. When Ann couldn't be outdoors because of the weather, she'd always loved playing in that room herself as a little girl. She loved her furniture made of cedar and the room's high windows displaying pine boughs and blue sky.

But most of all, she loved her mother's trunk, a gift given to her mother by Ann's grandparents. It sat at the foot of her bed and contained a few of her mother's most treasured possessions—her Bible, her dress gloves, elbow-length fingerless mitts, a linen cap, and two lace sleeve ruffles. Besides the waterfall, they were her only tangible reminders of her mother.

Very soon this wouldn't be her bedroom any longer. She would share a room and a bed with Daniel. The thought sent a pleasurable thrill galloping through her. It made her glad she was washing her face because she was certain she must have just blushed as furiously as a summer sunrise.

Ann lent Kelly one of her everyday gowns to wear but Artis insisted that her dirty work dress would suffice until she got home.

"Ye, William, and Nicole will be movin' in with Bear and me, of course," Artis told Kelly as she helped her into the gown, "until they can repair or rebuild on your place. The McGuffins are welcome too."

"Now is the time to get a home built exactly like you want it," Ann told Kelly. "Bigger and better."

Kelly chewed on her bottom lip, struggling not to cry. "It *was* exactly how I wanted it. Not only that, the smokehouse is gone with our winter hams, all my canning, the apple orchard, the fall garden we planted today, everything, even my Bible."

"Do na worry about havin' enough food for winter. We'll plant another fall garden and store the bounty in the fine new cellar Bear and Daniel just finished buildin'. And Bear can hunt enough fresh meat for all of us. The important thing is that we are all safe."

Kelly nodded and glanced down at Nicole. "You are absolutely right. That is the most important thing."

Ann knew how difficult all this must be for her friend and how much Kelly treasured that Bible. It was the only thing she had left that her mother had given her. "Oh Kelly, I can't tell you how sorry I am," Ann said. "We should postpone the wedding. You won't feel like celebrating tomorrow."

"Tomorrow?" Artis and Kelly both said.

Ann realized she hadn't yet told them. "Yes, Daniel wants to be married tomorrow. And frankly, so did I. But now I'm not so sure."

Artis and Kelly looked at one another and then Artis raised a questioning brow at Kelly.

"Perhaps it would get yer mind off yer loss," Artis told Kelly.

A hint of a smile found Kelly's lips and she said, "You know, Artis, you're right. A happy event is just what we need. If you want to get married tomorrow, Ann, then we shall have a wedding!"

"I think Daniel has already taken care of most of the arrangements," Ann said. "That pile of packages in the parlor are all for the wedding."

"Susie wants wedding," Nicole said, holding up the doll.

"Ann wants a wedding, too," she told the child and struggled to contain her tears of happiness. She reached out and wrapped an arm around both women and hugged her closest friends to her. Riley jumped up on Kelly, wanting a hug too.

Laughing, they all gave him one. Then they all sank to the floor, and chased away the day's horrific events in a playful pile of good friends, fur, and a giggling little girl.

BEAR ARRIVED AT ANN'S HOME a few minutes before William, Conall, and Daniel did. As they all suspected, the fire largely destroyed William and Kelly's farm but the flames did stop at the creek, sparing Highland. The men and militia determined that once the wind died down and the heat of the day lessened, the fire had largely burnt itself out as soon as it reached the web of neighboring creeks and streams that fed the Kentucky River. Fortunately, only two other homesteads fell to the fire's wrath but the families were both able to escape safely.

The group of them gathered in the parlor and the McGuffins got there as her father poured a brandy for those who wanted one. Ann didn't drink strong liquor often, but after the day she'd had, she accepted it gratefully.

Everyone fawned over Mrs. McGuffin, but she shooed them away saying she had only fainted from fright.

"It was more than a mere faint," Doc said. "Although it will take more than a forest fire to bring down my plucky wife."

"Keep buttering me up and I just might put some jam on your bread," she said with a saucy grin.

Doc let out a hearty chuckle, held his glass up to his smiling wife, and took a long sip of the tea he was drinking.

"How did Mr. Snyder take the news of his son's death?" William asked Bear. Little Nicole was now asleep in William's arms and he was rubbing her tiny back. An exhausted Riley was also asleep on the floor, his head resting on Kelly's feet.

"He was stricken with grief, but I do na think he was surprised," Bear said. "Evidently, Tommy Dooley and Ed Sanderson had told him that his son was going to William's place. They said Snyder planned to find Ann and take her to New Orleans to marry her before Daniel did. They tried to stop him, but he wouldn't listen to reason."

"He never did," Ann said, staring down at her hands. Hands that had been forced to kill a man. Regrets and sadness assailed her and she shook her head and then swallowed the rest of her brandy.

Bear continued, "Mr. Snyder even thanked me for bringin' his son's body back and he offered his apologies to you, Ann, after I explained the circumstances of his son's death."

"That was decent of him," Daniel said.

Bear added, "He plans only a small private service and will bury his son on his home place. I offered to help dig the grave, but he said Dooley and Sanderson could do it."

"Helen has taken herself to bed," her father told them. "I don't think she took the news of Snyder's death well."

Suddenly, Ann wasn't taking it very well either. Her thoughts became jagged and painful. Her vision colored gloomily with the memory of how it felt when she plunged the knife into Charles' chest.

"I'll speak to Helen later," her father said. "As for me, I'm incredibly proud of you Ann. You showed tremendous strength and courage."

Ann couldn't respond. A suffocating heaviness abruptly centered in her chest. She clasped her hands together and stared at them, hoping the feeling would pass.

"I agree," Daniel said. "I'm proud of her too."

"Thank you both for going after my daughter," her father told Bear and Daniel.

"I just wish she'd let me take the bastard's head off," Bear said, sounding truly disappointed.

Ann let out an exasperated sigh and tried to shake the feelings of remorse and guilt. "Let's just forget about him and all the trouble he caused. I only want to think happy thoughts on the eve of my wedding." She swallowed the lump that lingered in her throat.

Daniel tugged her close to him and wrapped his arm around her. Even though he smelled like smoke and gray soot covered his face and hair, he'd never looked more handsome to her. His warm smile made her feel better and she wanted to kiss his lips again. But that would have to wait until tomorrow night. He'd be cleaner then anyway.

"I can see the sadness you're trying to hide," Daniel whispered.

She felt an instant squeezing hurt as the wound on her heart opened again.

"You can't hide it from me, Ann. Come here." With a hand on her waist, he guided her into a quiet corner and said, "You had no choice, Ann. If you hadn't killed him, I would have. Or Bear, if Snyder hadn't killed Bear first. You likely saved my father's life. And consider what he was just about to do to you. He deserved what he got."

She recalled the sickening sensation of feeling his hand on her breast and his manhood pressing against her. He'd come shockingly close. "He *did* deserve it. I just wish it hadn't ended that way."

"It could have ended in your death. Or mine. Or my father's."

That possibility shook her to her core.

"I've come to believe all things work together for good," Daniel told her quietly. "Let's put this behind us. We have a wonderful future ahead of us and the only one who tried to take that away from us is gone. Let's be sure he stays gone." His face was full of strength and shining with hopefulness.

She vowed to herself to put the day's dreadful events behind her for good. "You're right, of course." She took a deep breath and forbade herself to think of Charles or what he did to her ever again. She knew that would not be easy. Often, the events that hurt us the most are the hardest ones to forget.

"So, guess who is going to be my best man," he said to change the subject.

"I have no idea," she answered.

Daniel took her elbow and they rejoined the others. He cleared his throat to get everyone's attention. "I am proud to announce that Conall will be my best man," Daniel said, loud enough for everyone to hear. "He's been a big help already." Daniel smiled meaningfully at Conall. "And there is the fact that he saved my life."

Everyone chuckled and congratulated Conall for both reasons.

"We set the time for the wedding at 4:00 tomorrow afternoon," Conall announced and glanced at Daniel and Ann. "And the groom and I took care of everything—food, musicians, wine. And Judge Webb will be there to conduct the ceremony. Daniel even bought me a new shirt and cravat."

"Well, you *do* have to look the part of a best man," Daniel teased. He went to the corner, picked up the gown and jewelry packages, and placed them in front of Ann after she took a seat. "And these are for you," he said, "for tomorrow when you get dressed." He turned to Bear. "Lucky will shoot something for you to roast tomorrow."

"Aye?" Bear said. "Then we are guaranteed a feast worthy of a MacKay wedding!"

Ann noticed a terrible red spot on Daniel's arm. "What's that on your arm?" she asked, alarmed. "I thought your shirt was just torn, but I saw a patch of red underneath."

"It's just a burn. Nothing to worry about."

Doc took a look at Daniel's arm. "There will be something to worry about if it festers," Doc said. "Artis has some of my special ointment for wounds. Just as soon as you get home, I want you wash it well and then put some ointment on it and again in the morning and every day for a week."

"I'll see that he does," Artis said.

"So I will," Ann said. Then she glanced up in surprise when Mother Helen strode into the room. She braced herself for what must be coming. The tension in the room loomed between them like an oppressive fog.

Her stepmother nodded at everyone and said, "Hello everyone. Forgive my absence. I laid down for a moment and fell asleep." She marched up to Ann and took her hand. "Ann, dear, I owe you a profound apology. Instead of wanting what would make you happy, I pushed for what I believed would make me happy. I was so wrong. Can you ever forgive me?"

Ann wrapped her arms around her stepmother's back and said, "Yes, of course I will." The friction between them melted in that heartfelt hug.

Mother Helen stepped back, still holding her hand. "Conall said those packages there are for your wedding."

"They are," Daniel answered.

"Did you buy her a veil?" her stepmother asked him.

"No, I never thought about it," Daniel said. "I'll buy one tomorrow."

"No need, Daniel. Ann, I want you to wear mine. It was my mother's before it was mine and you are now welcome to it. Someday, you can give it to your daughter. I'll dig it out of my chest in the morning and we'll try it on you. You are so beautiful I know you will look like an angel in it."

"Oh, Mother Helen," Ann told her. "You've made me so happy. Now my wedding will be complete."

"It's getting late now," her stepmother told everyone. "A bride needs her beauty sleep. And every one of you looks dog-tired, even the dog."

"I'll need to borrow a wagon from you, Colonel," William said, "to take Mrs. McGuffin, Kelly, and Nicole home."

"And Riley," Kelly added, patting the dog.

"I'll help you hitch it up," her father told him. "But first, finish up your drinks, all of you, while Daniel takes Ann outside to say goodnight." Her father winked at Daniel.

They all chuckled, even Kelly and William, as Ann and Daniel left hastily, hand in hand.

Chapter 34

The next morning, Daniel thought Highland rather resembled a bee hive there was so much activity. Last night, Kelly, William, Nicole, Doc, and Mrs. McGuffin, and Riley had all come back with them and were given rooms upstairs on either side his room. Exhausted, they'd all gone to bed at once.

But this morning, Artis buzzed here and there, giving everyone assignments to get tables draped and set for a buffet, wildflowers arranged, floors swept and mopped, and water for washing up put in each bedroom.

Bear kept telling Artis to take it easy since she was with child, and she kept ignoring him.

It amazed Daniel how the family was able to quickly regroup from the fire, helping one another not only to cope and recover, but to prepare for a joyous celebration. This was what family was all about and it pleased him to be a part of it.

The burned forest would quickly recover as well and would soon overflow again with beautiful wooded spots brimming with life. Lucky had told him earlier that fire was a necessary part of the cycle of life in the wilderness. Life would not only go on, the forest would benefit from the fire. The flames left large patches of ground open to the sun. Seeds released from heated pinecones would take root and begin to grow. He remembered from his science classes that nutrients from ash helped new vegetation to prosper. Wildflowers would be abundant by the following spring and the grasses a rich green.

Thankfully, though, the fire spared Highland—a home large enough for all of them to share until homes could be rebuilt.

Daniel joined Bear and Lucky on a grassy area well away from the big house. The meat Lucky brought hung from a tree branch. Daniel mostly watched and helped a little as Bear and Lucky skinned the wild boar that Lucky shot sometime during the night. The aging hunter said wild hogs roamed the forest during the night and there had been enough of a moon for him to spot one in the woods to the south, in an area the fire did not reach.

After they finished removing the animal's hide and entrails, they were going to soak the meat in brine for a couple hours, and then mount the whole pig on the roasting spit by running a rod through the pelvis, down the spine and out through the mouth. Afterwards, they said they would use soaked braided rawhide to tightly fasten the pig to the spit. Lastly, they would tie a rope to the spit handle with a heavy block on the rope's other end to lock the spit handle in position whenever it was turned during roasting.

Bear explained that he would turn the meat every quarter hour for the next five hours, after which it would be ready to eat.

"At each quarter turn, Lucky and I will share a wee droppy," Bear said. "It's a Scots tradition when roasting meat."

Daniel laughed, suspecting that his father might have made it his own tradition. "I'm looking forward to learning more of our Scottish traditions. But can a drunk Scotsman cook? That is the question, Sir."

"Although they sometimes consume more than their share, Scots do na get drunk. Whiskey is like water to us. That's why we call it the breath of life. I promise ye, the meat 'twill be moist with a nice smoky flavor and crispy skin," Bear said. "And by that time, Lucky and I will be feelin' no aches in our bones." Bear and Lucky exchanged a companionable smile.

Lucky nodded. "Pour me a little of that lightning rod," he told Bear as Lucky finished the first rotation.

"Just keep that whiskey away from the fire," Daniel advised. "I'll be back soon. I'm going for ride."

DANIEL MARCHED OFF, SADDLED SAMSON, and headed toward Whispering Hills. He felt responsible for the fire, because he hadn't succeeded in stopping Snyder, and he wanted to see if anything could be salvaged from the main cabin.

When he arrived, he found both cabins still smoldering. After tying Samson, he made his way to the larger of the two cabins. He stepped through the piles of ash and partially burned logs, carefully avoiding spots with the faint glow of embers that might still be hot. The scent of burnt wood and ash quickly invaded his lungs. What once was a cozy cabin now resembled a black skeleton. The roof had completely crumbled in, but most of the thick log walls still stood, charred, blackened, and emaciated.

He didn't know what he hoped to find or why he was even here. But something compelled him to keep looking. He kicked over a partially melted metal pail. Then he spotted an overturned iron pot—Kelly's Dutch oven. Its lid lay nearby. Neither had melted. Maybe the pot was what he was supposed to find. Although probably not significant or sentimental, at least Kelly would have that. He turned it over. The sight before him made him kneel on the charred ground.

A small Bible.

The intense heat had cracked and crinkled its cover and singed pieces fell off in his hands when he picked it up. But miraculously the inside was still completely intact. All those beautiful words refused to burn.

The Bible had been saved. Just as his own scorched heart had been saved from the flames of grief and the shame of illegitimacy. He thanked God for saving both.

Daniel stood up, clutching the Bible. He opened it to the first page and read the inscription. *To my beloved daughter Kelly.* It was signed by her mother. But how did it survive? He studied the spot and could see what looked like the remnants of a table. Kelly must have been reading it in her kitchen. When the table burned, both the pot and the Bible must have slipped to the floor at the same time and the pot covered the precious book.

His face creased into a sudden smile.

WHEN DANIEL RETURNED AND STABLED Samson, he dusted his breeches and boots off with a rag, trying to remove all traces of ash. He still had some soot under his fingernails, but he would get that out later when he bathed. Before he'd left Whispering Hills, he'd retrieved a small piece of doe skin from his saddle bag and carefully wrapped the Bible to protect it. He reached in and withdrew the package from the saddle bag and headed toward the house.

He found Doc hard at work out back because he'd volunteered to wash everyone's smoky smelling clothing. He told Daniel that he insisted that his wife take it easy today.

Daniel grinned when he walked in the back door and heard Mrs. McGuffin insisting that she do something to help. Artis sat her down in the kitchen to peel potatoes.

Conall had told him that he would arrive early and bring the packages with the doll and candy. There hadn't been enough time last night to have Ann open the packages with her dress and jewelry to see if they were all right with her. He hoped they would be and that the dress would fit.

He couldn't wait to see her in the lovely gown he'd bought. Even more, he couldn't wait to take it off her. For a moment, he imagined what she might look like with nothing more than her silky tresses to adorn her shapely body. It wouldn't be long before he found out.

Earlier, Artis had given Kelly one of her gowns to wear today and Kelly sat in the parlor making minor alterations to it. He decided to wait until the wedding to give Kelly his precious find. Then the entire family could share her joy.

Daniel had loaned William some of his own attire. When William had tried them on, they were a little loose-fitting, but at least they were clean. Bear leant Mr. McGuffin one of his shirts and a pair of breeches he could use. The shirt was too big in the shoulders and the pants were a bit tight in the waist, but they would have to do. Mrs. McGuffin, being a rather portly woman, could only wear one of Bear's large night shirts until her own gown was washed and dried. They would all look a little ragtag at the wedding, but no one seemed to care.

Daniel stored the Bible in his room and hurried downstairs again. As he walked through the house, headed toward the front, William glanced up. His uncle's face and shirt were sweat-soaked from mopping the large front room and the rest of the downstairs.

"You missed a spot," he told his Uncle and pointed.

"I'll show you a spot!" William threatened and chased Daniel out the front door with the mop dripping a wet trail behind him. William chased him until they both had to quit they were laughing so hard.

Bear and Lucky continued to feed the gently burning fire all afternoon and occasionally swathed the boar with a mixture of butter and herbs. After a couple of hours, the roasting meat's succulent smell filled the air, making everyone's stomach growl. But the strong, delicious aroma was welcome because it covered the lingering scent of the forest fire.

As they kept watch over the roasting meat, Bear and Lucky began singing songs. Here and there, he could hear the other members of the family humming along with them.

He spent an hour or so helping Doc with the dirty laundry, wringing out and hanging the clothes to dry on the fence. Then he used the same large iron washtub to heat bathing water for everyone. He hauled bucket after bucket of the warm water into the only bathtub located in Artis and Bear's wash room, adjacent to their large bedroom. Each person in the family took turns in the tub and every person, with the exception of Nicole, emptied the tub by throwing water out the window onto Artis' flowerbed.

He finally took the last bath himself and never enjoyed a bath more. He washed and scrubbed until his fingertips started to wrinkle. Then he used a pocket knife to remove the ash from under his nails. Finally, he washed his hair with some of Bear's hair soap.

"Are you going to soak in there all day?" Conall called. "You'd better come out soon or you'll miss your own wedding."

Daniel laughed, sprang up, and grabbed his towel. "I'll be out in a flash."

The two were soon upstairs in his room dressing for the wedding.

"Has the baker's delivery arrived?" he asked Conall as he finished shaving. "And the wine?"

"Well, when I arrived, I witnessed twelve wine bottles lined up like soldiers on the table. I also observed six pies and a cake mustering for a celebration so I would surmise that the evidence suggests that your delivery did in fact arrive."

"You sound like a lawyer already," Daniel said. "And that is *not* a compliment."

Conall gave him a lazy grin and said, "Judge Webb told me lawyers are like coyotes because they talk so loud, so long, and so much, without saying anything. I've been practicing."

"Speaking of saying something, you know you have to give the best man speech at the wedding don't you?"

Conall smiled. "Yes, that is the traditional *modus operandi*."

"You're becoming annoying, Conall. Perhaps you should go to architecture school instead of law school."

Conall shook his head. "I can't draw a straight line. Do you have something you want me to say?"

Daniel grew serious and thought for a moment. "Yes, there is something. When I left Philadelphia, aside from a few close friends, I had nothing…except wealth."

Startled, Conall released the cravat he was in the process of tying in front of the mirror and turned around to face him.

"Now, I have everything. A father and a family. But most of all, Ann. And I want to share my good fortune with all of you."

"How?" Conall asked.

"For you, I want to pay for your legal education in Lexington, including your room and board there."

Conall gasped and his mouth fell open. "You mean to say you're actually rich?"

Daniel nodded and pressed on. "For William and Kelly and the McGuffins, I will offer to pay, if they'll let me, for their new homes to be built. For Kelly and Mrs. McGuffin, in anticipation of enjoying their delicious pies for years to come, I will order one of Benjamin Franklin's new stoves."

"They will be thrilled," Conall said.

"I have another idea. For Bear and Artis, Stephen and Jane, and Sam and Catherine, I will buy each couple a fine thoroughbred mare which we will breed first to Artis' Glasgow and the following year to Samson. They're both exceptional stallions from good bloodlines and if we breed them to quality mares, we can have a real family horse race in two or three years. And we can start selling their offspring. There will be a big demand for quality horses as the country expands westward and after talking to Artis and Sam, I believe we have the makings for a strong family business that could be quite lucrative."

Conall merely stared, tongue-tied and astonished. "Your generosity is… completely overwhelming. I don't know what to say, except thank you."

"I didn't earn the money to do this. My father in Philadelphia, John Armitage, did. And I know he would be pleased if I use it now to help my new family. He was a generous and kind man who loved my mother even when most men would have shunned her for carrying another man's child. That child was me and I owe it to him to use a portion of his life savings to show others a similar generosity and goodwill. It will be in his name that I do all this. I loved him. And it would be difficult for me to say all that in front of everyone. My grief is still too fresh and I know I will be thinking about him at the wedding. So, I would be grateful if you would do it for me."

"I would be honored, Daniel. I'm also honored that it is you who is marrying my sister. In an hour or so, we'll not only be friends, we'll be brothers."

"When you have completed your studies in Lexington, perhaps we can practice law together somewhere where Ann wants to live, here in Boonesborough or in Lexington or Louisville. I don't care, as long as she's happy. I lack only a few courses and I have decided to finish my studies early next year. We can both go to Lexington and meet Edward and Mr. Tudor. Bear and William said their law school should be open by January."

"Yes, that's right. But what about Ann? Will you take her with us to Lexington?"

"Of course. You don't think I'm going to let my new bride out of my sight do you?"

Artis called up to them. "Daniel! Ann is here!"

At last. Daniel started toward his bedroom door, his heart already racing.

"Oh no you don't," Conall said, grabbing his elbow. "I've been ordered to keep the groom up here until summoned by the bride's father. He's a colonel, you know, and we must follow orders."

Chapter 35

Daniel took a step toward the door. "Conall, I am going to go greet my bride. Right now! Please stand aside."

Arms outstretched, Conall blocked the door. "No. I am my sister's brother and she wants a chance to freshen up before you see her. She's just finished a thirty minute wagon ride. And you know how women are. She wants to look her best."

Daniel threw his hands up in the air. "The woman couldn't look any better if she were bedecked and bejeweled by a dozen queen's attendants."

Conall eyed him with little sympathy but he lowered his arms. "You've waited this long, you can wait a few more minutes."

Daniel began pacing the room to cover his annoyance. Even though the bedroom was spacious in size, he felt trapped. He was about to be married and the last thing he wanted to do was wait. He suddenly wondered if Judge Webb was there. "Did you see the judge?"

"He came with my parents and Ann."

"What about the musicians?"

"They arrived while you were bathing. When you were soaking for so long, they were practicing and Bear and Lucky were singing along. Your father has quite a nice baritone by the way."

Daniel opened the window and he could hear them even though his room faced the back of the property and the musicians were in the front.

"What did you do with Nicole's doll and the candy?"

"It's still in the bag and sitting on the table near the wine. You can give it to her later this evening."

Daniel nodded. "Have we thought of everything?"

"Do you have a ring?" Conall asked.

"I've ordered a fine one but it will be a few weeks getting here."

Clearly aware of Daniel's growing annoyance, Conall tried to coax him into a better mood. "Look at it this way. Once the wedding is over you will only have to put up with all of us for a few more hours."

That didn't help. He wanted Ann all to himself now, not later. And besides, they were having to spend their wedding night in a house full of people. He didn't like the idea one bit and Conall became the victim of his glare.

His soon to be brother-in-law quickly looked away. "Perhaps I should go get some of Bear's whiskey to calm you down."

"I don't need any whiskey. I just need to marry Ann."

Someone tapped on the door and when Daniel told them to come in, Bear and Colonel Byrd stepped in. Both men wore their best clothing and polished boots. The Colonel wore a navy blue and gold military styled coat and Bear wore a well-made green coat with gold buttons down the wide lapels. Bear's dark red hair was wet and combed neatly. And for the first time since Daniel's arrival, he was also clean shaven. His father's smart appearance made him look quite the gentleman.

Bear took a long appraising glance at Daniel. "Ye look as handsome as a prince. Are ye ready?"

Conall laughed. "He's as ready as a racehorse at the starting line."

"My daughter looks as beautiful as a princess," Byrd told him. "And she's awaiting you."

"At long last!" Daniel said as he rushed out and raced down the stairs followed by the other men.

William stood in the front room waiting for them.

"Wait!" Bear called, stopping him. "I have a wee gift for ye."

Daniel turned and took a few steps back. He watched as Bear grabbed something off the mantel.

"'Twas my father's. 'Tis yours now. A *sgian-dubh*."

He took the small, single-edged knife with an antler handle.

Bear pointed to the blade. "'Tis a traditional part of Scottish Highland dress. And I'd be pleased if ye would wear it on your weddin' day. Ye can tuck it into your boot or hose."

"It would be my honor. Thank you," Daniel said. He was truly honored to be given something that belonged to his grandfather. He glanced down at the knife again. "What was his name?"

"Daniel Alexander MacKay," Bear answered with a sudden sparkle in his eyes. "A truly good man."

"Then Ann and I shall give our first born son that worthy name." He bent to the top of one of his tall boots and used the clip on the knife's sheath to attach the *sgian-dubh* to the inside of the boot. He gave the knife a heartfelt pat and then gazed affectionately at his father.

Bear swallowed and cleared his throat.

"And the name of your second son?" Colonel Byrd prodded.

"John Byrd MacKay, of course," Daniel said.

Colonel Byrd grinned broader than Daniel had ever seen him.

It came as no surprise when Conall asked, "And your third son?"

"Now hold on. I'm not even married yet," he told him.

"I'd say 'tis time to get on with it then," Bear said.

"I'll lead the way," William said.

The five of them exited through the front door and moved off the porch. They would hold the ceremony where it would be cooler under the shade of the larger hardwood trees in the front of the house. And in the front, Bear and Lucky could also keep guard over the pig still slowly roasting nearby over a low fire. They didn't want to risk any area bears or other troublesome varmints trying to sample it.

Colonel Byrd quickly stepped over to stand beside his wife and Conall stood next to his father. Bear joined Artis and William stood beside Kelly, who held Nicole's tiny hand. The little girl held a small bouquet of wildflowers in her other hand. The McGuffins were both standing behind Nicole. Lucky and Judge Webb waited with the others.

They all stood there awaiting Daniel. But where was Ann?

The musicians, sitting on log stools clustered off to the side, started playing a soft romantic melody. The notes stirred the air and filled the woods. The entrancing music sounded so lovely that Daniel was sure that even the birds must be listening. The strong rays of the setting sun streamed through the trees and their shafts of light lit the ribbons tied around the largest trunks. He found it hard to believe that just a few miles to the west, what was left of the forest stood scorched and blackened. But here, the setting seemed magical.

And, as if she were conjured by some fairy, Ann stepped out from behind the trunk of the largest pine.

Daniel froze, unable to move. Before him, stood the most beautiful woman in the world. Her eyes looked like green opals and gleamed with tiny tears that glistened like diamonds. Her cheeks glowed with heightened color. Her full mouth curved in an enchanting smile. She truly did look like a princess. When he'd seen the ivory satin gown in the store it was lovely, but adorning Ann's body it was positively stunning. And the necklace and earrings he'd bought to match seemed even more exquisite displayed on her slender neck and perfect little ears. Her stepmother's lace veil draped from her head to her chest, framing her face.

Just as he felt the first time he laid eyes on her at the ball, Daniel was drawn to Ann with a force so powerful he would rather die than resist. His breath quickened as he closed the distance between them and reached for her hand. Her excitement must be as great as his because he could feel a slight tremble as he took her hand in his and led her toward the others.

When they stood before everyone, he looked intently into Ann's face. "Before we marry, I want to say that it would be easier to count every grain of sand in the ocean than to tell you all that you mean to me. I will love you each minute of every day for the rest of my life." He gazed into her sparkling eyes and squeezed her hand.

Ann took a deep breath and said, "It would be easier for me to count all the stars in the heavens than to tell you all the ways I love you. I will treasure every moment with you for the rest of my life."

A breeze that seemed to whisper the love they shared lifted the edges of her veil. He softly kissed the top of her head, claiming her as his, now and forever.

After a nudge from her mother, Little Nicole toddled over to Ann and handed her the bouquet.

"Thank you my little wedding angel," Ann told her.

Bear said a heartfelt prayer asking for God's blessing on their marriage and then Judge Webb proceeded with the ceremony that would make their union legal in the eyes of man.

As soon as the judge finished, he kissed Ann for the first time as her husband, a moment he would remember forever. He pressed his mouth to hers, kissing her devouringly. When he released her lips, he slipped an arm behind her back and tugged her toward him. "I love you."

"And I you," she whispered.

Everyone gawked at the two of them for a moment and then clapped. As soon as Artis filled each person's glasses, the wedding festivities began with toasting.

Bear was the first to raise his glass. "I congratulate ye both on yer weddin' and pray that the best of happiness, honor, and fortune will always be with you."

Everyone toasted and then Bear continued, "Daniel, ye should know that bein' the husband of a strong-willed lass with an independence of spirit is na an easy task." He eyed Artis and said, "Believe me I know." Everyone chuckled and Bear continued, "I have but one piece of advice. If reason fails, do na try force. Kisses work far better."

Artis called out, "Aye, they do!"

Daniel laughed so hard he nearly spurt out the sip of brandy he'd just taken and Lucky cackled and guffawed so much he fell off the log stool he was sitting on.

"Ye see what I mean lad? But I know ye are up to the task, Daniel. My lovely wife and I wish ye both much happiness and many blessin's." Bear held up his glass yet again and said, "To a man after my own heart, my son, and to his bride Ann whose beauty is only exceeded by her bravery."

Daniel nodded his thanks and raised his own cup. "When I first arrived here and met all of you, I didn't know if I could ever feel like I belonged here. You were all so close to one another and I felt like a stranger in a place I didn't belong. I very nearly left."

Everyone gasped, especially Bear, and their smiles faded.

"But your overwhelming love and generous spirits brought me into your family's circle little by little." Daniel glanced at Bear and swallowed his emotions before he could continue. "And my father's affection was so great, he even gave me his proud name. Not only will I honor the MacKay name, I will teach my children and their children to do the same. You are all blessed to have a devoted and loyal family and the more I got to know all of you, the more I grew to respect and love you."

"We love ye too," Artis said. "And our family's bond and faithfulness will never leave you, even when we have gone to live with our maker."

"Here, here," William and Kelly said, raising their cups.

"It is my wish to repay that generosity. I have come up with a plan to honor the memory of my father in Philadelphia. I have asked Conall, my best man, to share with all of you how I plan to do that."

Conall began by welcoming him into the Byrd family too. "I could not be more pleased to have this fine man as my new brother." After that Conall told them all of Daniel's plans to share his wealth.

Ann appeared to be the most surprised. Her eyes and mouth both flew open.

Then Conall explained how Daniel wanted to help his new family.

When Conall finished, Kelly and William, carrying Nicole in his arms, rushed over. Smiling broadly, Kelly hugged him and William shook his hand. "You have no idea how grateful we are," William said.

"Wedding," Nicole said, pointing at Daniel.

"And we're grateful too," Mrs. McGuffin said. "I thought Doc and I were going to have to live in his apothecary in town because we did not want to impose on Bear and Artis for too long. And a Franklin stove! I promise you the first pie I bake in it."

Daniel chuckled. "I am already looking forward to it, Mrs. McGuffin."

"And Nicole gets the first cookies," Mrs. McGuffin told the child.

"Cookie?" Nicole said.

"Uh oh," William said.

Daniel came to the rescue. "Guess what I have for you, Nicole?"

"Cookie?" Nicole asked, her hopeful face as sweet as a cherub's.

"No, it's even better. A present just for you." He took her by the hand and they went to get the doll. He wouldn't give her the candy until after she'd eaten her dinner. Her eyes widened at the sight of the pretty doll. He sat her in a chair to play with it while he raced upstairs, retrieved the wrapped Bible, took it downstairs, and set it aside. He returned with the smiling little girl carrying the doll in her arms and handed Nicole back to William.

Artis and Bear joined them. "Thank ye for the gift of a mare for Glasgow," Artis said. "Thanks to you, our family will raise some fine horses together here in Kentucky."

"You are welcome. I'm looking forward to a prosperous partnership."

Colonel Byrd said, "Helen and I thank you for your generous support of Conall's legal education. I thought I was going to have to beg an out of town banker for a loan. Our local, pompous banker refused to lend to me unless I would agree to let his son marry Ann. I turned him down, of course. He made repeated offers, each time offering me a little sweeter deal."

Daniel's smile vanished, wiped away by his astonishment. That explained why Snyder kept thinking he would eventually have Ann. He was counting on his father to negotiate a favorable marriage contract.

Judge Webb appeared outraged. "That banker is contemptable. To think he would try to use a young woman in exchange for a loan."

"I've come to realize his scruples, along with his son's, must be locked up in his bank," Mrs. Byrd said.

Everyone nodded their agreement.

"He must have locked up his common sense too," Colonel Byrd said. "He believes the militia will not be needed in the future because of the peace treaty with the natives."

Bear shook his big head. "Nay, the militia and an army will always be needed. Strength is our best defense. And Sam says our troubles with Britain are na over."

"I am of the same opinion," Judge Webb said.

Daniel nodded. "Diplomatic relations between a soundly trounced archaic monarchy and a young upstart republic are not likely in the coming years. Britain will seek to even the score. War is inevitable."

"I believe that as well," the Colonel said. "In fact, if you are agreeable, I was hoping you would start training my militia in the use of a sword. The state of Kentucky is paying for a sword for every volunteer militiaman. But they will be useless without the proper training."

"I would be happy to do so," Daniel said. "But Conall and I will be leaving for Lexington in January. Can we start training your militia right away?"

"Absolutely," Byrd said. "The sooner the better."

"Enough of politics!" Artis said. "'Tis time for celebratin', eatin', and drinkin'. And I wish ye would get on with it! Bear's babe has made me famished."

She was right. It was time to eat, drink, and rejoice. But he needed to do something first. In a loud voice, he said, "Artis, please give me just a minute or two. If you could all gather together and wait here for a moment." Then he spun around, retrieved the Bible, and raced outside again. "Kelly," he said and motioned her forward. "This is for you." He handed her the wrapped book.

She unfolded the doeskin and with widened eyes stared down at the Bible for a few moments. When she glanced up, she asked, "How?"

"It was some kind of miracle, I guess," Daniel said and told her how and when he'd found it. "I have a friend in Philadelphia who is a book binder. If you would like, we can ship it to him and I'll have a new cover put on it for you."

"Oh Daniel, I can't thank you enough. My mother gave me this," she said, her voice breaking as she wept for joy. "It's all I have of her."

Mrs. McGuffin wrapped an arm around her stepdaughter's shaking shoulders.

"She was so happy the day she bought it for you," Doc said. "I'll never forget that day."

Kelly smiled at her father as if she were a child again.

Ann and Artis both hugged Kelly too and Bear said, "Kelly, if ye do na mind, may we use that Bible to bless the food?"

Kelly handed it to Bear and he placed a hand on the Bible as he said a heartfelt blessing and then handed it back.

Kelly carefully rewrapped the book and took it to her room for safekeeping.

Ann's eyes bathed him in admiration. "That was so kind of you."

"I merely found it. God or her mother saved it for her."

She gave him a quick kiss. "Shall we eat, husband?"

Bear and William started carving the roasted pig and from the looks and smell of it, Daniel was certain it would be the best meat he'd ever tasted. Kelly and Artis began pouring wine and slicing bread while Mrs. McGuffin served up the corn she'd been boiling in buttered water. Doc made sure everyone had a plate and eating utensils.

But food was not what Daniel was hungry for. Just a few more hours and he would be able to truly make Ann his wife. The thrilling notion flooded him with warmth, both arousing and poignant.

When everyone finished eating, the musicians began playing again and he led Ann to the area Bear cleared earlier in the day for dancing. He took her into his arms, marveling at the great beauty he held. The setting sun cast her in a warm light that only accentuated her lovely features and made her dark hair shine like polished glass. The lacey veil now rested on her bare shoulders like a delicate net that had captured his bride for him.

As their bodies swayed to and fro, he asked her, "Are you happy, my darling?"

"Yes, Daniel, very very happy."

Chapter 36

Daniel and everyone else momentarily paused their celebrating to look toward the road when a Barouche turned into the path leading up to Highland. The fancy four-wheeled carriage had a fold-up hood at the back and with spacious inside seats that faced each other. Daniel could see a well-dressed man and woman with smiling faces riding inside the carriage.

"William, look!" Bear cried. "'Tis Edward and Dora!"

The coach driver snapped the reins to hurry the horse team along and soon the dusty carriage pulled up to all of them.

So this is Edward, Daniel thought, the brother who recently relocated to Kentucky and now lived in Lexington.

"Are we in time for the ceremony?" Edward called out to Bear, even before his boots hit the ground.

Bear enveloped Edward in a massive hug. "Ye just missed it, but ye did na miss the celebration!" Bear stepped over to help Dora down from the carriage and then hugged her too.

In the next couple of minutes, Artis, William, Kelly, and the McGuffins were also hugging the new arrivals and Lucky, the Byrds, and Judge Webb all enthusiastically shook their hands.

Like Daniel's other uncles, this man was tall and quite handsome. A fine sword hung at his side and his pistol appeared to be well made. He wore a nicely tailored double-breasted tailcoat made from brown linen—the fabric undoubtedly a concession to the uncomfortable summer heat. A fashionable top hat covered his head rather than a cocked tricorne. Daniel knew that in the last few years, gentlemen began to replace the tricorne with the top hat, but he never cared for the new style of hat.

Edward's wife was truly lovely. Her splendid royal blue gown complemented her auburn hair and warm skin color.

Judge Webb told Edward, "I see you made it. I was beginning to worry."

"We left as soon as I received your message this morning," Edward said. "It took us about two and a half hours. We went into Boonesborough first to arrange for a room and clean up from the trip before we came here."

Daniel wondered how Edward managed to acquire a room when he hadn't been able to.

Judge Webb folded his arms and a glint of humor crossed his face. "Actually, the inn was full, but I persuaded the owner to hold his best room for you for two nights. He owed me a favor."

"Ye invited Edward and Dora?" Bear asked the judge.

Judge Webb nodded. "Indeed I did. I thought it would be a great surprise for all of you after all the trouble you've been through lately. I had a rider going to Lexington this morning anyway to deliver some legal documents for me."

"This *is* a terrific surprise," William said. "Edward and Dora's visit here on their way to Lexington was far too short."

Bear glanced toward Daniel and Ann. His father motioned them forward. "Edward and Dora, I'd like ye to meet my son, Daniel, and his bride and brand new wife, Ann."

The four shook hands and then Edward hugged them too. "What a great pleasure it was to learn that Bear had a son."

Daniel smiled at his new uncle. "I've been looking forward to meeting you. Bear and Artis speak fondly of you both."

Dora glanced toward Ann. "Congratulations on your marriage. We're newlyweds as well. We married earlier this summer in Boston before moving here to be closer to Edward's brothers and their families."

"I'm so glad ye did," Bear said. He put a hand on Daniel's shoulder. "And now, with my son here too, our entire family is reunited."

"That deserves a toast," Edward said. "Can a man get a beverage worthy of a toast here?"

Bear laughed. "Aye, that can be arranged. And call yer coachman over here. He's welcome to eat and drink too."

As soon as each person held a drink, Edward raised his cup and told Daniel, "I am honored to welcome you and your lovely bride to our family, Daniel."

Everyone cheered and then took a sip of their drinks.

Edward swallowed a couple of swigs before he said, "I pledge to help you in any way I can, nephew. I hope you and Ann will consider coming to Lexington for your honeymoon. It's a fine city with many pleasing attractions. What once was a rough, wild settlement in the wilderness has transformed into what many call the Athens of the West. Dora's father, Douglas Tudor, and I are founding an institute of higher education and a law school. Then Mr. Tudor will become the 'tutor' to the west."

Daniel and Ann chuckled, amused by Edward's play on words. It seemed Edward and William shared a tendency to create witty puns.

Judge Webb stepped forward. "I enjoy going to Lexington. I haven't been to your home town, Daniel, but I'm told the main street of Lexington now resembles Market Street in Philadelphia on a busy day."

Daniel glanced at Ann. "What do you think about honeymooning in Lexington? Shall we take Edward up on his offer?"

"Sounds wonderful!" she said. Her cheeks colored under the heat of his amorous gaze.

"It's settled then," Edward said. "Dora and I have purchased a fine big home with a guest house in the back. You are both welcome to honeymoon in the guest house for as long as you like."

"That is exceedingly gracious of you," Daniel said. "We can stay for a week, but then I want to get back to help with rebuilding the homes we lost to the fire."

"Yes, we could smell the fire as we got closer. How far away was it?" Edward asked.

"Just a mile or two north and west of here," Bear said. "We lost William and Kelly's place to the fire and Doc and Mrs. McGuffin's cabin there too. And the homesteads of two other families burned."

"How dreadful," Edward told William.

"We'll all pitch in and help rebuild," Daniel said. "I'll also need to get back to help my father build a smokehouse here at Highland and a new one at Whispering Hills. Bear is going to teach me to hunt." It came as a bit of shock to Daniel that he already had an understanding of the urgent need on the frontier to prepare for winter and he wanted to do his part. "And, Colonel Byrd has asked me to start training the militia on the use of a sword."

Edward placed his hand on the hilt of his sword. "I've just taken up fencing lessons. Perhaps you can give me some pointers while you're in Lexington."

"We heard about the fire from people at the inn," Dora said. "I'm so sorry for the loss of your home William and Kelly."

Daniel was certain that William and Kelly were both still in shock. Undoubtedly it was difficult for them to come to grips with the enormity of their loss.

Edward told William, "Losing your home must be exceedingly difficult."

"It is, but thanks to Daniel's kind generosity, we'll be able to rebuild," William said, with a glance at Daniel.

Edward raised his brows and smiled.

Bear held up a hand. He was about to say something when William added, "We needed a bigger home anyway. Kelly just told me she's expecting our second child."

Mrs. McGuffin squealed and Doc yelped with joy and clapped his hands.

"'Tis outstandin' news indeed!" Bear said. "And Artis and I have good news as well. I am very proud to say that Artis is also with child."

Daniel could almost see his father's chest swell with pride.

"It must be something in Kentucky's water," Edward said, "because Dora is expecting a babe too!"

Everyone hugged Kelly, Artis, and Dora and joyously congratulated all three fathers.

"Our bairns are comin' faster than a family of rabbits. Pretty soon our babes will be hoppin' all over." Bear said, laughing, and slapping Edward heartily on the back. "Congratulations, Edward!"

Edward's eyebrows shot up and his breath flew out of him as he was thrust forward by the powerful whack. "Bear," Edward barked, "I see you haven't yet learned to control your strength."

Bear grimaced. "I'm sorry man. I was just so happy for ye. And for William and me too. Three babes! Just imagine!"

After everyone absorbed the news of the coming babes, the wedding celebration resumed and the musicians started playing music once more. Mrs. McGuffin said she would show Edward and Dora where the food was and help them fill their plates while Daniel poured each of them some wine.

As Daniel picked up a wine bottle, he heard Judge Webb and Lucky involved in a political discussion again. Bear and William and their wives went off to dance and Little Nicole continued to sit in Doc McGuffin's lap, where she'd spent much of the last few hours. Daniel could tell that the man was over the moon for his darling granddaughter.

As Ann spoke with her parents and Conall, Daniel could not keep his eyes off of her. Surely she was the most beautiful bride ever. Her dark hair swung about her shoulders as she spoke excitedly to her family, who was now his family as well.

Daniel filled Dora and Edward's wineglasses and strode toward them. He could already tell he was going to grow fond of Edward. The man seemed to be a prince among men. Refined, polished, and gallant, Edward was unlike his other brothers, especially Sam, who was a far more rugged individual. Sam was the type of man you would want to protect your back in a fight. He suspected Sam possessed the same refined qualities as Edward, but only exhibited those traits when the occasion required it. Stephen and William's demeanors were somewhere in between Edward's and Sam's. And his father seemed to possess the strengths of all of them. Maybe that explained why Bear was such a titan of a man.

"Thank you," Edward said accepting the glass. "Have you arranged for a place to take your bride tonight?"

"No, Sir, I have not. The inn was full when I inquired about a room and...well other choices in Boonesborough are nonexistent."

Edward reached into his elegant embroidered waistcoat pocket and handed him a key.

"What's this?" Daniel asked.

"Our wedding present for you and Ann," Edward said. "Our room at the inn is yours for the next two nights."

Mouth agape, Daniel stared at him. "I'm so grateful. I don't know what to say."

Edward smiled and said, "It's a decent and fairly private room at the end of the hall on the second floor. When you get to Lexington, the guest house will be far nicer, but at least you'll have a room for your wedding night." He took a slow drink of his wine. "I brought our bags with us, figuring we would want to stay the night after celebrating."

"Are you sure?" Daniel asked. "I don't want to take your room."

"We'll stay here with Bear and Artis—in your room I suppose. I'd like to spend some time with Bear and William anyway. And then day after tomorrow, Dora and I will return to Lexington and you are welcome to travel with us. We can let the ladies ride in the carriage and I can ride Ann's mount."

Inclining his head, Daniel said, "Thank you, Edward. Perhaps someday I can repay your kindness."

"You are most welcome. Judge Webb tells me you have nearly completed your legal education."

"Yes, I plan to attend your school in January if it's open by then. Conall, who just graduated from William and Mary, wants to attend as well, but he is just beginning his legal education."

"Dora! We have our first two students!" Edward called over to his wife who joined them at once.

"Really?" she asked Edward. "That's wonderful."

"Yes, both Daniel and Conall plan to attend in the fall. Daniel to finish up and Conall will be starting his legal education."

"Father will be so pleased when we tell him," Dora said. She turned to Daniel. "My father was a well-known Boston lawyer. He moved to Kentucky with us because I refused to leave him behind. But he was also ready for a change. He will be your primary professor. Judge Webb has also agreed to teach part-time. And we're trying to persuade a professor in Boston, one of father's friends, to join us."

William strode over to them. "Edward, I heard what you called over to Dora. Did you include me?"

"Are you planning to study law as well, Sheriff Wyllie?" Dora asked.

"I have studied law books for years. Part-time, of course. My duties as sheriff require most of my time. And yes, I do plan to formally study at your new school as well if you can allow me to come one or two days a week."

"For you, William, we will make whatever accommodations you need," Edward said.

"What possessed you to sell your businesses in New Hampshire and move to Kentucky?" Daniel asked. "I visited your store. It was impressive. Bear tells me you were enormously successful there."

Edward took a sip of his wine and furrowed his brows in thought. "When Sam and Catherine came to visit earlier this summer, I realized just how much I missed my brothers. I knew I could be successful here in Kentucky too, given a little time. I'll establish another mercantile or two in Lexington as well as serve as the administrator for our school."

Daniel's respect for the man escalated even further. It appeared Edward was business savvy, confident, and loyal to his family.

Edward put a hand on William's shoulder. "I finally reached the point in my life when I realized family was far more important to me than wealth or my big fine home."

Daniel knew exactly what Edward meant.

Chapter 37

Daniel quickly packed a small bag and Ann grabbed the one she had brought and left in Artis' room while Edward unloaded their bags and instructed the driver.

As they departed in Edward's fancy carriage, sitting side by side in the rear seat, they both waved as the rest of the family shouted their goodbyes. Their families and friends would all likely continue celebrating long into the night, except for the Byrds and Judge Webb, who said they would return to Boonesborough soon.

As they left Highland behind them, the light provided by the roasting fire and candlelit house quickly disappeared. In the darkness, with her arm tucked securely around Daniel's elbow, Ann smiled up at her new husband. She couldn't believe she was now a married woman—Ann MacKay—and her husband was the most handsome man she'd ever laid eyes upon. He was even better looking than all of his attractive uncles. Good looks definitely ran in their family. But more importantly, they were all good men as well.

The wedding celebration was all she could have hoped for and more. When she'd stepped out from behind the tree, hoping to surprise him, his look of enchantment thrilled her. Daniel's appearance surprised her too. Cut to shoulder length, his wavy hair gleamed and his beard had disappeared revealing a face so handsome she worried her knees might buckle under her. He wore the fine clothing of a gentleman and his beautiful, gleaming sword hung at his side.

But Daniel's revelation that he was wealthy, and apparently extremely generous, was an even bigger surprise. She wondered if he had any other surprises for her.

Keeping her voice low so the coachman wouldn't hear, she said, "Other than the fact that you are even more handsome than I thought, now that I can see your entire face, and that you are clearly quite wealthy, do you have any other major revelations in store for our wedding night?"

Daniel gave her a mischievous grin. "Ah, indeed, I do. However, you will have to be patient. But I promise it will be worth the wait. Do you really think I'm handsome?"

In answer, she raised her mouth to his and he eagerly took her lips. She drank in the softness and warmth of his kiss. It made her shiver despite the sultry night.

When he finished kissing her, he brushed his lips across her forehead and kissed the top of her head. "I love you, Mrs. MacKay," he said.

She squeezed his hand. "And I love you, Mr. MacKay."

Ann glanced away, blinking away tears of happiness. Everywhere she looked it was peaceful and picturesque. The moon was shining bright over Kentucky although a few shy stars hid behind wispy clouds. The woods on either side of the road were a mixture of dark shaded areas and open lighter spots painted by moonbeams.

So much serenity in the fire's wake seemed out of place. Only a few miles behind them, this same forest stood blackened and wasted. Wasn't it just yesterday that their world had exploded into chaos?

But Daniel had refused to give in to that bedlam, letting nothing get in the way of their marriage. Likewise, his family quickly put it all behind them so that the wedding could proceed as planned. One day her world was exploding in violence and flames. And the next, she married the man she loved in a peaceful wooded setting surrounded by family and friends. *How swiftly life can change.*

Love not only conquered all their difficulties, it opened a path to their future.

As THEY STOOD FACING EACH OTHER in their room at the inn, Ann's heart filled with tenderness and a yearning for something she didn't even understand. But from the look in Daniel's smoldering eyes, she soon would.

He took his jacket, waistcoat, and tricorne off, and poured wine from the bottle Edward and Dora thoughtfully left in the room for them. As he poured it into two crystal glasses, Ann read the note left with it:

"We share this fine wine with you with our compliments and our hope that you will both share a lifetime of happiness and love. Edward and Dora."

"I think I'm going to love Dora as much as Kelly and Artis," she said. "She seems intelligent, well-educated, and charming."

Daniel nodded. "I would say the same for Edward. Except I would add thoughtful. I still can't believe he gave this room to us."

"Indeed."

They held their glasses high and then drank. The red wine had a smooth texture on her tongue and its deep flavors tasted far better than anything she'd ever drank before. "That's heavenly."

Daniel nodded his agreement. "They must have brought it with them. I have a bottle packed in my bag, but this is far better than anything available in Boonesborough. Although it's not labeled, clearly it's a fine wine. It must be French."

"French?"

"My father in Philadelphia imported wines from France and he taught me much about them. The finest wines come from France, but only some are labeled. The methods for label construction are still crude and involve designing the wine label on a stone then passing an ink roller over it to produce the label."

"Then how can you tell that it's a French wine?"

"Because of its richness and color. Some of France's vineyards date back to the time of the Roman Empire. The roots grow exceedingly deep and draw rich minerals from the earth."

She held her glass up. "Here's to the Romans! And the French!"

"No, here's to you. Without you here to enjoy this with, it might as well be a common ale."

Ann toasted, took a sip, and then sat down in a cushy chair thinking about how sophisticated and educated her new husband was. She admired his obvious intelligence but it was his compelling character and refined qualities that captivated her. "Daniel, you're so polished and cultured. Are you sure I'll be able to be the wife you need? I'm neither well-educated nor refined. And as I warned, I tend to rebel against what is considered appropriate for women."

He grinned and said, "Ah, but it is that very spirit that I admire in you. Culture and education can be acquired, if you have any interest in doing so. But I love you just as you are. There were plenty of sophisticated women in Philadelphia. But not one of them was as clever or as appealing as you. And you're courageous, adventurous, and strong."

His words cheered her and wrapped her in an invisible warmth. Soon she would be wrapped in his arms as well. At the thought, her heart thudded wildly in her chest.

"Ann, I have two wedding gifts for you. The first, you will have to wait for. I've ordered you a fine wedding ring and it should arrive in a few weeks."

She let out a little squeal. "Really? What does it look like?"

"You will have to wait and see. I will say that it will be beautiful. Like you."

Her insides jangled with excitement, amazed at how he continued to find new ways to make her happy.

"And…" he started and broke into a wide smile.

"Yes?"

"The waterfall you took me to—Bad Branch Falls—it and all the acreage around it is yours!"

"What!"

"I bought it. All the land around it too."

Ecstatic beyond words, she could only stare. Then she leapt up, flung herself into his arms, and hugged him fiercely. Unable to believe it, she said, "But...but Mr. Breedhead said he wouldn't sell. My father tried to buy it from him years ago."

"I did some research on the spot at the Land Office. They told me Breedhead had owned it for a long time, but never built on it or improved the property. I remembered that when I was in his store, Breedhead said he probably owed his life to Bear. So, I took my father with me when I made my offer. One look at Bear's beseeching eyes, and Breedhead accepted my offer."

Ann giggled with glee, envisioning Bear's pleading face. "Oh Daniel. I will never, ever, be able to thank you enough. That is the kindest thing anyone has ever done for me—by far. I don't know what to say."

"Just say you love me."

"Oh, how I love you. When we wed, I didn't think I could ever love you more, but now I know I do." With this gift, he struck a chord deep within her that made her soul dance. Feeling lightheaded and giddy with joy, she sat down again. "Are we going to live on the land?"

"If you would like. Or we can live in town. Or even in Lexington if we both like it."

"Daniel, I would love to live there at the falls. Then my mother's spirit will be able to share in our happiness and be a part of watching our children grow up."

"Then we shall live there! In a fine home. We'll start building it as soon as I finish my legal schooling in Lexington." Daniel took a seat in another chair across from her. "But right now, my most perfect wife, I just want to stare into your beautiful eyes and enjoy this wine for a bit. Afterward…"

"Yes?"

"I'm going to take you to that bed over there and show you…"

Shyly, she inclined her head toward him. "Show me what?" She *was* innocent in the ways of marriage and she knew it. But she could still have a little fun with him. "Mother Helen said I was to just lay back and let you have your way with me. What is it you want to do with me?" She gave him her most demure look.

"Perhaps we should refrain from mentioning Mother Helen again."

"Should I tell you what father said instead?"

Daniel sighed heavily and gulped some of his wine. "No, please don't."

Ann took a sip of wine and then another. Suddenly, she couldn't stop the giggle that escaped her chest.

Daniel rose and stood in front of her. "You've been teasing me!" He gazed down at her, his eyes burning with both mock indignation and desire. He reached for her hand and tugged her up.

"Yes," she confessed. "But my ignorance is real. I truly have no idea what I should do."

"Are you nervous?"

The wine seemed to relax her, but she did feel a bit like a bird afraid of flying for the first time. "A little. I just know I want you more than I've ever wanted anything."

He moaned a little and then quickly removed his shirt. He looked so powerful—his chest broad and his arms muscular. And his stomach muscles rippled at his narrow waist as he bent to remove his tall boots. The sight quickened her pulse and kindled strange sensations in her body.

But when he took off his breeches, she swiftly emptied her wine glass.

THE THOUGHT OF BEDDING THIS gorgeous angel who was now his wife was exciting enough. But the fact that she was a chaste woman, innocent in the ways of lovemaking made the prospect of bedding her all the more thrilling.

Her purity meant she could learn little by little and it pleased Daniel to know he would be the one to guide her as she learned the meaning of passion. He reminded himself to take it slow—to bring her along only as fast as her desire, not his, grew.

Layer by layer, Daniel helped her remove her clothing, stroking her arms and her slender back and planting kisses on the side of her neck as he did so. After he eased her out of her stays and petticoat, she stood before him wearing only a thin silk chemise he could see through. For the first time, he glimpsed her magnificent breasts. He swallowed. "You are breathtaking!"

She smiled modestly, keeping her hands over the spot between her hips.

She would shortly learn that the spot she was embarrassed for him to see would be the very place he would linger to bring her great pleasure. For he intended to pleasure Ann as a woman should be pleasured—gently, tenderly, lovingly—without shame.

He poured them each some more wine and he studied her face as she took little sips while looking up at him. Curiosity and wonder filled her eyes. When she licked a drop of wine from her lips, his whole being flooded with desire. It was time.

"Would you mind removing the pins from you hair?" he asked.

When she finished, she shook her head and a mass of black waves hung beautifully against her creamy white shoulders.

He was certain no mortal man had ever gazed upon such a heavenly face. He gently wove his fingers through her hair and kissed her. Then he led her to the bed, his own heart beating wildly, and tossed back all the covers. He wanted nothing in the way. Gently he lowered them both and tugged her on top of him.

He wanted Ann to feel in control until she was at ease.

Even through her chemise, the feel of her luscious form against him sent a pleasurable quiver through his entire body.

"Hold me," she said, "and never let me go."

He wrapped his arms completely around her. "I could never let you go. Our love is written on the pages of my heart in an ink that will never fade."

He kissed her letting her read the words of his heart on his lips.

She returned the kiss, tentatively at first. Then, as her desire grew, he let her take the lead and he opened his mouth for her. Soon, as she continued to kiss him, her hand ventured to his chest and then his stomach, causing his muscles there to tighten. Spellbound by her touch, his skin tingled under her fingertips.

When her hand shifted lower, he gasped. Her gentle, light touch felt exquisite and sent shockingly powerful waves racing through him.

Ann's timid lovemaking soon flared into a bonfire of uninhibited passion. The intensity of her ardor stunned him. Her desire was clearly overriding all her shyness and inhibitions.

Leaving her straddled across his legs, he sat up to meet her. He trailed kisses down her neck as he stroked her back, letting one hand massage the fullness of her hips. Then he lightly trailed his fingertips down her bare shapely leg and back again. He repeated the path on her other leg, followed by both of her arms.

The light massage made her quiver and her body and neck arched back.

He quickly slipped her chemise over her head, leaving her flawless rounded breasts bared and ready for his caresses.

Her breaths became rapid and she began releasing long whimpers.

A moan of ecstasy slipped through his own lips at the sound and his impatience grew as scorching passion rose within him. The soul-reaching ache to join with her became more than he could bear.

"You're ready, Ann, and I am too. It may hurt a bit at the beginning, but the discomfort will ease as your body accepts mine for the first glorious time." He kissed her long and hard. "Are you ready to experience the fullness of love, my darling?"

She placed her hands on either side of his face and gazed into his eyes. "Yes, my husband. Let's soar together."

Chapter 38

After spending two blissful nights and one day at Boonesborough's inn, leaving only to eat, Daniel helped Ann climb into Edward's carriage.

During their stay at the inn, the driver had spent his time visiting relatives in the area. He came back this morning and would take them first to the Byrd home, so Ann could pack, and then back to Highland. There they would pick up Edward and Dora and say their goodbyes to Bear and Artis before leaving on their honeymoon.

Once the coachman loaded their bags and they were all seated, the driver turned to face them. "Good morning, Mr. and Mrs. MacKay!"

"Good morning," they both replied at once.

It was a good morning, Daniel decided as the carriage took off. Earlier, they made love one more time before giving up their cozy room. Each time they coupled, he'd shown Ann just a little more, gradually exposing her to the wonders of the marriage bed. Not only was she a quick learner, she managed to teach him a few things. He'd learned that enjoying lovemaking to its fullest requires being with someone you love. And genuine passion comes from an instinctive response that cannot be taught. It can only be experienced. For the rest of his life, every time he passed this inn, he knew he would look up and smile.

Daniel instructed the driver to take them to the fort and wait for Ann while she packed for their trip to Lexington. As Ann entered, Conall was just leaving to ride somewhere and he said his goodbyes to Ann.

Leading his horse, Conall strolled alongside Daniel across the enclosure toward William's office. "Thank you for asking me to be your best man," Conall told him.

"It was my honor to pick you." *No one could ever replace the brother he had lost, but he was learning to love Conall as a brother.* "I know I have few friends in Boonesborough, but that was not the reason I asked you. I admire and respect you, Conall, and expect us to be great friends in the future."

"I agree." Conall gave him a lopsided grin and nudged him playfully on the shoulder. "And let's not forget you owe me your life."

"Maybe someday, I'll be able to pay you back."

"Let's hope you won't have to," Conall said.

Behind them, the morning sun's rays splayed across the sharpened logs of the high stockade on the fort's eastern side. It promised to be another sweltering day. In Philadelphia, the weather was a constantly changing mix—everything from the fury of hurricanes to the soft, rolling mist of fog. Here it seemed ever the same, hot and dry.

When they reached William's office, Conall tossed the reins over his horse's neck.

"Where are you headed?" Daniel asked.

"I'm riding out to see what kind of help the two families who lost their homes could use. One of the burned places belonged to the father of the girl I brought to the dance. Some of the militia have volunteered to join me later after their drills."

They both glanced over and, for a few moments, watched the men's maneuvers in the center of the enclosure as they followed the orders of the militia's lieutenant. Why did it seem that men were always either fighting wars or practicing for them? Daniel guessed it was because there were equal amounts of evil and good in the world.

He drew his coin pouch out of his waistcoat pocket and handed two gold pieces to Conall, one for each family. "That should allow you to help both families a bit more."

Conall stared at the gold glittering in his hand. "I'm sure it will!"

"Don't tell them where it came from. And let me know if you need more," Daniel told him. "I'll see you in about a week then."

Conall nodded. "Take good care of my sister."

"I intend to. For a very long time."

Conall mounted and waved goodbye as he rode through the fort's gates.

Daniel stepped onto the wooden porch in front of William's office. "Hello!" he greeted as he opened the creaky door.

William stood up from his paper-covered desk and smiled. "Good morning, Daniel. Haven't seen much of you the last couple of days."

Daniel chuckled a bit.

"How was your room at the inn?" William asked with a sly grin.

Daniel suspected that his uncle wasn't actually asking about the room but was too polite to ask anything else. "It could not have been better. How is Kelly? Is she still grieving the loss of your home?"

William answered with a nod. "I'm afraid so. We were so happy there." Suddenly glum-faced, he sat down and slumped in his chair. The strain of losing their home obviously weighed heavily on his uncle's shoulders.

"Have you been back since the fire to inspect it?" Daniel asked.

"Yes, Bear, Edward, and I all went over there yesterday. It had cooled completely. When I saw the destruction up close, I found it hard to believe." William looked sickened. "But the charred smell, gray ash, and black cinders everywhere made it hard to deny. It broke my heart." He sighed loudly, releasing his disgust.

Daniel bent his head and studied his hands. "I am so sorry, William."

William raked his fingers through his short, straight blond hair. "Everything we had is gone. All of the beautiful trees closest to the cabin are burnt down. The smokehouse is reduced to ashes as is most of my barn. And our cabin and my in-laws smaller cabin are damaged beyond repair."

"I know. I saw it when I found the Bible."

"Thank you for that. Kelly was beside herself with joy. For her, it took a lot of the sting out of the situation. But I was so furious when I saw it all that I wanted to murder Snyder. And I would have if Ann hadn't already killed him."

Daniel had to sympathize. "It's difficult to extract revenge from a dead man."

William took a deep breath and straightened his shoulders. "Rebuilding will be like starting from scratch. But most of the settlers here in Kentucky have done just that. We can too. We can turn the acreage that was burnt into good pasture land since it is now virtually cleared. We can build a house big enough for more children and we'll need a bigger barn too for that mare we're going to breed. Thank you for that as well."

Daniel nodded. "It will be exciting to see what kind of horses we can all raise."

"Fortunately, about a third of the orchard was spared and so were all the woods on the north side of the creek bank."

"William, I want you to hire a fine housewright right away, and whatever craftsmen he'll need. Have him go out and speak with Kelly about what she would like in her new home. Here," he said sliding a folded piece of paper toward William. Earlier that morning, he used a piece of the inn's stationary to write down the estimated cost given to him yesterday by one of the local housewrights. He'd visited with the man while Ann napped since she'd gotten little sleep the night before. Daniel added ten percent to the total knowing that it was just an estimate. "That amount should cover everything. I'll arrange for the transfer of funds from my bank in Philadelphia while I'm in Lexington."

William unfolded the slip of paper and then swallowed hard. "Daniel, this is far too generous. We only had a modest cabin with a loft. Not a big house. This is enough to build two houses. I can't let you do that."

"Remember it's how I chose to honor the memory of my father in Philadelphia." *It would be in his good name, even though it was no longer Daniel's name.* "He would want you to build a fine home and an adjoining house for Doc and Mrs. McGuffin. They deserve a nice place to live."

"Daniel, I simply can't believe the extent of your generosity. It's… overwhelming."

"As I explained at the wedding, it's my father Armitage you should thank. He worked hard all his life and amassed a fortune. I didn't even know how wealthy he really was until he died."

"I will certainly remember him in my prayers. And you."

Daniel smiled. "I would be grateful for that."

William continued to stare at the piece of paper. "Edward offered to help some too, but he's invested most of his wealth into building the new school and buying their home in Lexington."

"Yes, Edward told me the same thing. I told him I could take care of the expense of hiring a housewright. If your housewright is really good, we'll use him to build our home too after I finish up my studies."

"Bear would be a better judge of his skills. He is actually a fine builder himself. I think we told you that both he and Doc helped to build Sam and Catherine's home."

"Yes, I remember."

"Their home site is so remote, near Cumberland Falls, that there were no housewrights available. So Bear and Doc lived there for some time while they helped Sam build the house. That's where Doc met his wife—she was Catherine's cook. You should see their house—and I'm sure you will at Christmas—it's spectacular. Bear used a housewright to help him build his own home at Highland because he was in a hurry to get it finished so he and Artis could wed. But Bear did much of the work himself."

"That's great news. They can both assist with the rebuilding. And, of course, I'll help just as soon I return from our honeymoon."

"Please take all the time you'd like. You only get to take a honeymoon once," William told him.

Daniel certainly hoped so. He prayed God would grant Ann and him many years together. He would consider it a great blessing if they could grow old together. So many men lost their wives to childbirth. He prayed that Artis, Kelly, and Dora would all deliver their babes safely.

The door to William's office flew open and Deputy Wallace rushed in. "Sheriff! I just saw Tommy Dooley and Ed Sanderson gallop across the enclosure over to the Byrd home. That can't mean anything good."

Chapter 39

Daniel leapt up from his chair and so did William. He rushed past the deputy and bounded off the porch. "Ann is there packing for our honeymoon," he told them as they took off running. The three of them raced across the north side of enclosure.

Daniel reached the Byrd home first and he threw open the door, not bothering to knock. "Ann!" he shouted before even clearing the entry.

"She's in here, Daniel," the Colonel called to him.

Daniel, William, and the deputy stampeded inside.

Ann and her parents sat in their parlor with Dooley and Sanderson pointing their flintlocks at Ann.

"What is going on here?" Daniel demanded, withdrawing his sword.

William and the deputy hastily drew their pistols.

Sanderson ignored Daniel and looked at William. "We were just about to take her to you, Sheriff Wyllie."

Dooley used his pistol to point at Ann. "Mr. Snyder wants Miss Byrd arrested."

"She's Mrs. MacKay now!" Daniel swore and stuck the sword's tip against Dooley's neck. "And if you wave that weapon at my wife again, your head comes off!"

William stepped closer and snarled, "Put your pistols away. Now! Or my deputy and I will shoot them out of your greasy hands."

Dooley and Sanderson both tucked their pistols into their belts.

Daniel stepped back but did not sheath his sword.

Dooley rubbed the spot on his neck pricked by the sword tip, smearing a few drops of blood.

William asked smoothly, "Why does Mr. Snyder want Mrs. MacKay arrested?"

Dooley stuck his narrow whisker-covered chin out. "For murder."

"Murder!" Daniel and William both barked at once.

Dooley almost jumped, but he managed to say, "She murdered Mr. Snyder's son and our friend."

Still holding his pistols, rage bristled through Daniel and he hardened his eyes. "She killed him, but she did not murder him. She defended herself against that brute."

"Mr. Snyder thought the same thing until we told him what we saw. And we explained what Charles was just tryin' to do," Dooley said.

"That's impossible. You weren't there," Daniel told them.

"Yep, we were. Charles told us to meet him up on that hill where we camped sometimes. We were almost upon it when Ed and me spotted you and Mr. MacKay coming from two different directions. Ed and me, well we got nervous 'cause Mr. MacKay looked like some kind of crazed warrior about to take Charles' head off. So we rode into the woods real quick and hid our horses behind a big boulder. But we peeked around and saw the whole thing. Charles was on his knees…"

Wide-eyed, Sanderson took over and pointed accusingly at Ann. "And then we heard her shriek like a banshee. Her unearthly cry did herald a death—just like real banshees. He never had a chance. We saw her plunge a knife right into the middle of poor Charles' chest."

Byrd's eyes flashed with outrage. "He was about to attack my daughter!"

Dooley shook his head. "No, Colonel! I'm sure he was just tryin' to give her a kiss. He would have let her get up once he got one. Before Charles left to go get her, he told us he was gonna take her to New Orleans and marry her. He asked us to go with them and be his witnesses. He loved her something fierce. Could hardly think or talk about anything else. He would never hurt her."

When Dooley paused for a breath, Sanderson added, "After she murdered him, and they left, we waited a while before we headed back to town. We wanted to wait until we were sure the fire wasn't coming into Boonesborough anyway. The next morning, we helped Mr. Snyder bury Charles. He grieved a couple of days and we did too before we told him everything. Then Mr. Snyder decided Ann should pay for killing his only son. We thought so too. We sure did. And we told him so. He told us to go get her and take her to you, Sheriff Wyllie."

"Mr. Snyder said he would come to your office to press charges just as soon as the bank closed," Dooley said.

Mother Helen gasped and grew even paler.

"That conniving bloody…" Daniel started.

Ann leapt up, her green eyes blazing. She faced them belligerently. "Liars! He wasn't just trying to get a kiss. I attacked Charles because he was about to violate me. He thought he could keep Daniel from marrying me if I was defiled. His hands were so strong. But I fought back. He didn't like that, so he decided to kill me just as soon as he had his way with me. He was going to use Daniel's own pistols to shoot me. When he aimed one of the weapons at Bear, I leapt up with my knife. If I hadn't killed him, he would have killed Bear, used the second pistol on Daniel, and then finished his disgusting assault on me."

"I hate to call a lady a liar, but…" Dooley started.

"Then don't!" Daniel shouted and raised his sword.

Dooley eyed the deadly weapon warily.

The colonel vaulted toward the two men, fists clenched, but William flung an arm against Byrd's chest stopping him.

Dooley and Sanderson both peered expectantly at William.

Daniel's anger boiled to a scalding fury within him. Even his eyes felt hot. He forced himself to put away his sword to keep himself from slicing these men in two. But he wasn't above beating them senseless. "This is beyond preposterous. How dare you bloody no goods distort the truth and dishonor my wife!" For the sake of Ann and Mrs. Byrd, he didn't want to say he'd seen Charles' breeches down around his knees. And from what Bear had told him, his father, who got there a few moments before Daniel did, saw worse than that. "Step outside you devil's spawns and let's see what you say after I beat the truth out of you."

"They do deserve a sound thrashing," William said. "But that won't be necessary, Daniel. Mr. Dooley and Mr. Sanderson, you should have come to my office and told me that Mr. Snyder wanted to file charges against Ann. Instead, you forced yourself into this home and held a family at gunpoint. You two agreed to meet Charles while he was in the act of perpetrating a crime. You also knew of his plans and failed to report them to me. That makes you both accomplices in the abduction and brutal attack upon Miss Byrd and in the total destruction of my property and the homes of two other families. In addition, Mrs. McGuffin nearly died. It is you who should be charged with arson and attempted murder."

Sanderson looked confused. "Perpetrating?"

Dooley's voice hardened. "Accomplices?"

"That means it is you two who have broken the law—yet again—not Ann MacKay. You were known cronies of Charles Snyder and I can now charge you with several crimes. Once I charge you though, what happens to you is up to the judge, not me. You have two choices, gentlemen. One, I can arrest you now, charge you with multiple serious crimes, and put you in front of Judge Webb. By the way, he's in a particularly prickly mood today. Or two, you can leave Kentucky, and never, ever, come back to Boonesborough. Perhaps you can find a new life and become decent citizens somewhere. What is your choice?"

The two men looked at each other, then Dooley said, "We'll leave. I've been wanting to go back to North Carolina anyway."

William inclined his head toward the door.

Dooley and Sanderson practically tripped on each other trying to reach the door first.

"You handled that well, sheriff," Colonel Byrd said.

"The very idea!" Mother Helen said. "Thank you, Sheriff Wyllie."

"I'll handle Mr. Snyder too, just as soon as he steps foot in my office," William said. "Come on deputy, let's go wait for that banker."

DANIEL RELEASED A LONG SLOW breath and drew Ann into his arms. "Are you all right?" he asked, his eyes searching her face.

She smiled up at him, remarkably composed. "Of course I am with the bravest men in Kentucky here to defend me."

"You have proven that you are quite capable of defending yourself," Colonel Byrd said.

"Have you finished packing?" Daniel asked. "I'd like to get going before something else happens!"

Ann put her hands on her hips. "I only had a few minutes before those two dimwits showed up and forced their way in here. I have to pack for a week, but I dress pretty simply. It should only take me a few more minutes."

Daniel suspected that her wardrobe might be quite limited. While they were in Lexington, he intended to buy her all the frilly gowns or riding habits she wanted. A woman as beautiful and loving as Ann deserved to be pampered.

"Will you saddle Whitefoot in the meantime?" Ann asked him.

"Yes. If it's all right with you, Edward said he would ride her to Lexington so you could ride in the carriage with Dora. We can tie her onto the back of the carriage until we get back to Highland."

"I can't wait to leave!" With a springy step, Ann left with her stepmother to finish her packing.

"Have your militias' swords arrived yet?" Daniel asked Byrd.

"I expect the shipment next week. About the time you'll be getting back from Lexington. I'll muster the militia just as soon as you're ready to begin their instruction."

"I will come to the fort eight or nine days from today," Daniel told Byrd.

The colonel placed a hand over Daniel's shoulder. "In the meantime, take good care of my daughter. This will be the first time she's been away from the fort since she was born. She has little knowledge of the ways of the world."

"I will, Sir. You have my word."

Ann's father raised his graying brows. "And you have my plucky daughter," he said with a chuckle. "God help you!"

"He already has. He gave me a new beginning with Ann and a new family. I will thank the good Lord the rest of my days."

Epilogue

Riding next to Edward, Daniel was getting to know yet another new uncle he didn't know he had before coming to Boonesborough.

As they rode north, he felt as though he truly belonged here in Kentucky. The road to Lexington passed through limestone palisades, rolling hills, tree-studded fields, pine woods, spring-fed peaceful ponds, and cascading waterfalls. Here and there stone or split-rail fences marked the occasional settler's farm. The lush scenery and open air strengthened Daniel's heart and awakened his senses making him feel fully alive. But it was more than the countryside and the impressive vistas that stirred his soul.

What hastened the healing of his grief ravaged heart the most was Ann becoming his wife. *He was married!* Everything about his life now seemed more substantial and somehow more significant. He was no longer the frolicsome, carefree bachelor enjoying a frivolous life. He had someone to live for. Someone to dream with. Someone to care for.

During their ride, he carried on a thought-provoking conversation with Edward about the new law school, offering his uncle several suggestions based on his years at The University of Pennsylvania Law School. Then they turned to discussing Edward's New Hampshire businesses and what had made them so successful. Daniel wanted to learn all he could from Edward. The man possessed a sharp mind and a quick wit and he asked Daniel many astute questions about his Philadelphia father's shipping business.

After some time, the heat forced them to stop at a spring-fed pond to water the horses and themselves. After they all drank from the crisp, clear stream that fed the pond, Edward took Dora's hand and the two strolled into the woods saying they wanted to stretch their legs while the horses rested for a bit.

Daniel tied Samson and Whitefoot onto the back of the carriage, and the coachman led all the horses a little further up the road to let them rest in the shade under a large tree.

"Are you ready to honeymoon in Lexington?" Ann asked as they both sat down by the pond's edge.

That morning, Daniel had packed his cravat and dress coat away, a concession to the heat of late July, but he was still hot. He splashed water onto his face and neck and dried off with his shirt sleeve. Located beneath a canopy of tree limbs and thick vines that shielded the pond from the strongest rays of the sun, the blue-green water was surprisingly cool.

He bent his head and kissed the back of her hand. "As long as you're with me, I'm ready to go anywhere."

She smiled and then they both gulped a few more handfuls of water.

Daniel could not resist kissing the droplets of water that clung to her moist lips. The taste of her sent a shudder of desire racing down his spine. He glanced up to be sure they were still alone. They were, so he tugged her into his lap. "You realize we've started our honeymoon," he breathed into her ear.

A blush raced across her cheeks. "Daniel! As much as I want to, we can't. Dora and Edward will be back soon and the coachman isn't far off."

"I'll wager my newlywed uncle and his wife are preoccupied themselves. And the coachman has his tricorne pulled down over his face. I think he's catching a quick nap," he said. "I'm just going to give you a small sample of what awaits you tonight."

Keeping a lookout for Edward and Dora's return, he slipped his hand beneath her skirt and gently explored his wife's softest flesh. She gasped, buried her face on his shoulder, and began to squirm until his caressing stroking made her smother her ecstasy against his neck. As she recovered, an easterly breeze stirred the air, drying the beads of lust induced moisture on their faces.

When her breathing returned to normal, they stood and brushed off their clothing. He heard something in the distance. "Could that have been thunder?"

They both searched the sky and Ann pointed to an enormous thunderhead looming to the south in the direction they'd just come from. "I think it was! It's growing darker too. Is it coming this way?"

He studied the horizon. "It seems to be centered over the area around Boonesborough!"

"Rain! At long last! Hurrah! I hope it rains the entire time we're gone." Ann dusted a few more leaves off the skirt of her gown.

"Bear and Artis and William and Kelly will be happy," he said as a bolt of lightning shot across the dark gray clouds.

As they watched, the storm mushroomed right before their eyes. Billowing dark clouds spread out in several directions from the main thunderhead. This did not appear to be a fleeting shower.

"It looks like the drought will finally be banished by a thunderous storm," he said. "I'm glad that carriage has a cover. We'd best get it pulled up and get going."

"I can't wait to see Lexington. It sounds impressive from their descriptions."

"It does. And a week away will do us both good after all the turmoil in Boonesborough."

"I hope you're not planning to relax overmuch!" she said with a grin and gazed at him longingly.

"Not even a minute," he said, tugging her into his embrace and kissing her soundly. Brimming with love, he gazed at her upturned face for a long moment.

"Just before she died, my mother told me that if I found my father, I would find a new beginning."

"She was a wise woman. Your new life will be a good life, Daniel," Ann said. "Full of happiness. I promise you that."

That new life included his father—Daniel Alexander MacKay Sr. His mother had been right about Bear too. His father was a good man. And he gave Daniel his good name. He would no longer carry the scandalous brand of bastard. He pitied those forced to live with that label their whole life through no fault of their own.

Having his own identity so abruptly and unexpectedly stripped away, had left him feeling vulnerable and nameless. His whole life became unstable, shaky as a branch in a strong wind. But when he'd left to find his father, with each step Samson took onto Kentucky's soil, little by little, his balance returned. The search for his true father became far more than a promise he'd made to his mother. It became a quest to uncover his true identity and begin life again.

He could never have imagined that he would find so much more. Most of all Ann. And, a loving new family.

This was home now. An entirely new place—Kentucky—the first frontier.

A perfect place for love's new beginning.

Dear Reader,

I hope you truly enjoyed reading

LOVE'S NEW BEGINNING
Wilderness Hearts – Book One

Thank you for selecting my novel to read. If you enjoyed reading Daniel and Ann's story, I would be honored if you would share your thoughts with your friends. Regardless of whether you are reading print or electronic versions, I'd be extremely grateful if you posted a short review on the *Love's New Beginning* page on Amazon.com. Reviews are so helpful to both authors and readers. It helps the works of authors to stay visible on Amazon and it helps readers find books they will enjoy.

If you would like to contact me directly, please send me a note through my website http://www.dorothywiley.com under the 'Contact' tab. Under that same tab you can also sign up for my Newsletter to receive special offers for free or discounted books.

To receive notifications of my new releases follow me on Amazon at www.amazon.com/author/dorothywiley.

If you are interested in reading my other novels, they are listed on the last page.

Thanks for your support!

All the best,
Dorothy

P.S. For a memorable Christmas novel, be sure to read *Frontier Gift of Love*, a poignant story about Sam, Catherine, Little John, and the rest of the family.

Interesting Facts Behind this Story

PHILADELPHIA WAS OUR NATION'S FIRST capitol and is the birthplace of the Constitution of the United States which laid the foundation for the American system of government and our belief in liberty and freedom. It will forever remain one of the greatest documents in human history.

Philadelphia was also at the forefront of legal education in our country. In 1790, James Wilson, one of the signers of the Declaration of Independence and a framer of the Constitution, delivered the University of Pennsylvania's first lectures in law to President George Washington and all the members of his Cabinet. Later he became a member of the first U.S. Supreme Court. The University of Pennsylvania Law School in Philadelphia officially traces its foundation to Wilson's lectures. For this novel, Wilson is mentioned as one of Daniel's Philadelphia law professors.

For more information on swordsmanship and fencing in colonial America and Daniel's Philadelphia instructor in this gentleman's art, Jean Baptiste Lemaire, please see:

http://ahfi.org/wp-content/uploads/library/estafilade_fencing-in-america.pdf.

The colonial medical community did not know the source of Yellow Fever, a viral infection spread by the Aedes aegypti mosquito. For more information about Philadelphia's Yellow Fever pandemic see: https://en.wikipedia.org/wiki/1793_Philadelphia_yellow_fever_epidemic. And the excellent article, "A Short History of Yellow Fever in the US," by Bob Arnebeck at http://bobarnebeck.com/history.html.

The American eagle became the national emblem in 1782. Benjamin Franklin did indeed want the turkey to be our national symbol. He wrote, "For a truth, the turkey is in comparison a much more respectable bird, and withal a true original native of America … a bird of courage, and would not hesitate to attack a grenadier of the British guards, who should presume to invade his farmyard with a red coat on." For more information please visit the American Eagle Foundation at https://www.eagles.org/.

Kentucky is filled with amazing natural beauty including many majestic waterfalls. For the purposes of the novel, I made Bad Branch Falls close to Boonesborough. It is actually located in Letcher, KY, about 130 miles from Fort Boonesborough State Park.

Kentucky has some of the country's most beautiful woods and forests. For a map of the Daniel Boone National Forest go to: http://www.fs.fed.us/ivm/index.html. And the link to the USDA Forest Service web page for the Daniel Boone National Forest is: http://www.fs.usda.gov/dbnf/. According to that website, "The Daniel Boone National Forest embraces some of the most rugged terrain west of the Appalachian Mountains. Steep forested slopes, sandstone cliffs and narrow ravines characterize the land."

Big Bone Lick is located just 100 miles north of Fort Boonesborough and is mentioned in the story as a place Bear and Lucky found while hunting. In 1807 Thomas Jefferson sent General George Rogers Clark to Kentucky to collect fossils. Big Bone Lick is the site of an ancient salt lick that once attracted Pleistocene-era mammoths, giant ground sloths, and giant bison. Some of these animals died near the salt lick when they became trapped in the surrounding bogs, leaving a rich heritage of fossils. In his letter of 1807, Jefferson directed the General to have the bones that Rogers collected packed and shipped to a New Orleans collector, who would then forward them to Washington. In a letter written the next year, 1808, Jefferson described to the French naturalist Bernard Germain de Lacépède the details of Clark's expedition, and offered the bones and other examples of American wildlife to the National Institute of Paris. To see an image of Jefferson's letter, go to:

https://commons.wikimedia.org/wiki/Category:History_of_Kentucky#/media/File:Thomas_Jefferson_to_George_Rogers_Clark_fossils_1807.jpg

I believe that fictional stories become richer when they are woven with facts and true history. In doing so, the reader is more likely to be transported to the time and place of the characters.

I sincerely hope you loved your visit to 1800 America!

Titles by Dorothy Wiley

AMERICAN WILDERNESS SERIES

Book One — the story of Stephen and Jane:
WILDERNESS TRAIL OF LOVE

Book Two — the story of Sam and Catherine:
NEW FRONTIER OF LOVE

Book Three — the story of William and Kelly:
WHISPERING HILLS OF LOVE

Book Four — the story of Bear and Artis:
FRONTIER HIGHLANDER VOW OF LOVE

Book Five — A story of Sam and Catherine and the entire family:
FRONTIER GIFT OF LOVE

Book Six — the story of Edward and Dora:
THE BEAUTY OF LOVE

WILDERNESS HEARTS SERIES

Book One — the story of Daniel and Ann:
LOVE'S NEW BEGINNING

Wilderness Hearts Book Two — Releasing 2017

All titles available in print and ebooks from Amazon
at www.amazon.com/author/dorothywiley

ABOUT THE AUTHOR

Amazon bestselling novelist Dorothy Wiley is the author of seven books, including her highly acclaimed debut novel *Wilderness Trail of Love*, the first in her American Wilderness Series Romances. Wiley blends thrilling action-packed adventures with the romance of a moving love story to create highly engaging page-turners. The novels of this popular award-winning author are enjoyed worldwide by readers of historical romance, westerns, and classic American adventures.

Like Wiley's compelling heroes, who from the onset make it clear they will not fail despite the adversities they face, this author is likewise destined for success. In 2014 and 2015, her novels won six awards, notably an Amazon Breakthrough Novel Award Quarter-finalist, a Readers' Favorite Gold Medal, a USA Best Book Awards Finalist, and a Historical Novel Society Editor's Choice. Her books continue to earn five-star ratings from readers and high praise from reviewers.

Wiley's extraordinary historical romances, inspired by history, teem with action and cliff-edge tension. Her books' timeless messages of family and loyalty are both raw and honest. In all her novels, the author's complex characters come alive and are joined by a memorable ensemble of friends and family. As she skillfully unravels a compelling tale, Wiley includes rich historical elements to create a vivid colonial world that celebrates the historical heritage of the frontier.

Wiley attended college at The University of Texas in Austin, Texas. She graduated with honors, receiving a bachelor of journalism, and grew to dearly love both Texas and a 7th-generation Texan, her husband Larry. Her husband's courageous ancestors, early pioneers of Kentucky and Texas, provided the inspiration for her novels. After a distinguished career in corporate marketing and public relations, Wiley is living her dream—writing novels that touch the hearts of readers.

YOU ARE INVITED TO CONNECT WITH THE AUTHOR

WEBSITE:
www.dorothywiley.com

authordorothywiley

WileyDorothy

dorothymwiley

FOLLOW DOROTHY WILEY ON AMAZON AT:
http://www.amazon.com/author/dorothywiley

Also look for Dorothy Wiley on YouTube
to see her beautiful book trailers

And look for Dorothy Wiley on Goodreads

ACKNOWLEDGMENTS

A huge thank you to all my loyal readers. I am so grateful for each of you! I especially want to thank those of you who take the time to write such kind reviews on Amazon. They truly motivate me! And your reviews help other readers find and enjoy my books. Your ratings and reviews, no matter whether they are just a few words or several paragraphs, are enormously appreciated. To write a review, go to the *Love's New Beginning* page on Amazon. Scroll down to the box that says "Write a customer review." Just a sentence or two is all that is needed. Afterwards, send me a message using the "Contact" tab on my website http://www.dorothymwiley.com so that I can personally write you a note of thanks!

I would also like to thank my husband, the hero in the story of my life, for always having faith in me. My husband's brave ancestors inspired these novels.

And my thanks to my dear talented sister Maria and my fellow author and friend Deborah Gafford for their help in polishing this manuscript. I also received many helpful suggestions from JoAnne Weiss who reviews for http://romancing-the-book.com/.

I am also grateful for the talents of designer April Martinez at Graphicfantastic.com for her design of the cover and interior.

And Facebook friends, thank you for liking and sharing my posts! And to those super fans, who are always there on Facebook encouraging me, you are my book angels—watching over my writing career! I love hearing from you! Finally, please follow me on Amazon. Just go here http://www.amazon.com/author/dorothywiley and click "Follow" under my picture.

Many thanks!

Dorothy

21635189R00167

Made in the USA
Columbia, SC
19 July 2018